LOUELLA BRYANT

SHELTERING ANGEL

A NOVEL BASED ON A TRUE STORY OF THE TITANIC

Black Rose Writing | Texas

ISBN: 978-1-68513-240-8
PUBLISHED BY BLACK ROSE WRITING
www.blackrosewriting.com

Printed in the United States of America
Suggested Retail Price (SRP) $23.95

Sheltering Angel is printed in Book Antiqua

*As a planet-friendly publisher, Black Rose Writing does its best to eliminate unnecessary waste to reduce paper usage and energy costs, while never compromising the reading experience. As a result, the final word count vs. page count may not meet common expectations.

Praise for
SHELTERING ANGEL

"Bryant's passionate storytelling will captivate readers and bring a fresh perspective on a maritime tragedy that still reverberates in the twenty-first century."
–Jacquelyn Lenox Tuxill, author of
Whispers from the Valley of the Yak: A Memoir of Coming Full Circle

"*Sheltering Angel* tells the true story of several lesser-known individuals whose lives were impacted by the Titanic disaster. The stories of Cumings, Cunningham, Siebert and the others are engrossing, and Bryant's passion for the source material shines through on every page."
–Tad Fitch, author of
Recreating Titanic & Her Sisters: A Visual History

"This tale of an unlikely friendship between two people from worlds a galaxy apart is not just a good read. It's a beautifully told and poignant backstory to a piece of history we all know. Bryant is a master at finding such great true stories and bringing them to life."
–Sylvester Monroe, co-author with Peter Goldman,
of *Brothers: Black and Poor—A True Story of Courage and Survival*

Dedicated to the memory of
Lea Cumings Reynolds Parson
1925-2020

May God grant you always a sunbeam to warm you,
a moonbeam to charm you, a sheltering Angel so
nothing can harm you. And whenever you pray,
Heaven to hear you.
–Celtic blessing

Every age is a tragic age. Wars kill youth, disasters maim the living, and storms sink great ships. We cling to our meager blessings and to those left for us to cherish. But it was not always so for me, Florence Thayer Cumings. In what seems so long ago it must have been another life, there was feasting and laughter. There was joy. That life was before the cruel night, under a starry universe, my beloved was ripped from my side. Only the friendship of one humble man gives me courage to travel back to the time before the iceberg.

SHELTERING ANGEL

BOOK ONE

World's largest ship
RMS *Oceanic* Sets sail
The Liverpool Mercury, 1889

The grime and soot of Liverpool seeped through Andrew's jacket, through his shirt and trousers, and stuck to his skin. It was a different filth from the coal dust of Scotland. At least there the heather was abloom on the hillsides. But here, even on a bright June morning the dominant color was gray. Horses clip-clopped and wooden wagon wheels rumbled over cobblestones. The air carried a muddle of odors — the greasy pong of frying sausage and treacle wafting out of windows, the fishy tang from the docks, and the earthy stink of manure from horse-drawn carriages, all riding on salty breezes from the Irish Sea.

Since it was still early, he wandered up Waterloo to Regents Road, past Princes Dock to Millers Bridge and the docks where the great ships were tied awaiting passengers traveling to America. As a boy, he used to pretend the family house was afloat in the harbor waiting to weigh anchor and sail off somewhere. On nights when wind rattled the window glass, he rocked himself to sleep as if his bed were sailing over billows. He had always wanted to go to sea.

An ocean voyage was a fantasy beyond reach unless he could work on one of the big ships. He was forthright and honest, a good listener with a genial temperament. His mother always said he had a grounded quality, but he wouldn't let himself get doughy like some Scotsmen whose bellies hung over their kilts. If he could control his temper, he would work hard without complaint.

In front of the office of the White Star Line, he swallowed hard. With barely a shilling in his pocket, he was either going to catapult into a new life or skulk back to Scotland, tail between his legs. Fate had better smile on him today.

When he pulled open the door, essences of linseed oil and wood polish drifted toward him. Promising scents. The strong perfume of some exotic flower must have come from the rouged secretary sitting behind the counter and reading *The Halfpenny Marvel*, a magazine for school children. She must not have been too clever. He approached, shoulders back, feigning confidence.

"Beg pardon, madam," he said. "I'm here about employment."

The woman glanced up from the magazine. Shuffling papers on her desk, she pushed a form and a pencil toward him.

"Fill this out." She motioned toward a wood chair. "Over there."

The chair was horribly uncomfortable, and he shifted while he answered the questions.

Name: Andrew Orr Cunningham
Age: 22
Height: 5 feet 11 inches
Eyes: blue
Hair: brown
Nationality: Scottish
Employment experience: Thomson's Mercantile (He had worked at the mercantile, stocking shelves and sweeping up, and had a note from the storeowner in his pocket in case he needed a reference.)
Physical limitations: None
Distinguishing marks: A.C. and Union Jack tattoos on right arm. (The tattoos had been a splurge, but he had wanted to memorialize his move to England, his new home. If White Star objected, he would keep the ink covered while he was working.)

He finished completing the form and checked his answers. They were honest, at least, if not suitable. If he didn't measure up, he would have to languish in the cramped room he rented until some other prospect came along—unless he ran out of money first.

If only he had a cup of tea to calm his nerves. Should he get an interview, it had to go well. His options were running out—and so was his money.

Finally, the receptionist pointed to a wide desk with a gentleman sitting behind it.

Be cannie noo, he told himself. Everything depended on the way he presented himself in this moment.

The man's eyes glazed with dullness. How many others had he questioned for a job? How many others as desperate as Andrew Cunningham? Under his whiskbroom mustache the man's teeth were bucked, but he had a kind expression that set Andrew at ease.

"Thomas Brady," he said, standing. When he offered his hand, Andrew took it with a firm grasp. His Da had taught him that—a firm handshake shows confidence.

He gave his name and handed Brady the application. Andrew was a good head taller, which worried him. He didn't want to slouch, but he certainly didn't want Brady to think of him as superior and was glad when the fellow waved toward the chair opposite his desk.

Brady glanced at the form.

"What part of Scotland do you hail from?"

"Aye—er—" Andrew corrected himself. "From the Lanarkshire region, sir—Shotts specifically."

If Brady knew anything about the area, he would understand that any man who stayed in Shotts was expected to work in one of the smutty industries and surrender to the inevitable black lung disease that would take him slowly and bitterly. For a century the land in Lanarkshire had been torn by steam engines ripping out black nuggets of coal, and foundries melting ore into metal tools smudged the sky with malodorous smoke belching through their chimneys. Coal dust settled on roofs and yards turning the entire town an oily black. For a young man with ambition, the only option was to leave.

Brady rubbed his chin. At first Andrew had thought him young, but now he could see the chap had a good number of years under him—thinning hair, mustache flecked with silver. Pushing fifty—the age of Andrew's father.

"Any relation to Sir Charles Cunningham?" Brady asked.

Andrew racked his brain. "Afraid I don't know the name."

"Rear Admiral of the Royal Navy last century."

"It is possible we are descended from the same clan, but I'm not aware of a family line with that Cunningham."

"Pity. He led navies during the American War of Independence and the Napoleonic Wars. Quite a hero, he was."

As far as Andrew knew, there were no heroes in his family unless one considered struggling to pay bills a heroic task. If he had claimed to be a relation of the rear admiral, Brady might have been none the wiser and hired him based on his ancestry. Wasn't that how the rich got ahead—the privilege of birth?

He worried his ignorance about Sir Charles might dash his chances of employment.

"Of course," he said, "I should be proud if the admiral and I were related."

He tried not to flinch as Brady studied his application. The next questions came like buckshot.

"Your father's occupation?"

"Joiner, sir—making cabinets and such." Was he stuttering? Andrew wasn't ashamed of Da. His profession was a noble one and he was adept at it. Even though Andrew had no desire to saw and sand, he respected his father for what he did.

"And did he not train you to follow in his footsteps?"

"He tried." Here Andrew allowed his face to relax. "Not cut out for it, I'm afraid."

"Why are you interested in a steward's position?"

Ah—a steward. Is that what he was applying for? Better that than swabbing decks or shoveling coal. If the cruise line needed a steward, he could be a steward.

Don't hesitate. Don't mumble. Look the man in the eye.

"I feel my character suits the job, sir. And I am very eager to serve on a ship." It was an understatement, but he didn't want to push too hard.

Brady looked at his shoulders, his chest.

"Tall for a steward, aren't you?"

Andrew gambled a smile.

"I'm supple for my height, sir. Work out most mornings."

The interviewer made a note on his form and frowned at the paper. He hesitated so long Andrew thought the bloke had forgotten he was sitting in front of him. The fellow was a tortoise, a sloth. Most aggravating creature on earth. But Andrew would lie in wait—a patient predator.

After what seemed eons, Brady dipped his head and regarded Andrew from under his brows.

"You are able, of course, to read and write?"

"I completed secondary school with high marks, sir." Actually, his marks were the highest in his class. He had been an honor student.

"From your appearance, it seems you practice good hygiene. Hygiene is essential."

"Certainly." Andrew's palms were sweating. He didn't want to make a mistake.

"In order to perform the duties efficiently, you will be required to follow a strict schedule."

"I—" He cleared a tickle in his throat. "I am able to follow a strict agenda."

"Our passengers pay dearly for transport aboard our ocean liners. Everything must be done precisely."

"Precise—I understand." He felt like a runner who sprints the last yards to the finish line, spirits soaring.

"I advise you to slow your speech," Brady said. "Enunciate clearly. The language spoken aboard ship is predominantly English, but it's essential you be understood."

"I will enunciate," he said slowly.

Brady handed him a booklet.

"We'll take a chance on you, Mr. Cunningham. Your position will be Assistant Steward in first class. You'll board the *Oceanic* on Tuesday. Ask for the Second Steward. He'll instruct you in your duties. The ship sails on Thursday, so you'll have no time to waste learning the ropes. Meanwhile, study this handbook. If we have any complaints about your service, you will be terminated."

All he heard was first class. *Clas àrd* in Gaelic. Magistrates. Lairds. Burgesses. None of the masterless class. He'd have to mind his manners.

Standing straight, he offered Brady his hand. "Thank you, sir. I won't disappoint."

Outside the offices Andrew blew out a breath, as relieved as a sloughing snake that has shed its too-tight skin. Everything felt fresh and new. He had a job. He was going to sea.

Even an overcast sky couldn't cloud his elation. He tilted the bowler cap on his head and did a little jig on his way back to Mrs. Butler's boardinghouse.

Susan B. Anthony establishes
International Congress for Women's Rights
Boston Daily Globe, 1888

Who was the dashing young gentleman sitting toward the back of the sanctuary at my father's Unitarian church? He must have been a Harvard student, or a recent graduate, since the church was next to the Cambridge campus. The fellow deserved credit for not missing the last month of Sundays. One week he slid into the pew behind Mother and me, second row from the altar. I enjoyed his tenor voice during the hymns and especially enjoyed the sensation of his gaze on my back. My skin warmed as if it were midsummer instead of early spring. Carefully, I raised my hand to my necklace. It was made of glass, not real pearls. Papa and Mother had given it to me for my last birthday—sixteen years. Living with my parents in the parsonage was drudgery. Time was a turtle in its pace, and I wished for more excitement than housework, reading, and prayer. Hoping Mother wouldn't notice, I crept the necklace around so the golden clasp was at the back. The clasp was a tease on my part, but I figured my Unitarian lad should have something to hold his attention besides my father's bearded visage at the pulpit.

Following the service, at fellowship hour I sidled up to the cookie table where that very young man was studying the selection—molasses crinkles, hermits, and cinnamon dreams. When he reached for a hermit, his arm bumped mine.

"Very sorry," he said. "Clumsy of me." He was close enough that I could smell his hair tonic, a geranium scent so masculine I had to force the slowing of my breath.

"You're forgiven," I said, wishing he had bumped me earlier. "I believe I shall live."

His lips curled into a smile that made my heart flutter. "I dearly hope so. And may it be a long and thrilling life."

"That has yet to be seen." I glanced at Papa, relieved to see he was occupied with a member of his congregation.

The fellow blinked at me. "The long part or the thrilling part?"

I chose a cinnamon dream and held it up for effect.

"Both, of course." Then I dipped my head and took a bite.

Weekly the gentleman complimented my father on his inspiring homilies. Papa was so impressed he invited him for supper on a Friday night. It was not unusual to have guests at the parsonage—visiting fat-bellied clergy with stinky breath, straight-laced Unitarian officials, and timid divinity students who took Papa's ethics class at Harvard and read—or skimmed, I imagined—the six volumes he had written on the morality of armed combat. Saturday nights were reserved for polishing his Sunday discourse, but visitors scooted themselves up to our table most other evenings. Mother and I kept the cottage clean and the table set with the English bone china handed down from my grandmother.

On Friday afternoon I changed my dress three times and settled on a simple walking gown, pink with white stripes. I cinched the waist tie and pinned up my hair loosely, hoping a tendril would droop to fascinate our guest. Papa said his name was Bradley Cumings and his family was well respected in Boston. I tried out the name Mrs. Bradley Cumings. Florence Cumings. It had a nice ring.

When a knock came at the door, Mother called from the kitchen for me to greet our guest. The mantel clock said a minute before six. He was punctual—I liked that. And there he was— gray suit, four buttons up the front. When he saw me, he slipped off the derby and held it over his chest.

"Mr. Cumings, I presume?" I said.

"You presume correctly, Miss Thayer."

"You've heard of the naturalist John Muir, I take it?" I had read his work as part of a botany project at Winsor School.

He looked confused. "Vaguely, yes."

"Then you might know his standing on presuming. He said the idea of the world being made for men is not supported by all the facts. Presumption is often erroneous."

His forehead crinkled. "And I suppose the world was made for women?"

"That would make more sense, would it not?"

He covered his mouth with his hand. If he were laughing at me, I hoped he was enjoying the banter. When he raised his russet eyes, I took a step back as if Edison's electric current had surged through me.

"Is it erroneous, Miss Thayer," he said, "to presume that eventually you will invite me in?"

I glanced toward the dining room then back to our guest. "Very sorry," I said. "Please do join us."

Taking the chair across from Bradley Cumings, I tried to think of something clever to say. The words wouldn't come, but he kept the conversation flowing, speaking mostly to Papa. At the boarding school he had attended in Rhode Island, he explained, the boys were taught that privileged young men had a duty to serve their communities and their country—honor and service above all else. I was delighted to hear of his desire to serve. He would make a good partner for my own intentions to help the poor. Papa nodded approval.

Mr. Cumings had two sisters, he said, but his boarding school was all boys. I blinked when he glanced at me over the roast.

"If a boy had a chance even to glimpse a girl in those days," he said, "it was at a dance organized with the all-girls Wheeler School in Providence."

"Under strict supervision, of course," Papa said. He was uncomfortable with table discussion regarding boys meeting girls, having married Mother at their parents' insistence even though they barely knew each other. Of course, I would want Papa to accept the man I loved but I intended to make up my own mind in matters of the heart.

"When I finished my Harvard studies," Mr. Cumings said, "I took an internship at a stock brokerage in Boston."

He would be a stockbroker, then. I hoped he wasn't preoccupied with money when there were more pressing struggles like equal rights for Negroes, Indians, and women. I had to give him the benefit of the doubt, though. Unitarians supported reforms, and the fat bill he dropped into the offering plate every Sunday gave me the impression he was in favor of Unitarian activism.

Bradley and Papa talked about their years at Harvard, which left me out. What was I to speak about—fashion? Books I was reading? *The Scarlet Letter* and *Sonnets from the Portuguese* were too titillating to discuss at the supper table although I'd have liked to send our guest one of Browning's poems. "I love thee to the level of every day's / Most quiet need," I would write him. As for my own needs, they were growing less quiet by the day.

Queen Victoria
surpasses grandfather
King George III
as longest reigning monarch in British history
The Liverpool Mercury, 1895

Andrew spent three days memorizing the steward's manual—hundreds of regulations, etiquette, table settings, servicing a stateroom, general cleanliness. He kept himself clean and neat, but cleaning other people's messes—that was another matter.

By Tuesday morning he was ready. At the dock he stared up at the monstrous ship. Her two massive funnels slanted toward the stern, making her appear to be plowing into the wind even tethered to cleats. *Oceanic* had been christened before her maiden voyage only a year earlier. She had won the Blue Riband by crossing the Atlantic in fewer than six days. The largest engines in the world propelled her with the most lavish first-class accommodations. Andrew thought himself honored to serve on such a ship.

He had swum in the Firth of Forth and had contemplated the North Sea, but he had never seen an ocean. Now he would be crossing one on a liner named for the breadth and depth of such a body of water. He felt a rising panic. What if he couldn't measure up? The captain wouldn't unload him in the North Atlantic, would he? Or leave him on the Manhattan dock without an American cent in his pocket? No—Andrew Cunningham would follow the steward's manual to the letter. He'd prove himself. Within a few days he'd be smartly dressed in the White Star uniform and on his way to New York, the most glamorous city in the world.

He jerked his jacket straight, wiggled his hat, and lugged his duffel across the gangway.

In the first-class lounge he might as well have been standing in the room of a palace. Murals above the mahogany walls glittered with gold leaf. Velvet draped windows and upholstery, and chandeliers dripping with cut glass dangled in midair. Fourteen feet above the dining saloon, a glass dome filtered daylight that fell to the thick carpeting like fairy dust. The aromas of wood polish, carpet wool, and fresh paint were untainted by the stink hovering over Liverpool. For Andrew, this ship offered a new start far from the coal dirt of his boyhood.

Behind him, an indignant voice called, "See here, sir!"

Andrew twirled around to find a corpulent fellow pointing a finger at him.

"State your business." He was wearing a uniform and must have been a ship's officer.

Andrew broke from his trance. "Name's Cunningham. I'm to report to the chief steward."

"You're one of the new ones, then." He tilted his head as if to say he should have known. "I'm Mayes. You were meant to report to the bunkroom." Without waiting for Andrew to ask where the blazes the bunkroom was, Mayes said, "Follow me and be quick about it."

For such a wide bloke, Mayes moved like a rhinoceros on a charge, and Andrew stumbled behind him down a flight of stairs—ladders, the handbook called them—and through an alleyway. The bunkroom was little more than a storage space crammed with bunks, one bed sardined above another. Mayes assigned him a top mattress, and Andrew worried that with his tall frame he'd overspill and land atop the unfortunate bloke below. But he intended to spend as little time as possible in these smothering quarters.

Other stewards were settling in and tossed their names at him, most of which he quickly forgot. One warned him about seasickness.

"You feel sick, press the inside of your wrist," he said.

"And if you chunder," another added, "you'd bloody well not funk up the glory hole with it."

The handbook hadn't mentioned chundering, and he supposed the glory hole was the bunkroom. It was clear he had a lot to learn—and he had better learn fast.

Mayes took his hands, looked at the palms, and turned them over to examine the backs.

"I see you don't wear a ring—that's good. Keep your nails trimmed and clean and use a pumice stone to rub off nicotine stains."

"I don't use tobacco," Andrew snapped. Bugger the man for making assumptions about him.

"All the better." Mayes sniffed. "Never wear cologne, and be sure your clothing and especially your underclothing are clean and fresh."

Andrew wouldn't intentionally do anything that might offend a guest, and he bristled at Mayes discussing his undergarments. Gritting his teeth, he nodded agreement. A steward was respectful of his superiors.

"Be observant and alert at all times," Mayes said. "Do whatever the passengers request of you. And don't dawdle about it."

Andrew had read how to make beds, clean chambers, and answer bells when passengers called for service. Mayes needn't worry about his deportment.

"Do you have any questions, Cunningham?" Mayes asked.

Sure, Andrew had questions. Where would he eat and when? Could he use the ship's library and the gym? Or was he to make himself invisible unless called for? But he didn't want to get on the officer's bad side and held his tongue.

Mayes handed him a uniform. "Put this on and keep it spotless." The white jacket hit just at the waist, the black trousers made of scratchy wool. Then Mayes launched another sting. "The cost of the uniform will be subtracted from your wages."

Blast it—how long would it take him to make up for the cost?

"Third class boards at the stern," Mayes said. "Irishmen and Eastern Europeans mostly. Immigrants are White Star Line's bread and butter. They'll be six to a room, but it'll be clean and dry, and the food will be better than anything they had in the old country." He mumbled the final comment. "Long as they stay put in steerage where they belong, we should have a smooth sail."

The words "where they belong" slapped him. If Andrew were a paying passenger, he'd be squeezed in with the immigrants at the lowest fare. Likely it was only the uniform that set Mayes apart from steerage himself. They both should count themselves lucky.

On boarding day, Andrew watched the third-class passengers arrive, men wearing clean woolens, women with scarves over their heads and shawls around their shoulders. Their faces shone with a mixture of awe and terror. Most of them already were farther from home than they had ever been, and the *Oceanic* might as well have been a spaceship to another galaxy. Andrew knew how they felt. He would not have been surprised if the propellers levitated the ship above the water and up into the stars. As it was, navigating such a vessel across so vast an ocean seemed nothing short of magic.

Before first class boarded at the forward entry, Mayes lined up Andrew with the other stewards and barked at them to be courteous.

"Always say 'sir' and 'madam,' and if you must address them by last names, use their titles—Doctor, Miss, Judge, *et cetera*. Understood?"

Mayes stood beside Andrew, jabbing his ribs with an elbow to remind him to stand straighter, give the passengers submissive nods, and keep a pleasant expression on his face — no small task with his blasted ribs aching.

With all classes aboard, luggage delivered, and passengers settled, finally the dockworkers loosed *Oceanic's* lines. As the ship started to move, Andrew went to the rail and felt his first thrill at setting out from land. He had a tingling of raw energy, like an axe driven into the frozen lake of his small life.

The *Oceanic* threaded its way down the River Mersey into the Irish Sea, through St. George's Channel and out to the open ocean. Fully underway, it cruised at twenty knots, the ship's three engines each pumping ten cylinders that consumed twelve tons of coal every hour. The bow cut the water's surface like a saber, but except for the barely perceptible vibration of the engines, it felt as if the ship were hardly moving.

Sea birds rode the crisp air with hardly a movement of their wings. What more could a lad ask for than this ship, this sea, this clear morning? Andrew wasn't sure what he'd find on the other shore, but he was sure of one thing — he was ready for whatever was to come.

President of Harvard To Sign Parchments
of the Fair Graduates
The Boston Globe, 1895

For the next two years, Bradley Cumings came calling every week. Mother offered him tea, sometimes supper, and often when the weather was agreeable he and I walked around Cambridge. Bradley, as he asked me to address him, showed me the Harvard Campus, which I already knew well, but I enjoyed how his voice swelled with pride when we reached Soldiers Field.

"Sport," he said, "is an art."

"Some might disagree with you," I said. "Sport is akin to war. There are winners and losers. In art, no one loses except those who ignore it."

"That's rather deep thinking." He gave me a quizzical look.

"Oh, sorry. Would you rather I keep to the shallows?"

He laughed. "You have a quick mind, Florence. You might consider the Harvard Annex for study."

"Might I?"

"Radcliffe College, I believe they've named it. Harvard professors give lectures to women students there."

"My dear Mr. Cumings," I said, "I leave it to you to lecture me. Whether or not I listen is another matter."

"My dear Miss Thayer," he responded, his tone matching mine in playful formality, "I expect you will exert your will in lectures as well as in all other matters."

If he only knew that my will was that this comely companion walk by my side for a lifetime.

Some evenings Mother and Papa left us alone in the parlor. There was never a strain being with Bradley. He could talk on any subject, and when I had nothing to say, he filled in the gaps. We had been seeing each other for three years when he surprised me by sliding off the divan and getting down on one knee.

He pulled a box from his coat, a small one just the size to hold a ring or a bracelet. The box was black velvet suggesting whatever was inside was expensive. When he fumbled the box and dropped it to the carpet, I stifled a giggle—he seemed so earnest. Scooping up the box, he cleared his throat. Then, realizing his tie was crooked, he tried with one hand to straighten it and nearly dropped the box again. This time he captured the misbehaving thing and centered again on the mission he had undertaken.

"Florence Thayer," he began. He had taken to calling me Florrie, which I thought intimate and dear. To address me by Florence was serious business indeed.

"Would you do me the honor—"

"Yes, of course," I said before he finished. I might have gotten down on my own knee if he'd waited any longer.

I was nineteen, and Bradley suggested we hold off the wedding until I turned twenty and he was twenty-four. A year of engagement seemed appropriate. In the meantime, he would take me to meet his parents at the Cumings summer home in York Harbor, Maine. He was sure they would love me. I was sure I loved him.

Down Boston's School Street, Bradley stopped in front of the Parker House Hotel.

"Let's go in," he said.

"I'm not dressed for such a fancy place," I said.

"We'll just have a slice of Boston cream pie. It was invented here." He took my elbow and led me to the hotel restaurant. "What do you think?"

I regarded the wood paneling and the high ceilings, the crystal chandeliers.

"Very nice."

"I've reserved it for our wedding," he said. "We can have as many guests as we please—hundreds, if you like."

"What do you mean you've reserved it?" Why hadn't he consulted me before he made such an important decision?

"There's no better setting in Boston for a wedding. You've heard about the Saturday Club that met at Parker House, haven't you? Emerson was a member, Hawthorne, Whittier, and Henry Longfellow, too. Oliver Wendell Holmes recited 'A Christmas Carol' here."

"I don't want to be married here," I said.

"Why in heaven's name not, Florrie? It's the quintessence of posh."

"I don't need posh, I don't want posh, and my father can't afford posh. We're Unitarians, Bradley."

He planted his fists on his hips. "What is it you want, then, my Unitarian darling?"

"My father will perform the ceremony at College Club of Boston. The drawing room will do very well," I said. "I've already made the arrangements."

"That brownstone in the Back Bay? How in blazes will we get the guest list down to—what, a hundred?"

"More like fifty. And no lunch—just afternoon tea."

"Florrie," he said, kissing my cheek, "if I didn't love you so much, I'd find you absolutely infuriating."

If Bradley wanted names dropped, I could have mentioned Mark Twain, Sarah Bernhardt, and Lucy Stone as previous guests of the College Club. But he wouldn't have approved of Stone, the suffragist who kept her own name after she married. I couldn't fathom what difference it made whether I kept my father's name or took my husband's. I could be Mrs. Cumings and still hold my own convictions.

One of those convictions involved the dress I would wear on my wedding day. Mother wanted me to use her own wedding dress from twenty-three years earlier, but I found the gaudy thing flouncy with far too many layers of lace ruffles around the plunging neckline. Queen Victoria would have approved, but it wasn't at all my style. Mother had blanched when I suggested the gown might be remade with a high neck and a glossy line, a touch of lace, if I must, at the shoulders. And I would wear white gloves with buttons at the wrist. I conceded about the veil that fell to the floor, and Mother was adamant that my dress be white. She would not hear of her daughter being married in a dress of even the palest blue. I damned Queen Victoria for setting the trend that brides always wear white.

And so a compromise was reached. I walked down a chair-flanked aisle at the College Club of Boston and joined my heart with the heart of the man I loved in front of seventy — at Bradley's insistence — of our family and closest friends.

"As you stand beside each other," Reverend Thayer announced, "may your love be as constant as the ocean tide, waves flowing endlessly from the depths of the sea. Just as water is an eternal force of life, so is love. Love is the force that allows us to face fear and uncertainty with courage."

The ceremony was intimate and unpretentious, exactly the way I had wanted.

Late that night, after the vows, the congratulatory handshakes and kisses on cheeks, after the champagne, the dancing, the farewells, in the mirror of a hotel dressing table I watched my new husband while I brushed my hair. Long and dark, it reached nearly to my waist. I had not let it down in front of him before, but we were married now and he would have to take me for how I was — flaws and strengths as well. My hair, I believed, was one of my assets.

Bradley was in bed propped against a pillow, the table lamp shedding light on some financial paper he was reading. He had on striped pajamas. I took delight in seeing him like this, relaxed, the white shirt with the stiff front hung on the back of a chair. His eyes slid from the paper to my back where I could feel the silk of my gown clinging to my skin. I had drawn my hair over my shoulder and brushed the strands across my breast. One of these evenings when we were both beyond the shyness of the first nights as man and wife, maybe he would come to me, take the brush from my hand, and groom my hair with a gentle hand. Surely that would be when finally he realized I was his—completely his.

For now, I wound my hair into a loose braid, my fingers nimble but shaking at the prospect of slipping under the crisp sheet beside him.

Liverpool Population Grows to over half a million
Liverpool Echo, 1897

One morning before the breakfast service Andrew climbed to the boat deck for a few quiet moments. The brisk air burned his cheeks as he stood at the railing and stared across the vast field of blue water. Was it possible to love something and fear it at once? The ocean was deeper than the skyscrapers of New York are tall, vast enough to hold the largest creatures on earth, and fierce enough to sink the largest ships ever built. When he was a bairn diving into the firth near his grandparents' home, he opened his eyes under the blue-green water. Deeper down, there was no light except the luminous flicker of a passing fish. He had learned to be a strong swimmer. The tide came in fast and could carry a boy out to sea or pull him under if he didn't have enough fight in him. Andrew could keep his head above water or hold his breath a full minute if the current pulled him down. But his mum taught him to be wary of the sea. Its waters are more powerful than anything on earth, she had said. But even then he was lured by its mysteries as if he were one of its own creatures. If by some great mishap the *Oceanic* should founder, he would sprout gills and fins. He would grow a fantail and glide back to England. The sea would not conquer him.

Thinking of shipwrecks was not conducive to rest, and at night he wrestled with thoughts of disaster, turning one way on his narrow mattress and then the other, flipping his pillow, then squeezing it. He knew he'd be his own shipwreck if he didn't get at least a few hours of sleep. But willing sleep made it more elusive.

During the day, he performed every duty like an actor in a play. He had memorized the script and knew his lines perfectly. His audience were the well-heeled who never applauded his performance except for the few thin dollars they pressed into his hand at the end of the voyage. He hid his resentment while he cleaned up after cocktail parties, doctored ailments with medicinal teas, sympathized with the tearful lonely, and pacified complaints with whatever soothing remedies he could concoct. Their staterooms suffocated with the fragrance of flowers sent by well-wishers. He had to find vases for the parade of bouquets that came aboard, enough to furnish a florist's shop. Water had to be changed daily, stems clipped so the blooms would last all the way to New York. He worked seventeen-hour days, moving bundles and baggage, serving, polishing, and keeping an ear out for call bells. On the busiest days, he took his meals standing up in the pantry, careful not to drop a crumb on his impeccably clean uniform. He knew enough to play the steward's game in order to reap the biggest rewards.

While he trudged up and down ladders to satisfy whims, Andrew cursed the birthrights of the leisure class. His own father was as good as any of the rich toffs he waited on. Better, even. The senior Cunningham worked hard for what he had. For his Da—and for Andrew as well—work was not a game. Work was survival. And survival was on the line.

At breakfast one morning Andrew failed to ask a passenger if she wanted powdered sugar with her porridge. Scots always salted their porridge—porridge was meant to be breakfast, not dessert. On top of that, at the dinner service he had neglected to serve the Scotch broth before the cold salmon with mayonnaise. Whenever he had the opportunity, he took a cup of the broth himself to ward off any illness he might pick up from the toffs. And it served against the joint pain he felt during the first days at sea from unaccustomed lifting and bending.

Mayes pulled him aside and delivered a reprimand about the broth mishap, ordering him to study the steward's handbook yet again.

In the room he rented for respite between launches, Andrew was so entranced with the diagram of dinner lay-up for the officers' mess that he hadn't heard the knock on the door.

Mrs. Butler, a stout, gnome-like landlady, tapped once and turned the knob without waiting for a response. Andrew jumped to his feet as if she had caught him in his union suit.

"Oh," she said. "Thought you were out."

"No, I'm very much in, as you can see." The woman was a simpleton in Andrew's opinion.

Behind her was a narrow fellow, his coat drooping around his spare frame. With hair the color of seasoned firewood and shimmery gray eyes, he seemed unearthly, as if he'd been plunked down from a flying saucer.

"Sorry, but—" the lad blurted to Mrs. Butler. "It doesn't look as if this room is available."

"There's two beds," she said. "Ample space."

"I wonder," the youngster said, "if you have another room— one I might occupy alone."

Andrew wanted his privacy as well. He had shared a room with his younger brother most of his life, and now he treasured the peace and quiet of his own space.

"Oh, dear me, no. These days rooms is scarce as hen's teeth. The city's bulging at the seams, what with everyone moving in to work on the big ships. Bless yer lucky stars there's this one bed." She jerked her chin toward the extra cot.

"I suppose there's no choice." The new bloke shrugged toward Andrew. "If it's all the same to you."

It wasn't all the same to Andrew.

"The rent will be half each," Mrs. Butler interjected.

Half rent—an appealing offer, what with Andrew being gone so much of the time.

"In that case," he said, "we might manage."

"He's a shop assistant." Mrs. Butler tilted her head toward the skinny chap, as if he should be fortunate to work in a shop.

"I see." Not that Andrew gave a whit about what the bloke did as long as he was quiet about it.

The landlady backed out of the room. The youth—not more than a teenager, Andrew reckoned, stuck out his hand.

"Siebert—Sidney Conrad Siebert. The first."

Andrew smirked. "And not the last, I assume?"

"Remains to be seen, doesn't it?"

Andrew offered his firm handshake, aware of the lad's spindly fingers.

"Andrew Cunningham," he said.

"A highlander, are you?"

An inane question—of course he was a highlander. And if his being Scottish was a problem for Siebert, he could wallop the bony fellow with one hand.

"If I keep my mouth shut, maybe I won't give myself away." Andrew was making an affable effort.

"Fine by me. I don't mind doing all the talking." Siebert tossed his leather suitcase onto the second bed, took off his coat and threw it over the suitcase. Then he flopped into the only stuffed chair.

Andrew leaned against the door, arms akimbo. "How long have you been in Liverpool?"

"What is it—June? Well then, that would be most of the spring and now into summer. The landlady at the last place was a mite stingy on the portions." He patted his middle. "Surprised I haven't dwindled to skin and bone."

Andrew laughed. Had Siebert ever looked in a mirror? He was reminded of Irving's story of the lanky schoolteacher of

Sleepy Hollow whose skeleton—as he remembered the tale—hung loosely beneath his hide.

The younger fellow held up a finger.

"What say we invest in a spirit stove and kettle? Then we can have a cup of tea whenever we like. Might as well start off as chums."

"I expect there won't be much time for tea."

"Always time for tea. Or do you Scots prefer whisky?"

"I don't go in for whisky—or any alcohol for that matter." Andrew knew he sounded curt, but he wanted to get back to the handbook.

Siebert tented his fingers under his chin. "If you don't haunt the pubs, what keeps you busy?"

When Andrew didn't answer, Siebert got up, ambled to Andrew's bed, and picked up the book.

"*Ship's Manual?* What's your business with ships?"

"I steward on a cruise ship. First-class cabins." He was boasting, but he wanted Siebert to know he wouldn't be sleeping next to a steerage steward. He grabbed the book from Siebert's hand. "We sail again in a couple days. I'll be gone for two weeks, and you'll have this mansion to yourself."

"A steward—that's virtually a servant, isn't it?"

"I suppose you could see it that way." Andrew leveled his eyes at Siebert. "Not much different from being a shopkeeper."

"The shop is more of an amusement." Siebert twisted his mouth to the side. "Landlords require their tenants to have a means of support. An allowance from a generous aunt has set me up in this elegant lodging—until I land upon my next course of action. A place like this—" He flapped his hand around the room. "Who would want to linger here?"

"Can't argue with you there," Andrew said, thinking who would want to linger with Sidney Siebert? At least with this pompous arse as a roommate, he'd look forward to getting back aboard *Oceanic*.

"The thing is, Cunningham, I'm rather stuck at the moment." Siebert dropped back into the chair, curled his fingers inward, and examined the nails. "I am debased by the company I keep—social climbers, all of them. People aspiring to the upper levels without the right of entry by birth. Oh, one could marry an American, I suppose. But any proper Englishman should be suspicious of American women."

"Seems you have strong opinions."

"Indeed," Siebert said. Banging his fists on the armrests, he added, "And my current opinion is that we should sit ourselves at Mrs. Butler's table for our evening tea. Shall we, Cunningham?"

Andrew snorted. By happenstance, Siebert might have become his first "chum" in Liverpool.

While on land, it became Andrew's habit to go out for coffee at a café on Pudsey Street. His New York passengers preferred coffee over tea and he'd gotten used to the bitter taste. He bought a newspaper and skimmed the headlines. The mogul J. P. Morgan and the prosperous Rothschild family had saved America from economic ruin by lending the government millions in gold—with significant interest, he reckoned. Once the London market opened, bonds had sold out in minutes. From his knowledge of passengers aboard *Oceanic*, it seemed America had enough rich toffs to keep it afloat.

When he turned the page, an ad for the White Star Line popped out at him. They were hiring more crew for the *Oceanic*. Business was apparently better than the company had anticipated.

The paper snapped in front of his nose and when Andrew lowered it, he found a grinning Sidney Siebert.

"How'd you find me?" Andrew asked.

"Followed the redolence of haggis."

"Very amusing." Andrew smirked at him.

"Oh, come on, chappy — don't be so solemn."

"It's solemn times." Andrew put his finger on the article about Morgan and Rothschild. "America's in an economic *maim*."

"Mime? Translation, if you will?"

"Gaelic for panic, mate," Andrew said. Sometimes his native language crept up on him.

"America, America." Siebert slid out a chair and sat down even though Andrew hadn't invited him. "You've caught New York fever working on that big tub, mate."

Andrew could feel Siebert hurtling into a rant.

"Most of Europe wants to be part of the United States. Everyone is lining up to be American. Before you know it, the entire globe will be one great America."

"Have you been to the States?" Andrew asked.

"Once to New York on one of your cruise ships. My mum took my brother and me. We were barely in our teens, but I shall never forget it. The smell of the sea wakes a man from his daydreams. If I could manage it, I'd live on a cruise ship."

Andrew had no reason to reach out to Siebert, but he wouldn't mind witnessing whether the young Brit could live up to his arrogance. He folded the newspaper.

"I might be able to make that daydream come true."

Siebert tilted his head down and raised a brow. "And how do you propose to pay for said passage?"

"The *Oceanic* is hiring crew." Andrew pushed the newspaper across the table.

"Crew? I don't crew."

"You could be a steward," Andrew said. "You might even meet one of those rich American women you so distrust."

"A steward? How vulgar."

Andrew shrugged. "Suit yourself. But the monthly wage is two pounds, fifteen shillings, plus gratuities. And the first classers are generous. If they like you, it could mean another ten pounds each way."

Siebert rubbed his chin. "Generous, you say?"

"Generous, yes." Andrew smirked at him.

Siebert slapped his hand on the table. "Good enough, then. My guardian will be happy I've found a hobby that actually gives compensation."

"That's the spirit. Have a cup of tea, Sid." Andrew signaled the waiter. "It's on me."

"Cunningham," Sid said that evening, "take a gander at this application, will you?" He pushed a piece of paper across Mrs. Butler's tea table. "You know—just to make certain I haven't overlooked anything."

"Sure, mate." Andrew peered at the sheet of paper.

Name: Sidney Conrad Siebert

Age: 19

Height: 5'9"

Weight: 135 pounds.

Andrew guessed the bloke hardly reached ten stone, but what was a little fudging if he could get away with it?

Hair color: Brown

Eye color: Gray

Education: Secondary school certificate

Address: Liverpool

Previous address: Brightlingsea

Birthplace: Battersea

Father's name and occupation: Conrad Siebert, chairmaker

Experience: Yacht block maker, Brightlingsea shipyard.

Skills: Making yacht blocks by sawing, drilling, planing.

Yacht blocks were for running lines through. Making them required skill and a degree of artistry. Andrew was impressed. But he wasn't about to reveal that to Sid.

"I don't know about this last bit," Andrew said. "They might put you in with the stokers."

"Stokers?" Sid scowled.

"The firemen who shovel coal into the furnaces. Revolting work, that."

"Sod off." Sid reached for the application and started to tear it, but Andrew grabbed it away.

"Never mind, mate. I'll put in a good word for ye."

Andrew used his sway with White Star to get Sid hired as steward aboard *Oceanic*. First class, no less. Within a few days, with their duffel bags in hand, the pair stepped onto the *Oceanic's* deck. Sid admitted to being a touch anxious, but he was up for the challenge.

"I've asked the maid to leave a bottle of port in our room." He poked Andrew's arm.

"The only swallie you'll have will be the leavings from the first classers," Andrew grumbled.

"Then bless them, and may they heave their appetites overboard."

Even if stewarding didn't suit him, once Sid took in the inlaid ivory and gold in the ship's paneled walls, he came around.

"Rather homey, don't you think?" He ran a finger over the scrolled woodwork, drawing a laugh from Andrew.

"Is there any limit to your arrogance, Siebert?"

Andrew put Sid to task straightening staterooms when passengers were out. When they were in, he was to attend to their every wish, even when their demands were tedious. "Bring me a nail file. A hairpin. A fresh toothbrush." Andrew made him go at a run but warned him not to sweat—perspiration was unseemly in a steward.

He tutored Sid in helping with the dinner service as the newcomer recited rules of etiquette under his breath.

"The sterling flatware is placed in the order of its use, those to be used first placed farthest from the plate. The salad fork to the left of the plate, then the meat fork. Just to the right of the plate is the meat knife and on the outside, the salad knife." He lifted the fish knife. "Now where the blazes—"

"The meat knife replaces the fish knife after the first course is withdrawn," Andrew said. "You must execute the table setting seamlessly."

"I can be pressed into seamlessness," Sid responded, mocking him.

"It's like choreography, mate."

"Then I'll dance my way around the table." He executed a comical demi-plie.

Andrew tried not to laugh. "This is important, Sid. You can't afford to make mistakes." He gestured to the setting. "The cutting edge of each knife lies toward the plate lest the diner cut herself from carelessness."

"Right. Clumsy toffs," Sid growled.

Andrew ignored him. "Outside the knives are the soup spoons. Dessert spoons and forks are centered above the plates."

"Think you're bleeding clever, don't you, mate? Or as the toffs would say, in-tell-ee-gent."

"As I've often been told." Andrew jerked up his nose toward Sid. "Now remember the order or you'll muck up." Andrew went on describing the placement of goblets and napkins while Sid murmured "bloody hell." The lad would get used to the table setting after a few crossings—or so Andrew hoped.

While passengers smoked and gossiped in the lounges, he and Sid rushed to turn down beds. Later in the evening when bells rang and he was weighed down by weariness, he scooted

Sid along to bring one a nightcap, another a quinine or an extra towel. "No dragging heels," he barked. They answered questions about the next day's breakfast service—pastries and coffee ready by eight o'clock, full breakfast by nine—and willed most of them to sleep in.

It was near midnight when the stewards dropped into their bunks, but daylight had not yet shone through the porthole when Andrew jostled Sid awake and ordered him to hop into his uniform. Then he set Sid to dashing up and down ladders to answer calls.

"You never cease to amaze me, lad," Andrew told him. To his surprise, Sid had learned nautical terms and navigational routes and had seen to every detail of his duties. After passengers disembarked, he changed linens, removed trash, and even dusted lampshades and picture frames. When a new group boarded, Sid delivered their luggage, put fresh water in the flower vases, and directed them around the ship—dining saloon, smoking room, purser's office, promenade deck.

"When you're familiar with every nook and nuance of the *Oceanic*," Andrew told Sid, "you'll have the advantage over newly boarded first-class passengers. The trick is to make them feel superior and tuck your smugness into the sleeve of your serving jacket."

Of course, complacency wouldn't do. The passengers were a steward's bread and butter. The better they served, the more generously passengers pressed their palms with gratitude when they disembarked.

The first-class travelers were among the most notable people on two continents, including members of Parliament and the U.S. House of Representatives, and Andrew made sure Sid kept on his toes. British Lord Beresford wanted coffee in his chamber at dawn, a bottle of wine in the afternoon, brandy at night and tea and scones in between. William Hargreaves composed music hall songs, and when they shuffled him off in New York, his song "Burlington Bertie" rang in Andrew's head for days. *I'm Burlington Bertie, I rise at ten thirty, then saunter along like a toff. I walk down the Strand with my gloves on my hand, then I walk down again with them off.* He couldn't afford to hold a grudge against toffs, even the ones who looked down on him for working a menial service job. Most were clueless about the real world — at least about Andrew Cunningham's world.

Boola Boola Yale Fight Song
New York Times, 1901

At the Brookline Free Women's Hospital, I gave my body over to the baby about to be born. My own agony was nothing compared to the work the poor little thing was undertaking to enter the harsh light of the world after three-quarters of a year tucked snugly in my womb. Now, in late summer 1897, the child was ready to make an appearance.

When finally the nurse put the infant in my arms, a pink and healthy boy, I hadn't imagined it possible to love another being as much as I loved Bradley. But here was a tiny version of him, twice as much to cherish.

When he came into the delivery room and stood beside the bed, Bradley's eyes misted over.

"We have a son," I said.

"A boy?" he answered, wanting to be sure.

"And we'll name him after you — John Bradley."

His mouth moved, trying to get out the words. He moistened his lips with his tongue and tried again.

"All right," he whispered. "But we'll call him Jack."

My husband had never said no to me. He once told me I was everything a man could wish for in a wife — grounded, intelligent, well spoken. I had been embarrassed he thought of me in that way, a minister's daughter with no impressive pedigree. But that day I had given him the most generous gift I could bestow — a child who would bear his name.

Bradley's stock brokerage was doing well, and befitting his success he had joined the very best groups—Racquet Club, Metropolitan Club for spa and fitness, and the Riding Club for exploring Back Bay's bridle paths. He worked long days to provide for us, but I'd gladly have lived like a pauper just to be with these men—father and son—both of whom I adored.

Two years following, a second son joined our clan. Whereas Jackie had the demeanor of his grandfather, studious and thoughtful, Wells took after Bradley. He was playful and talkative, imitating sounds even before he could form words. I doted on my boys with no regret for the hours they demanded of my attention.

I was happy Bradley fell into the thick of the fatherhood business. Not that he had much to do with the work of babies. He wrestled with Jackie and rocked Wells in his arms, but as I had heard it said—and it was very true—two were twice as trying as one. If I hadn't gotten involved in the new settlement movement for women in Boston's South End, I could have been better at domestic tasks. But relief work was important to me. Once in a while my mother would watch the children, and Papa donated some of his books to help set up a South End library. I hadn't mentioned the settlement work to Bradley. Not yet, at least.

A couple evenings a week, Bradley stopped at the Racquet Club after work for a tennis match with a New Yorker he had befriended. They had drinks afterward, and by the time he came home for dinner, I had fed the boys and gotten them ready for bed. I didn't begrudge Bradley. But my energy was depleted, and I let him lead the conversation over our late meal.

"This chap Bert Marckwald is gracious enough to let me wallop him on the court," he said. "Even picks up the tab at the bar afterward."

"You mean your friend from New York? I'm sure he's a fine fellow." I couldn't summon more enthusiasm than that.

"Florrie, I'd like to have him for dinner."

"Dinner? Here?"

"Tomorrow night. You'll find him most entertaining."

"Bradley—" I had hoped to attend a talk about public baths in the South End. The women needed sanitation for the settlement houses.

"You're overworked, darling. But not to worry—I've hired help for you. We can afford it, and the woman—name's Hannah—will see to the boys, do a little cleanup, even start our supper. Bert recommended her."

I looked at the boys' dinner plates still on the table and peered toward the parlor where they had left toys scattered over the rug. It was beyond me to clean up enough even to have help come in.

"Leave everything," Bradley said. "Hannah will start tomorrow morning. She'll have the place shipshape by the time Bert gets here."

I admit being both relieved and agitated. He might have passed these decisions by me, but I was grateful for the offer of help. It might even be refreshing to have a dinner guest. We hadn't entertained in—I couldn't remember when.

"Bert won't be any trouble for you," Bradley said.

No trouble for you, I wanted to say. But I held my tongue.

Bradley was right about Albert Marckwald. The only thing to criticize was that he had gone to Yale instead of Harvard.

Bert, as he insisted I call him, propped an elbow on the mantel and lifted the tumbler of whisky Bradley had poured him.

"My pops calls it poor man's Harvard but as far as Ivies go, Old Yale suited me. Yale's less stymied by tradition than your

Harvard and more tolerant of a young fellow kicking up his heels."

"Stymied?" Bradley said.

"Tradition has its place—don't get me wrong. But my money's on innovation and forward thinking."

I watched my husband ball his hands into fists. Not that he'd ever lash out or let a disagreement come to fisticuffs. But Bert was treading on sacred ground when it came to Harvard. Fine-looking with an aristocratic forehead and limpid blue eyes, his pillowy lips were always on the verge of a sneer. He was enjoying baiting the host.

"Junior year when the Yale Bulldogs needed a fight song, someone had to step up," Bert said. "The words came to me one night at a club party."

"Influenced, no doubt, by the gin you imbibed," Bradley said from the Morris chair.

"Bradley, stop," I said. Then to Bert, "Won't you sing it for us?"

Bert cast his eyes at the ceiling as if trying to recall the words.

"If you insist." And he launched into "Boola boola, boola boola, boola boola—when we roughhouse poor old Hahvahd they will holler, 'Boola boo!' Oh Yale, Eli Yale!"

Bradley scowled. "Now look what you've gone and done, Florrie."

"I'm sure Bert was an excellent student." I looked at him for affirmation.

"I didn't shirk my studies," Bert said. "Earned honors in Disputes and considered studying law. But that meant more schooling, and I was ready to move on. Harvey Fisk offered me the job here in Boston, and I couldn't very well turn it down. Your city is stodgy compared to New York, but at least you have a few respectable clubs in the Back Bay." He gave a quick nod to Bradley. "A few respectable gentlemen, too, even if he did attend Harvard."

"You are forgiven for your poor taste in colleges, my friend," Bradley said.

I broke in. "Could you please cease the chest-thumping? You're both intelligent, competent, and more fortunate than you realize." I was thinking of the poor who considered themselves lucky to have a bed in a settlement house. If only Bert and Bradley could understand how blessed they were, they might stop squabbling.

"I suppose I'll never be invited back." Bert hung his head, feigning shame.

"Nonsense," I said. "You're welcome as often as we're able to convince you to come."

As it turned out, Bert Marckwald was entertaining indeed.

"We're going to be late, Florrie." Bradley was dressed in evening clothes. I hadn't changed from shopping on Madison Avenue. Wells was growing like a weed and needed new shoes, and Jackie had worn out the knee on a pair of knickers. For myself, I favored practical outfits for daywear, a simple skirt and blouse and walking boots.

"Late for what, darling?" I asked.

"Did you forget? I have tickets for the opera tonight. Caruso's singing *La Bohème*."

"Honestly, I don't feel up to it. Really I don't." I dropped into a chair by the hearth. "Couldn't Bert go with you?"

"Why in heaven's name would I want to attend the opera with Bert?" He sounded annoyed. Bradley enjoyed opera, and here I was spoiling his evening. But I couldn't muster the energy for a night of Italian drama.

Bradley's expression changed to concern. He perched on the edge of the divan next to me.

"Are you ill, Florrie?"

"I don't think so. Maybe a little." I didn't feel feverish—just tired. So tired.

"Well," he said, "there's nothing strenuous about sitting in the theater. Be a brave girl and get ready. Puccini awaits."

He would never beg, but he had a way of infusing me with his enthusiasm. Even so, I found arias interminable and getting dressed for the opera was beyond me.

When I didn't hop up, Bradley frowned. He must have suspected something more serious than the fatigue of chasing down two rambunctious boys.

"Shall I call for the doctor?"

"No—it will pass." I didn't need a doctor. I needed to rest.

He stared at me. "I've seen this look before, my dear."

"What look?"

"How old is Wells now?"

"He's just four." What a strange question. Bradley should have known our younger boy's age. We had taken him to Lexington Avenue for an ice cream sundae on his birthday.

"Then I believe you felt this way a little more than four years ago."

"Did I?" I stared at the diamond pattern in the carpet. "Oh, dear. With chasing Wells around I haven't been paying attention." Of course that was it. How could I have missed the signs? But hadn't we agreed that two children were as much as we could manage?

"How can we do this again?" I asked.

"Old hat. We have the hang of this parenting business."

Bradley curved an arm around me and I laid my head on his shoulder. Usually I liked the smell of his shaving cream and hair tonic, but now the aromas made me nauseous.

"Maybe I should ask my mother to move in with us."

Bradley flinched. "Hannah is working out fine. I'll hire more help—a housekeeper to cook and clean. Don't worry, my girl. Three is a lucky number, and with one more for the Cumings brood, Bert will be hard pressed to catch up."

"If it's a girl," I said, "we'll call her Ella for my mother. If another boy, do you object to the name Thayer? My father would appreciate that."

"Absolutely no objection. Let's make the minister proud." He stood up. "Now, then—the opera?"

I was exhausted, yes, but exhausted for a good reason. Together we could raise three children. Of course we could. Three was a lucky number indeed.

"Just give me a few minutes to get ready for Mr. Caruso," I said, "if you don't mind my leaning on you."

"Mind? Not at all, darling. I can't think of a greater privilege."

The *Oceanic* Sinks a Coasting Steamer
Collides with the *Kincora* in the Irish Channel
New York Times, 1901

In his middle twenties, healthy and strong, Andrew believed he could accomplish anything. He just had some things to figure out. He couldn't live in a boarding house forever and although Sidney Siebert was a good bloke, he wanted a wife and a family. The question was — on which continent would he find her?

Even if stewarding didn't suit his mate, Andrew decided work did Sid's soul good. He had to climb up and down vertical ladders and distinguish textures and temperatures by feel in case lights failed or — heaven forbid — a fire broke out. He crouched, kneeled, crawled, and practiced pulling a fire hose to full extension. He knotted the ties of flotation devices on Andrew while the Scot squirmed to make the task more difficult. White Star Line insisted its stewards be well trained.

Once underway, Andrew rolled out of bed at 5:30 a.m. to take a few laps in the ship's pool before it opened to travelers. Sid told him he was going to wear out the water, but Andrew countered that he needed the exercise to keep from getting stiff. He roused Sid at six and led him to the Chief Housekeeper's office, signed in for the morning shift, and picked up passkeys to their assigned cabins. Fetching a trolley from the supply office, he loaded it with fresh towels and cleaning materials and reminded Sid to greet each passenger respectfully.

"The courtesy will be worth your trouble," he reminded the Brit.

As soon as a stateroom was vacant, Andrew worked on the main chamber and sent Sid to clean the loo.

"The toffs must spend half their lives doing their toilettes and they're bloody well slovenly about it," Sid grumbled.

Toffs were a messy lot, to be sure, but the work had to be done and done correctly.

"You're welcome to go back to Liverpool and work in a shop, mate," Andrew told him, which shut Sid up.

They changed bed linens, supplied clean drinking glasses, and replenished the ice bucket. While Sid ran the carpet sweeper, Andrew checked the water closet to make sure he had hung the towels properly and left things spotless.

"Maid Marian herself couldn't have done it better," he said.

"I'm not that sort of maid," Sid said. "More of a gentleman's butler."

Andrew repressed a grin. "As you wish, mate."

When they finished their round of staterooms, they broke for lunch in the crew's kitchen. The galley cooks took good care of the stewards. All they wanted to eat, top drawer quality, and no bill to pay at the end of the meal.

Between one and four in the afternoon, the two stewards answered bells. A jeweler wanted shoes shined, and Andrew instructed Sid in applying polish followed by buffing.

"Use a velvet cloth to give the leather a sheen," he advised.

When the priest of a New York church asked for a whisky brought to his room, Andrew watched Sid in case he was tempted to help himself to a quaff of the father's liquor before delivering it.

Sid assisted Andrew in serving afternoon tea at four in the first-class saloon and offered cakes, biscuits, bread and butter. When Andrew reminded Sid teacups and saucers were placed to the upper right of the cake plates and serving was always done from the right, the new steward scoffed.

"I'm not a rustic straight from the farm." Sid punctuated his defense with a salute of his nose.

At five, passengers began arriving in eveningwear for cocktails, and Andrew coached Sid in the turndown service, replacing damp towels with fresh ones, removing used glasses, tidying the W.C. again. They placed the daily programs on the table so guests would know the menus and on-board activities for the next day.

And so it went for weeks that melted into months, first-class passengers demanding, stewards obsequious but peevish behind their backs.

On one launch day after *Oceanic's* passengers were settling in, a heavy fog crept over the harbor. By the time to set loose from the dock, the weather had not improved.

"When will we shove off?" one fellow asked. "I have meetings in New York."

"I didn't pay passage to sit in the harbor," another complained.

"The captain will cast off when he knows it's safe to sail," Andrew told them, feigning cheeriness. "Better to be out of harm's way here than in the middle of the foggy channel."

The passengers weren't the only ones keen to start the voyage. The mail had to be delivered to New York, and each hour of delay was money lost for the cruise line company.

All night *Oceanic* strained at her dock lines as if she, too, were eager to get underway.

"If the captain checks the calculations, he should be able to navigate through the channel when the tide is full, even with such poor visibility," Andrew told Sid the following morning. The fog still had not lifted, and Captain Cameron passed word among the crew to prepare to set sail.

For an entire day, the ship crawled forward, sounding its foghorn. Because there was nothing to see from the decks or portholes, passengers sedated themselves with the ship's whisky. The more they swilled, the more their courtesy toward the crew turned to indignation and anger. They blamed the captain and the stewards for the slow progress and even accused the stokers of laziness. They played endless games of whist and talked of their travels, their businesses, and their influential friends, their boasts growing more exaggerated with each drink. Andrew was hard pressed to appease them and kept his head down, focused on his tasks.

Tides rose and fell. As much as he had wanted to go to sea, Andrew could hardly bear the odor of the Saint George Channel, a rotten-egg stench caused by decaying seaweed and bacteria feeding on plankton. Fish found their food, oddly enough, by smell. The stink tainted everything—food, tea, even the air he breathed. Neither salt nor water itself carried any scent at all, and once the ship reached open sea, the odor would evaporate. He hoped by all that was holy the ship would break free of the channel soon.

The third day dawned like a shroud. The ship had crept forward less than two hundred miles from Liverpool. Andrew hated the fog. The horn that blew into the steely darkness every thirty seconds clawed at his brain. There was another sense, too—a dread that gave him jitters. He was all too aware that the *Oceanic* wasn't the only vessel in the channel. Freighters carrying coal and ore made regular trips from Limerick around the coast for trading in Liverpool. In daylight he had seen the long, low ships navigating the watery passageway. They were like trains leaving the station loaded with cargo. Freighters always yielded to the enormous cruisers but without radios, skippers had to rely on foghorns and lights to know when another ship was nearby.

The August air was warm and the water cold, producing an impenetrable fog. Fog was a bigger menace than any monstrous creature of the sea. In dense cover such as this, light was distorted and sound deceptive. A man's senses could betray him. He had to stay alert.

He estimated *Oceanic* was approaching Tuskar Rock lighthouse, a beacon set on a craggy island halfway through the channel. The island was a captain's biggest challenge. In a gale, its sharp rocks had torn open the hulls of ships that had been blown too close. The water's sandy bottom was a cemetery for ruined boats.

On the open sea, the captain found his way using charts, logbooks, and sextants to navigate by the stars. In rivers and channels, navigation was done by sight and the simple depth instrument that was often inefficient. Fog, especially after sunset, was like slogging through gravy.

Late that night, whenever Andrew flirted with sleep, the ship's horn startled him awake. Frustrated, he rose and wandered out to the boat deck. The ship was traveling at six knots, creeping through the mist. The tide was at half flood, so even if the ship came near Tuskar Rock, there should have been plenty of clearance to pass. Plenty of clearance, that was, unless a freighter obscured in fog happened to be in the way.

The sickening crunch of metal tearing and buckling reached him before the impact threw him backwards. He rolled against a chair, knocking it over. When he landed hard on the deck, pain ripped through his hip. He got up, rubbed his side and wobbled to the railing. The hum of the engines had stopped.

It was useless to make out anything in the cloudy darkness, but he heard a frenzy of bellows coming from the bow. *Oceanic* crewmen, some of them still climbing into their clothes, raced past him toward the commotion.

"What is it?" he shouted at an officer.

The man swiveled his head. "Rammed a freighter," he said. "Give us a hand, will you?"

"*Mhac na galla*," Andrew cursed in Gaelic — son of a whore. The steward's manual had told him how to serve tea and set the crease of a sheet in the exact center of a bed, but it hadn't said anything about a goliath of a ship tearing into a helpless vessel.

When a crewman aimed lights off *Oceanic's* bow, Andrew made out the wedge-shaped hull of the liner, designed to cut through obstacles in its path. At the bow, Captain Cameron called for more light, and a crewman brought torches. It looked to Andrew that the dark hulk of the freighter had been hit square on the port side with such force that the vessel was impaled on the sharp edge of *Oceanic's* prow, as if a great charging rhinoceros had plunged its horn into the side of a small antelope.

In the moving light, he could discern three of the freighter's men in the water. They either had leaped from the freighter or the jolt of the collision had tossed them into the channel.

"Get the ladders over the side," the captain called.

Sid approached next to Andrew, looking stunned. He peered over the deck railing.

"What the bloody hell?" he muttered.

"Help me get these lines out," Andrew ordered.

When they had tossed rope ladders to the freighter's crew, six men crawled up the side of the *Oceanic* to safety.

"Cappy's still on the boat," one man panted.

"Call to him to climb the ladder," Captain Cameron shouted. "Do it now."

"They're going to lose the ship," Andrew told Sid. If it released itself, the freighter would go down. If it didn't release, the boilers could explode. Either way, he saw disaster unfolding.

The man, drenched and shaken, cupped his hands around his mouth. "Cap'n Powers! Grab the ladder and come aboard."

The freighter's captain looked around as if counting his men. When he found no other sailors on the boat, slowly Powers began crawling up the ladder.

Freighter captains seemed decades older than their actual age. Graying and swarthy, Powers was no exception.

There were at least six men in the channel that Andrew could count. They'd have to be rescued. He had made several crossings without a mark against him. Stewarding had been mostly uneventful—a few spills or a temporary inconvenience. Nothing like this. Nothing that risked lives.

He looked at Sid, the younger steward's face furrowed with confusion. Sid was about to learn hazards were just as much a part of life at sea as teacakes and civility.

"Senseless," Sid muttered. He shook his head but never took his eyes off the action below.

Captain Cameron ordered lifeboats to the grisly task of searching for a trace of the lost men. No doubt some of them were hurt—if they were alive at all.

"Careful," Cameron called after them. "The freighter could break loose any minute." Suddenly he gasped and pointed toward the freighter. "There's another sailor!"

Powers looked down. "Collins!" he called. "Grab a line! Climb, man!"

The crewman's voice sounded like an echo from the bottom of a cave. "Got to shut down the boilers."

"If the boilers blow, at this close range, it could rupture the *Oceanic's* hull," Andrew told Sid. "Both ships would go down."

"Great God," Sid said.

Powers shouted for Collins to forget the boilers and save himself.

"Aye, Cap'n. After I tend to somethin' below," Collins said.

"George—" The captain used the man's given name, the captain's good friend George. "I'm giving you an order!"

Collins disappeared from the freighter's deck. Water rushed through the gouges on its side, and the hull turned upward the way a whale does when it waves a fin above the water. Through the fog, Andrew could just make out the freighter's name painted on the bow — *Kincora*.

The water had to be in the holds by now — the engine room, too, channel water weighing heavily on its bulk. Within minutes Andrew watched the *Kincora* tear itself from the *Oceanic*'s prow. As it sank, bubbles rose around its wound. And then like a sounding whale it dove into the depths, taking George Collins with it.

The crew aboard the cruise ship seemed to hold its breath. In the silence, Andrew heard his blood pulsing — waiting, waiting. But there was no explosion — just the collective exhalation of relief.

Kincora's captain wagged his head. "Collins is our best fireman," he said. "He's got five young ones at home. What in the name of the Almighty are they to do?"

Sid buried his face in his sleeve and his body heaved with sobs. Ship disasters went hard on any man. Each time Andrew set foot on deck, he knew there was a chance he wouldn't be stepping off. Nature was pitiless to the pleas of men on its waters.

Sid had a lot to learn.

"We'd better go below," Andrew said. "The passengers will want to know what's happened."

In the first-class saloon, Andrew and Sid served food and hot coffee to the rescued *Kincora* crew. A pair of the men were stowaways, not unusual on freighters. Sea passages cost a dear sum, and those without the fare were known to hide out for the few days of the trip to Liverpool, their pockets stuffed with food to sustain them. But all the Kincora survivors deserved the same respect as his millionaire passengers. Their wives would rejoice to welcome them home, but the wives of the seven dead men would be left to the mercy of neighbors and charities. When they had married sailors, they must have known about the frightening power of the sea, but for the sake of love or desperation, they had no choice but to accept the possibility their men would not be returning home.

If anything were to happen to him, Andrew wondered who would give him a second thought. But he shook that notion from his mind. It was ill luck to contemplate disaster.

As morning dawned, the ship made its way to Queenstown to deposit the *Kincora* crew. Passengers from first-class gathered in the lounge, and one of them collected donations for the widows and orphans of the drowned men. Andrew dropped half a dollar into the hat and Sid added a fistful of shillings. In short order, Captain Powers was handed an envelope containing one hundred sixty pounds, small recompense for so great a sacrifice.

The *Oceanic's* bow had suffered only dents and scrapes to its steel plates, and Captain Cameron determined the ship was sound enough to continue its journey across the Atlantic. He ordered the engines cranked to full speed to make up time. Ocean crossings were expected to be swift, and they were days behind schedule.

For the rest of the crossing, Sid was unusually quiet. Except to prompt him to be more thorough and work quickly, Andrew left him alone.

Race riot breaks out at Columbus Avenue
AME Zion Church
Boston Globe, 1903

"That iron ship—what was its name?" Mrs. Hart poised her teacup halfway to her mouth. "The one that sank last week off the coast of England?"

"*Kincora*, I believe it was." Mrs. Baldwin lifted her nose in a knowing manner.

"It must have been badly damaged to go under,"' Mrs. Hart said.

I listened as the wives at the Metropolitan Club prattled about matters that didn't concern them. Better than boasting, I guessed, or having them air the trivial details of their privileged lives. Anyway, I had read of the freighter's foundering.

"There were no passengers," I said. "Just crew, and most of them were rescued, thankfully."

"It's getting dangerous to sail at all these days," Mrs. Baldwin said.

"Nonsense," Mrs. Hart put in. "The new ships are absolutely safe. Mr. Hart and I sailed to France on the *Oceanic* just last year. A charming voyage. The real danger is here in the city with so many sullen Negroes demanding jobs."

Mrs. Baldwin added, "Absolutely. Creating work for them is an exercise in futility."

"Not to mention the expense," put in Mrs. Hart.

I felt my Unitarian blood rise to a boil. "They have rights as we do."

"Some of them are hostile. Things could get violent." Mrs. Hart slid her teacup onto a side table. "You must face reality, Mrs. Cumings."

"I'm not sure my reality is the same as yours, Mrs. Hart." I forced a pleasant expression even though I wasn't feeling at all pleasant.

When I got home, Hannah was at the kitchen sink washing lunch dishes. I picked up a newspaper from the counter, one I hadn't seen before. The masthead read *The Guardian*.

"Is this your newspaper, Hannah?" I asked.

"Oh, sorry. Didn't mean to leave it about." Hannah dried her hands on a dish towel.

I opened a page to the editorials and skimmed an article calling discrimination against Negroes the most damning degradation in America. "Do you agree with this opinion?"

Hannah patted her hair, done up in a neat bun. "I don't believe it means to say all white people discriminate." She was looking at a spot where the wall met the floor, avoiding my eyes.

"But some do." I was thinking about the women at the club and turned a page of the newspaper. It looked as if all the articles dealt with aspects of Negro business affairs. I stopped reading at an announcement.

"There's a notice here that Booker T. Washington is coming to Boston next week to speak to a gathering of the National Negro Business League."

"Yes." Hannah stood straighter. She was a tad taller than I. "Mr. Washington is said to be a powerful speaker."

"I'd like to hear him." I touched my fingers to my lips, thinking. "Maybe the boys and I will tag along with you."

Hannah opened her mouth to speak but seemed to decide against it.

"If it's a problem—" I started.

"I'll not be going," Hannah said. "The church is apt to be—" She glanced toward the bedroom where Thayer was napping. "Crowded."

"Jackie will help with Wells and Thayer, then."

"Of course." She considered a second. "But sometimes the discussions can be, well, heated."

Hannah's mouth twitched.

"Thank you for the warning." I had made her uncomfortable, but I was determined to hear the talk. After spending hours with people of color at the settlement houses, I wanted to know what the future held for them between the doctrines of these two powerful leaders. "But Mr. Washington's talk will be an education for Jackie and Wells."

That evening after dinner I brought up the editorial with Bradley.

"The *Guardian* is considered a quality paper," he said. "What concerns me is the attitude toward Booker Washington."

"Mr. Washington is well known, isn't he?" I asked.

"Monroe Trotter edits the paper. He and Washington both want to improve conditions for Negroes but they don't agree on how to go about it. Washington's interest is the rural south—sharecroppers and such—and Trotter, well, he was in my class at Harvard, one of the few Negroes in the college." He glanced at me. "He's from a wealthy Hyde Park family. Graduated magna cum laude. I recall him speaking out in favor of higher education for Negroes."

"I'm in favor of that." Everyone deserved an education, in my opinion. But if a woman wanted educating, she had few options other than the Seven Sisters—Wellesley, Smith, Bryn Mawr and the like. Otherwise there were seminary schools, if one didn't mind Bible studies. My grades at Winsor School had been excellent—even better than my sister Elaina's, but Papa said there was money for only one of his children to attend college. "Cultivate poverty like a garden herb," he was fond of saying. Well, poverty may have been fine for old Mr. Thoreau who wrote that line, but who would choose to be poor? As far as I was concerned, poverty was not an idealistic state. Didn't everyone deserve to live well?

"What else do you know about Mr. Trotter?" I asked.

Bradley didn't answer. I was afraid he wasn't taking me seriously. We both were born two decades after the Civil War ended, and news of beatings, lynching, and other gruesome atrocities had made its way to Boston. I thought he should be more engaged in talking about matters of race.

"Bradley—what about Mr. Trotter?"

He looked at me over the paper. "We've been on different paths, Trotter and I. My nose was always in financials. I'm not good at soapboxing."

"What does he have against Mr. Washington?"

Bradley peered at me. "You're seriously interested in the Negro situation?"

"Yes. And I'd seriously like to give those ladies at the club a different perspective."

"Well, then. Washington accepts segregation and believes Negroes should be educated and successful by their own means." He shook the newspaper. "Trotter preaches that business leaders ought to be color blind when it comes to working with Negro businessmen." He cleared his throat. "You might tell the biddies at the club that Andrew Carnegie supports the Negro Business League. That should pull some weight."

"I'd like to take the boys to hear Mr. Washington," I said. "I want them to understand about these things."

"That's not a good idea, Florrie. I know you're an idealist, but I wouldn't want to predict what might happen if Trotter shows up."

"We're in the Twentieth Century now, Bradley. It's time things changed." It was my belief that life is a sacrament, to be lived with justice and compassion for all races. And it was with that philosophy I tried to raise my sons. If my way of thinking made me an idealist, then so be it.

I asked Hannah to have a plate of food ready for my husband when he returned from work. Then I started to write him a note to tell him—what? I had never lied to Bradley. And he hadn't forbidden me to attend the talk. Anyway, by the time he finished his supper, we would likely be home. I wrote, "Boys and I ate early. Gone for a walk. Back soon." That was all.

I put Thayer in the stroller, Jackie and Wells walked next to me, and we marched most of a mile to the Columbus Avenue A.M.E. Zion Church where Booker T. Washington was to speak. The church was a pretty brick building that until the previous year had been a synagogue. From outside the open door, I saw a crowd had gathered.

"We'll leave the stroller outside. Jackie, you take Wells's hand." I lifted Thayer and led the way up the stairs. Nudging ourselves in, we found a space at the back where a group of ladies stood. The women wore Sunday hats and spoke in low voices, their heads inclined toward one another. Occasionally they turned and glared at my boys and me and rolled their eyes. Several reporters carrying notebooks wrestled their way toward the stage to get the story. It was an odd sensation, being so out of place. I didn't feel threatened, not physically, at least. But unwelcome, yes—an awareness I'd never had before.

"Why are we here?" Jackie asked. I guessed he was feeling the same.

"A man's going to be speaking," I said. "Turn around and show respect."

Most of the men in the room wore suits even in the late summer heat. They shifted from foot to foot muttering to each other as they waited for Washington to take the stage. Sweet aromas of talcum and hair tonic wafted through the crowd.

When a robust gentleman came through a side door, I heard murmuring. The man's hair was cropped, and his piercing eyes had a look of intelligence. He waited to be introduced, grazing the audience as if assessing their mood. They stood mesmerized and taut, as if they had come upon a bear in the forest and were unsure whether it would attack or amble peacefully by.

The air around us tightened, and I put my hand on Wells's shoulder.

"I can't see, Muz," he said.

"Then just listen." My attention was on the guest speaker. This was Trotter's territory, and surely Washington knew that. What might he say under the circumstances?

A fellow came to the lectern and announced, "We are grateful to have Mr. Washington with us today. He is a founder of the National Negro Business League, a leader of the Tuskegee Institute in Alabama, and a prominent figure in our community of Negro leaders."

There was polite applause, a rustling of agitation, and low murmuring.

As Washington stepped forward, I thought of what Bradley said about Mr. Trotter being unpredictable. Wouldn't Trotter be courteous to Washington, a man born into slavery who now was a spokesman for Negro pride and dignity? When he began to speak, his baritone voice projected the weight of his conviction.

"We must not agitate for political or social equality," Washington declared, "but both races will determine the future of our people to end subjugation of the Negro."

"Compromise has failed," someone yelled out. Another voice called, "Resist!" Dozens more shouted with fists raised.

"We demand equality."

"We'll take what we deserve!"

Washington tried to continue his speech over hisses and boos.

"Muz, please can we go?" Wells took my hand. His face had fear in it. My prickle of worry turned to dread, especially when a fellow stepped onto a chair to shout at the speaker.

"Segregation is an abomination! Uncle Tom is dead!"

"Tell it, Trotter," someone shouted.

So that was Trotter, his face etched like a bronze statue from ancient Greece. He had a determined gravity about him and the bearing of a leader. I suspected that when a dynamic person like Trotter fuels the fire, a group could quickly turn into a mob.

Chairs scraped across the floor and men shoved each other and punched the air, their hands clenched as if ready for a fight. Women shrieked and men's voices roared. Washington put out his hands as if trying to calm a wild beast. When he tried to speak, protests drowned him out. The melee escalated, and I realized there might be violence.

"Missus C?" When I turned toward the voice, I saw a pretty young girl—just a teenager.

"Georgia!" It was one of the women I worked with at the settlement house. I was teaching her to read, and she was making stunning progress. She was bright and held such promise.

"These your young men?" she asked. I was happy she recognized me, but this was no time for pleasantries.

"They are."

"Then you all follow me. And stay close."

The women I worked with at the settlement house were strong and dogged. They had survival skills I'd never had to learn. They knew how to get along on bare necessities, never asked for anything, but accepted what was offered. And they took care of one another. Their loyalty to people they liked was fierce. I was glad to be on Georgia's friends list—especially at that moment.

She cleared a path through the jostling crowd. Just as we reached the exit door, policemen with billy clubs pushed past us on their way in.

"You be fine now," Georgia said. "Go on home." And before I could thank her, she whirled around and went back inside.

"Looks like my classmate Trotter may spend some time in the Charles Street jail," Bradley said at breakfast the next day.

"Oh?" I said.

"The news is calling last night the Boston Riot."

"Really?"

"I don't suppose you'd know anything about it?"

I set a cup of coffee in front of my husband.

"Just that it seems a horrid way to treat an honored guest."

He gave me a knowing look from under his eyebrows. "Indeed," he said.

Fire Warms a Frigid Hogmanay
New Year's celebration
Highland News, 1903

The weather in New York had been unforgiving—hurricane-force winds and driving rain. Back aboard ship, Sid suggested when they reach Liverpool they sprint to a bar to while away their hours off, but Andrew told him it was a waste of their hard-earned gratuities. Sid countered with "What better way to waste them?"

Andrew, too, was ready to get off the ship's decks and away from docks, but the deeper they sailed into the St. George's Channel, the less he was able to see. By the time the ship should have been passing between Dublin and Holyhead, the shore had dropped into an abyss of gray.

The engines stopped, and there was a peculiar calm. The first-class deck dissolved like a lump of sugar in hot tea. On the boat deck, water droplets clung to Andrew's face.

"I've been in London soup," Sid told him, "but nothing like this." He had come to the deck and stood beside Andrew. When he lit a cigarette, its glow cast a red glimmer in the fog.

"Might have rained here last night causing what's known as radiation fog rolling off the land," Andrew said. "When the air's warm like this, even for December, and the water's cold, it's ideal conditions for fog."

"I suppose you know all about fog, mate?"

"Sure. Near shore you're bound to encounter this muck." Andrew's voice hung in the cloudy silence. "In daylight the captain can pick through the rocky shoals, but not in this cloud.

The ship could get hung up or worse—" He was thinking of *Kincora*.

"I suppose we're better off waiting it out," Sid said, "but I'm going barmy to get off this tub and tip a pint."

"Just listen," Andrew said. "A foghorn carries over water. That'll tell us if another ship is close."

"You're giving me collywobbles, mate. I can't take another freighter bashing."

"There's not a breath of wind, Sid. If the sun broke through, it might lift the fog. But it's dusk now. We could be out here for a good spell. Better get below."

With five staterooms to care for, they had to be sharp, put on a friendly face, assure passengers there was nothing to worry about. Below, they ushered some to the library, set up chessboards, pulled decks of cards from drawers, and served snifters of brandy. Hours passed and still the fog refused to let up. Even in the dark of night, water beads glistened on porthole glass. With enough whisky in them, the passengers stumbled to their staterooms. It was near midnight when Andrew fell exhausted into his own blessed bunk.

By morning, the stubborn pall over the water had not budged. At breakfast Captain Cameron wandered from table to table, playing the blithe spirit.

"We're very near Cleveleys on the Fylde coast," he said. "Nice area. Just a brief postponement and we should be in Liverpool shortly."

After so many years and so many crossings, to Andrew the passengers were cardboard shirts, stiff tuxedos, and corseted mannequins wrapped in Parisian cloth. The first-classers were courteous and offended each other only in the subtlest manner that might be taken as a compliment. One woman to another—

"What a lovely frock. I do hope you didn't overpay." Or the winner to the loser of a hand of cards — "Oh you are a good sport. I admire that in a man." Andrew made a point to keep his opinions to himself. Or better yet, not to have opinions at all. How the toffs admired or belittled each other was none of his business.

The second day passed and the third dawned with no sun. Christmas came and went without celebration. Someone played a few carols on the parlor piano, but few were inclined to join in singing. It was impossible to tell morning from evening or east from west. Some carped and others endured with the help of bottled spirits and sleep medicines. With firemen idle in the engine room, fights broke out between stokers quaffing bottles of wine as if it were honey water. Not that Andrew could blame them — he felt ready to throw a punch himself.

The *Oceanic* was built to carry seventeen hundred passengers and three hundred crew. On this crossing, a few first-class cabins were vacant, but there were still a thousand mouths to feed. The storerooms were running low on provisions and captain ordered the cooks to cut back on portions at meals. Stewards were to be stingy even with the cognac — no more than a finger's width in the glass.

Andrew went about his duties, but his nerves were frayed. If a pot clanked in the galley or a suitcase fell from a shelf, he braced for a ramming. The stress was exhausting and he shuffled through his duties like some sluggish sea mammal.

How ironic that up on deck the air had the wormy aroma of land, even though the coast was swaddled in gray batting. Andrew was taking a break with Sid when he heard a voice through the mist off the starboard railing. He knew if a voice came from the water, it would be too late to avoid a collision.

"Halloo!" a man called. And again, "Halloo there, I say!"

Slowly a dark mass took shape. It was — yes — a boat. A flat-bottom boat, the type of large sturdy tub used to haul freight and passengers on inland waterways. The flat hull made the boat stable in calm water, and it could float easily over shoals.

"Hello yourself!" Andrew shouted.

"Fogged in, are ye?" the skipper called from the boat.

"Yes. Four days now." What use was a flatboat? There was no way a flatboat could hold a thousand people.

"Lucky you held up here. You've nearly run aground," the skipper said. He must have been able to detect more than the *Oceanic's* lookout in the crow's nest.

"I'll get the captain," Sid said.

Captain Cameron arrived and leaned on the railing. "Identify yourself, sir," he called.

"Name's Peter Harrison, captain of this fine vessel *Alice Linda*. Happy to guide you into harbor if you'd like."

The captain glanced back at the decks holding his impatient passengers. They were days behind schedule and others were waiting to board in Liverpool.

"If you want to get to the dock, you should accept Harrison's offer," Andrew told him. But trust was a tricky thing, like jumping from a cliff into darkness. Somewhere in one's soul, there had to exist a belief that things would turn out well. As Andrew saw it, Cameron had little choice except to trust.

The engines started up and following the *Alice Linda's* lights, the steamer crept slowly into harbor. Safely tied to its slip, *Oceanic* released its captives. When Cameron reported Harrison's help, White Star officials rewarded the skipper with a pair of the best binoculars made in England, and the captain gave the crew an extra few days of shore leave. Just what Andrew needed to let off a little steam.

"Where the deuce are you taking me, Cunningham?" Sid scrolled his eyes over Andrew's plaid kilt and heavy woolen sweater. He had shoved Sid onto the train but kept tight-lipped about their destination.

"You haven't lived until you've done a New Year's Hogmanay with a Scotsman, mate."

"I dearly hope this Hogmanay has some pubs," Sid said.

A cold wind blew off the firth as they stepped off the train at Edinburgh's North British Hotel. Sid drew a silver flask from his waistcoat pocket and raised it to his lips.

"Keeps me from icing over." He saluted Andrew with the raised flask.

Mobs crammed the street, some staggering drunk, others shouting with holiday spirit. Men in kilts paraded with torches, lighting up the night. Others swung fireballs of chicken wire stuffed with oil-soaked rags.

"Fire wards off evil spirits in this darkest of seasons and invites the sun back to the land," Andrew said.

"Then welcome, fire!" Sid yelled.

Drums and bagpipes tore through the air over a boisterous wave of humanity. Andrew felt euphoric — no one asked him for favors, no one made demands on him, and he let the tide of people carry him along. He knocked shoulders with revelers, most of them three sheets to the wind. Even so, the walk was better than a stroll along the promenade decks of a cruise ship and its fantasy of indulgence. Here among these hardy and raucous countrymen, he felt more alive than he had in months.

In the revelry, Andrew lost sight of Sid. Where the blazes had he gone? Off to the right he noticed a young woman jostled by the crowd, an orange muffler wrapped around her neck. Probably couldn't hold her liquor, he guessed.

As the clock struck midnight, he linked elbows with strangers, and they sang Auld Lang Syne, all of them swaying in rhythm. No matter how far he traveled or how many millionaires he waited on, the song reminded Andrew that he was Scottish, through and through. He always grew misty at the verse, "seas between us broad have roared, since auld lang syne." The sea had separated him from his roots for so long, and it felt good to be back in the heather.

When the song ended and the partiers began to disperse and wander away, he realized the person on his right still held his arm. He looked over and in the firelight saw that her eyes were brimming with tears. It was the lass with the orange muffler, her cheeks red from the cold.

Her nose had begun to run, and Andrew pulled a handkerchief from his coat pocket and offered it to her.

"It's the song—so moving." She took the handkerchief and dabbed at her nose.

Even in the shadowy light he could tell she was pretty— awfully pretty. From her accent, not Scottish. What was she doing in Edinburgh alone at midnight?

"I know what you mean," he said, his voice tender. "It moves me as well."

When she shivered, he said, "You're cold." Nothing seemed to be open, not even a pub where he could buy her a hot tea.

"I'm all right," she said.

"Somehow I doubt that." He put an arm around her and felt her lean into his chest.

"Do you live here in Edinburgh?" At least he could offer to walk her home.

"No," she said. "I came from London to visit my aunt. Her husband's a Scot. They live in Newington. Do you know it?"

"Not far, is it?" They were north of Holyrood Park near Royal Terrace Gardens, the center of town.

"No, not far if you enjoy a walk."

"I do enjoy a walk," he said, trying not to sound eager.

She turned her head as if looking for a recognizable landmark.

"To be honest, I'm not sure of the way."

Another opportunity to be of help. It was truly an auspicious night.

"Can you see Arthur's Seat from your aunt's house?" Andrew asked. Arthur's Seat was the dormant volcano that watched over the city. Young lasses were said to climb the hill on May Day and bathe their faces in the dew to make themselves more beautiful. But this lass had no need of dew.

"Arthur's Seat? No, I don't believe so."

"Let's go through the park then," he said. "We should have a good view of the moon if the clouds clear out." He willed the sky to clear. He wanted to glimpse this miss in moonlight.

They started around Regent Gardens, past the hairpin curve of townhouses, their shadows circling around them as they passed under gaslights.

"It feels warmer when we keep moving," she said.

"Yes," he agreed, wishing to be better at conversation. But he liked the comfortable quiet between them.

"Should auld acquaintance be forgot," she said. "Have you lost someone?"

He had nearly forgotten about Sid. "As a matter of fact, I have. We've a train to catch tonight."

"I'm being a bother," she said. "Go and look for your girl. I'll be fine."

He was being coy with her, but the disappointment in her voice thrilled him.

"Come with me," he said. "We'll check the castle first, then the university."

Andrew glanced at her as they walked. Her hair was pulled to the back of her neck, wisps like slender tongues of gold escaping the clasp. As slight as she was, she had a robust quality about her. He believed she would have looked as at home in silks as she did in winter woolens.

By the university they fought a brisk breeze through George Square, Andrew keeping an eye out for a sign of Sid. When Sid wasn't at the castle, he turned the lass up North Meadow Walk. The wind was aggravating, and he pulled her into an alley to get out of the cold. She looked up at him, and he drew her against his chest.

"Better?" he asked.

She stopped shivering.

"Yes—much."

He lifted her chin and slowly brought his lips to hers. She didn't resist at first, then pulled away.

"What about your girl?"

"Don't worry about him," he said. "I'm sure he's fine."

"Ah, a fellow — how fortunate."

Again he sought her lips. They were soft and cool, and he wanted to sink into them. He put his hands around her face, warming her ears, and felt the vibration of a low moan in her throat. When he kissed her again, his tongue tasted the essence of licorice on her lips, which electrified him.

"Do you have a name?" he breathed. "Or are you an apparition?"

"I'll gladly be an apparition if it's a warm one. My name is Emily."

"Well then, apparition named Emily, you've charmed this old fellow."

"Ah — very sorry, sir."

"Never ye mind. But charm me again, won't you?"

As he bent to kiss her, he heard someone yell, "Cunningham! I say — Cunningham!"

It took all Andrew's might to pull away from Emily and look toward his graceless mate. At first he was relieved Sid had found him. Then he saw the bloke's arm firmly around a woman.

"Look who I found wandering about," he said. "She says she knows you."

Andrew's blood boiled when he recognized his own sister Lizzy — with his mischievous mate.

"Get your hands off her, Siebert — you scaffbag!" He bolted toward them and shoved Sid against the wall.

"Calm down, Cunningham. I was just thawing her out while we looked for you."

It had always been Andrew's duty to watch over Lizzy. Since he'd been away, she had grown into a woman — but not a woman for the likes of Sidney Siebert.

"Lizzy, go to the hotel and wait for me." Andrew threw his head toward Emily. "And take her with you."

"Andy, tis nae what ye're thinking," Lizzy started.

Sid pulled on his arm. "Say, mate—let's talk this out."

Andrew's temper flared. Whirling around, his fist caught Sid's jaw. Sid fell against the building, smacking his head on the stone. Blood dribbled onto his sweater and he bent over, his hand against the wound.

"Look what ye've done!" Lizzy shouted. She started toward Sid, but he barreled past and rammed against Andrew, knocking the breath out of him. Andrew went down, and Sid straddled him. The Brit was strong for such a bag of bones.

"You'll listen to me now, you porridge wog," Sid shouted. "Your precious sister wants nothing to do with me."

Lizzy broke in. "Andy, ye've been away. Do ye nae know I'm spoken for?"

As angry as he was, Andrew felt a twinge of delight at hearing Lizzy's accent—the lilt of home he had smothered in order to sound more English.

"Who?" he huffed, hoping Sid wouldn't plug him while he was down.

"Liam Godfrey. I've been with him all night. His ma was ill, an' he caught the last train out. Sidney and I've been searching for ye."

"Liam? My mate from Calderhead School?"

"Aye." She pulled Sid's sleeve. "Let him up afore he expires."

"Not going to hit me again, is he?"

"He's nae goin' ta hit ye, are ye, Andy?"

Andrew shook his head.

Sid let him up. "Misunderstanding. Happens to the best of us." He stuck out his hand. Andrew hesitated, brushing himself off. Sid was still standing with his hand out. A few seconds passed. Then—slowly—he took it.

"Limey bastard," he said.

Now it was Emily's turn to be concerned. "Your name's Andy, is it? Well, Andy—are you all right?"

"Just peachy," he said.

"This is—your sister?"

"The same." Andrew didn't trust Sid and kept one eye on him.

"Hello, Lizzy," Emily said. "What a way to meet."

"Ye'll have ta pardon my brother," Lizzy said.

"I think I can manage that." Emily raised an eyebrow at Andrew. "Now, can we all please go somewhere to get out of the horrid wind?"

At the North British Hotel, Sid and Lizzy dozed in lobby chairs while Emily and Andrew laughed at silly things—the curly pattern in the hotel's carpet, the chandelier that looked as if it were dripping ice, tipplers staggering into the lobby slapping the cold from themselves.

Far too soon, sunrise blushed outside the tall windows signaling the first train due to pull in.

"I should call you a taxi before our train arrives," Andrew told her.

"Oh, it's all right. I told my aunt I was going back to London. She'll send my things so I don't have to bother with luggage."

"We take the London train to Shotts," he said, his hopes soaring. "Come home with me. My mum will make us something to eat."

"Your mum?" Her brows lifted. He told her about moving to Liverpool and working on a ship, about the steward's job and the famous passengers.

"What a fascinating life you live," she said.

"It would be fascinating if you'd stay with me a little longer." He touched his lips to her forehead. "I've only just found you, and I'm not finished drinking you in."

"In that case," she whispered, "I suppose London will wait."

At dawn, even a mining town looks cloaked in velvet. Or maybe it was Andrew's mood. The four celebrants stumbled off the train and weaved like drunkards down the narrow road toward the Cunningham house.

"I have a sense this new century is going to be a good ninety-nine years," Andrew declared.

Sid grimaced. "Optimist."

"Why not be an optimist? We have work. We get to wander around New York, and as long as ships float, we're in business."

"I'm a realist," Sid said. "Ships sink, hearts break, and hopes are dashed upon the rocky shoals."

"How poetic," Lizzy said.

"On the contrary." Emily grinned at Andrew. "It's dreams that keep us alive."

Lizzy hesitated at the front door. "We need a first-footing to set our good fortune for the New Year."

"Bollocks," Sid complained, "not another bizarre Scottish ritual."

"Tradition asks for a tall dark stranger to set the first foot over the threshold in the New Year," Lizzy said.

"Sid's strange," Andrew suggested. "He'll have to do."

"I trust the act does not involve violence," Sid said. He winced when he touched the raised knot on his head where his skull had hit the wall.

"The Viking invaders had blond hair, so a dark man is preferred. You don't have Norse blood, do you, Sid?" Lizzy asked.

"Born and bred in England."

Emily giggled. "Sid may be all we've got at the moment."

Andrew opened the green door. "After you, my dear fellow, and may your foot crossing our threshold bring tides of richness to us all."

Jeanie Cunningham was frying sausages when they arrived, and the house smelled delicious. Her mouth fell open when she saw her son, and she reached up to curl her arms around his neck.

"It's time ye came home to roost, son," she said.

"I'm just here a short time, sad to say." Andrew kissed his mother's cheek and introduced Sid. Emily lagged behind, and he took her hand and pulled her next to him.

"Emily Jones, this is my mum."

Jeanie Cunningham looked from Emily to Andrew and back to Emily. One of the qualities Andrew loved about his mother was that she asked no questions but quietly approved whatever her family handed her. Andrew had never brought a girl home before, and surely she suspected this one was special.

"Your father's in the workshop," his mum said. "He's got a pressing project to finish."

His Da was like that—wood called to him as the sea did to his son.

"He'll be in later." Jeanie winked at Emily, a seal of acceptance.

They ate the breakfast she placed on the table—eggs, bangers with mushrooms, beans, and toast with marmalade. For Andrew, it was a meal of substance, of comfort, of home. His eyes welled with gratitude.

Sid stared at him, cleared his throat, and sopped egg yolk from his plate with a slice of toast. "This meal will last me 'til afternoon tea," he said.

"I doubt that very much." Andrew had seen how his mate could eat.

After the meal, Lizzy took Emily to her room for an hour's rest before time for the London train. Andrew led Sid to the bedroom he shared with his younger brother Jessie who was probably off somewhere with his own lassie. Sid said he'd grab a few winks, but Andrew couldn't imagine falling asleep with

Emily just down the hall. She was so close, and he cursed the wall that separated them. Even so, he must have dozed off because it was noon when he rose. He shook Sid awake.

"Want to come for a run, mate?"

"You're bleeding mad." Sid rolled over and pulled the blanket to his chin.

The house was quiet and Andrew felt a frisson of pleasure to think Emily was under the same roof. She had walked on the worn rug he had played on as a lad and which his mother had braided with her own hands from wool remnants. She had sat on the sagging sofa and eaten at the table his father had made, nicked and scratched from the years of Cunningham meals. She had hugged his mother whose fingernails in spring were brown with garden dirt. Emily had seen him at the core, without adornment. Even when he lost his temper, she had not walked away.

He tiptoed into Lizzy's room and nudged Emily awake. When she opened her eyes, he shushed her with a finger to his lips.

"Meet me downstairs," he murmured.

It was time he saw his town again, and he wanted to see it anew through Emily's eyes. The scruffy town defined him. To be ashamed of where he came from was to be ashamed of himself. She would have to understand that.

She came down looking fresh, her amber hair tumbling down her back. Andrew watched her slip into her coat and lift her hair with one hand, letting it fall over her collar. Such a simple action caught him with a pleasure that was nearly painful.

"Ready?" he asked.

"For anything," she said, and he believed her.

Along the avenues, houses squeezed together—like its citizens, frugal, practical, neighborly. On this winter morning, chimneys spouted black smoke carrying from the kitchens aromas of leek, turnip, mutton, sausages, and apple tarts. He led her past the refineries belting black smoke to the outskirts of the village where Kirk O'Shotts stood like a medieval stone monument. He always found the hillside peaceful, but with Emily he was tempted to playful devilment.

"I don't mean to scare you, lass, but it's said giants tramp these hills." He shifted his eyes toward her to gauge her reaction. "They live in caves and come out when they're hungry."

"Oh, do they now?" She swatted his arm.

"Sure they do. And they have a taste for human flesh. Mum always locked the doors at night so they wouldn't plunder the house and steal her children. Bairns are their favorite lunch."

"And did you ever meet one of these giants?" Emily was playing along, which delighted him. He pointed across the meadow.

"See those boulders? The fiends toss them around when they're in an ugly mood."

Emily gave him a side-eye. "I suppose their moods are always ugly?"

"Right you are. I'd keep an eye out if I were you."

"I'll keep an eye out. Both eyes, in fact," she said. "But isn't it awfully pretty here, even in January?"

She stopped and pivoted on her toes, regarding the rocky hillsides dotted with golden gorse and wooly sheep munching meadow grass.

"In the spring, the fields yellow with rapeseed," Andrew said, "and the moors are covered with pink heather." He had forgotten how winter light sparkled on the frost at Blawhorn Moss and enchantment settled on the windswept moor.

He guided her to the graveyard behind Kirk. "Mum and Da have a plot here." Instantly he regretted the sad comment. "But who can say where or when fate might catch us up?"

"I don't like such talk," she said, "especially since I've just found you."

Was he going mad? After a single night he saw this lass as a timid bride, a mother nursing a child, her hair graying, the fullness of a life, her hand forever in his. As sure as there is coal dust in Shotts and water in the ocean, Andrew knew he was meant to travel through life with this woman. When Emily squeezed his hand, he knew she felt it, too. He wanted to show her everything—the splendor he'd seen on the ocean—dolphins leaping from phosphorescent waves, whales frothing the water with their sounding, pink sunrises and golden sunsets. It was uncanny how comfortable he felt with her, as if he had birthed her from his own rib.

He shook his head. It was crazy to think such things. But there was no doubt about it—he was crazy in love.

When they returned to the house, Mum was in the kitchen.

"How about a cup of tea?" she asked.

"Yes, but I can help myself," Emily said. With a mug in her hands, she peered out the kitchen window at the garden, dried up and brown now. Andrew thought of the flowers his mother had planted—blue hydrangeas, iris, lavender, primrose—and wished by some magic their color would blossom for Emily's pleasure. It seemed natural for her to be with his mother at the sink, these women at ease with each other.

"Must you leave today, son?" Even as Mum asked, Andrew knew she envied his freedom, his lust for the sea.

"Afraid so." He looked at Emily. "We'll need to be at the station soon."

"Why don't you go along without me," Emily said. "I'll just stay here and apprentice with your mother. I'd like to learn some of her cooking skills."

"That would suit me fine," Mum said. Andrew was pleased they had taken to each other.

"Is Da still in the workshop?" he asked.

Mum nodded. "You'd better go out there."

His father was the smartest and toughest man Andrew knew. He feared he would never become the man his father was. Whereas Da was outgoing and made friends easily, Andrew tended toward shyness. He had only one or two boyhood friends, which was all he needed. He shunned the vulgar jokes of his classmates and turned away from quarrels even though his father had taught him to fight boldly if he were backed into a corner. Even so, his father had a heart of butter, and Andrew knew that heart would melt at learning his eldest son was leaving again.

In the workshop, he had his head down, sanding a newel post.

"I've come to say goodbye, Da."

The elder Cunningham dipped his head deeper. Slowly he set aside the sandpaper and looked up, leveling his eyes at his son.

"Ye can still work with me if ye'll give up that ship business."

Andrew rubbed his jaw. They'd had this talk before. His father was as rooted to the earth as the trees whose boards his hands worked. When Andrew didn't answer, his father gave a shrug of resignation.

"I'll ask just one thing of ye," he said.

"Sure, Da."

"Remember where ye come from. Ye've got Scotland in yer blood. Always be proud of that." He pointed a finger at Andrew. "And if ye need a hand, send for me."

"It's a promise," Andrew said.

When his Da clapped him on the shoulder, Andrew was glad that his father was still an inch taller than he. It seemed fitting that he should stand above his boy.

"And may the best ye hae iver seen be the warst ye'll iver see."

It was an old expression Andrew had heard him say a thousand times. He'd nearly forgotten it.

"Thanks, Da. May it ring true in the New Year for you, too." He took a step forward and wrapped his arms around his father. The older man's chest heaved and then his hands were on Andrew's back, strong hands that wrestled hard oak into useful things pleasing to the eye. In his father's embrace, he promised to do his best not to disappoint him.

Historic Winter Storm
Buries Boston
Boston Globe, 1903

In February the weather in Boston turned horrid. Temperatures dropped to near zero, and I couldn't get the house warm enough. I lit fires in every fireplace, and the boys huddled in front of the flames. Then snow began to fall.

"Muz," Wells said, "Hannah says we haven't a scrap of food in the house."

"Nonsense, Wells. There must be something." When I checked the pantry, I saw that Hannah was right. We hadn't even yeast for bread, and we were down to a single egg. I should have seen about getting supplies before the bad weather moved in.

Certainly there would be no deliveries today, and I hadn't the heart to send Hannah out into the cold. I would have to go. I remembered walking to school in Cambridge winters, but I was younger then and skipped my way along the sidewalks. There would be no skipping today, though—not in deepening snow and savage wind.

I secured a hat with a scarf tied under the chin, another scarf around my neck. My boots were made for city walking, but they would have to do. I pulled on leather gloves and my warmest fur coat, hoping the fur wouldn't be ruined in the driving storm. At least I would be warm—or so I hoped.

Outside the window, snow blew sideways and I grabbed an umbrella to use as a shield, kissed my sons, and summoned the will to leave the shelter of the townhouse.

When I opened the door, snow blew in and settled on the entry rug. Holding my arm in front of my face, I leaned into the wintry attack. Before I was down the front steps, my fingers began to sting. The storm was worse than I had thought. Bradley's office should have closed on such a day, but he had gone out early and was lucky to find a carriage to take him to the financial district. If this snow kept up, he'd be better off finding a couch to sleep on tonight rather than braving the elements to come home. From the look of the steely sky, the weather showed no promise of improvement.

Our townhouse was on Commonwealth Avenue near Hereford Street. In the spring the divided road would have greenery growing in the median, but now I couldn't see more than a few yards. The wind blew with even more ferocity here. It was nearly too cold to breathe, and I nudged the scarf to cover my nose. There were no carriages, and I crossed the avenue without looking.

Now my toes were aching and gusts sliced into me. The umbrella was useless, and I dropped it in the snow to free my hands and hold my coat closed. My eyes watered and my cheeks felt as if they had been stuck with needles. Even though tied on, my hat threatened to catch like a kite. I should have turned around. What if I couldn't make it home, and Hannah alone with the boys?

My blood grew sluggish in the cold, and my hands and feet were ice. I hoped the buildings on Newbury Street would block the squalls, but the buildings formed a tunnel and wind assaulted me, screaming like a malevolent ghoul. The gusts hesitated, gathering strength for another onslaught, but I dipped my chin to my chest and kept walking. Snow reached above the tops of my boots and packed inside them. I thought how rabbits and ermine huddle into snowbanks for warmth, and I envied them.

Was I walking on the sidewalk or the road? Everything looked foreign in a storm, and I had no sense even of where I was. On my right I could make out steps leading to a door with a roof covering. When I grasped the railing and pulled myself up, I huddled against the brass plaque that read St. Botolph Club. Women were not allowed in the club, but Bradley was a member. Surely the men would give respite to a desperate female soul. I tried the door and with great relief found it unlocked.

Inside, a few gentlemen sat deep in leather chairs. In one of them I recognized Bert Marckwald. He looked up to greet who had come in.

"What in Lucifer's name are you doing out in this beast of a blizzard?" he said.

I couldn't speak. My jaw was frozen.

"Come in and sit by the fire, you wicked girl. Your husband insisted on going to the office. I doubt we'll ever see the demented chap again."

Never was I more grateful that Bert was a chatterbox so I didn't have to make excuses for my foolishness.

"A body can catch hypothermia in no time out there. Even a bloody horse could freeze to death."

I nodded and attempted to pull off my gloves which by now were stiff with ice. My hands were numb and clumsy, and Bert pinched the tip of each glove and dropped the pair onto a bench by the fire. Taking my cold hands, he rubbed them between his own warm palms.

"Out for provisions, are you?" he asked.

"Yes," I said, surprised at the sound of my own voice. "I had no idea—"

"No idea it was so grisly awful out there?"

I nodded again, grateful my skin was thawing.

"Even if they're open, markets most likely are sold out. But wait here." He shook a finger at me. "Don't move a muscle until you warm up."

He hurried through a door and I scrolled a look at the dark paneled wood and crimson walls bedecked with painted portraits of men in suits. By the windows, thick drapery fell from the high ceiling to the carpeted floor. The fireplace was nearly big enough to stand in, and the stone surround radiated heat. Over the tall mantel hung an autumn landscape and behind an upholstered sofa, a grand piano. I almost laughed at the idea of playing with fingers that had no sensation.

When I regained feeling, I loosened my coat. I could have sat by the fire the rest of the day, but there were the boys. And Bradley—why had I let him leave the house that morning?

Bert returned carrying a canvas bag bulging with foodstuffs.

"The cook was happy to load you up from the larder. None except the most rugged—including old Bert Marckwald—will be at lunch today and he didn't want his fine cuisine to go to waste."

I thanked him. "I would invite you home for a meal, but I'm not sure how I'll get back myself. The storm is not letting up."

"I'd have you stay, but your young men are probably hungry. I've asked our driver to bring the sleigh from the stable and the stoutest nag to pull you home. He'll have a blanket for you."

Bert had saved me. Even if it took years, I would find some way to recompense him.

It was well past the dinner hour when Bradley stumbled through the door. His face was blue with cold. The wind had let up, but the temperature hovered near zero. There had not been a single carriage for hire, he said, and he had walked the three miles from the financial district through snow drifting to his calves. Ice clung to his hair and his brows, and his teeth chattered.

In the bedroom I helped him out of his clothes and into bed.

"Jackie, get some more logs for the fire," I commanded, "and tell Hannah to bring tea and a plate of food."

"And whisky," Bradley rasped.

"You've had us all worried sick," I said. "You could have caught your death. In the morning I'm going to ask about getting a telephone. I don't know why we've waited so long."

Jackie added wood to the firebox and pumped the bellows over the embers to raise the flame. The bedroom began to warm, and Hannah brought food. After Bradley had eaten and drunk the tea and the whisky, I got up and closed the door. Then I lay beside him and rubbed his shoulders, his chest. I blew on his hands, still stiff with cold, and kissed his fingertips. Through the blanket I touched his feet, massaging them until I felt warmth flowing back into them. I kneaded his calves and his thighs. When his breathing deepened, I laid my head on his chest. I could hear his heart and thanked the Almighty for its beating.

"Come to bed," he said.

Cursing the hooks of my dress, I wriggled out of it, aware of my husband watching me. Shoes kicked off, stockings rolled away, knickers discarded on the floor. When I was down to the chemise, I slipped under the blankets beside him. I kissed him, and the whisky on his lips made me lightheaded. The strength with which he pulled me to him surprised and excited me. At that moment I desired nothing except this man, his hands searching me, his face against my neck, his fullness filling me, matching my need with his own.

British Museum Acquires Greek Series
Daily Mirror, 1903

Opera singer Enrico Caruso was exactly Andrew's age, and if he had had a single artistic skill to develop, their destinies might have been reversed. Signor Caruso was his most pompous passenger on the voyage, and Andrew told Sid he'd serve the tenor himself. The singer expected two baths a day, one before breakfast and another before tea. Maybe he believed the steam helped his vocal chords. Twice a day Andrew brought a kettle of hot water from the galley and made sure the temperature was to his liking—toasty but not scalding. Towels were to be fluffy and warm.

One afternoon Andrew answered the signor's bell and nearly choked on the vapors of menthol and cologne inside his cabin. He looked pale—probably seasickness. Caruso was a portly fellow with thin lips pulled into sneer and a vacant glaze to his eyes. He asked for a teapot of steeping water with lemon.

"Right away." Andrew started to walk away.

"And cognac," Caruso added.

"Of course, Signor."

Andrew brought a tray with the snifter of cognac and the teapot, cup and saucer, sugar cubes, and cream pitcher. When he put the tray on a table and tried to make a quick exit, the singer pointed to the cup.

"Lemon?"

He had forgotten about the bleeding lemon and had brought cream instead.

"Right away, sir," he said. He wished he could tell the tenor he'd have to sing for his service, maybe a song from *La Bohème*. The *Oceanic's* library had books about opera, and he had thumbed through a few late in the evenings. The stories were so ridiculously dramatic that they helped him nod off to sleep.

When he retrieved the lemon, he found Caruso sitting at the small table, his back straight. He didn't speak, either indignant about his steward's ineptitude or saving his voice for his next performance. Carefully Andrew poured the water, grateful steam still rose from the pot. He pinched a sugar cube in the silver tongs and hesitated for the chap to nod before he dropped it into the cup. He placed the snifter to the right of the saucer. To keep his hands steady, he pictured Caruso dressed in the clown costume from *Pagliacci* and reminded himself that he had waited on more noble gentry than this Italian whose voice alone had kept him from laboring in a Naples foundry that manufactured public fountains.

When he finished serving, Andrew stood waiting to be dismissed. He had more important things to do—like daydream about Emily Jones.

"*Che sarà sufficiente,*" Caruso said.

Although Andrew didn't know Italian, he could understand with great relief that his services were no longer required.

"What's gotten into you, Cunningham?" Sid perched on the edge of his bunk watching Andrew pace between the beds.

"Gotten into me?" Andrew stopped pacing and leaned against the top bunk.

"You've fumbled a dinner plate. When you went to answer a bell, you got distracted and forgot which passenger had rung. I had to save your arse with a lame excuse when the chief steward caught you staring out a porthole at horsehead clouds drifting across the sky."

"I don't know, mate," Andrew said. But he did know. He was too merry. His feet barely touched the deck.

"Well then," Sid said. "How's about you figure it out. Otherwise I'll be pulling all the weight around here."

It wasn't like Andrew to slack off. He was Sid's superior — he should have been on his toes.

"I need some time off," Andrew said. "I'm going stir crazy on this beastly Pequod."

"When we get to Liverpool," Sid said, "there'll be a few days before the next sailing. How's about we go down to London?"

Andrew wanted to go to London, yes. But not with Sid.

"If it's all the same to you, there's a little business I need to attend to — alone."

"Aha." Sid stood up and clapped him on the back. "I believe I have an inkling of just what sort of business that might be."

Andrew's gut knotted when the London train chugged into Euston Station. What if Emily had decided she deserved better than a ship's steward? He thought maybe he should traipse around London and write her later that he hadn't been able to get away. But he was aching to see her, to hold her. She must have felt the same about him — at least her letters made it seem so. Summoning his confidence, he stepped out onto the platform.

Overhead, the train shed's network of iron crisscrossed like a metallic spider's web. Andrew imagined a spider dropping down and winding him in her sticky silk. If it had been Emily's web, he wouldn't have minded.

He walked through the station's grand hall with its soaring ceiling and marble pillars and exited onto the wide walk.

London reeked of coal smoke and manure. Steam rose from a wagon as a man shoveled piles of horse shit from the cobblestones. Clouds hovered overhead like black fists, and mist dribbled onto the brim of his cap. Under the trickle of rain there was a mad bustling of people hurrying one place or another.

Emily had given him her address at Hampstead Heath, but which direction was he to head? He dared not spend cash on the underground train, so despite the drizzle he started walking, thinking he might find a shop where he could ask directions.

The junction of Shaftesbury Avenue and Regent Street teemed with traffic. He reckoned he was in the center of Piccadilly Circus. Horses shook their soggy manes and their harnesses jingled as they clip-clopped in front of carriages. Automobiles careened around them. An engine backfired, causing a horse to rear up, and the rider yelled an obscenity. Blackened buildings stood like scorched titans, and ash-smudged signs advertised Guinness beer and Dewar's whisky. Clammy soot drained color from the city except for one red scarf plastered to a woman's head.

Atop Shaftesbury Fountain, the statue of a naked boy holding a bow watched over the circle. Wings rising behind him reminded Andrew of the myth of Eros, son of Aphrodite, whose arrows pierced people's hearts and made them fall in love. But the statue's arrow had been stolen or rusted off. More likely it was buried deep in his own throbbing heart. Where in damnation was Hampstead Heath?

A woman with a kerchief tied to her neck sold fish from a cart, and cats rubbed themselves against the wooden wheels. The fishy smell turned his stomach, and he quickly moved on. By the time he reached Cheapside marketplace, rain was falling steadily. He ducked under a shop awning and paid a vendor a farthing for a plum. He hadn't realized how hungry he was until he tasted its juice on his tongue.

Near St. Paul's Cathedral, men in top hats and wool overcoats pushed their brollies against the rain and rushed by ragged men collecting rubbish in dustcarts. A dustman was a base way to live. Andrew would go back to the Scottish coalmines before he'd deal in rubbish, and he counted himself fortunate to have a job where he could wear a crisp, clean uniform.

Shadows lengthened over the street. Having no notion of where he would lay his head that night, he wandered to the east end's Whitechapel area. A tramp wearing a tattered coat held out his rumpled hat. At least Andrew was better off than that poor bloke, and he dropped a haypenny into his hat.

Pedestrians stepped over a guttersnipe lying on a bed of newspapers. A tarry sweet smell came from a pipe the poor sap cradled—opium, Andrew suspected. Ragamuffins ran barefoot through puddles, and a legless mendicant sat on the walkway with a tin cup in front of him. The dregs of humanity tumbled from doorways, and he nearly gagged at the stench of human waste.

A man wearing baggy clothes stood under a porch roof with a tray of baked goods atop his head. Andrew handed him a penny for a pastry knowing full well he'd have to be cautious with his money.

"Any idea which way is Hampstead Heath?" he asked the man.

"'Ampstead 'Eaf? Where the toffs live?"

"I suppose so, yes."

"Norf of 'ere. Past Regents Park."

"I'm very grateful." At least Andrew had a solid direction out of this hellhole.

As he scuttled toward the river, voices rang behind him.

"Spare a lit'le fer a poor soul, mate?"

"Fin yer better'n us, ya basta'd?"

No—he wasn't better. Just luckier.

Mist hovered lazily above the Thames. His feet ached, but his sights were set on Regents Park. Surely Hampstead Heath couldn't be much farther.

Rain let up as he came to a well-groomed neighborhood — no tattered beggars here. A green was rimmed by rows of tidy five-story houses. When he found the address Emily had given him, he stood in front of the tall door, straightened his jacket, took off his hat, and ran his fingers through his damp hair trying to look presentable. What if she wasn't home? Why should she hang about waiting for some Scottish bloke? But here he was, win or lose.

He knocked softly and waited half a minute. Just as he started to turn away, the door opened and a woman wearing a small white apron stood at the threshold.

"Yes? What is it?" Her curt question made him wonder if she thought him a vagrant.

Andrew hadn't expected the Jones family to have a maid. He was out of his depth in courting this woman. Essentially he was a ship's butler, and he knew better than to get above himself. He should have apologized, said he had the wrong house or some other lameness. Instead, he stood straighter and took a deep breath.

"Might Emily Jones be home?"

"Will Miss Jones be expecting you?" the woman asked.

"I believe she is expecting me, yes." He held his hat in front of him as a show of courtesy and earnestness so the maid would see he was a gentleman. He *was* a gentleman.

The woman lifted her chin and moved aside for him to enter.

The foyer was all mahogany — stairs and banister, trim work, floors, all dusted and polished. A glass chandelier hung overhead nearly as grand as on the great cruise ships. He was glad not to be impressed. The trappings of wealth were second nature to him.

"May I have your name?" the maid said.

He should have given his name immediately. An oversight. He had to be more careful.

"Andrew Cunningham." He thought a second and then added, "Emily — Miss Jones," he corrected, "is acquainted with me." He might have said, "She *was* acquainted with me." Hogmanay was months past. Who knew what she had done since the letters she'd sent? By now she may have written him off as a fleeting lapse in judgment.

"This way, Mr. Cunningham." The maid led him into a parlor with old but elegant furniture, a small fireplace with marble surround, and an ancient Persian carpet. The room was comfortable and inviting, like Emily herself.

The woman had not asked him to sit. Damn the English. Even the maids thought they were superior to the Scots. Emily was different — at least that was the way he saw her.

He examined the photographs on the mantel, all in silver or gilded frames. A family portrait with two children — a boy and a younger girl. He recognized Emily even so young, the round face, sharp cheekbones, her hair burnished in the picture. Her mother stood by her father, the family in formal clothing. Another picture showed young Emily leaning uncomfortably on a chair, her hair in braids, a grumpy expression on her face. He would watch for grumpiness — she might have a temper. In a photo of Mr. Jones, he guessed it was, he wore a Royal Navy officer's uniform, his thin face sporting a generous mustache. Three stripes on his cuff identified him as a commander. Was he still in service, Andrew wondered? And would he approve of the son of a man who worked with his hands?

After a few moments he heard the creak of the stairs. Then a voice said, "Thank you, Sally."

He stopped breathing when she appeared. Her hair was hastily pinned up, flaxen tendrils falling around her tiny ears. He wanted to see her tresses down, falling past her shoulders, resting over her breasts. Yes, he would witness that — or die with longing.

She must not have expected him and had dressed so hastily in a white blouse and long skirt that she was still adjusting the belt at her slim waist. She was more beautiful than he remembered.

"Andy! You found me." Pleasure spread across her face, giving him a sense of relief.

"I had some difficulty navigating my way through London's labyrinth." It was all he could think to say. But, yes — of course he was here. He had spent the last months wanting more than life itself to be exactly here.

She looked him up and down as she might if she were buying a horse.

"No kilt, Laird Cunningham?"

He liked the way she taunted him.

"When in London, I dress as Londoners. Did I do all right?"

Her laugh was a tinkling bell. "You did right indeed."

When she withdrew her hand from a fold of her skirt and hovered it in front of him, Andrew took it clumsily, bent and touched his lips to the soft skin. He didn't care whether kissing her hand was proper or not and let his mouth linger, breathing in the scent of almonds and honey.

"You must be hungry," she said. "Would you like tea?"

"I am hungry, yes, but not for tea. Not even for cake." He pulled her to his chest, his arm around her waist, and glanced at the staircase. Were her parents home? The brother from the photograph? Burying his nose in her hair, he whispered, "Where can we be alone?" He wanted to bite into her, to devour her. He was predator and she was prey — tantalizing, delicious prey.

"Come with me," she whispered and climbed into her coat. She donned her hat with a quick adjustment in a wall mirror.

Outside the rain had stopped, but the air was dense with moisture — not like the salty scent of the ocean but tinged with the aroma of earth. Andrew looked to the sky. It would rain again that afternoon, he was sure of it. For now, he was glad to feel the hard cobblestones under his feet, the ground that didn't shift and sway over billows.

Pedestrians shuffled along the sidewalks. Someone jounced his elbow. Another jostled his arm. Too many people. If he didn't get this enticing woman to himself soon, he would surely lose his mind.

When she slipped her arm through his, he felt her warmth seep through her coat. He didn't care where she was taking him as long as he was with her. She offered him a coquettish look and he blurted, "Your eyes are green." Why hadn't he noticed their color before? "I'd like to drown in those eyes."

"Please stay afloat a little longer," she said, flirting with him.

"Right. Then I'll paddle for my life in your sea of green."

She led him past Regent's Park, through the campus of University College, down Bloomsbury to Great Russell Street. If anything, the sidewalks were busier here, but he held his tongue. It should be enough to walk beside her, listening to the swish of her skirt against her legs.

"Here," she said, stopping in front of the British Museum.

What in heaven's name did she want with a museum?

"It's not so much as it will be in a few years," she said. "They've bought the surrounding houses and will be adding new wings. The museum is fairly bursting with fascinating things from the past."

"I'm more interested in a fascinating thing here and now." He winked so as not to seem roguish, not wanting to frighten her off.

She sniggered. "You are silly. Let's go in."

Andrew had seen his fill of lifeless art, but he hadn't seen it with Emily. Wandering among the artifacts, he watched her point out the Parthenon sculptures which, in his opinion, would have been better left in Athens—and the Rosetta Stone, an indecipherable hunk of black marble. This woman, too, was unreadable, but he vowed to decipher her before he left London.

Beyond the Rosetta Stone were old books, coins, medals, and drawings. Nothing but cold, dead things that interested him not in the least. But he enjoyed watching Emily sigh over a piece of old jade, a chipped vase.

She walked him through a rotunda lined with statues and stopped in front of a woman sculpted from marble.

"Here she is," she said. The woman was naked, crouching, covering herself with her arms.

"Who might this be?" The sculpture had aroused Andrew's interest.

"Aphrodite. She was about to take a bath and someone surprised her." Emily walked around the pedestal, looking up at the stone woman. "Do you see how shy she is? How vulnerable?" She pointed to Aphrodite's hands. "How could the sculptor get such a delicate effect from such a hard substance?"

Andrew ran his fingers along Aphrodite's thigh. The marble was cool and smooth. Except for her blank eyes, she seemed almost able to move. But next to her was another woman, this one pink and stirring. He pulled Emily into an alcove. Holding his mouth to her temple, he murmured, "Aphrodite is stone. You are alive—and much lovelier." Then he kissed her, his tongue flicking over her lips that now tasted of tart cherries. It was all he could do to control his desire for her. What was the power this woman had over him?

A guard passing the alcove announced, "Museum closing in ten minutes."

"We have to go," she said, her voice deep.

"Yes," Andrew said. "We've got to go."

Outside the museum, rain had begun again and there was not a public car to be hired. Showers in London were always a sure bet—why hadn't he brought a brolly?

He took off his coat and held it over Emily as they slid along buildings back toward Regent's Park. Off Wigmore Street, they turned up Langham Place and he tugged her under an awning.

She was trembling.

"You're cold," he said.

"A bit, yes."

He had to find a place to get his girl warm and dry. Attached to the building behind them, a plaque read "Langham Hotel." By a stroke of luck, they were standing smack in front of the hotel's door.

"This place is bound to have a tearoom," he said.

"I may be too chilled even for tea." Her hat drooped, and her hair had fallen around her face. Strands stuck to her cheeks. "I must be a sight."

Then he had an idea. Not a new idea at all but one he had dreamed of many times in the last weeks at sea.

"Wait here," he said. "I'll be just a minute."

At the reception desk, Andrew asked if a room were available.

"I have a young lady who needs a place to get dry and perhaps a hot bath," he told the clerk.

"Yes, there's one room," the clerk said. "Fourteen shillings, including dinner."

Andrew flushed when the clerk added, "and breakfast if you require it." He hadn't intended to stay the night, and fourteen shillings was nearly a month's rent in Liverpool. But now was not the time to be parsimonious.

He paid for the room and reached for the key. Back outside, he took Emily's hand and led her in. The clerk gawked as they walked past the desk, but Andrew was of age and what he did was none of the clerk's affair.

When they started up the carpeted stairs, Emily raised her eyebrows. "Is the tearoom on the second floor?" She was toying with him again.

"In a manner of speaking," he said.

When they reached the chamber — a simple bed, a desk, mirror over a bureau — he fell into the steward's role.

"Let me help you." He peeled off her wet coat and hung it by the firebox. She sat on the bed and took off her hat. He kneeled and removed her shoes and stockings.

As he rubbed her feet, she crooned, "Oh, that feels very nice." When she let down her hair and it tumbled about her like heavenly wings, his heart nearly burst from his chest. He swallowed and thought of what to say.

"Shall I draw you a bath?"

"Andrew Cunningham, you are not a servant. And I don't need a hot bath. If I did, I could draw it myself. I simply need to get out of these sopping clothes and under a blanket."

"I'll leave and give you privacy." He stood, doubtful he could leave her even though it seemed the chivalrous thing to do.

"Don't be daft. You're wetter than I am." She reached for his vest and began undoing the buttons. "It's my turn to help you."

The tie next, then the shirt.

"Not exactly bashful, are you?" He swept a coil of damp hair from her shoulder.

"This is no time to be coy. We could catch dreadful colds." She struggled with the buttons of his trousers. "This would be easier if you were wearing the kilt."

"I'll remember that if ever you plan to trap me in a storm again."

When she succeeded with the buttons, he let the trousers drop and stepped out of them. Down to union suit, he was aware of his arousal.

"Oh dear," he whispered and plopped onto the bed to hide his mortification.

While he bent to loosen his sock garters, she must have undressed herself and had slipped between the sheets wearing only her chemise.

"How long do you suppose before the clothes are dry?" he asked, climbing in next to her.

"If it keeps raining, they'll be drenched again as soon as we go outside." She shifted her eyes toward the window.

"Then we'd better wait 'til the rain tapers off." He nuzzled her neck and cautioned himself to be patient.

"That may take all night." She stroked his hair, his cheek.

"With any luck," he said and kissed her.

Suddenly she broke away. Sitting up, she chewed her bottom lip.

"What is it?" he asked. She had changed her mind—he had moved too fast. Damn him for being too eager.

"There are things you should know about me," she said at last.

"Such as?" He tried to keep his voice from quavering. Did she have some dreadful disease? No—he'd never seen a healthier looking woman. Was she married to a soldier away on duty? Of course not—she'd have told him, wouldn't she have?

"I'm twenty-three years of age. Would you like to know why I haven't wed?"

"If you think it's important," he said with great relief.

"I am a very nice person—"

"I'm relieved to know that." He stroked a lock of her hair.

"But I'm obstinate. I don't like to be told what to do."

"I am not in the habit of telling people what to do. In fact, I usually take orders."

"Then we shall be compatible." She smiled crookedly and then her face was serious again. "I harbor no illusions about perfection in life or love, Andy, and I'm willing to work hard for what I want."

"I understand." He was feeling so happy he could barely keep a straight face. He wanted to burst into laughter, but Emily was solemn and he wouldn't dare to break her mood.

"What is it you want, Em?" he asked.

He watched her study his hair, his ears, his lips and wondered if she had an answer.

"Since you asked," she said at last, "I'm ready to have a family and I want to make a pleasing home."

"How odd," he said.

She scowled at him.

"What is odd about that, Mr. Cunningham?"

He stretched his lips into a lazy smile. "That's exactly what I want."

This time she kissed him. Most girls he knew were silly and awkward. But not Emily. Touching her seemed natural, as if they had touched before and would touch again and again, an unspoken pledge between them.

When he trailed his fingers along her arm, he felt her tremble. He lifted her chemise and ran his hand up her thigh.

"Get out of that ridiculous undergarment," she growled softly.

Never had a man shed a union suit more swiftly.

She pressed her cool hand against his chest, and he was glad for grabbing a few precious moments in the ship's gym, proud even, that he had no ugly fat around his middle. Then she touched the Union Jack tattooed on his arm.

"I like this," she said. "It makes me feel at home in your arms."

He leaned on an elbow and looked into her green eyes, his ache threatening to overpower him.

"Where do we go from here?" he asked.

"Where would you like to go?" Her voice was husky.

He pushed back the sheet and took in her perfect form. He touched her round breasts, the impossibly smooth skin of her stomach, the mound between her legs.

"Is it all right?" he asked, barely able to speak.

"Nothing has ever been righter," she answered and pulled him to her.

Andrew had not been aware of falling asleep, but when he awoke, light was seeping through the window. He got up and pulled back the curtain. Dawn. How had they slept so long? The rain had stopped, at least. He woke Emily and they dressed slowly and went out, stumbling in the half-light through Regent's Park.

When they reached her house, he said, "Should I see you in?"

"Better not," she said. "Mother will be out, but Father will be angry enough—that is, if he even knows I've been gone. He hardly notices me at all."

"How could anyone not notice you?" He pinched her cheek playfully.

"When will you call on me again, Andy?" she asked.

He realized he'd be aboard ship for the next two weeks—an eternity—and cursed the *Oceanic*.

"After the next crossing," he promised. "Will you wait for me?

When she didn't answer at first, he was afraid she was annoyed. But when her bewitching face lit up, he knew she would pardon him.

"I suppose I'll wait," she said. "I seem to have waited all my life for you, Andy Cunningham."

BOOK TWO

Cumings and Marckwald
Form Wall Street Stock Brokerage
The Financial Commercial & Chronicle, 1903

Our boys had taken to their father's New York friend. Wells leaned against Bert Marckwald's knee and studied his face.

"How old are you, Mr. Marckwald?" he asked.

"That's not a polite question, Wells," I said.

"First of all," Bert said, ignoring me, "you're to call me Uncle Bert from now on. Now—how many years are you?"

"Five," Wells answered, holding up his palm, fingers extended.

"Then I've got about two-decades jump on you." He patted Wells softly on the head.

Wells looked at me. "What's decades, Muz?"

Bert chuckled. "Muz, is it? I like that."

Thayer had been asleep for hours, and after I put Jackie and Wells to bed and the modest weeknight dinner was over, the bottle of Sauterne Bert had brought emptied, I sat at the piano and filled the parlor with melodic Chopin etudes.

"Your Florrie is talented," Bert told Bradley. "Fine-looking, too. You can do better than Boston for her and the boys. Your city's old school."

"Now see here," Bradley said. He was Boston born and bred and wasn't about to let anyone—especially a New Yorker—criticize his birthplace.

Bert interrupted. "New York has the Vanderbilts and the Astors," he said, setting his brandy snifter on a side table. "Why not the Marckwalds? We should start our own firm there." He shook a finger at Bradley. "Marckwald and Cumings—Wall Street."

I stopped playing. Bert was impulsive, but he had a point. Bradley said Bert was a savvy broker, and even I knew that Wall Street had more reach than Boston's financial district. I had been in Boston all my life. New York—just the sound of it was enticing.

"I'll give it consideration," Bradley said, "but if we're going to be partners, Cumings and Marckwald has a better ring to it."

"You know, Brad," he said, "you're six years my senior, and I suppose you have more experience in finance."

"True." Bradley dipped his head. Under his brows his eyes caught mine. "And a family to support."

Bert nodded. "And a fine family at that. I suppose Cumings and Marckwald is as good a name as any."

"Right you are," Bradley agreed.

And in that manner, the partnership was settled.

I had come to expect Bert for supper at least once a week—and we three lingered at the table after a meal. According to Bradley, his only faults, aside from going to Yale, were that he hailed from New York and he rooted for the New York Giants. In anticipation of moving to the glamorous city, he suggested we sign with a realtor to look at houses in Manhattan.

"If you insist on living on Manhattan, find a place in the Lenox Hill district," Bert advised. He had grown up on the outskirts of the city and knew the neighborhoods well.

"Which section is Lenox Hill?" I asked.

"Upper East Side. It's a cozy neighborhood—if you don't mind mingling with the outrageously rich and stuffy. Find a place close to Central Park. South of the park is where the rubbish live—if you call it living."

"In that case, I should see about ways I can be of help with what you call rubbish," I said.

"If you must," Bert said. "Just be careful not to catch some dreadful disease."

Bradley wisely changed the subject. "Who is Lenox Hill named for?"

"A Scotsman who made a windfall trading with the West Indies." Bert nodded at Bradley. "We ought to investigate that. Could be profitable investments there."

"A Scotsman, was he?" Bradley said. "My ancestors date back to the Middle Ages in Scotland. We Scots stick up for one another. Florrie, we're going to live in Lenox Hill."

The realtor found a brownstone on Sixty-Fourth Street a block from Central Park. He described the architecture as Italianate, but to me it looked like a column of cold stone. Boston and Cambridge were all I knew. Even though the streets wandered along paths cows had trodden nearly three centuries earlier, I had never been lost in Boston. How was I to get along in New York?

"Manhattan is an island," Bradley said. "You're either uptown or downtown. Streets and avenues are numbered. You'll always find your way."

But even Central Park seemed enormous, and one could get confused on the circuitous trails winding through the eight-hundred acres.

The realtor encouraged us to explore the brownstone's interior. Eleven steps led up to slender twin doors capped by a stained-glass window. Inside the five levels were five bedrooms. Reaching the top level was like climbing to the stars. Was this the way New Yorkers lived, I wondered, crushed up against one another? Fortunately, the walls were thick enough to muffle sounds from neighbors on both sides. Crown molding and wainscoting were of a polished wood. Soft afternoon light filtered in through tall windows, and the mornings would stay dark and cool. The master bedroom wallpaper was of a pattern like ones I had seen in stylish magazines. What was it called— Art Deco, if I recalled correctly. Green leaves and lavender blossoms vined and curled on a lattice of crossed rectangles.

"Good Lord," Bradley said. He was studying a detail in the wallpaper. "Are those ladies' corsets?"

"Bradley, they're flowers." But I had to agree that in places the design might have suggested undergarments. In fact, I would never again regard the wallpaper any other way. "Bustiers, then—if you like."

"I like very much," he said and gave me a playful squeeze.

Bradley put down a deposit, and I let Jackie and Wells choose their rooms. I would decorate one of the remaining two bedrooms for overnight guests and the smallest was for little Thayer.

If the brownstone lacked width, at least it was deep and roomy enough for my piano, and I decided the new Cumings accommodations would do. In the evenings the parlor rang with my melodies. Bert suggested Bradley join the Knollwood Country Club where he was a member and they could challenge each other in golf and tennis. And Knollwood had a women's club for tea and croquet tournaments, Bert said. Not that I'd have time for croquet if I were to help poor women, but I would enjoy making some New York friends.

Once we were settled in, the boys enjoyed watching shepherds stop morning traffic on Fifth Avenue to herd sheep for grazing in Central Park's meadow and halt traffic again in the afternoon to lead them back to wherever they were held. Lenox Library, only a few blocks away, was a quiet space for the boys to study. Lenox Hill felt rustically urban, and I decided New York might do for us quite well.

Our sons would have at most a dozen years in New York before we sent them off to boarding school. Bradley insisted—as he and the Cumings men before him had been sent away for their education. His traditions were too deeply rooted to break, but having my boys leave home so young crushed my heart.

Bert secured a townhouse near Brooklyn's Prospect Park where he said the air was fresher.

I gave him a wicked smirk. "In that case, Lenox Hill will have to struggle by without the benefit of your sprightly company."

One evening Bert came to the house straight from the office to set an earthquake in motion.

"An anarchist has shot President McKinley," he said, his face blanched.

"Shot?" I said. "Is he alive?"

"Barely," Bert said. "The news came over the stock ticker before *The Times* hit newsstands." He looked at Bradley, who had arrived home before him. "I could use a whisky if you've got one."

He spouted details while Bradley poured for him. "McKinley had been at the Pan-American Exposition in Buffalo when an anarchist shot him twice in the stomach. The vice president is standing by."

I had heard Roosevelt was a savvy politician. He would probably be a good leader at the helm, but I hoped it wouldn't come to that.

"I met Teddy at a resort on Saranac Lake in New York," Bert said. "He fishes the lake and haunts the big hotels there. That's where he was when he got the news about McKinley."

"McKinley supports American business," Bradley said. "What do we know about Roosevelt? Stock markets are likely to plummet if McKinley doesn't pull through."

"Our brokerage has barely gotten off the ground," Bert said. "We could lose our shirts." He swept his hand over the table set with our wedding gifts of silver and crystal. "And you'd have to give up all this, Florrie."

While I set another place for our guest, Bert added, "Anarchists are rioting against the upper classes in Europe, accusing them of exploiting the working poor. It's a wonder the assassin didn't shoot the whole lot of us."

"Oh no!" My hand went to my collarbone.

"No one's going to shoot us, Florrie," Bradley said. "We're not rich enough."

"You're not exactly living in one of those settlement houses in the Tenderloin," Bert said.

"You'll have to ask Florrie about settlement houses." Bradley pointed toward me.

Relief work was important to me. I had already spent several hours teaching women to read as I had in Boston. Most hadn't finished primary school. A few immigrants barely spoke English.

"Poor women need work, a place to live, and social interaction as much as we do," I said.

"My wife has given two of those poor women employment with the Cumings household," Bradley said. "In fact, you're about to enjoy Ciara's authentic Irish stew, my man."

"The problem with money—" Bert said, sitting down at his usual place. "—is that when one doesn't have it, he has nothing to lose. With it, everything is at stake."

"Whatever happens with the markets," I said, "I hope we have enough in reserve to live on. If not, we may have to squeeze in with my parents at the parsonage." I was only half joking. My reserved father was too old to tolerate a trio of rambunctious boys.

"Florrie," Bert said, buttering a roll, "if it comes to it, there's always one of your settlement houses."

Daring Robberies Plague the Tenderloin
New York Times, 1903

In New York Harbor, tugs guided the *Oceanic* into its berth. Passengers scurried across the gangway after which the stokers tumbled off the ship, their duties done once the ship's engines were shut down. Andrew hardly recognized them polished of their grime and smelling of soap. Their pockets were full and their gullets dry. He suspected they would plant themselves in the nearest establishment that slid liquor across the bar.

After they had set the staterooms aright, he and Sid had only one night for savoring the delicacies of America's most glamorous city.

"I think I'll stay on board," Andrew said. "I want to get a letter off to Emily."

"Come on, mate," Sid prodded. "I'll buy you a lemonade, you teetotaler."

Sid could always lead him down the garden path, and Andrew followed him into Manhattan. In their street clothes they could have been any Richard Roes come to the big city for some excitement. An odd duo they were, though, Andrew robust and nearly six feet and Sid resembling the one-third of Britains emaciated and living in desperate straits. There was no doubt he ate well aboard ship and his good wool suit and rooster-like strut showed him anything but impoverished.

At Fortieth Street and Fifth Avenue, the Theater District buzzed with tourists. Museums and galleries were closed this late in the evening, but Sid seemed to have other ideas. He turned down Sixth Avenue and marched Andrew toward

Broadway. Night had fallen, and little ones played in pools of light dripping from streetlamps. Rouged women leaned against pediments, smoked, and eyed men who looked as if they had deep pockets. When one found a likely candidate for a tryst, she waved him inside.

"We'll find a classier lot than these wenches if we play our cards right," Sid said.

"I'm not interested in playing either with cards or wenches, Sid," Andrew answered.

"Don't be daft. Cards is the last thing we're going to do tonight."

"Are you sure you know where you're going?"

Sid swished his hand at Andrew. "I've done my research, man. Trust me."

"Trusting you is a dangerous prospect, mate."

As they moseyed toward Thirtieth Street, music drifted through windows and onto the pavement. Sid stopped in front of a respectable looking theater with a small sign over the door that read "Haymarket."

"This is it," Sid said.

"This is what?"

"Cunningham, you are about to have the experience of your life. Give the nice doorman twenty-five cents — we're going on a bash."

They were on the edge of the city's financial district. Inside, smoke drifted in air thick with flavors of hair pomade and perfume. Shrieks of laughter and strident voices pealed over a band's fast music.

"Ragtime," Sid yelled. "It's the latest. Gets your blood pumping."

Men in top hats ogled women high kicking and swirling, lifting their skirts to their thighs. Others in various stages of drunkenness hung over the railing of a mezzanine. A woman in a low-cut bodice escorted a well-dressed gentleman up the stairs and through a thick curtain.

Andrew leaned toward Sid. "What sort of den of iniquity have you got me into?"

"Try to relax, Cunningham," he shouted.

"Buy me some champagne, fella?"

Andrew spun around to find a lady smiling at him, red lipstick smeared across her mouth. Twists of hair escaped from a clasp, and she smelled so strongly of cologne that he coughed into his fist.

He signaled to Sid. "What do I do?"

"Buy her a drink." Sid was sidling up to a wench of his own.

The woman pinched Andrew's sleeve and pulled him to a small table. She pointed to a chair, and when he sat, she plopped onto his lap, her skirt spilling over his legs. A waiter brought them glasses of a bubbly liquid, and he wriggled his wallet from his vest and pulled out a dollar. She took the bill and stuck it down between her breasts.

"Name's M-Maizie." She wrinkled her eyes in a kittenish manner. He suspected she had made up the name on the spot. "What's yours, handsome?"

It didn't seem wise to give his real name in such a place.

"Conrad." He had just finished reading Joseph Conrad's new book *Lord Jim* about an outcast sailor tormented with guilt about abandoning his doomed ship. There had been seven lifeboats for eight hundred passengers, and Jim had felt the sea was waiting to swallow him up. Nothing could have saved all of them, Jim believed. Andrew hoped Sid or someone else would save him from this *boireannach gun nàire*, as she'd be called in Shotts—a shameless hen.

The woman raised her glass and tapped it against his.

"Here's to you, Conrad. You look like a real gent." Her voice was saccharine.

He set the champagne down and slipped his wallet into his coat pocket. The woman must have weighed ten stone, and he wished she would get her arse off his lap.

"C'mon now, Conrad. Be a good boy," she said, lifting the glass to his lips.

"I don't indulge," he said.

Maizie tossed her head back and laughed, but the sound was lost in the noise of the room.

She leaned in and spoke to his ear. "What is it you do, Conrad?"

The situation required anonymity. He wasn't going to give her any information to use against him, should she be that sort.

"I—I do—I do whatever it is I'm asked to do."

"Well, then. Such a decent fellow ought to be rewarded." She tossed her head toward the stairs. "I'm asking you to take a walk with me, and you oughtn't refuse."

Andrew changed his mind about the drink. His mouth was dry, and he took several gulps. It tasted watered down, probably to get a lad to buy more.

Maizie lifted herself from his thighs, much to his relief, and took his hand.

"Come along, Conrad." She nodded toward the stairway. He glanced back at Sid. His mate gave a wink over his own lady's shoulder.

Upstairs, Maizie pulled back the heavy velvet curtain and entered a darkened room ahead of him, letting the curtain fall against his shoulder. He dipped his head and followed, more curious than aroused. Try as she might, there was no way Maizie could summon the charm he felt for Emily Susan Jones. But here he was, and it would seem rude to retreat now.

His mind was foggy. Was it something in the drink—or the smoke of incense floating through the chamber? In the dim light of a sconce, the details of the room blurred. The walls were painted dark gray—or maroon, he couldn't tell which. On the wall a gilded frame held a mirror. In the reflection he didn't recognize the fellow following a strumpet into a tiny alcove behind another curtain — a reflection of himself.

The alcove held only a fainting couch, and he dropped onto it, afraid he might pass out. A cloth had been draped over a small lamp. Maizie put her hand on his neck, her chubby fingers pulling his face toward hers, her breasts nearly falling out of the low neck of her dress. She was going to kiss him, this woman he had no desire to kiss. He swallowed a bilious uneasiness and thought for an instant he was back in his steward's uniform. If she had been one of his passengers and he kissed her — or more — his life could change in the blink of an eye. He might be put out on the streets begging for his dinner — "Spare a ha'penny fer a pitiable bloke, mate?" If he resisted, she might accuse him of some advance of which he was completely innocent. Without witnesses, her word would be taken over his. He felt he had no choice except to stand his ground.

Her lips were dry and her breath smelled sickeningly sweet, like paint thinner. More like overripe fruit. He recognized that odor from visits to the dentist. It was ether — he was sure of it. A vial of ether could cause an explosion if not handled carefully. Drunk with the vapors, this woman was as unpredictable as whatever substance had her under its power.

Andrew struggled to his feet and edged past her.

"Sorry, miss," he said. "Must be going."

"Aw," she groaned. "Give us a hug, then, will you, darlin'?" She pushed herself against him and rubbed his sides. He could feel the stiff corset under her dress, and her breasts pressed into his chest like boules.

Back outside the heavy curtain, Andrew looked around for Sid, who seemed to be enjoying his lady's company. He stumbled down the stairs and yanked Sid up from his seat.

"Pardon, madam, but my gentleman friend has business to attend to. Good evening to you."

"Spoil sport," Sid said as Andrew ushered him outside.

"Barely made it out with my dignity," Andrew said, sucking in the night air.

"Dignity be damned. You're missing out on a great deal of fun, my mate."

"Not my cuppa tea." Andrew patted his coat and frowned. "I seem to be missing more than fun."

"That's what happens when you leave a woman unsatisfied."

"Oh for fuck sake!" He punched the air. "I'll be a bawheid!"

"My word," Sid said. "I didn't know you were capable of such invective."

"Don't be funny, Sid. I had two crossings worth of tips in that wallet."

"Want to go back and pat down the offending damsel?"

"Not on your life. I'd be lucky to get out with my socks."

Sid clapped him on the back. "That's all right—I'll spring for the rest of tonight's delight."

"Never mind, Siebert," Andrew said. "I've had enough of your brand of delight."

"Night's young, Cunningham." Sid shot Andrew a crooked smile. "We've one more stop tonight. And worry not—there'll be no lustful trollops. I promise."

Walking back toward Broadway past brothels and gambling parlors, Andrew wanted to be anywhere but here. This wasn't the New York he had seen on his own, the Astor-library New York. But he'd already lost everything of value, so what difference did it make?

At the corner of Broadway and Thirty-Fourth Street, Sid paid the admission for Koster and Bial's Music Hall, and Andrew followed him up the marble stairs to the cheap seats in the gallery. Two places in the orchestra would have set them back four dollars, a sum too enormous even for Sid. The hall must have had seating for nearly four thousand. Cigar and cigarette smoke floated above the audience below, and slurred voices rose louder by the minute.

At the front of the theatre, red velvet curtains hung from the ceiling down to a stage. The two found a chair and within a few minutes the curtains opened to reveal a tall white screen that took up one whole wall of the building.

Sid must have seen the quizzical look on Andrew's face.

"Vitascope," he said. "Watch this—"

The lights dimmed and a man at a piano began playing a sprightly tune.

The curtain opened and four enormous female dancers pranced onto the screen. High stepping, they kicked up their legs to show their bloomers.

"Ha!" Sid laughed. "Ever seen anything like it?"

The audience cheered so boisterously that Andrew had to yell over the noise.

"Can't say'z I have. Is it real?"

"It's an illusion, old chap. The magic of film."

The image on the screen was black and white and gray, and the women's movements were jerky. They rustled and flapped their skirts, turned around and showed their white ruffled knickers to the audience.

Men in the audience guffawed and waved their hands in the air. The tick-tick-tick of the projector was off time with the piano music, and the auditorium seemed about to erupt into pandemonium.

Andrew felt he could barely breathe. His head was a balloon about to burst. He had to get out.

"I've had enough," he said.

"There's more, mate. Just watch."

"Do what you like." Andrew got up and gave him a salute. "I'll see you in the morning."

"Wait—let's get set up in a hotel. I'd rather not brave the docks with thugs lurking in the shadows."

"We'll be all right once we're aboard ship." He didn't like arguing with Sid, but Andrew wanted to sleep in his own bunk—what was left of the night.

"You mean if we get there in one piece," Sid said.

"We survived the Tenderloin, didn't we? The docks'll be like walking into a candy shop."

When they reached the harbor, it was near midnight and pitch black except for ships' lights. From behind them, Andrew heard footsteps running. Someone pushed him forward and he tumbled to his knees. When he turned to accost whoever had done him such rudeness, two men stood over him, sleeves rolled up to their beefy biceps.

"Give us yer dough. All ov it," one of them growled. In the faint light, Andrew couldn't make out their faces. "You deaf? I said hand it over. Now!"

Andrew got up and balled his hands into fists but Sid stepped in front of him, ludicrously thin next to the hulking thieves.

"He doesn't have any dough," Sid said, mocking the robbers. "He's already been mugged."

The shorter man sneered. "You don't say." He pulled a knife from his pants and waved it in the air.

"I'll handle this, Sid," Andrew said. He wasn't going to die tonight, not if he could help it. He elbowed Sid aside.

"Wait—" Sid reached into his pocket. "Here, you felchers— take this." He pulled out a handful of coins and tossed them on the pavement—all English shillings.

The smaller man picked up a coin.

"Say—what is this? You'll pay for that, limey!" The man with the knife came for him. When Sid lunged out of the way, the blade caught his shoulder and slit his coat.

"You pikey arse!" Sid yelled, hands clenched in front of him. "Come at me again, will you?"

Just as the knife wielder started again for Sid, a strong arm wrapped around the brute's neck and whipped him backward. A scorched, scarred arm. Salvadore Caveney had Jimmy Birdsall and several other stokers with him.

"We'll see who's g'wan ta pay, ya bag o' shite!" Jimmy roared.

Fists flew and Andrew heard the dull thud of knuckles hitting flesh. A robber's head jerked back when Sally punched his jaw. At the next punch, the thief fell to the ground. Jimmy buried his fist in the stomach of the other man. When he doubled over, the wind knocked out of him, the stoker grabbed the knife and stood solid as a two-legged pillar, blade in one hand, the other curled tight as a cricket ball.

"Didn't mean no harm," the now knifeless man choked out.

Sally stuck the knife into his belt and raised his iron paws, daring the attackers to come at him. Andrew was sure he had never seen a more beautiful, horrible face than Sally's. He wanted to kiss those burnt cheeks. Once the ship got under way again, he would bring the stokers so many buckets of cool water they'd fairly shiver.

"Don't let me catch ye near the docks agin," Jimmy said, "or ye'll know what yer in fer." The robbers scrabbled to their feet and dissolved into the night.

When they were gone, Sally turned to Andrew.

"They followed ya from the Tend'r-line, likely. Don't be goin' down there agin wifout us stokers. Hear?"

"Thanks, Sally," Andrew stuck his hand toward him. When the fireman took it, he nearly crushed the bones, but Andrew didn't mind.

Crewmembers were required to be back on board a day ahead of setting sail. Fires in the furnaces were started the night before to be sure there would be a full pressure of steam at least an hour before shoving off. With a launch, everything had to be synchronized. Everything had to be in order.

On launch morning, Andrew leaned against the deck railing and watched Sid smoke. Above them, the captain stood on the bridge while winches chattered, windlasses clinked, cables squealed around the capstans, and the docking gang worked the warps.

"I could use one of those fags," Andrew said.

"Haven't you picked up enough bad habits this trip?"

"Shut up, Sid, and give us a smoke."

After what he'd been through, Andrew guessed a cigarette wasn't going to kill him. Sid cupped his hands around a match and lit the cigarette for him. Andrew coughed his way through the first puffs. After that, he watched the ash glow between his fingers.

At last the *Oceanic* was set loose from the dock and slowly made her way through the busy harbor and out into open water.

Isabella Kilpatrick Weds Albert Marckwald
Brooklyn Daily Eagle, 1903

"I had hoped to walk to Wall Street, Florrie, but Bert neglected to tell me the office is more than six and a half miles from Lenox Hill." At the kitchen table Bradley fumbled with a pat of butter poised above a slice of toast.

"Let me do that." I took the butter knife from his hand. "You shouldn't walk anyway. It's not safe." From working with the poor, I had learned my way around Midtown. The women there gave me protection and I didn't dare linger after giving them reading lessons. "You'd have to go through SoHo, Chelsea, and the Tenderloin. Those areas are rife with brothels and muggers."

"Muggers? Wherever did you hear that word?"

I had picked up a few terms from women in the shelter houses. Apparently my husband did not approve. "It's the new slang, darling."

"New or not." He shook a finger at me. "Promise me you won't use slang in front of the boys. It's difficult enough to get them to speak proper English. Anyway, the new underground train is faster than walking, and time is money. Besides, the ride gives me a chance to peruse the *Herald* and check the latest stock market trends."

"Will you stop at the club for a match with Bert tonight?" I nuzzled into his chest and kissed him.

"Oh," Bradley said, patting my back, "I've been meaning to tell you — Bert says we ought to think about a trip to Europe on one of those grand steamers."

"Sailing to Europe?" I took a step back. I had longed to visit Paris and the Italian city I was named for. Europe meant history, the Renaissance and La Belle Époque. Architecture, art, music, and industry. There would be so much to show our boys. "Can we afford it?"

"I'd like to wait until the brokerage takes a firmer hold on the money market. No sense in going unless we book first class. You deserve nothing less, my darling." He pressed his cheek to mine and whispered, "Be a good wifey, won't you Florrie, and tell Ciara I'd like chops for supper."

"Chops it is," I said, handing him a plate with the buttered toast. "You deserve nothing less, dearest."

"I don't like the news about tensions in Asia and Europe." Bradley's nose was buried in the Sunday morning paper.

"The country ought to build a few of those new torpedo boats to protect our harbors—just in case."

Bradley put down his coffee cup and looked over the *Times* at me.

"What do you know about torpedo boats, Florrie?"

He knew I had been attending meetings of the Women's Suffrage Association, but he may not have realized we spoke about reforms like the women's vote, child labor laws and, yes, world affairs. I hadn't bothered mentioning the topics of discussion to Bradley.

"What do you think I do all day, Mr. Cumings?" I said. "I bear a good brain, you know."

"I well know the quality of your brain." He regarded me through slit eyes.

"The subsurface boat is nearly invisible above water and can get within five hundred yards of its target."

"I've heard of it." He looked at me as if I were some rare curiosity. "Maneuvers faster than a bulky submarine."

"Umm-hmm. And virtually unsinkable." I enjoyed surprising him with my newly acquired knowledge. Certainly I could read the newspapers as well as any man.

"Here's an article," Bradley said. "Listen — 'The boat's upper hull is in effect a float divided into cellulose-filled compartments.' Cellulose swells when it's wet, so if a shell should go through one of the compartments, the cellulose would expand and fill the hole, keeping the boat afloat. It could indeed be unsinkable."

"Has the company issued stock?"

"Good question. The article says a million and a quarter shares at twenty-five dollars. You could build a fleet of these subsurface ships for the cost of one destroyer." He put the paper down. "Investors will like the idea of harbor protection, and the stock's bound to shoot up."

"Sounds like a good investment. If the market cooperates, the torpedo boat could make enough money to send the boys to good schools." And, I thought, there was the prospect of the cruise to Europe.

"I'm going to ask Bert about purchasing some stock in this new boat company," Bradley said.

"What a wonderful idea, darling." What was the harm in letting my husband think he had come to the conclusion on his own?

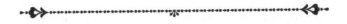

Bert stopped by the brownstone on Sunday afternoon after a stroll through Central Park. I liked seeing him dressed in the casual cardigan jacket. He looked somehow vulnerable without the stiff shirt and tie of his business suit. When Bradley asked him about the torpedo boat idea, Bert said it sounded like a solid venture and he intended to buy some shares himself.

"I'm glad we agree on that," Bradley said. "Now, on another matter — what are you now, Bert — twenty-six years?" Bradley handed him a glass of beer.

"Precisely, old man." Bert drank standing, elbow up.

Bradley pulled his mouth to the side. I knew he didn't like to be called old. He was thirty-two now and with three sons. I was nearing thirty, too. Bert was nearly a generation behind us. Where had the years gone?

"Isn't it time you found yourself a wife?" Bradley bounced Thayer on his lap. "Investors don't trust single men your age."

"And where am I to find suitable wife material?" Bert said.

I actually felt sorry for him. A prosperous stockbroker wasn't going to find the right kind of lady sitting on a park bench.

"Bradley and I met at church," I said.

Bert grimaced. "You Unitarians are more liberal than we Episcopalians. I'm convinced that young ladies at Trinity Church wear chastity belts."

"What exactly are you insinuating, Mr. Marckwald?" I pursed my lips at him.

"Oh, don't take offense, Florrie. You know what I mean."

"You need a woman of good breeding," Bradley said. "She should have some intelligence — like Florrie. And it wouldn't hurt if she were damned attractive."

Damned attractive was Bradley's expression for a woman who could play tennis, canter her horse on the bridle paths, and tolerate a scamp like Bert Marckwald. But who had time for that sort of foolishness? And as for Bert Marckwald, I wished him only the best.

"If only Florrie were on the market," Bert said, winking at me.

"I'm afraid my wife has all she can handle with four men in the house, my dear fellow," Bradley said. "So don't get any ideas."

I knew Bert well enough not to be flustered by his compliment. "This is New York," I said. "There must be lots of qualified women."

"My father is friends with a New Jersey judge." Bert lifted his glass in salute. "And I believe the judge has a daughter. She could be just the ticket."

"Then I suggest you consult your father for nuptial advice." I gave him a smug grin.

As it turned out, the judge's daughter was of marriageable age, and he considered a Yale man to be a fair match for his darling Isabella. Bert found Isabella acceptable, and after a brief courtship they were married in an elaborate ceremony followed by an extravagant reception—four hundred guests and champagne-and-lobster sort of extravagant.

"Old Bert wants to make sure Isabella—and the rest of New York—know that she married well," Bradley told me at the reception dinner.

Bert's wedding was not the way Bradley and I had started our marriage, but we were Bostonians and tended not to overindulge. Bradley remained true to his Scottish roots of waste not, want not. But if I were being honest, I had to admit I enjoyed the sumptuous evening.

"Are you jealous of all the pomp, Florrie?" Bradley asked during the shrimp cocktail.

I sighed. "I suppose I am, yes." But it wasn't the pomp I envied—it was the bride. Before the engagement, Bradley and I had enjoyed Bert's exclusive company. He was clever and kindhearted, a perfect dinner guest—almost a member of the family. Now things would be different. He might still be Uncle Bert to the boys, but undoubtedly he and Isabella would have children of their own before long. I was going to miss those evenings in front of the fireplace on Sixty-Fourth Street.

As a wedding gift, Bradley gave the couple two tickets for the best seats at Hilltop Park to watch the New York Highlanders play, even though he purchased the tickets through gritted teeth.

"I was tempted to give them tickets to a Boston Red Stockings game," Bradley told me, "but Bert probably would have tossed them in one of his fireplaces."

Bert had purchased a house across the river in Short Hills as a residence he and Isabella would use during the week. An impressive second home in Bedford Hills served as a weekend retreat with a two-story brick guesthouse for weekend visitors. Both neighborhoods were marked with sprawling mansions of the rich.

"Now," Bradley advised his friend, "get busy in one of your many bedrooms. Take it from me — offspring keep a man on the right track."

I knew who was keeping Bradley on track, but I wasn't about to gloat about it.

Emily Susan Jones Weds Andrew Orr Cunningham
The Daily News and Reader, 1905

While the railcar swayed over the tracks, Andrew considered Emily's last letter. She wanted to talk to him — *had* to talk to him. Because of the loss of his wallet, it had been eight weeks since he could afford a trip into London. At least it sounded as if she had forgiven his absence.

Crossing the city on foot, he wavered between expectation and apprehension. In front of the door, he thought about the story of the lady or the tiger. Emily's house had only one door, not two, so Andrew had no choice to make. He heaved a breath and lifted the knocker. After what seemed like an eternity, a stern looking woman opened. Dressed in a ruffled blouse and a long skirt with vertical stripes, she seemed taller than she was. Not the maid he remembered, she had pale eyes and a longish nose with nostrils that flared.

The tiger.

"You must be Mr. Cunningham." Her face was cast in iron.

"I am, yes. I'm here for Emily Jones." He pulled off his cap. He was glad Emily had spoken about him, but the woman had such a threatening presence his voice nearly cracked.

She did not ask him in, and Andrew stood on the doorstep fearing he might swelter in the August sun. At that moment Emily's voice came from inside the house.

"Mother, is it Andy?"

"Mrs. Jones, I take it?" Andrew offered his hand. She did not accept it but stepped aside for Emily to join her in the doorway.

His darling's face was pallid, her eyes swollen. He expected her to beam with the pleasure of seeing him after so many weeks. Instead, she glanced at her mother.

"I'll be going out for the evening." Then she looked at Andrew, her mouth set. "I'm ready."

The sun was blinding, unusual for London. Thin puffs of clouds floated high above. If only he had a carriage—a ride through the countryside would do them both good. A picnic on a blanket, ripe berries and cheese. But he had no carriage—not even the means to rent one.

They walked without speaking and at such a pace Andrew had trouble keeping up with her. He reached for her hand and she didn't resist. When he pulled her arm through his, he slowed to an amble. She felt small next to him. He wanted to ask what was wrong but summoned patience. Frustrating, maddening patience.

The noises of the city swirled around them—a horn, the clatter of horse hooves, wheels rumbling over cobblestones, someone playing a squeezebox on the sidewalk. A walkway snaked across the meadow of Regents Park, and they followed it.

At the boating lake, Emily said, "Shall we sit?"

He led her to a bench and sat with her, pretending to be mesmerized by the water. A woman with a small dog on a leash came down the walk. She wore a lavender dress with puffy sleeves, the sort of casual gown one of Andrew's first-class madams would don for a stroll on the promenade deck. Across the grass, a mutt sprinted toward the woman and her dog. A boy chased the mutt and called after him, "Rascal! Come here, boy!" But Rascal ignored him and made for the little dog, a terrier of some kind. The mutt stopped at the terrier and sniffed its tail.

"Oh!" the woman exclaimed. "Stop that!" She yanked the leash. "Come, Buttons!"

The terrier growled and snapped its teeth at Rascal. The woman dragged Buttons by the leash until Rascal's owner came at a sprint and grabbed his dog by the collar.

"Sorry, miss," the boy said. "He got away from me."

Andrew turned to Emily. Her mouth was open, her eyes pasted to the scene.

Is that what had happened, he wondered? Had he gotten away from himself? No—he had kept his head. It was his heart that had lost control.

When the dogs were gone, Emily sighed. "This used to be a hunting park. Deer and small game. After that, plots were let out for farming gardens."

"Probably there were no lawns then." Andrew pictured wildlife loping over the meadows. They were talking about nothing that had to do with the thing they came together to discuss.

"Have you been to the zoo?" he asked.

"Yes, many times." They sat side by side, gazing ahead of them, speaking to the breeze. "Would you like to go?"

"To the zoo? Not particularly." He had no interest in caged animals. He wanted to run his fingertips over her bare skin as he had that night months ago.

"The babies born this spring will still be with their mothers. They're awfully snuggly little things." She was still staring at the lake, a wistful expression on her face.

"Babies usually are snuggly, aren't they?" he said, not expecting she would burst into tears. Oh—what a fool he was. What a bloody stinking fool.

This was not the surprise he anticipated. He offered her a handkerchief. She took it and he put an arm around her.

When he didn't speak again, she breathed a sob. "What are we going to do, Andy?"

He swallowed the lump in his throat. "We're going to do whatever it is we need to do."

An expression of horror came over her face. "I can't give it up—I can't!"

"I didn't mean—I mean, there's so much to consider. Can you go through with it?"

"Can I? You mean alone?"

Right—he was part of this thing, too. If it had been Sid, he probably would have gotten up and taken the first train back to Liverpool. But Andrew Cunningham was not like Sidney Siebert. Andrew Cunningham would step up and take responsibility.

He pressed Emily against his chest.

"Of course I don't mean alone. I'm in this with you, Em."

"Andy, I'm so relieved."

He was glad to hear her cheer up. Maybe things weren't so bad as they seemed.

"I thought maybe I was just another girl you'd taken up with."

Another girl? Where would he have found another girl? Not on a six-day cruise. And he had outgrown the hens in the mining town he'd come from. There was no way he would ever go back.

"There are no other girls, Em. Only you."

After a minute, a rowboat came by on the water—a man with a small boy.

"You'll make a wonderful father," she said.

Father—how strange that word sounded. A little one on his knee, calling him Da or Papa. He felt a tickle in his gut to think of it.

Emily's tears were dry now. "There'll have to be a wedding, of course."

"A wedding?"

She dared a glance at him. "Nothing fancy. Just our families. The sooner the better, I think."

He blinked at light shimmering on the water. He wanted to be accountable. The fault had been his, at least partly—but marriage?

He leaned forward, elbows on his knees. "You don't want to marry me, Em."

"What do you mean I don't want to marry you?" She grimaced. "Don't you understand? I'm going to have a baby—*your* baby."

"I ken. Really I do. It's just that—"

"It's just what, for mercy's sake, Andrew?"

Her use of his formal name made him bristle. It was Emily who didn't understand. How could she?

He heaved a sigh.

"We're from different worlds, you and I. In the long run, you'd see that." He spoke to the lake. Water was a familiar environment. On the ship, he felt safe. He knew the rules and what was expected of him. Mostly, his passengers were courteous—at least until they got what they wanted. If they had to live with him day after day, year after year, the civility would break down. He wouldn't be able to bear Emily's scorn.

She let her hand fall from his arm. "You're not going to get away with that."

"Away with what?"

"The different worlds nonsense. There's only one world, and we're both part of it."

Emily was a woman who had no tolerance for self-pity—he knew that much about her.

"Look at me, Andy."

Slowly he twisted toward her.

"Somehow we found each other that night in Edinburgh. And then through some magic, there you were on my doorstep. We were in the same world then, weren't we?"

She was right. He had taken her home to meet his mum, and she had eaten at the table his Da had made with his own hands.

She had seen him for what he was, a salt-of-the-earth Scotsman. And she still wanted him, even so.

He slid off the bench and bent on one knee. Staring into her eyes, he said, "I haven't much for you, Emily Jones, but I'd like you to be my wife. Will you?"

Her face melted into a grin. "Well now, Mr. Cunningham, you're finally talking sense. I'd ask you to let me think about it, but I'm afraid you'll change your mind. Therefore—" She let the word linger on the air. "I accept."

There. It was done. Andrew's mind was whirling. She pulled him onto the bench and took his hand.

"You take some convincing, don't you?" she said.

"What do we do now?" he asked.

"Well—"

He dreaded what came next.

"I suppose you'll have to ask my father for permission." She hesitated. Then she blurted out, "But only if you love me."

He focused his attention across the lawn. It would take all his gumption to confront Commander Jones. Even more gumption to convince Emily's father he was capable of taking care of his daughter and the child she was expecting. But first he had to convince himself.

"You do love me, don't you, Andy?" It was more of an imperative than a question.

A wave of trepidation pressed the air out of him. His tongue felt like lead in his mouth. He licked his lips and fixed his eyes on hers. Today they were almost translucent, a sea green.

"Em, you are the most wonderful woman I know." He kissed her lightly. "Of course I love you." And he meant it. He had loved her every day, every hour, from the moment he met her.

He tried to picture himself as a married man. How could he possibly handle ocean crossings with a wife and child? He'd have to be a better steward, work harder, be friendlier, on his toes every minute. An obedient puppy dog. Good service was in the details—shoes polished, jackets whisked of any trace of lint. Hustle and charm would earn bigger tips for his family.

His family. Mum would be thrilled. Da might think it time. He had been much younger when his own first son was born. Andrew would show his father that he was handling the situation like a man.

"You'll see about the wedding details, won't you, Em? I've got to shove off again within the week."

"So soon?"

Her question irritated him. "I have to earn a living—especially now." He could never earn as much working with Da in joinery, and in any other profession he'd be starting at the lowest level. He had to keep stewarding, at least for now.

"If you want to get married here in London, my folks will need time to travel down from Scotland. Set a date and I'll let them know."

"Of course." She hesitated. "Your parents won't hate me, will they, Andy?"

He laughed. "Of course not, girl. They'll be mad about you. But—"

She waited for him to finish. When he didn't, she said, "But what?"

"I'm not so sure your father will feel the same about me."

Commander Jones's temples were streaked with white, and his trimmed beard was mousy gray. He seemed a viceroy of a man even though, standing, he was exactly Andrew's height. In his den, surrounded by shelves of books on navigation and astronomy, he shook Andrew's hand and pointed to a leather armchair.

"My daughter informs me you and she are interested in each other." There was no warmth in the commander's eyes. He was a man used to giving orders and having them obeyed.

"We are, yes, sir."

"And you work with a naval service, she tells me."

"Not exactly, sir. I'm with the White Star Line of cruise ships."

"You're an officer on a ship?"

Andrew hesitated. No — not an officer. "Steward, sir." And he added, "First class compartments."

The few seconds of silence that followed gave him grisly anxiety. He wished to have Emily's hand on his shoulder, settling him. But this was his task. He had to face it alone.

"Your family is in Scotland?"

"Yes." Andrew felt like a criminal being interrogated, testifying in his own defense. "My father works in wood. My mother is from Largo — Fife."

The commander's face lit up.

"Know it well. Birthplace of Alexander Selcraig — the pirate Robinson Crusoe. Scenic country. I've passed it many times sailing to Edinburgh."

Andrew rankled at the suggestion that his mother's birthplace manufactured pirates, but he said, "She's always loved the sea."

"Of course. It makes sense you'd seek work aboard ship."

That seemed a reasonable comment. Maybe all was not lost.

"Mum has tried to convince my father to move to the coast, but he's not got the sea in his blood as she does. I guess I have it in my veins, too."

"I see." The commander studied his hands, fingers woven together on his desk. "And if you marry my daughter, what will she do while you're at sea?"

Andrew looked around the room. Weak light struggled through thick window curtains.

"We thought she might continue to live here."

In the sudden hush, he could hear the ticking of a clock. It was late afternoon. The commander pulled his watch from his pocket and glanced at it. Andrew's head hurt. He wished old man Jones would offer him a drink, even an alcoholic one. Under the circumstances, he could have used some liquid courage.

When Jones slipped the watch back into his pocket, Andrew realized it was the watch that he'd heard ticking. Each tick sounded like a small explosion.

The commander cleared his throat.

"In light of the circumstances, I agree the best course is for my daughter to continue living at home."

Of course they both were well aware of the circumstances, yet they continued the bluff. Unfortunately, the elder gentleman was holding the winning hand.

"Commander Jones, will you give us your blessing?" Andrew was taking a risk, raising the bid.

The commander tapped his desk with his index finger. There had been no discussion of love, for which Andrew was grateful. Love was not an issue he wanted to discuss with Emily's father. He looked at the man with the hoary beard. Had the commander loved his wife? Had they married under a similar state of affairs?

When he still had not spoken, Andrew took a deep breath. If the commander wanted to play, he was not ready to fold.

"I am willing to take care of your daughter, sir," he said. "Financially, I mean." He fumbled for words. "I mean, I'll make a good life for her."

The elder man stroked his beard. "Hmm," he croaked. Then he leveled his eyes at Andrew as if peering through a rifle sight.

Finally, he said, "I suppose there are no other options."

Andrew felt like a condemned man up against a wall, firing squad aiming at his chest. Undeniably, he was guilty but he refused to flinch.

"You will treat my daughter well," he said. It sounded like a threat. "You'll see to her needs."

Still Andrew wouldn't cower. "I will, sir."

"Then—it's settled."

When Jones stood, Andrew sprang to his feet and thrust his hand toward the gentleman. The commander accepted it.

"I look forward to getting to know you better, Mr. Cunningham," he said.

"And I as well you, sir."

At the moment, a little white lie seemed the best option.

In late August on a Wednesday morning, Andrew stood at the front of London's Saint Luke's Church. In the grand brick edifice with sunlight pouring through the rosette windows, he was ready to receive his bride. Sidney Siebert stood beside him as best man.

A church organist played some music Andrew didn't know, and then Emily entered on her father's arm. She was draped in black from neck to ankles looking like a scorched angel. He wished the situation were different. Emily deserved the cottony fairy princess wedding all little girls yearned for. But a black wedding dress was not unusual, so he'd heard, and more practical than a white one. A white dress was fine for photographs, but she could wear black again to a funeral if such a sad event were to occur. The veil was white, though, and fell around her nearly to the floor. She carried a small basket of blooms and looked so beautiful Andrew nearly wept with joy. He had employment, a beautiful woman who was about to become his wife, and a child on the way. What more could a man want from life?

After the brief ceremony, his mother and sister Lizzy welcomed Emily into the Cunningham clan with proper cheek kisses. He saw Mum wipe away a tear as she turned toward Mrs. Jones to give a brief embrace. Andrew doubted there would be holiday gatherings with the two families, which he thought just as well. Da took the hand of Commander Jones in his own rough paw as a sign of mutual agreement. The deal was sealed.

His father had engaged a room for the newlyweds at the Langham Hotel, their best suite. He could ill afford such an extravagance, but Andrew knew it was his Da's way of sanctioning the marriage. When they checked in, Andrew chortled when the same desk clerk raised his eyebrows. This time their clothes were dry. They were official now. The beginning is the most important part of the work, Plato had said. Andrew had read it in a book in the ship's library. He knew the importance of beginning well, even if they'd gotten things a little out of order.

When finally they were alone, he held Emily gently, mindful of her expanding waist.

"Hello, Mrs. Cunningham," he said.

"Hello back, husband," she answered.

He sat on the bed with his wife. "Em," he said, "All I have, I'll share with you. I'm not rich, but I have sufficient to make you comfortable. I hope you'll be content with it."

"I am content, Andy. Having you, I have enough. No—more than enough."

He kissed her then, and kissed her again. They did not leave the room that night, not even for supper. All that existed were the silk of her skin, the alabaster of her breasts, and the intoxicating scent of her. He wanted her to seep through his pores so he could carry her with him all the way to New York and back.

BOOK THREE

White Star Line Moves International Service from Liverpool to Southampton
Southampton Press 1908

In late fall Sid brought Andrew a message from the wireless office. Before handing it over, he held the envelope up to the light. "Must be important," he said.

Andrew had never received a wireless before. He took the paper out of the envelope and read it aloud: "Baby girl born 3 November. Congratulations." He read the message again and puckered his brow at the paper.

"Crikey — I'm a dad again." He had been at home when his son Sandy was born and took leave from a crossing to enjoy fatherhood. But a daughter — that would be another story.

"Well, well. Things will be different now, mate," Sid said. "There's more at stake."

Andrew handed the paper to Sid.

"Not signed with love, eh?" Sid said.

"Emily's mother must have sent the telegram." Nothing about how things had gone. Nothing about the baby, how big she was. There was no love between Andrew and his mother-in-law. Damn little could be said in a wire anyway.

Sid pumped Andrew's hand. "If you like, I'll work a double shift on the next cruise."

Andrew rubbed his chin. "Thanks, mate. Emily wants to name her Gloria. It has a ring, doesn't it?"

Sid leaned against the bunkroom wall. "Speaking of rings, while you were fiddling about with your little clan, I paid a visit to Brightlingsea."

"Nothing like a trip home," Andrew said. "How's your family?"

"Didn't dally with family. I was more interested in a little crumpet named Winnie. Winnie Savage."

"A crumpet, is she?"

"Things took a sharp turn in our courting." Sid raised his eyebrows and gave Andrew a fish-eating grin.

"What do you mean?"

"I mean we tied the knot. Mrs. Sidney Conrad Siebert—now, that's a name with some weight to it."

"Sid, old boy! I would've stood up for you, mate."

"You had your hands full, so Winnie's brother Charlie did the honors. It was all quick, what with me being at sea so much."

"Emily will be pleased."

"Good—she and Winnie can keep each other company in Southampton."

"What do you mean, Southampton?" How the Brit always got the news before anyone else was a mystery.

"Say farewell to Liverpool, mate. We'll be sailing from Southampton with the other cruising ships. Winn's looking for a place down there now."

Southampton would be much better than Liverpool. No more St. George's Channel to navigate. Just a short stretch of the English Channel, and then clear to the open ocean.

Sid thumped his chest. "Now we'll see if I'm able to generate a brood."

"If you like, I'll lend you my pajamas," Andrew said. "They have a tad of magic in them."

"My strategy doesn't involve pajamas, old boy."

Andrew hissed and shook his head. "A clever one, aren't you?"

"Let's get our new toffs aboard," Sid said. "Then we'll celebrate with a drink in the lounge. With any luck, we'll find something that packs a punch."

Emily took to the idea of the move, and Andrew was glad to get her out from under the watchful eye of her parents. Lined with elegant shops, Southampton's High Street led to the waterfront. She found a red brick rowhouse for rent on Charlton Road a short walk from Southampton Common. Only two bedrooms, but Andrew said Gloria's crib should be in their room for the time being. And there was a back yard—albeit tiny.

"Could we have a garden?" Emily asked. "Like your mother's?"

"If you like." He put his arm around her. "But what do you know about gardening?"

She laughed. "Not a thing."

At the Charlton Road house, Andrew considered that he had two bairns to support now, but leaving was torturous. He had discovered the meaning of home, where the rooms were filled with happiness and warmth. The Southampton house gave his life meaning.

Charlie moved Winnie into a rowhouse a block away on Harold Road. He worked as a third-class steward, and when he wasn't at sea, Charlie lived with Sid and Winnie. He was a friendly fellow and easy to chat with. Andrew liked his Essex accent, the way he talked about Sid as his "bruvah-in-law" and his promise to look after "ole Winn" while Sid was at sea. He and Emily invited the three to supper at least once when they were all in port, and the table resounded with laughter and good will.

If a man is fortunate, he ends up with the right woman, one who will reform him and coach him in abandoning his wilder ways. Winnie was that sort. She was serious — even a tad stern, in Andrew's opinion. Sid minded his manners around her. Not a single "bloody hell" or "sod off" issued from his lips in Winnie's presence. He most certainly was in love.

Austria-Hungary Border Troubles Mount
New York Tribune, 1909

Bert purchased an automobile and brought it by the brownstone for our sons to ogle. Bradley ogled as much as the boys.

"Easier for getting across the bridge to Short Hills and the little woman," Bert said with a wink.

"Rather risky purchase with tensions at the Austria-Hungary border. Especially if Taft gets the U.S. involved." Bradley scowled at the auto, but I knew he was envious.

Wells either didn't hear or ignored his father's comment. "How much did it cost?" he asked.

"That's not a polite question, Wells," I said.

"Not to worry about that. American commodities are dominating world markets with exports," Bert said. "My investments are paying off."

Bradley was working his way around the car, checking the wheels, the shiny interior. He glanced at our sons and then at me. He knew I had other ideas about how to spend his profits.

"What's com—commo...?" Wells asked. A good question, I thought.

"A *commodity* is a product used in commerce," Jackie said. My eldest son was astute about so many things.

Wells screwed up his face in confusion.

"The wheat in your dinner roll," Bert explained, "the silver in the gravy boat, and your morning orange juice are all commodities."

Wells crinkled his nose. "Are spinach greens commodities, too?"

"Absolutely," Bert said. "Tell you what, Wells—how about you and your brothers come down to the brokerage next week and I'll show you how things work there, including commodities."

"Really?" Wells said. "Gee—can we, Muz?"

I raised my eyebrows at my husband.

Bradley sniffed. "Jackie seems to have taken an interest in the market. I suppose it's not a bad idea to show the boys around."

"Don't get lost, Wells." I held Thayer's hand as we worked our way down Broadway through throngs of people. Jackie strode in front gawking at horse-drawn carriages trotting between streetcars and people scurrying across the road. Pedestrians hurried six abreast on the sidewalk. It was a warm day, and the smell of horses, wool and sunbaked stone mingled with the loud backfiring of automobile engines. Modern contraptions were an annoyance, in my opinion.

Finally, our entourage stopped at Trinity Church so the Cumings boys could find the gravestones of American dignitaries—Revolutionary War general Horatio Gates and American statesman Alexander Hamilton and his wife Elizabeth.

Jackie stopped at a granite square lying flat on the ground. The plaque held a star honoring the deceased for his service in the War of 1812.

"This is Robert Fulton," he said. "Didn't he invent the steamboat?"

"Not a very impressive stone for someone famous," Wells said.

Jackie stooped to look at the dates on the marker. "He died nearly a hundred years ago. There were lots of diseases back then, like consumption and yellow fever, and they had to get them in the ground before the epidemics spread."

Thayer looked up at me. "I don't want to die, Muz."

"Oh, you'll die one of these days, Thayer," Wells said. "Everybody will."

Thayer scrunched up his face. "No I won't. I won't die."

"No one is going to die," I said. "And don't traumatize your brother, Wells." I didn't like to speak of death and its inevitability either. My parents were aging. Papa was in his seventies now and had retired from preaching. I knew their time on earth was growing short—but not just yet, I hoped.

"Look at this church, boys," I said, distracting them from the unpleasant subject. "Isn't it magnificent?" The soaring neo-gothic spire was like a pointed crown on a giant stone king ruling over Wall Street.

When we stepped onto Wall Street's cobblestones, the road was narrower but with fewer people and horses to dodge. I rolled my eyes up the edifice of the Gallatin Bank where the offices of Cumings & Marckwald were housed. Across the street, a brass placard identified J. P. Morgan's place of business. Next door, a statue of George Washington guarded the U.S. Treasury. These ancient buildings in New York's oldest section stood as symbols of the nation's economic power. The fact that managing such prosperity was a prodigious task did not escape me, and I admired my husband for his ability to make money for his clients—and money to support the Cumings family.

Inside the building, I paused to check my hair in the lobby mirror and then started toward the stairs.

"I want to take the elevator," Wells said.

I eyed the automatic door. "I suppose we can—if we all fit."

Jackie pressed the call button and within a minute the door slid open. A man in a gray uniform shoved aside the collapsible gate for the four of us to enter. When the elevator lifted, Thayer whispered that his stomach felt funny.

The door opened on the eighth floor and Wells erupted, "Boy! That was keen!"

In the office, I overheard Bert talking about rumblings of war in Europe.

"We should propose convertible bonds holders can trade for common stock when things calm down, Brad," he said. "American Telephone convertibles could be a profitable endeavor."

"And how are your torpedo boat stocks doing, my dear Mr. Cumings?" I interrupted.

"Florrie!" Bradley said. "What a pleasant surprise."

Jackie and Wells said hello to Uncle Bert, and Thayer climbed onto a leather chair and swung his feet, which did not reach the floor.

"The stock is at a hundred dollars a share," Bradley said. "We quadrupled our investment."

"He's making money faster than you can spend it, Florrie," Bert said.

"Well, then," I said, "I think I'll shop for new shoes on the way home."

"Say—" Bert perched his rump on Bradley's desk. "There's a house for sale in Short Hills just a jaunt from our bungalow. Why don't you and Bradley think about moving the family out of the urban jungle into the open air? Wouldn't you like that, fellows?"

Wells nodded.

"No, thank you," Jackie said.

I imagined my eldest son had gotten his fill of rural solitude during summers at the house in Maine. I wasn't interested in living in New Jersey, either.

"I'm happy in the city, Bert," I said. "And so is Bradley, aren't you darling?"

Bradley hesitated. I suspected he was thinking about the prospect of a piece of land to reward his hard work.

"Leave the city?" Wells said. "What about Central Park and the zoo and, and—"

"The brownstone suits our needs," I wasn't about to upend my family just to be close to Bert Marckwald.

"Jackie will be away at boarding school next year," Bradley said finally, "and we'll send Wells off before long. Thayer has plenty of room to rattle around. We don't need more square footage."

"I see." Bert tapped a pencil on Bradley's desk. "Then rather than sit on your plump bank account, why don't you take that cruise? Florrie would enjoy Paris. Isabella and I had our honeymoon in France—very romantic, if young Albert Junior is any measure. In fact, maybe we'll go along with you. I could do with another romp down the Champs-Élysées and have a ride on one of those new grand cruise ships."

I didn't care about how grand the ships were. It mattered more to me that the new liners were safer than the older ones. And I supposed it would be a good idea to visit Europe before some nasty war broke out.

"We'd be gone a month," Bradley said. "I'll have to set things in order before we plan a trip like that. And Bert, I'll need you here to keep up with the market and answer to the clients."

"Cumings, you dog," Bert said, "you have all the fun."

Edward VII Declares his Daughter
The Princess Louise Duchess of Fife, Princess Royal
The Morning Post Gazette, 1909

There were moments Andrew had an almost intolerable impatience with the first-class passengers, the way they looked through him when they barked orders, as if by some magic he could instantly make their whims materialize. The men were all kings of their countries, the women their princesses. When he brought the the tea, the caviar, or sandwich, he was dumbstruck if he received a single word of thanks. It was undignified for people of their caliber to thank a servant for doing what he was paid to do. That's how they regarded him, a hireling unworthy of their gratitude. *Dè fo ifrinn*, his father would say — what the hell.

Whenever he had a few moments, Andrew stood on the boat deck and fixed his eyes on the razor-sharp line where sky met water. To the sea, he was no less than the millionaires. The ocean was indifferent to wealth. One reason he loved the sea was that to her he was as noble as any man on the ship. If he happened to let the Edwardians plunge him into the depths of self-pity, he visited the boiler rooms as a reminder that his circumstances could be worse.

Steamships ran on the muscle of the black gang, as the stokers called themselves. Greasers took on the messy task of keeping the mechanisms oiled, but firemen had the hottest job — feeding the furnaces. For the entire six days at sea, the stokers worked in the hellishly blistering belly of the ship, brutal toil that covered them in greasy soot and turned their eyes a devilish crimson. They each took two shifts a day, four hours at a go, one constant shovelful after another until the ship reached harbor.

The *Oceanic* had twenty furnaces manned by thirty strapping firemen who muscled coal in temperatures not less than one hundred twenty degrees Fahrenheit and sometimes as hot as a hundred sixty degrees. A stoker fed four furnaces, spending a few minutes at each fire. When he finished a round, he rushed to the air pipe to breathe fresh air before the furnaces called to him again. The stokers wore gray flannel undershirts drenched in sweat and clinging to their bodies. Every few minutes they peeled them off and wrung them out before struggling back into them. They were brutish men, their muscled biceps covered with burns, scars, and tattoos of tall ships, anchors, and scantily-clad women.

When Andrew went to the boiler rooms, he took a bucket of cool water in each hand. Even before he shouldered open the furnace room door, the throaty gush of heat reached him. Every step took him deeper into the oven, nearly suffocating him with the heat of fiery tongues licking inside the red-hot jaws of the furnaces.

Sally Caveney looked over when Andrew came in, and he opened his lips in a delighted grimace. His teeth were like pebbles on a rocky beach, but Andrew owed Sally his life after the night on the New York docks. He set down the buckets.

"Dere's our boy. Brought us some relief, 'ave you?" Sally knelt on one knee and when he stuck his head into the pail, the water turned gray.

"Ah," Sally said. "'At's better." He rubbed a gnarled paw over his head. "Be good to da stokers. We're dark cherubs what feeds the beast. She goes 'ungry an' you'll rot out on the sea an' the sharks'll pick yer bones clean."

He and the others had cloths tied around their necks. When one stopped to take a drink, he put the cloth between his teeth to keep from gulping water and getting stomach cramps.

"Want to 'ave a go at the shovel, lad?" Jimmy Birdsall said.

"Thanks, Jimmy, but not tonight. You're doing fine enough."

"Look at them lily whites," Jimmy said. "Used to 'ave 'ands like that. Now look a' me. All crust and char, inside an' out."

Usually third-class stewards brought the black gang their supper — large joints of beef with diced carrots and onions. A few times Andrew made the delivery after a middle-of-the-night shift. Most of the stokers refused to eat a midday meal before going down to the stokehold in case the heat and labor made them sick. But whenever they were offered a tray of remainders from the saloon table piled with chicken carcasses, meat scraps, and cakes not pretty enough for first-classers, the food always disappeared.

"G'wan back up to clean air, m'boy," Sally said. "It does the black gang's 'eart good ta see ya."

Andrew was wary of the stokers. They were unpredictable when they were half drunk, which was most of the time. The galley made sure they had all the red wine they wanted for courage to keep at the fires, and the heat could drive them to madness. What would lead a man to work down in a ship's bowels when two decks above him stewards served after-dinner mints in the smoking room and rich men lit cigars while they leaned back in upholstered chairs? How did the first class sleep so soundly above the torment of men toiling at the furnaces below them? But they didn't know. How could they? For them, the ship's propellers whirled by some magic that took them from shore to shore with as much decadence as they could wallow in between continents.

Visiting the boiler rooms kept Andrew humble. And it kept his mind off Emily Jones and his family.

Burpee Uses Aeroplane
To Drop Goods onto *Olympic* Deck
The Weekly Colusa Sun, 1911

Packing for a European vacation was no simple task. I had months yet to get ready, but it was not too early to begin planning. Paris would be pleasant in the spring, but the North Atlantic crossing would require woolens. Oh, it would be much more efficient to fly across the sea in one of those new aeroplanes, but how could a flying machine lift so many trunks off the ground? On the ship, I would be expected to change outfits four times a day—and without a maid like other first-class women. Bradley said bringing Ciara was a waste of the fare when he could help me dress. As complicated it was to get into these outfits, I hoped he could live up to that promise.

Breakfast required a tailored suit of tweed or worsted wool in gray or brown colors—practical and designed for traveling comfort. Younger women followed the new fashion trends, but at my age, well, no one expected a thirty-four-year-old woman to dress extravagantly. I packed low-heel boots to wear with the suit.

As I understood, lunch was rather formal. With several courses, the meal could last hours, so I folded in several dresses with high waistlines, V-shaped necklines, and a chemisette to cover the chest for modesty.

Bradley might want to skip the afternoon tea service and have the steward bring tea to the stateroom, but I'd take another dress just in case. Heaven forbid I wear the same frock twice during the voyage.

Attendance at the evening meal was not negotiable. No heavy jewelry—I preferred a single strand of pearls. Less was more, I believed, and if the dresses were of highest quality fabrics, there was no need for fancy embellishment. Fortunately I had one special dress, the one I had worn to the opera. With luck it would still fit even after my third pregnancy.

Since the sail was scheduled for March, I would, of course, need a winter coat of thick wool trimmed with fur. Some of the first-class women would bring several coats, but one coat with mink cuffs and collar suited me.

I couldn't leave my favorite brooches behind. And gloves and hats—but no ostrich feathers. Nothing outré—that wasn't my style.

Bradley would need a tuxedo—the one with the swallow-tail coat and linen waistcoat—and bow tie. A dinner jacket, wool suits, calf shoes, cravats, and, of course, hats. I'd try to talk him into leaving the straw topper behind because it took up so much room, but he'd likely wear it. And he would need a walking coat.

I pressed the dresses into the trunk—too many to close the lid so I took several dresses out. How was I to know what was appropriate to wear until I was on the ship itself? Nothing felt right for a week-long cruise and a month abroad. I'd have to do some shopping and expect a shop clerk to assist me.

As much as I tried to scale down the luggage, there would be a few trunks to negotiate. At least we would have help—no one would expect us to haul our own baggage.

The time away would surely rekindle a bit of romance between us after having our sons. Thinking of evenings alone with Bradley gave me a thrill. After all these years, I was still deeply in love with my husband.

When finally the time came to board the ship, Bert offered to drive us to the dock, a chance for him to make one last plea for Bradley to let him come along. But first, Bradley and I said goodbye to Wells and Thayer. Jackie was away at boarding school, and our capable Irish employees Ciara and Shauna would take care of the two younger boys, make breakfast, get them off to school, and in the evening fix them dinner and get them to bed.

"How long will you be gone?" Wells asked.

I bent to eye level with him. "The ship takes a week to reach France. And a week to return."

"So you'll be back in two weeks?"

"Wells, darling, Daddy has some business in Europe, and that will take a few weeks." I wasn't lying. Bradley intended to investigate how his international investments were holding up, but that certainly wasn't the primary purpose of the trip. What was the purpose? To please me, I thought. To expose me to a part of the world I'd only read about. To show me how much he loved me.

"Hurry back, Muz," Thayer said, tears in his eyes.

"Daddy and I will be back before you know it." I understood children always need their mothers. Of course I had wanted to go, but now that the trip was upon us, I was having misgivings. Six weeks was ever so long and so much could happen in that time. So much on either side of the ocean. But the die was cast. Tickets purchased, trunks packed, ships waiting at the dock.

Bradley checked his pocket watch. "We have to be at the dock by noon," he said.

I glanced at the Irish women then turned to my sons. "You will both be well taken care of."

"We'll be fine, Muz," Wells said. He was my brave one. Between school and piano and tennis lessons, I knew he'd be fully occupied.

Thayer wrapped his arms around my waist. He didn't speak and I suspected his heart was breaking. In half a dozen years my youngest would be off to boarding school and we'd see him only during holidays and summers. Our boys were young men now, alarming as it was to realize.

"I expect you to be heads of the house," Bradley said. Wells shook his father's hand and looked to Thayer to do the same.

"We'd best get a move on," Bert said. "You don't want to cut it too close." He had already loaded our trunks into his vehicle. "Do you have your boarding documents, Brad?"

Bradley patted his chest pocket. "I do." Then he put a hand atop each of the boys' heads as if pronouncing a blessing. "Be good men," he said. "I'm counting on you."

Wells gave him a salute. Thayer's bottom lip quivered.

At the dock, I looked up at a ship larger than I had imagined. I couldn't fathom what it would take to get such a gigantic vessel across a broad ocean. One had to trust, I supposed — trust the designer, the captain and crew, and trust the good men who had built her.

"What's the name of this ship, Bradley?" I should have known, but there was trust again. I trusted Bradley to take care of details.

"*Oceanic*. She's been in service for thirteen years and has proved herself seaworthy."

"That's a relief," I said. But I didn't feel relieved. War could break out at any time, and battles would be fought on the sea. This voyage may have been a mistake. If I were a soothsayer and could be certain the sea would be clear both going and returning, my heart would be lighter.

Uniformed men directed us to roped-off lines. Ours was the shortest and I saw other lines were longer. Second and third class, I guessed. Really, could the accommodations be so much better in first class?

"Mr. Cumings, Mrs. Cumings?" A tall, handsome fellow in a white uniform greeted us at the elevated gangway. His eyes held warmth, a pleasant curve of his mouth under the thick mustache.

"My name is Andrew Cunningham. I will be at your service on the crossing to France. Allow me to escort you to your cabin. You'll be housed at mid-ship. Less rocking on the waves there."

I barely glimpsed a smile behind his generous mustache. He handed Bradley what looked to be a program.

"Here is a schedule of the afternoon's events and a map of the ship."

Was it foolish to put my confidence in a fellow I'd never met before? But strength and intelligence emanated from him. Besides, the voyage was just a few days, not forever.

"Very good, my man," Bradley said.

I had to admit the opulence of the ship's décor was more than I expected and not at all tawdry. Mr. Cunningham must have seen me pivoting my head to take in the carved wood and woven carpet.

"Do you find the décor impressive?" he asked.

In truth, I felt I didn't belong in such luxury. Bradley could be comfortable anywhere, but as long as the third-class passengers were relegated to cabins in the bowels of the ship, I would be burdened with guilt at such favorable treatment.

"I feel as if I've stepped out of my own skin and into someone else's," I said.

"The *Oceanic* is a point of pride for White Star Line," Mr. Cunningham said, opening our cabin door. "I'll bring your trunks shortly. Please let me know if you have need of anything at all."

"Well," Bradley said after the steward had closed the door. "It looks to me as if half the fun of seeing Europe will be getting there."

"Fun?" That wasn't the word I would have used, but there was no turning back now. "I dearly hope you're right, my darling."

White Star Line Names Royal Mail Ships with Launch of R.M.S. *Olympic*
The Daily Mirror, 1912

"The world is changing, Cunningham." Sid tossed his opinions over his shoulder as he pushed the cleaning cart down the alleyway. "Queen Vic's son Edward is now king of England, horsepower has four wheels and an engine, and before long passengers will be flying across the ocean rather than taking cruise ships. We'd better start looking for another sort of employment."

"There'll always be people who prefer slow and luxurious to quick and jumpy," Andrew said. He knocked on a stateroom door to start the cleaning and straightening. "Especially those who want pampering."

"Speaking of changes—" Sid nodded toward a woman in a stewardess uniform, a smoky-eyed looker with auburn hair swept atop her head.

"Hello, chappies," She marched toward the two men with the bearing of a knight in armor.

"I thought stewards were older before a hard crust formed around them," Sid murmured to Andrew.

"Good morning, Violet," Andrew said. "Sid, you remember Miss Jessop from our stewards' meeting yesterday?"

"Stewarding's a man's job," Sid snarled. "Anyway, I thought you were assigned to second class."

Violet flashed him the evil eye. Apparently she didn't think much of him either.

"Scottie, I can't find a thing on this bucket of bolts," she said.

Sid lifted his eyebrows. "Scottie, is it now?" Andrew ignored him. So did Violet.

"It's not laid out like the *Majestic*. If she hadn't had a bunker fire, I'd still be on her decks. As soon as she's fixed, you've seen the last of me."

"Sorry to hear that, Violet," Andrew said.

"Sorry my foot," Sid put in.

Violet gave him a sardonic smile. "You'll have to put up with me for a few cruises. But luckily the second-class cabins are on the lower deck, so you won't be in my way."

"I won't be in *your*—"

Andrew shoved a pile of towels at Sid. "Take these to the cabin and bring out the used ones."

Sid tossed darts at Violet. "Infuriating," he said.

If Poseidon were to rise out of the North Atlantic, Andrew had no doubt Violet would stare him down and send him packing.

"Scottie, do you have any idea what to do when an electric light burns out? I don't know why they're even used. The gas lamps on the *Majestic* are much more practical."

"I'll get you a fresh bulb," he offered, "and Sid will show you how to change it, won't you, Mr. Siebert?" He grinned at Sid as he brought out the soiled towels.

"I'd appreciate it if you'd hurry," Violet said. "These Americans always want things an hour ago. They're as nervous as cats."

"I find the Americans full of vitality," Sid said. He looked down at the petite lady. "We could all do with that sort of energy."

"Maybe you could, but my feet pay the price. It's hard to keep up with the Yanks."

"Try taking your vitamins." Sid threw the towels into the laundry cart.

"Sid," Andrew cut in, "go easy. The single women on board like having Violet to talk to."

"Your Americans suck the life out of me with their mad bell-ringing," she said. "And they all want to tell me how their ancestors came from England on the Mayflower." She shook her finger to punctuate the point. "That must've been a bleeding big ship to hold as many of their great-grandsires as they claim. Honestly, if they're so fond of the English, why did they go to America in the first place?"

"Maybe it's because English women are cheeky," Sid said.

Violet scowled. "More likely because Englishmen are dim."

"I trust you're not including Scotsmen in that appraisal," Andrew said.

"Scots, they're a different can of beans." Violet winked at him and added in a mocking Scottish accent, "Ye cannae leap in the air when ye have nae but fresh air under yer kilt. Ye'll frighten the lassies."

Andrew laughed. "Violet, how do you know what a Scotsman wears under his kilt?"

She turned and shouted back, "*Coma leat!*"

Andrew's mouth fell open.

"What'd that charwoman say?" Sid barked.

"It's Gaelic for none of my business."

"Not exactly a shrinking violet, is she? You'd better get that bulb for her, Cunningham, before she takes over the ship."

When *Oceanic* was well underway, Violet came into the stewards' galley where Andrew was heating water for tea.

"Where's your churlish sidekick?" she asked.

"Sid? I suspect he's either napping or out on a romp."

She sat down and pointed to the kettle. "I'll have a cup of tea while you're at it, if you don't mind."

Andrew got an extra cup from the shelf.

"How long have you been on this metal beehive, Scottie?" she asked.

He thought a minute. "What is this, 1912? Good Lord — nearly half my life." He spooned tea leaves into a pot and poured the steaming water over them. It always gave him joy to watch the black and golden leaves dance in the hot water, rehydrating from their parched days in the tin.

"How about you, Violet? Was the *Majestic* your first assignment?"

"Oh, no." Violet chewed her lip while she thought. "Let's see — this one makes five."

"Five? How is that possible?"

"I don't let grass grow under my feet." She guffawed at her own joke.

Andrew had thought she was older than the twenty-three years she claimed. Working on a ship ages a person, though — he knew that right enough.

He brought the teapot and cups to the table. "I'm surprised that such a — " He tried to find the right way to say what he was thinking. " — such a wee bit of a girl can handle all the lifting, carrying, and climbing. You must be stronger than you look."

"Right — don't trouble yourself about that."

Violet was an odd one. She could lure a man with her attractiveness and then slice him with her razor tongue. He turned his attention to the tea.

"You ever think about getting married and settling down?" he asked.

"I don't know what it is to you," she said, "but I vowed never to marry for money, especially to a man as old as my father. The proposals I've gotten have been from rich old geezers, so I've rejected them all."

"I dare say, there's a restless spirit in your blood."

"Sounds to me like you could do with a change yourself," she said. "Half a lifetime on the same ship year after year must be a drudge."

"The *Oceanic* and I have rather grown up together." He poured the tea through a strainer into the cups, added two sugars and cream to each, and pushed one to Violet.

"These liners don't last forever—twenty-five years at most," she said. "Like as not, she'll be outfitted for military duty when war breaks out—if the sea doesn't claim her first." She toasted him with her cup. "You don't want to be aboard when that happens."

He frowned. "I haven't heard anything about war."

"There's rumbling in the Balkans, and Russia is rearing its head. King George has a wary eye out for trouble."

"Who has time to keep up with King George? All I hear from the first classers is fashion and finance." He blew into his cup to cool the tea.

"Then you're probably not aware that White Star is building three new ships. Bigger and more elegant than this vessel. The *Olympic* is going to be the swankiest ship in the fleet. Four funnels and a twenty-thousand-ton hull. I'm putting in to crew on her."

Andrew could hear excitement in her voice. She leaned over her cup.

"Her sister ship *Titanic* is scheduled to launch in a few weeks and *Brittanic* after that. The pay'll be higher and gratuities are bound to be better." Violet tapped the table with a finger. "Think about it, Scottie."

He had never considered moving to another ship. There would still be the social chasm between stewards and passengers, and he would still bring cool drinks to fancy women lounging in deck chairs. As it was, he fairly fell asleep on his feet each night. A day's routine put him in a state of mental numbness. All he lived for was getting back to Southampton.

On the other hand, Violet had given him something to think about.

Days later, after Andrew had disembarked some of his first-class passengers in Ireland, *Oceanic* turned its bow toward France. The Cumings couple had asked little of him during the voyage. Rarely was he sorry to bid passengers farewell as they left the ship, but those New Yorkers had a special quality. Couldn't put his finger on it precisely, but he would swear he had met them before.

Once docked in Southampton, he had a precious few days to spend with his family before he was back aboard ship and tending travelers on their way to New York. When they docked, he planned to meander into Manhattan and purchase some gifts for his bairns. A gift for Emily, too, and he was in need of a new pair of socks. His toes were poking holes in his old ones. Not that the passengers paid heed to anything but their own needs, which was fine with him. He had no desire to get personal with the toffs.

He was about to amble to Sixth Avenue when a steamer sailing into the harbor caught his attention. Not just any steamer. It was White Star's magnificent new *Olympic*, the largest ship Andrew had ever seen. She was sleek and clean looking, a modern island of a ship. Three of her four chimneys spouted black smoke as flocks of gawkers waved from shore.

Once she was tied up, her captain, a white-bearded fellow — Edward Smith, Andrew believed it was — welcomed the admirers to tour the ship. As eight thousand lined up to board, Violet Jessop scooted up beside him.

"Well, I declare," she said, putting on an American accent. "My Scottish pal has come to check out what the hubbub's about, have you?"

"What do you think of the *Olympic*, Violet?" he asked.

"I'll be on her when she leaves New York. You'd better sign on, too, Scottie."

Andrew had a sixth sense about vessels, and instinct told him to steer clear of the *Olympic*.

"I'll know when the time's right," he said.

A few days later when *Olympic* was set loose for the eastbound leg, ten thousand cheered. Andrew had to admit being a tad envious of the ship's attention. He looked for Violet hanging on the railing, but she was lost in the throng. He admired how she crouched at the starting line, ready to spring ahead. He had been content to run in place, thinking only of the next herd of travelers and their trunks, their vases of roses, and their unending demands. Well, he could have used more of Violet's spunk. She had wanderlust in her, but he was content—for the moment, at least—to be anchored.

It was early spring when Sid burst into the stewards' lounge where Andrew was rushing through a cheese sandwich before his next detail.

"Good thing we passed up crewing on the *Olympic*," he panted.

"Why's that?" Andrew stopped the sandwich halfway to his mouth.

"A message just came across the wireless." Grabbing the edge of the table, Sid leaned in closer. "She's been wrecked."

"Calm down, mate. What do you mean 'wrecked'?"

"A collision. Off the Isle of Wight."

Cruise ships had to navigate around the Isle of Wight on the way to Cherbourg. But two ships could pass easily if a captain knew what he was doing. The *Oceanic* had often sailed side by side with another ship, passengers waving across the water to each other.

"The *Olympic* collided with another ship?" Andrew put down his sandwich. "Or did she run aground?"

"No, mate. She hit a warship. It had one of those rams meant to sink enemy ships. When the *Olympic* started her turn, the suction pulled in the warship. The ram tore two holes in the hull and nearly sank her."

"Nearly?"

"She got back to harbor on a wing and a prayer." Sid opened the refrigerator compartment. "Any more of that cheese?"

Mayhem made the lad hungry, but Andrew wanted more details. "How bad is the damage?"

"The *Hawke's* bow is smashed in like a pig's snout." Sid pushed the palm of his hand against his nose. "The *Olympic* nearly capsized her, but by some bloody miracle no one was hurt."

"Violet's on that ship." Andrew looked at him, afraid to ask.

"Anyone who's spent most of her life on a ship has to be willing to take risks," Sid said. "As Violet herself said, you never know when the thing will spring a leak. Don't worry about her. The hellcat will be back to prattle another day."

"Let's hope so," Andrew mumbled. He was fond of the damsel. She had brains, spunk, and the will to set out for what she wanted—against all odds. He hoped to work with her again on another ship.

Sid sliced some bread and laid a hunk of cheddar on top. "But she'll be out of work for a couple of weeks. They're sending the ship back to Belfast for repairs. It's going to cost White Star a pretty penny. And the warship may be out of commission for good."

"White Star's rushing to get these new ships ready," Andrew said. "There are bound to be kinks to iron out."

"Ismay knew what he was doing when he approved the design. The *Olympic* stayed afloat despite flooding on the lower decks. It's the captain—that fellow Smith—who's accountable." Sid took a bite of his sandwich.

"Captain Smith's an old salt, well respected in the seafaring world. Everyone seems to believe the *Olympic* is in capable hands."

"Salt's used for pickling, if I'm not mistaken." Sid spoke around the cheese in his mouth. "I hope Smith wasn't pickled when he took *Olympic's* helm."

It took a week for Southampton workers to patch the damage to *Olympic* well enough for her to hobble back to Belfast. It would be another few weeks before the ship could go back into service. Andrew expected Violet to join the crew on the *Oceanic*, but there was no word from her. A close call like that could unhinge even the most even keeled steward. *Olympic's* repairs would delay *Titanic's* launch. Already Sid had started badgering Andrew about jumping over to White Star's newest ship, but Andrew couldn't dispel a quibbling feeling that something wasn't quite right with these new vessels.

Helena Rubenstein Maison de Beauté Salon Opens on Rue Saint-Honoré
Le Matin, March 28

"Fasten me up, won't you, Bradley?" I had wriggled into a wool skirt for a shopping trip in Saint-Germain-des-Prés, hoping to find a Parisian souvenir to take back to New York for our sons.

"Mrs. Cumings, getting you into these outfits has taken up most of our vacation time," my husband said. I enjoyed hearing him call me "Mrs." After years of marriage, I was still not used to the name change. For two decades I had been Florence Briggs Thayer. From daughter to wife, one man's name for another's. I preferred Florence Cumings, closer to the beginning of the alphabet as if I had started anew, which I suppose I had. Wife, then mother, and now? New Yorker, I supposed, and European traveler. Although I owned all those titles, it was wife I held most dear.

I could feel Bradley struggling with hooks and eyes.

"Take your time, darling." I liked having his hands on my waist, the warmth of him so close. We had been married—what was it now? Jackie was fourteen, so it must have been fifteen years since I walked down the aisle of my father's church. Bradley had looked dashing in a morning suit. I was silly to worry that he'd change his mind at the last minute and escape out the back door. But no—he stood solid as a mast and has been devoted all these years.

He helped me into my jacket, and I chose a brooch to complement the outfit. Silly of me to bring several brooches. If anything happened to them, if they were stolen or lost—

especially the diamond piece that had been my grandmother's —
I'd be bereft.

"Let me do that, Florrie." Bradley took the brooch from me
and pinned it to my jacket lapel. "I want to make a special stop
after we've finished with your shopping business."

"Special?" I liked when he surprised me. What did he have
in mind this time? I hoped it was a visit to the new salon I'd read
about. When he touched my cheek with his fingertips, I felt a
quaver. Over the years we had found a place of comfort with
each other, our eyes fixed on an auspicious future.

"Why did we not have daughters, Florrie?" he said. "I should
like a miniature version of you." He kissed my forehead.

"I wouldn't trade our boys," I said. "What do you think
they're doing right now?"

"Not crying for their mother, I'll wager. More likely they're
playing some sport and not thinking of us at all. Don't fret about
them. In two weeks we'll be back on that cruise ship heading
home. You'll see the boys soon enough."

"You mean we'll see them?" I said. Our sons adored their
father. During summers at the house on the coast of Maine, he
had taught them to sail and ride horseback. He took them to
baseball games and Harvard College ice hockey matches. And
he made sure they knew the proper way to serve a tennis ball.
Their father was the center of their lives.

"Of course, Florrie." Bradley furrowed his brow at me. "Of
course that's what I meant."

The ceiling of Monsieur le Doux's studio floated high overhead.
I looked up but quickly lowered my eyes from the dingy webs
in the corners. Hard to reach so high to clean them out, I
supposed. Paint splatters dappled the scuffed floorboards. At
first I thought Bradley had brought me here to buy a painting,
but most canvases were perched on the worn floor and leaned

some several deep against the gray wall. White sheets draped over other canvases. At least the sheets looked clean.

My attention stopped at a high stool standing empty in front of an easel.

"What is this, Bradley?" I asked.

Monsieur le Doux said a few words in French—a greeting I didn't catch. He wore a white shirt, standard uniform for Frenchmen I had seen, and asked me to remove my jacket.

"No need," I said. "I'm not too warm." Indeed, the studio wanted heat, and I crossed my arms over my chest. Insistent, Monsieur le Doux tugged my jacket from my shoulders and I surrendered the woolen, which he hung on a hall tree.

It was past the noon hour and the smell of chemicals mixed with the oily scent of paints assaulted my lungs, an acrid sensation that deadened my appetite. The artist offered us each a glass of a pale liquid he poured from a bottle into what looked to be jelly glasses. I sipped, tasted flat champagne, and held in a cough.

"Monsieur le Doux is going to paint your portrait," Bradley said.

"He is?"

"Yes—a memento of Paris."

"Just me?"

"It will be like the paintings of beautiful women we saw on the cruise ship."

I recalled the images in gilded frames on every landing of *Oceanic's* central staircase, women in formal gowns, some with hats. I had thought them exquisite, but exquisite was not a word I would have used to describe myself. Sensible, perhaps, or tasteful.

When he saw me frown, Bradley added, "Monsieur le Doux has a very good reputation." I took that to mean the artist would improve my look. But I was being mawkish. Having a portrait painted was the fashion, but hadn't we enough framed portraits on the walls of the brownstone? Ancestors who died before we were born and about whom I didn't care. I never wanted to be thought of in that way. A modern landscape would have brightened up the house.

"How long will this take?"

Bradley spoke to Monsieur le Doux in French and winked at me.

"Just an hour, darling," Bradley said. "Then we'll take a stroll."

"A waste of the precious time, isn't it?" I said, hoping to change his mind. "And I'm not dressed for a portrait."

"Doesn't matter. He'll supply the dress—hat, too. Today he just wants to sketch your face."

The artist cranked the handle of a Victrola and lifted the arm onto a twirling record. Immediately I recognized Debussy. Clair de Lune was one of the first pieces of music I learned when I started playing piano.

When he left the Victrola and approached me, I took a step away. He swept his hand toward the stool and tapped the seat. I sat, chancing a look at Bradley. A nod of his head encouraged me to obedience, but I was apprehensive. What was involved with sitting for a portrait?

Monsieur le Doux pressed his hand to the small of my back to lean me slightly forward. Then he squeezed one hand to each of my shoulders and turned me to the right. His hands were dry and rough, the cuticles of his nails lined with indigo—paint, I suspected. His touch alarmed me. No man besides my husband had touched me in such a manner. Even Bert Marckwald had only pecked my cheek in greeting. But Bradley wanted a painting—expensive, I was sure, and unnecessary when he had me in the flesh. And such a large portrait. The canvas on the easel was three feet tall, I guessed.

"*Bleu*," he said in answer to the painter's question. Bradley wanted me in blue. "*Comme le ciel.*" Like the sky. A light blue.

Goodness—I had nothing that color. One gown maybe, but I hadn't brought that one. How could I not know he liked me in blue? I wore gray in the winter, cream or yellow in the summer and decided I must look for a blue frock in a shop—or have one made.

Bradley stood awkwardly in a corner, a crooked smile on his face. "I'll be just outside," he said. I shifted my eyes toward him, not daring to move my head or disrupt Monsieur le Doux's concentration. How disconcerting to be studied so closely by a strange man. Predators in the wild were not so particular about their prey.

Once the door closed behind Bradley, the artist spoke to me in rapid French then motioned to his own shoulders. He wanted me to expose myself. How dare he? I wished at that moment for Bradley to return, but most likely he was puffing on his pipe.

"*Pour la couleur de la peau*," Monsieur le Doux said. He wanted to examine the color of my skin the sun hadn't touched. The skin under the clothing, I think he said, is a different hue from that of the face.

When I didn't move, pretending I didn't understand him, he came around the easel and opened the neck of my blouse.

"*Alors, seulement ça*," he said. Only this. Then he stood straight and frowned at my chest.

I pressed my hand to my collarbone, but he waved at me to remove it.

The record skipped and the music ended leaving only the sound of wheels on cobblestones outside the tall windows, a faint scratching of Monsieur le Doux's charcoal on the canvas, the thrum of my heartbeat in my neck. His brows drew together as his dark eyes shifted from the canvas to my face, my neck. I resisted closing my blouse and willed my hands to stay in my lap, fingers laced together. Would he paint my hands?

As the minutes passed, I felt sympathy for models. Who would have known that being stone still for a period of time would be arduous and leave one so stiff?

Finally Bradley came in and handed Monsieur le Doux some money. I knew he'd never tell me how much, but I was sure the amount was exorbitant for artwork of which I was the lone subject. I'd much rather have had a painting of our sons and had it in mind to inquire about artists when we returned to Manhattan.

The painting could not have been finished within the hour, of course — or even the week. Monsieur le Doux told Bradley he would ship the canvas when he had completed the work, allowing time for the oils to dry. Home by then, we would have our own unveiling. We would make a ceremony of it and I would invite the boys' critiques. Thayer wouldn't have much interest and would rather a stormy seascape with a sailboat dashed by the waves. Jackie would approve to please his parents whether he liked the painting or not. Only Wells, my musician son, would remark on the light, the coloring, the neutral background that wouldn't overpower the figure. What a word — figure — as if I were no longer Muz or Florrie but reduced to two flat dimensions.

Launch of R.M.S. *Titanic* Delayed
After *Olympic* Collides with H.M.S. *Hawke*
The Sunday Times, March 29

Shoulder to shoulder, the stewards greeted new passengers at Southampton. Sid jerked his elbow against Andrew.

"Looks like I'm catching up, mate," he said. "Winnie's got a biscuit in the oven."

"That's excellent!" Andrew said.

"The little fellow should arrive in the fall, Winnie guesses."

When the chief steward cleared his throat and rolled his eyes toward Sid, he snapped back to attention.

"Sorry, sir," Andrew said. "A bit of good news here."

"We could use some good news," the chief said. "Word just came that the *Olympic* has gotten herself into more trouble."

Andrew had sensed it. Even the seemingly invincible have an Achilles heel. He hadn't heard whether Violet had gotten aboard, but it wouldn't have surprised him. Adversity wouldn't hold her down.

"What sort of trouble?" he asked.

"Propeller blade snapped off on the eastbound voyage. She's on her way back to Belfast. Looks like the *Titanic* sendoff is pushed back again."

Titanic's maiden voyage was set for late March, but if the *Olympic* needed a new propeller, likely as not she would get the organ transplant from her sister ship.

"Cunningham," Sid whispered, "when the *Titanic* sets sail, we're going to be on her decks."

"I don't know, mate," Andrew said. "We don't want to be hasty." The way things were going with the *Olympic*, he was more than ever set against joining the new brigade.

"With the baby coming, Winnie needs the extra dough," he said. "I've got no choice."

"It'll be April before the *Titanic*'s ready." Andrew was stalling about making the commitment. But maybe Sid was right. The builders probably constructed *Titanic* even stouter than *Olympic*. What could possibly go wrong?

"We've got a month to think about it."

"I don't need to think about it." Sid's mouth was set.

"Balls." Andrew gave in. "Then April it is."

Victor Hugo's *Hernani, ou l'Honneur Castillan*
Appearing at Théâtre du Châtelet
Le Rire, March 30

Outside our hotel, Bradley hailed a carriage and helped me in.

"Place de Vosages," he told the driver. "Dans le Marais." He tilted his head toward me. "Le Marais is where the French nobility lived for centuries."

"Not since the French Revolution." I may not have held the Harvard diploma my husband had on the wall of his office, but I knew some things.

"Yes, well," he said. "The neighborhood is still aristocratic."

Bradley didn't enjoy being outwitted, and I allowed him the last word. For my husband, however, it seemed there were never last words.

"Ever heard of the Hunchback of Notre Dame?" he said.

"That horrid story of the cathedral's bell ringer, the deformed monster?"

"Ah, my dear, you must do more studying. It's a love story, a sort of Beauty and the Beast tale."

"I see." I rolled my eyes at him and saw him stiffen as if he knew I'd come back with a rejoinder, but he could never be sure what it would be. I liked to keep him guessing. "Do you mean to suggest a parallel to our love story? You do hunch sometimes, my love."

Bradley harrumphed and kept silent until the cab let us out at Victor Hugo's apartment. The building formed part of a walled-in courtyard the size of a city block. The writer's quarters were housed on the second floor.

"After Napoleon's coup d'état, Hugo left France for a twenty-year exile," Bradley said.

"Twenty years away from home? I can't imagine," I said. Six weeks was difficult enough.

"Those were hard times, Florrie. Hugo's lucky he got out with his head. Besides—he probably buried himself in his writing."

I wondered if Hugo was too busy even to notice the Gothic furniture in the apartment and the colorful patterns on wallpaper that climbed and spilled across the ceiling. In his study, a small desk faced the wall. To block out distractions, I supposed. He must have written his masterpieces there with a feather quill pen. The room felt airless, a dark space that must have allowed Hugo to explore the inner soul of humanity as he wrote *Les Misérables*.

"Look at this, Florrie—" Bradley held out a paper he had picked up from a rack in Hugo's apartment. "It says the young Hugo wrote, "I shall be Chateaubriand or nothing."

"What do you think he meant by that?"

"Chateaubriand is the best cut of beef in a tenderloin. It's wrapped in cheaper cuts for grilling, and the cheaper meats are thrown out after the tenderloin has absorbed all their flavor."

I thought a minute. "So Hugo wanted to be considered of more value than his underlings?"

"I suppose. If that's the case, he succeeded."

"But Bradley—wouldn't it be better for Chateaubriand to raise the lesser cuts of meat to a higher level?"

"You do have a way of manipulating a metaphor in favor of those underclasses you work with, my dear," Bradley said. "But, yes, that's exactly what Hugo did. He was a humanist. He gave voice to the voiceless."

"Do you mean he had to become Chateaubriand in order to use his influence in helping the poor?"

"Precisely." Bradley slipped the paper back into the rack. "Now—all this talk about steak has made me hungry. What say we find a cozy proletarian bistro?"

Even when he outplayed me in a discussion, my husband made me laugh.

Sea Captain Edward J. Smith
Named to Lead Maiden Voyage
Of World's Largest Vessel
Star-Gazette, April 7

The morning Andrew was to report to *Titanic*, he rose early at the house on Charlton Road and got his things ready. When he had packed his duffel, he bent to look into his son's face.

"You're ten now, laddie. You'll have to be the man of the house 'til I get back. Will you do that?"

"I will," Sandy said. "But what about the sunbeam and the angel?"

Andrew had taught him an old Scottish blessing when he was starting to talk, and he was surprised his son remembered it now.

"A sunbeam to warm you," Andrew said.

"A moonbeam to charm you," Sandy added.

"A sheltering angel —"

Sandy's face took on a sweet expression. "So nothing can harm you."

Andrew hugged him. "I'm going to take the sunbeam and the moonbeam. I'll leave the sheltering angel with you and your sister."

"No, Dad," he said. "I've got Mama. You take the angel."

What a sweet boy he was. Andrew looked at him, memorizing his every aspect — the coppery hair curling at the ends and in need of a cutting, freckles on his nose, teeth too large for his narrow face, a hand shading his eyes from rare April sunlight. But there was also a glee the boy seemed barely able to contain, as if it would erupt from him any moment in volcanic peals of delight. And yet, he was growing so fast, worrying about his father's safety—even more than Andrew worried about his own. Did his son realize his father was getting on a ship that would hover above thousands of fathoms of water, a ship that might at any moment fall to the mercy of the sea?

"Aye, your mother is indeed an angel," he told Sandy. "Very well then, I'll take your sheltering angel."

Before he left, he planted tender kisses, one on each of the people he cherished most in the world.

From the dock, *Titanic* looked identical to *Olympic* with her four smokestacks and tall masts fore and aft. Three million rivets secured the hull, and the propellers were the size of windmills. The one-hundred-ton rudder was nearly eighty feet high, and her three anchors weighed a total of thirty tons. If stood upright on the tip of her bow, she would be taller than the Washington Monument, taller than the Grand Pyramid of Giza, taller even than New York's Woolworth building. She was a skyscraper of a ship.

On the concrete quay Andrew watched a towering crane load cargo into the ship's hold. The gangways were roped off until boarding day when third-class ticketholders would board after doctors examined them for diseases. Their cabins were aft where the engines were noisiest. The second-class gangway led to accommodations on E and F decks. An elevator was ready for first-class passengers to be escorted across an impossibly high walkway to their lavish cabins on A, B, and C decks.

When he boarded the ship that morning, the smell of fresh paint stung his nostrils. The builders must have been in a dash to get *Titanic* shipshape.

Without passengers, Andrew wandered the upper decks getting his bearings. In the wireless room, two Marconi operators studied the switches. Harold Bride introduced himself.

"Quite a ship," he said.

"Seems it," Andrew agreed.

"I was on the *Lusitania* before this, but what's the difference? All I ever look at is the inside of my cubby hole." He tossed his head toward the wireless equipment. "At least I've got a few days to get used to this tackle."

Behind Andrew, a group of men hustled by.

"These blokes all crew?" he asked.

"Sure enough. All seasoned seamen. We're in good hands."

"That's comforting."

"And there are five postal clerks, a window cleaner, and even a masseuse for soothing the aches of the elite. And with a dozen bakers and a hundred twenty on the catering crew, I dare say we'll eat well on this dinghy."

Bride, a handsome fellow with sad beagle eyes, could not yet have celebrated two dozen birthdays. Andrew remembered those days when his appetite was never satisfied and the next meal was his foremost concern.

"You're English?" he asked.

"I am," Bride said. "There's a handful of Irish on board, but you may well be one of the few Scotsmen."

Andrew was used to being in the minority. For so many years he had been the only Scottish steward on the *Oceanic*. Now here he was on *Titanic*, the ship at the head of its class for speed and luxury.

"I suppose eventually there will be ships flying across the water without ever getting wet," he said.

"No doubt," Bride said. "Well, good luck to you, Cunningham, and have a smooth sail." He turned to the Marconi machinery.

"You, too, mate," Andrew responded.

He knew *Oceanic* like the back of his hand, but he had a lot to learn about this new White Star vessel. And he had better learn fast because in four days *Titanic* was due to set her bow leeward toward New York.

Andrew was glad Violet Jessup had signed on. She was one of seventy-six stewards serving second class but as on *Oceanic*, she haunted the first-class stewards' galley.

"Well, well, lass," he said, "I'm glad to see you abandoned the maladroit *Olympic*. In fact, I'm quite surprised you're still in this line of work."

"I wouldn't want to miss any of the fun, Scottie. Besides, unlike your old vessel, everything's brand new here. Too new, if you ask me. The second-class women's bathroom isn't finished. Some of the sinks and toilets are still in boxes shoved against the wall." She leveled her eyes at Andrew. "I hear the loos in first class are made of marble. Is that right?"

"That would be correct, if you must know."

"Second class has porcelain. Better than third class, though. They set their bums down on iron. Horribly uncomfortable, I'm sure. But at least the loos flush automatically. Third classers aren't used to indoor plumbing and the bowls would probably overflow before they'd figure out how to send the slop away." Violet made a face of disgust.

"You've made a study of *Titanic's* water closets, have you?"

"Not complaining, mind you. The rest of the ship must be more promising than our privies."

"I'll endure the privies so long as the builders caulked the rivet holes tight." He expected a hitch or two on *Titanic*, but he had bitten off a hunk of the ship and had no choice except to chew it.

"Lighten up, Scottie," she said. "It's the opportunity of a lifetime to be on *Titanic*'s maiden voyage. We'll be part of history."

"Violet," he said, "I have no doubt that one way or another your name will be emblazoned across the front pages of newspapers all over the world."

She twirled around. "Must scoot along now — ta-ta!"

Andrew hoped there would be peace between the lass and his best mate. He wasn't in the mood for mollycoddling.

Because the *Titanic* was at half capacity, Andrew would be responsible for only five staterooms. He was to help male passengers dress — unless they had their butlers with them. For those who preferred to dine in their cabins, he would deliver and serve meals. Sid would make up beds, clean cabins and bathrooms, and freshen towels. Both of them would work in the first-class saloon, setting tables with linens and serving. And they would fill in wherever needed.

Andrew shared sleeping space on E deck with a dozen other stewards. But he usually was so exhausted at the end of a shift that neither a hard surface nor sawing of logs from a fellow steward would keep him awake. He should have been glad for the portholes that let in morning light, but since he undoubtedly would be on his feet before daybreak, the sea view was wasted on him. Violet said her own habitation was no better. She had no heat, and roaches climbed the walls.

He started unpacking his duffel, keeping an eye out for Sid. The limey had been assigned to his quarters, as luck would have it. When at last his comrade came in, he looked as if he had just rolled out of bed.

"Thought I might miss the boat," he wheezed. "Winnie has been feeling ill. I don't know why they call it morning sickness unless a bloke considers middle of the night the same as morning. It's enough to drive a chap mad. I had to get aboard ship so I can get a good night's sleep."

"You'd better catch up on your rest before we stop for boarding in France," Andrew said. "We'll be in for it then."

Sid jabbered on, unable to contain himself. "I'd like to get this *Titanic* trip done with and get back to my girl. And the tyke will be here before you know it. I tell you, Cunningham, it does a man proud to be head of the family."

"Well and good, mate," Andrew said. "But you're going to have to concentrate on this crossing. We'll have some of the richest people in America under our supervision."

"Excellent. And may they pass us their gold notes when they get off. If there's a good showing, I'll slip some to Charlie Savage in third class. Winnie made me promise to keep an eye on him, and with forty stewards down there, I doubt he'll get a farthing."

"We're scheduled to sail in a few days," Andrew said, "so get acquainted with the ship."

"Have you heard Captain Smith is playing chess with the crew? Lightoller was demoted to second officer, and one of the lookouts went back to the *Olympic*. I tell you, Cunningham, all this moving about makes me a tad skittish."

Andrew knew it was like Sid, even just having boarded, to have his ear to the latest gossip. "So long as we mind our own business," he said, "I doubt we'll have any worries."

J. Epstein Commissioned to Design a Memorial for Tomb of Oscar Wilde in Père-Lachaise Cemetery
London Times, April 8

"This graveyard covers over one and a half square miles, Florrie. Probably two hundred thousand souls are buried here." Bradley was skimming a brochure of Père Lachaise Cemetery. "We could wander these walkways all afternoon. In fact, we could spend days here if we didn't have to get to the dock."

We were due to catch the train to Cherbourg for our voyage to New York. I wasn't fond of cemeteries, but Bradley insisted we meander around Père-Lachaise, which he said was the most visited necropolis in the world. Necropolis, in my opinion, was a more agreeable word than graveyard.

At the grand gates, I craned my neck up at the two towering panels green with patina. We entered through a fortress of a wall, as if the corpses might try to escape their subterranean confinement. This afternoon a faint breeze carried a scent not altogether unpleasant but definitely not the sweet fragrance of spring. It reminded me of autumns in Boston when the leaves fell from the trees onto wet ground. Could the caretakers have been fertilizing the shrubbery? In that case, how odd it was that nurturing tender new life required the spreading of a substance that had the aroma of decay.

"A Jesuit priest—Father La Chaise—lived here in the seventeenth century," Bradley said, unfolding the brochure. "He was cloistered in a mansion on these grounds." He took my elbow, encouraging me in among the stone markers. "You'll enjoy the stroll, darling. Think of the cemetery as an art gallery or a museum."

I flashed a smirk at him. "Tombstones are not my favorite art medium."

My husband had methods of persuasion. I had eaten enough croissants and French cheeses to expand my waistline, and a walk would do me good. We had visited the Eiffel Tower and the Louvre, where I had hoped to see DaVinci's Mona Lisa. But I was disappointed to learn someone had stolen the painting the year before—right off the wall. And the mysterious burglary had yet to be solved. We had been to the opera at Palais Garnier and had seen most of the tourist sites. I supposed a necropolis would give us an hour or two of tranquility.

"Chopin's remains are buried here." Bradley pointed toward the field of towering white monuments.

"Frédéric Chopin?" The etudes were my favorite pieces to play on the baby grand piano at home.

"Yes—all of him except for his heart."

"You're joking. Or do you mean that metaphorically?"

"No, his actual heart. It was returned to Warsaw. I suppose that's all they wanted of him."

"How ghastly."

"This way—" Bradley swung his hand toward a bricked pathway then inclined his head toward me and whispered, "You'd think they'd have requested his hands."

When we found Chopin's tomb, I shielded my eyes from the April sun and gazed up at the statue of a muse weeping over a broken lyre.

"I can't imagine anything sadder than a body without a heart—except a body without a soul," I said.

"The soul leaves the body when it dies," Bradley said.

"Where do you think the soul goes? There must be a repository in heaven for spirits."

"Unitarians don't believe in heaven, dear — you should know that. Our purpose is to create our own heaven — on earth." He slipped an arm around my waist. "And you are my heaven, Florrie."

"What about the soul?" I pressed him gently away as if the spirits were watching our intimate moment.

"I can only speak for my own soul," he said. "When I'm in the tomb, my soul will rise and seek you out. You'll feel me near."

I rolled my eyes at him. "That's a comfort, darling, but let's not expect your passing within the immediate future."

"Shall we find the grave of the lovers Abelard and Heloise?" He opened the brochure to a map of the grounds, glanced at it, then nodded toward the west. "This way, I believe — or would you rather pay homage to Moliére? He wrote the plays *Learned Women* and *The Misanthrope*."

"One for each of us, I suppose?" I hid a laugh behind a gloved hand.

"Very amusing, Florrie." He grimaced at the brochure. "He's buried in the area for unbaptized infants. Moliére was an actor, and actors weren't considered holy enough to be laid in consecrated ground."

"How sad." Honestly, with so many soulless bodies interred so close together, I felt almost asphyxiated. Besides, the departed had nothing to say. I preferred to interact with the living.

"Could we go back to the hotel, darling? I want to write a letter to the boys."

"You'll be home before they get the letter, Florrie."

There he was again, leaving himself out of the reckoning. This time I didn't bother to correct him.

"All the better," I said. "I'll be able to witness their excitement."

In Near Mishap, S.S. *New York* Almost Rams H.M.S. *Titanic* at Launch
The New York World, April 10

Andrew went to the boat deck to watch the train roll in. The boat deck held officers' quarters, an open promenade, the captain's bridge, and wooden lifeboats. He counted forty-eight davits, but only sixteen held lifeboats. The company's chairman must have wanted to keep the deck clear so passengers could walk unobstructed in the fresh air. Sixteen lifeboats would hold a thousand passengers and crew, even though two thousand or more were expected to board. Of course, if some disaster were to happen, another ship would surely come to the rescue. But White Star shipbuilders had engineered a seaworthy vessel. He had no choice except to believe it.

It was a gray day with a nippy breeze but despite the threatening weather, all classes of people had gathered on the Eastern Dock, some bustling, some sauntering, some ruffled and cheeky. Andrew looked down on men's heads topped with bowlers, skimpy-brimmed trilbies, and the flatcaps of commoners. Rich women flaunted Parisian chapeaus aquiver with feathers, and poor women clutched hand-knit shawls over their heads. All of them chattered as they prepared to board. What they had in common was the largest moving manmade object in the world and the vast ocean they were about to cross.

Captain Smith came onto the deck to watch the boarding. A portly man with a round face, he was dressed head to toe in a navy blue uniform, epaulets on the shoulders. The trimmed beard made him look as fierce as an old lion. He must have been in his sixties, his lids drooping over tired eyes. Andrew had heard he planned to retire after this voyage, none too soon from what he could tell of the old fellow. Earlier Smith had inspected the watertight doors and airtight compartments, presumably passing his approval.

Of Andrew's passengers, only Mrs. Gladys Bronson, her daughter Emma, and Miss Bronson's governess boarded at Southampton. Mother and daughter were assigned to stateroom 91 on the starboard side of C deck. Andrew couldn't help but wonder why a girl who looked every bit a woman would need a guardian. There were so many things about the wealthy he failed to understand. Governess Daisy Bush took interior cabin number 125, near her employers.

Just before ten o'clock, six of the "black gang" pushed by him as they left the ship. Fireman Sally Caveney elbowed him.

"Goin' ta get in a last pint at The Grapes before we shove off," he said. "Care to join?"

When Andrew brought them buckets of water on the *Oceanic*, most of them were so blootered he was surprised they could find the furnace doors to shove in the fuel. He couldn't blame them. They had the most grueling and punishing job on the ship.

"Thanks, but no, Sally," Andrew said.

The *Titanic* was to sail at noon sharp. A quarter hour before noon, Andrew watched for the stokers to return, but there was no sign of them.

He heard the train approaching down the track and was about to return to his post when he spotted the firemen jogging in a lopsided line toward the dock. Sally Caveney and Jimmy Birdsall dashed across the rails just before the train chugged through. The other four held back to wait for the locomotive to pass.

The engine stopped, blocking the stragglers from crossing the tracks. When the train started up at a crawl and left the station, the last stokers sprinted toward the ship just as the dock crew swung the gangway aside. The officer in charge waved them off. They had missed their chance to serve at the boilers of the great *Titanic*.

With minutes before launch, the Blue Peter, an azure flag with a white rectangle in the center, climbed the foremast to signal all persons should be aboard. After three piercing blasts from the whistles, the ship let loose from the dock. A mass of passengers waved from the railing, and the ship's band played jaunty ragtime tunes.

Andrew had to admit the excitement was infecting him. Now—where in hell was Sid?

Just as he thought it, Sid found him, his face lit up like a child's. Below them, spectators cheered and handkerchiefs wagged. Newsmen snapped photographs.

"I'll bet you're glad you didn't miss this," he yelled over the noise.

"Thought you had some misgivings, mate," Andrew said.

"Not anymore." Rising onto his toes, he flapped an arm at the onlookers below. "It's something, isn't it?"

"It's something, all right." Andrew cocked his head. "You know, eight men died building this ship." He grasped the handrail as the cruiser floated slowly from the dock. "Imagine falling from this height."

"No bloke is going to die today," Sid said. "Besides, if *Titanic* rams anything, they'll get the worst of it. So could you be a little less gloomy, Cunningham?"

"I'll be less gloomy after we reach New York."

Even under the overcast sky, *Titanic's* decks shone with polish. Six tugs nudged White Star's masterpiece through the harbor. A fleet of cruise ships sat tied at the docks, one of them the *Oceanic*. Even though he knew of the coal strike, when Andrew saw her a shudder of regret rippled through him. If he had made the wrong decision about leaving the old girl, it was far too late to change his mind.

Even moving at a snail's pace, *Titanic's* powerful propellers churned the water. When the ship passed, its backwash sucked the sleek ship *New York* so that her lines snapped with what sounded like the report of a large caliber rifle. Her stern swung out, threatening to smack into *Titanic's* side. One of the tugboat crew saw the oncoming collision, jettisoned a line to *New York's* stern, and pulled her back into place.

Andrew heaved a sigh of relief. Calamity barely averted.

Passengers crowded the railings as *Titanic* glided along Southampton's reedy western shore. Her chimneys belched black smoke and the whistle, the largest ever made, sounded its deafening blast.

Andrew said a brief prayer for the fates to look favorably on the voyage, and the RMS *Titanic* was underway.

The Great Coal Strike Begins
The Daily Mirror, April 10

"Breakfast in France is a disappointment." Bradley stared at his tartine. "Would it kill them to soft-boil an egg?"

"*Le petit dejeuner* is the least important meal of the day, darling," I said. "Most French skip it and eat a big lunch. Try dipping your tartine into your coffee." The French either were too busy or running too late to sit down to breakfast. Or perhaps they liked to postpone gratification. My husband derived gratification from lingering over coffee in order to absorb the latest news — mostly news of financial matters. I admit the sliced baguette with butter and jam seemed like a waste of time, but we had the time to waste while we waited to board the *Oceanic*. Besides, the *café au lait* was delicious.

I allowed my gaze to wander to the window and the harbor outside.

"The sky is red this morning," I said. "What's the saying?"

"Hmm?" he buzzed.

"The saying about red sky in the morning."

"Sailors take warning." He didn't bother looking up.

"We're scheduled to sail today. In just a few hours, in fact."

"I'm afraid not."

"What do you mean?"

"Says here there's a coal strike affecting England and all of Europe."

"A coal strike?" I hoped the strike wouldn't reach New York. At least spring was blossoming and there would be no need for heating coal within the next several months.

"Worse news, darling. Most cruise ships have been docked. Not enough coal to fuel the engines. *Oceanic* is one of those out of commission."

"But we have tickets for the *Oceanic*."

He folded the paper and laid it next to his plate. "We may be stranded in Europe for a while."

"Bradley — we've got to get home. There must be some way."

He looked at me, his face without humor. "There is one slim chance. A new White Star ship has been allowed enough coal for a trans-Atlantic crossing."

"How new?"

He glanced at the article again. "If you're willing to book passage on the maiden voyage, we can leave tonight."

I had heard cautions against maiden voyages. At the very least, there would be wrinkles to iron out. I didn't want to think about the very worst.

"Is there a risk?"

"Folklore, Florrie. Every ship has to have a first launch, and very few of them have ended up in Davy Jones's locker." His eyebrows arched with optimism. "In fact, a first cruise is always a festive affair with parties and flowing champagne. And you might spot a celebrity — or at least an executive. A maiden voyage on a White Star ship will win you bragging rights for years."

I didn't need bragging rights. I wasn't a braggart. I just wanted to be home.

"What's the name of this new ship?"

"I believe it's —" He ran a finger over the newsprint. "RMS *Titanic*."

"*Titanic*," I repeated. I drew a deep breath and blew it out. "And a red morning sky."

"If there's a storm, we should be away from the coast before it lands." He patted my hand. "Don't worry, darling. We have a few hours yet. Why don't you write another letter to our boys while I see about tickets."

My Dear Sons,

France is beautiful in the spring. We loved the Palace at Versailles, Monet's gardens at Giverney, the medieval architecture of the Loire Valley, riverboats on the Seine. Daddy and I had a boat ride, and above us Notre Dame glowed with light and looked like a saintly castle. There is so much to see, and I know you will one day, and read about it in your schoolbooks, too. I trust you are behaving and studying hard. Your father and I want to hear all about your adventures when we return.

Very soon we will board the ship Titanic, named for Titans, the giants who ruled the earth until Zeus and the Olympians overthrew them. I'm sure you know the story from your lessons in mythology. As I write, across the harbor the ship's electric lights look like a constellation of stars fallen from heaven onto the water. I am willing Titanic to sprout wings and fly across the ocean with all speed. Oh, how I miss my sweet boys.

Vous êtes la joie de ma vie,

Muz

American Millionaire Astor
Boards *Titanic* at Cherbourg
Along with 150 Others in First Class
La Presse, April 10

The near mishap with the *New York* caused *Titanic* to be an hour late getting to Cherbourg. The French dock was not equipped to handle vessels as large as *Titanic*, so tender boats ferried passengers and cargo to the anchored ship. The first tender brought one hundred third-class travelers, mostly Lebanese and Armenians. When they were aboard, twenty of *Titanic's* passengers climbed onto the tender to disembark with their luggage, two bicycles, and a cage holding a canary. For them, Andrew thought, even the short trip from Southampton on the splendid new liner must have been a thrill to remember.

The larger tender *SS Nomadic* could carry a thousand, but on this trip it brought fewer than two hundred first and second-class passengers to the ship. Andrew assumed most of them were rich tourists fresh from visiting Paris. Even the wealthy were surely giddy with awe as they approached the ship.

While he watched passengers board, he thought of the endless string of trunks and crates being loaded into the hold. Ostrich plumes valued at ten thousand pounds, a rare copy of the *Rubáiyát of Omar Khayyám* bound in jewel-studded leather, cases of expensive cognac, and a red Renault motorcar nestled among the baggage. It was a more expensive haul of riches than on any crossing aboard *Oceanic*.

He stood at attention with Sid and the other stewards to greet the newcomers. Andrew looked for Pierpont Morgan. The most elegant suite on B Deck, designed specifically for him, had been readied with the best furnishings.

"You'll not see the tycoon Morgan on this trip," Sid said. "He canceled his ticket this morning. Said he was sick."

It struck Andrew as odd that the company's biggest investor was going to miss the maiden voyage of his finest ship. And if he was indeed sick, sea air cures many ills.

"How is it you're always the first to hear the latest news, Sid?"

"Could be I hang around the Marconi office," he said. "My ears have antennae."

"More likely you're just a meddler, mate."

Chief steward Latimer announced the names as travelers came aboard.

"Mr. Duff Gordon and Lady Duff Gordon, South Kensington, London," Latimer declared. Lady Duff Gordon, the London dress designer, was pushing fifty if she was a day. She was dressed in a coat of dark blue velvet with matching skirt that skimmed her ankles, no doubt one of her own designs. Emily had told him about the designer's fancy undergarment creations, and although Andrew would take delight in seeing his wife wear them, such frivolous things were beyond their budget.

Lady Duff Gordon and her distinguished-looking husband were to occupy two staterooms on A deck.

"Mr. Benjamin Guggenheim, New York, New York."

Mr. Guggenheim, a fetching fellow with piercing blue eyes, was a businessman assigned to B deck with his valet. Miss Aubart, his mistress, Andrew guessed, was conveniently housed down the alleyway from Mr. Guggenheim's chamber.

"Left his wife in New York, I'll wager," Sid whispered.

Andrew nudged him, a signal to hold his tongue.

"Major Archibald Willingham Butt, Washington, D.C." As military aide to President Taft, the major boarded in full uniform. His companion Frank Millet accompanied him, assigned to a room on E deck. Sid cleared his throat, which Andrew ignored. He didn't dare raise an eyebrow about the major's amorous preferences. Major Butt was followed by seven trunks of luggage, which Andrew dearly hoped would fit into his stateroom on B deck.

"Mrs. Margaret Tobin Brown, Denver, Colorado."

Andrew had heard about the wife of a gold miner who pulled herself up from dirt after her husband struck it rich. Even the working class were above where Mrs. Brown started out. Someone should have told her how to dress for a cruise, however. Her outfit was too elaborate for early evening, and her plumed hat barely fit through the hatchway. She was a tad homely, but Andrew liked the way she looked the stewards in the eye and shook their hands. She would be settled in the fore section of B deck.

"Mr. Bruce Ismay, chairman of the White Star Line." Ismay was a man not to be forgotten. At well over six feet in height, his head floated above the others with a self-satisfied grin under his handlebar mustache. Ismay spoke pleasantly with a lady and gentleman near him as he strolled up the gangway and stepped onto the deck. It was obvious that Ismay was a man who enjoyed his power, but Andrew saw an arrogance in his eyes that troubled him. Through his fine clothes and air of assurance, there was impatience in his movements, a quick darting of his eyes. This man who had led the charge to build such an exceptional fleet of ships exuded more cunning than charm. In Pierpont Morgan's absence, Ismay was assigned to the deluxe B-52 cabin. He would be a level above Andrew's assignment, which brought him a sigh of relief. He didn't trust the man.

"Here come the C-deck toffs," Sid snarled.

Andrew leaned in and muttered, "Stuff it, Sid."

"Colonel John Jacob Astor and Madeleine Force Astor, Rhinebeck, New York."

Old Astor owned more high-rise buildings than anyone in New York. He was awkward looking with a mousy face and strutted aboard like a tall bird with spindly legs. The press called him "Jack Ass," probably due to his spending buckets of quid on a whim. His wife was a teenager, and Andrew would not have been surprised if Astor were older than the girl's father. She was a sad-faced hen hanging on her husband's arm with one limp hand and leading an Airedale on a leash with the other. If Andrew was not mistaken, she was in a family way to boot. Even England flinched at the scandal of Astor's divorce and hasty wedding to the child bride. Out with the old, in with the new — he guessed that was the toffs' motto.

The Astors would stay in two staterooms in the fore starboard section of C deck with other cabins for the maid, the butler, and the nurse. Andrew pitied the stewards who had to look out for the couple and their entourage — and pick up the Airedale's messes.

"Mr. and Mrs. George Widener and Mr. Harry Elkins Widener, Philadelphia, Pennsylvania."

With his waxed mustache, Widener was a handsome chap. Mrs. Widener had an elegance about her but kept her gaze straight ahead, as if casting her eyes upon the *Titanic's* hired help would sully her. Their son Harry had the serious look of the privileged. He carried a volume with gold lettering under his arm — apparently he was a rare book aficionado. The Wideners took two staterooms on the port side of C deck.

"Mr. Martin Rothschild and Elizabeth Jane Rothschild, New York, New York."

Unlike some of the other toffs, Mr. Rothschild worked for a living. He was in the business of manufacturing clothing. Mrs. Rothschild wore a long, double strand of pearls around her neck and snuggled the Pomeranian dog she carried. When they passed the stewards, Mrs. Rothschild dipped her head and gave the pup a kiss. If the *Titanic* were sinking and she had to choose to rescue either the dog or her husband, Andrew believed the woman would scoop up her furry friend. The Rothschilds were assigned to the starboard side of C deck, along with the treasured Pomeranian.

"Cunningham and Siebert will be responsible for the following passengers," Latimer announced. Andrew corrected his posture. His job on the *Titanic* depended on how well he worked for the next six days.

"Mr. William Thomas Stead, Wimbledon Park, London. Stateroom C-121."

Everyone in London knew of Mr. Stead, England's most famous newsman. Andrew considered it an honor to wait on him. Mr. Stead paused in front of him. In his sixties, he looked like King Lear. Stead's piercing eyes sparked over his curly gray beard.

"What is your name, son?" he asked.

Andrew knew that Stead made anyone's business his own. "Cunningham, sir."

"Scottish, am I right?"

"Aye, sir."

"Then lang may yer lum reek."

"Thank you, sir. I'll see that you're settled in shortly."

When Stead passed, Sid murmured, "What was it he said to you?"

"It's an old Scottish expression. Means 'May you live long and stay well.'"

"The old fellow took to you, Cunningham."

Chief Latimer glared at Sid before he continued the introductions.

"Mr. and Mrs. John Bradley Cumings, New York. Stateroom C-85."

Bradley Cumings had a slight build. He was about Andrew's own age but had dancing eyes and a youthful look about him. Under his straw boater, his hair was slicked back and he sported a modest mustache. His wife was a few years younger and walked with a confidence that made her undeniably appealing but not at all inaccessible, rather like a queen radiating stateliness and warm reserve. Cumings bobbed his head, acknowledging the stewards before passing down the line. Mrs. Cumings hesitated and touched her husband's arm.

"It's Andrew, isn't it?" she said. "From the *Oceanic*?"

"Very good to meet you again, Mr. and Mrs. Cumings," Andrew said with a bow.

Bradley Cumings shook his hand.

"Well then," Florence Cumings said, "it will be a pleasant voyage indeed."

On the *Oceanic*, Andrew had felt a connection with the Cumings couple. And now here they were, as if some destiny had brought them to meet again. But that was inane thinking. They were on their way home to New York and he was doing his job. Anything else was pure coincidence.

"Mr. and Mrs. Warren Craig, Los Angeles, California. Stateroom C-89." Craig looked far too young to have amassed a fortune on his own.

"Inherited wealth, I'll wager," Sid murmured and nodded toward Mrs. Craig. "Married him for his money."

Another glare from Latimer. He was losing patience with Sid. But Sid was probably right. Andrew would have no problem remembering Mrs. Craig. She was beautiful in a melancholy way, her liquid eyes ready to leak tears. A steward would have to mind his place around a woman like her.

From his years of service on the *Oceanic*, Andrew knew better than to envy the rich. He had interrupted domestic quarrels to deliver food trays, heard weeping through the doors, and had waited on mistresses kept discreetly a few cabins from their rich lovers. He had comforted the lonely, the bitter, and the distraught on the verge of lunacy. As far as he was concerned, the toffs could keep their motorcars, their gold cufflinks, their rare books, furs, and pearl necklaces. Their worldly treasures didn't bring them happiness.

Eminent British Journalist William T. Stead, 63, Aboard H.M.S. *Titanic* Bound for New York
The Pall Mall Gazette, April 10

The grand saloon had space to spread out, but that nice steward Andrew showed Bradley and me to a table where Mr. Stead and other passengers were seated. Might as well get to know our fellow travelers, he must have thought.

"Thank you, Andrew," I said when he pulled out my chair.

"What's your family name, if I may ask?" Bradley said. That was one of the things I loved about him — his interest in people of all classes.

"Cunningham, sir."

"Cunningham —" he said. "Have we met before?"

"I served you aboard *Oceanic* a few weeks ago, Mr. Cumings," Andrew reminded him.

"Yes, I recall. But it's beyond that."

I saved my husband from embarrassment. "We've met so many people in the last weeks. But we're awfully pleased to see you, Andrew." A familiar face was comforting on a first voyage.

The Duff Gordons and Second Officer Charles Lightoller filled the other seats. Lightoller — Lights, as I had heard his shipmates call him — was a genial fellow a year or two older than Bradley. He had an air of confidence that set me at ease — not that I was worried. These ships were constructed in Belfast by the very best workers, so Bradley said. There was not a thing to worry about except which dish to order for dinner.

"What is your most recent investigation, Mr. Stead?" Officer Lightoller set the conversation wheels in motion.

"Morality, my good fellow. We've managed to raise the age of consent for sexual acts from thirteen years to sixteen. No small task if I do say."

"The Stead Act," Lightoller said. "I know of it."

Mr. Stead nodded approval.

"I understand your newspaper is taking on prostitution," I said. I had read Stead's paper in Europe. "Even in New York there are—ladies of the evening." I worked with women in the settlement housing who had resorted to prostitution to keep themselves fed. They were women with no other options, some of them even with small children.

"Prostitution is the oppression of desperate young women by the lewd impulses of men of privilege," Stead said.

"I doubt such topics are appropriate for public papers," Duff Gordon interjected.

"Sir, the press in a sense acts as our all-seeing Almighty. Gag the press and you destroy the last pillory by which it is possible to restrain the lawless lust of man." Stead's deep voice echoed from the glass dome of the saloon's ceiling.

Bradley coughed. He must have strangled on his wine at the mention of lust. I saw Lady Duff Gordon's feathers quiver.

"Mr. Stead would serve well as a preacher," I whispered to Bradley.

He rubbed his chin. "Is it not blasphemous to equate the press with the Almighty, Mr. Stead?"

"Bradley—really." I suspected my husband was baiting Mr. Stead. Or maybe his Unitarian feathers had been ruffled.

Stead leveled his eyes at Bradley.

"Society appears white and glistening—Mr. Cumings, is it? But within, it is rotten and littered with dead men's bones. The press alone can influence public opinion and government policy." When he bounced his fist on the table, the water trembled in the glasses. "Government by journalism is our salvation."

I wondered how Stead thought journalism could save prostitutes. Heavens — most of them could barely read.

Lady Duff Gordon broke in. "Mr. Stead, I understand you yourself paid for the company of a chimney sweep's daughter. She was thirteen years of age, if I recall."

Stead frowned but held his temper. I held my breath.

"Madam, I am a puritan and stand on principled virtues." He sat up straighter. "If you had read my articles on the topic of child prostitution, you would understand it was my intention to prove the ease with which anyone — even an old man such as myself — may easily purchase an innocent for his base pleasure."

"I know of your work, Mr. Stead," I said. In fact, I knew very little of it but felt the need to change the subject. "I understand that you also have an interest in spiritualism."

Stead's voice softened. "I have indeed received messages from the spirit world, specifically from an American temperance reformer and fellow journalist. I met Miss Julia Ames in 1890 shortly before her death."

"How did she communicate with you?" I asked.

"Through telepathy indirectly, and more directly through automatic writing."

"Please explain, if you would be so kind," Lightoller said.

I wondered if there was someone in the spirit world the second officer wanted to contact. My own parents were both still living although Mother was ailing. I dearly hoped I would have no cause to contact her spirit anytime soon.

"Simply put," Stead said, "a friend who has passed over can use my hand as her own. I mean, she moves my hand to write messages that I would otherwise have no way of knowing."

"Poppycock," Duff Gordon said.

"On the contrary," continued Stead. "Death does not interrupt consciousness. Personalities like yours, Mr. Duff Gordon, with so strong an identity, would have difficulty at first realizing you were actually — dead."

The world "dead" flopped in the air like a caught fish. Lady Duff Gordon's voluminous hairpiece had caused Stead to move his chair closer to mine in order to allow room for the fashion designer's plumage to quake. Her fancy costume combined with her husband's haughty attitude must have given Stead the idea the Londoners were social frauds. I felt no warmth from the Duff Gordons and was relieved their cabin was in a different section of the ship from ours.

"See here—" Duff Gordon protested. From their puckered faces, it was obvious the Duff Gordons thought Stead had stepped over the line of propriety. But what about the afterlife, I wondered? Could it be that spirits were trying to speak to humans, even to help them? Are those spirits what I found so unsettling at Père Lachaise Cemetery?

As Andrew served the first course, Stead kept talking. "What is certain," he said, "is that automatic writing often contains information about past events of which the writer could not be aware and sometimes perfectly accurate predictions as to events which have not yet happened." He stroked his beard. "I myself have been predicted to die either from lynching or drowning."

"In the absence of hanging trees in the North Atlantic," Bradley said, "I'd say you're safe for the next several days, Mr. Stead."

Lady Duff Gordon laughed. "Perhaps, but there's plenty of sea on this voyage for drowning."

Lightoller's face turned somber. "I personally will make sure no one goes overboard." I sensed he did not enjoy the joke.

Stead looked at Lady Duff Gordon. "Have you any foresight about your own demise, madam?"

"I should say not," she said. "And I have no intention of dying—lynching, drowning or otherwise."

"Well said, Lady Duff Gordon." I picked up my fork. "Now, I'm sure we can all agree this mousseline is positively heavenly."

Margaret Tobin Brown, 45,
Joins the Greatest Ship's Maiden Voyage
Denver Star, April 10

Andrew stood at the serving board, close enough to Stead's table to overhear the conversation.

"Is it not poor timing to talk of death when we're in the middle of an ocean, Mr. Stead?" Duff Gordon sneered.

Stead pointed a finger at him to drive home his point. "I have been speaking of the afterlife, which is very much alive."

What was very much alive for Andrew was the pain in his hip that ran down to his knees and back up to his neck. His body wanted sleep but more than that, it needed food. The smell of the roast beef was driving him mad. Since breakfast he hadn't had a chance to eat, and he was ravenous. When he looked down at his hands, he saw a spot of blood on his index finger. At first he thought he had cut himself, but the liquid was brownish — jus from the meat, most likely. Luckily he hadn't gotten any on his white jacket or he'd have to soak it in peroxide to get the stain out. He had to be more careful.

The meaty aroma raised saliva under his tongue. He swallowed and checked around the dining saloon. Maybe he could sneak a lick of the jus from his finger and savor its gaminess, but he dared not chance such a crude gesture. Not that anyone was watching — or even acknowledged him except to ask for second helpings. He could probably shove a sliver of beef into his mouth unnoticed, but he had learned to be disciplined. Even on this new ship he played his part like an orchestra cellist, no deviation from the score, coming in right on cue.

Taking a linen towel from the table, placed there in case of a mishap in serving, he wiped his finger.

From another table, Margaret Brown signaled for more roast beef. She was sitting with the Carters, the Wideners, and First Officer Murdoch. Andrew had arranged the place settings around the table at equal distances from each other, a little over fifty centimeters from the center of each plate lest diners be vexed with insufficient elbow room. Water glasses farthest from the utensils, red wine goblet closer in, and white wine closest. White wine the smallest, red larger, water the largest goblet. Mrs. Brown was drinking white wine from her red wine goblet. Now it was Andrew who was vexed.

He sliced from the rarest section, settled the meat on a silver platter, and delivered it to Mrs. Brown's table.

"That a boy," she said, helping herself to a hefty portion. A diner's elbow position suggested class. Hers were pinned to the table.

"Thank you, steward," Mrs. Carter said quietly as if correcting Mrs. Brown's manners.

When eating, slouching was unacceptable, not even for soup that threatened to drip. Mrs. Brown hunched over her plate, going off about ancient Roman society around bites of roast beef. Andrew recognized his signal to retreat, at least until he was needed again.

H.M.S. *Titanic* 3rd Class Holds 700
Mostly Central and Eastern Europeans
The Washington Post, April 10

Where had Andrew gone? I needed more ice for my wine. Parisians considered it gauche to add ice to wine. They served a bottle of white in a chiller of cold water. I liked mine colder than room temperature, and the bottle had been sitting for an hour growing warmer by the minute.

As I was keeping an eye out for Andrew to return to the serving table, a man staggered into the dining saloon dressed in a crumpled jacket, crooked bow tie at his neck. A flatcap sat rudely on the back of his head. He stood unsteadily between Stead and Lady Duff Gordon, who leaned away as if afraid some vermin might leap from the fellow in her direction. The rough man's face was leathery, his hands too large for his skinny body. The fingernails were chewed, some black substance under them. At first I thought he might have been a stowaway or a vagrant from the slums of London. He certainly wasn't attired like a first-class diner nor even like a steward. How had he even gotten on the ship?

"*Dobriy vyecher*," the man muttered. "Gude even-ink."

Russian, I suspected.

He slapped his chest. "Myee name Kozlov."

Conversation halted. Not even the journalist had a word to say.

Kozlov looked around the room. "Dees ees better den down in terd." His voice was sluggish and sounded as if he might swallow his tongue.

"See here, my good man." Lightoller stood up. "You need to go back to third class."

Kozlov grinned, slid off his cap and held it over his stomach. His dishwater gray hair was plastered to his head with what looked to be some sort of oil. He smelled of whisky and the rancid scent of a wild animal.

"Nyet. I eet here." He put his cap back on his head askew. If he had been sober, he might have been comical. As it was, he could be dangerous. And he was not going to leave peacefully.

When Lightoller put a hand on Kozlov's shoulder, the Russian thrust his forearm into the second officer's chest and pressed by him.

"My word!" Lady Duff Gordon spewed.

Kozlov went toward the serving table and reached for a hunk of beef from the platter. Andrew grabbed the man's wrist.

"You heard Officer Lightoller, Mr. Kozlov."

With his other hand, Kozlov pulled a knife from his pocket and waved it in Andrew's face.

"An' you heerd me."

I heard a gasp from one of the diners. From settling spats among my sons, I determined there was only one way to handle the situation.

"For heaven's sake, give the man some food," I said.

Andrew wrenched the knife from Kozlov's hand, and it clattered to the floor.

"Afraid not, old chum," Andrew growled. He outweighed the Russian by several pounds, and in his inebriated state Kozlov was slow to react. Andrew twisted his arm behind his back.

"No harm—no harm," Kozlov pleaded.

Andrew clamped his other hand on the back of the man's neck and drove him toward the saloon door, muscling him forward and down the ladders to steerage.

When they were gone, Bradley lifted his wine glass. "I believe we owe a toast to our intrepid steward, Mr. Cunningham," he said.

Stead raised his glass and proclaimed, "Here, here — to the heroic Mr. Cunningham."

"Very well," I said. "Now if someone would please get me a cube of ice."

In the dim alleyway of the steerage section, Charlie Savage was bent over, cleaning a putrid substance from the floor.

"Andy!" he said. "What brings you to the dungeon?"

"Your passenger seems to have lost his way. Hang onto him, will you?"

"As you see, mate, I've got me hands full. If they're not seasick, they're sick drunk and no portholes to pitch the foul mess out."

Andrew turned his head away. "Awful," he said. "Aren't there buckets in the cabins?"

"Aye, fer all the good it does. At least the lot of 'em are passed out. Tolstoy here must've gotten by when I had me back turned." Charlie was a solid, working-class bloke. No pretense about him. He got up, clutched Kozlov's vest and shoved him down the alleyway.

"Any chance the swallie will run out by tomorrow?" Andrew asked. "That should quiet things."

"No such luck. Sid says you're half empty up in first. We're full to the brim down here. I may not get a wink on this cursed voyage."

It was odd to think that people on this level actually slept underwater, a submerged mass of optimistic poor moving toward the prospect of riches in one of America's great cities. Andrew wished them well.

"Sorry, mate. Stay the course — I've got to get upstairs."

As he climbed back up to first class, Andrew thought how the *Titanic* was like Noah's ark. She carried a universe on board—nearly every race and nationality. Not that they were allowed to mingle. Heaven knew what might happen if blokes like Kozlov were invited to smoke and dine with the likes of John Jacob Astor. There were country borders, but class borders, too—even on a ship at sea.

Journalist Wm. Stead
to Address Carnegie Hall Conference on Peace
New York Tribune, April 11

"Good morning, Mr. Cumings, Mrs. Cumings." William Stead had his head out his cabin door and was checking up and down the passageway. His cabin was across the hallway from ours and down a few doors.

"And a fine morning it is, Mr. Stead," Bradley said.

"It seems to me this ship is not at full capacity," the journalist said.

"I believe full capacity is thirty-five hundred," I said. "Our steward Andrew said there are just over twenty-two hundred on board, including crew."

He stroked his white beard. "There's a coal strike. How is it that other ships are idle and the *Titanic* sails?"

"There's no need to worry about running out of fuel, Mr. Stead," Bradley said. "We have been assured the coalbunkers are nearly full and we'll cruise to New York at top speed."

"I'd think people would jump at the chance to cross the Atlantic on a ship like this." He was getting at something, but I wasn't sure what. If the man wanted nothing more than conversation, Bradley and I could afford a few minutes.

"Springtime is not the height of the travel season," I said. "France was bursting with flowers, but here in the North Atlantic, there's a bitter chill, wouldn't you agree?"

Behind Stead, books teetered on a small bedside table, writing paper spread on the bunk, sheets fallen to the floor. The gentleman must have gotten bored with his work and was looking for someone to distract him. Traveling alone was undoubtedly lonely.

"New ships tend to spew up annoying problems," he said. "Probably there will be technical glitches as well — the wireless and such. Wisdom dictates avoiding maiden voyages. An experience to crow about, though, especially on a vessel like the *Titanic*."

"Right, Mr. Stead," Bradley said, "and here we are, on our way."

"So we are. I'm sure this liner is as firm as a rock." Stead lifted his eyes above Bradley's head as if thinking. "However, a few years ago I published an article about a ship that collided with an iceberg in the North Atlantic. Odd that it was about this time of year, too." He mumbled as if talking to himself. When he shook his head and sighed, the trance was broken. "The ship *Majestic* came to the rescue and no one died in the mishap, I'm happy to say."

Bradley's stomach rumbled, and he heaved an exasperated sigh.

"We must get ourselves to breakfast, Mr. Stead," I said.

Ignoring my comment, Stead turned and looked back into his cabin. "I'm to address a conference on peace at Carnegie Hall next week. Working on it now." He motioned toward the spilled papers. "Speaking of which — I believe there has been a mistake."

"What sort of mistake?" Bradley asked.

"This is not the room I booked."

"Perhaps I could look at your ticket then?"

Honestly, my husband could have been less abrasive. This was a matter for the chief steward, not Bradley Cumings.

"Unfortunately, I seem to have misplaced my ticket," Stead said.

Ah, there was Stead's reason for his idle conversation. His stateroom was cramped, and with all his books and writings, he needed more space to spread out.

"The cabin next to ours is vacant, I believe," I said. "We'll have Andrew look into moving you."

"I would be most appreciative," Stead said.

As we continued down the hallway, Bradley leaned into me.

"I'm not sure having Mr. Stead as our neighbor is such a wise idea," he muttered. "We may be held prisoner for the rest of the voyage."

Andrew tracked down Latimer and asked about Stead's stateroom. Latimer checked the chart.

"He's in one-twenty-one."

"That's right," Andrew said.

"That's an inside room. He paid the cheaper fare."

"I understand. But he finds the quarters a bit — confining."

"That's usually a maid's cabin." Latimer lifted the sheet and studied the list under it. "Stead's been nominated for two Nobels and he may bloody well win the Peace Prize this year. He's the most famous passenger on board. We can do better for him." He flipped the top sheet down again. "Eighty-seven's empty. Move him there, between Cumings and Craig. He'll have a view of the swells."

"I'll move him straight away."

Before the ship anchored at Queenstown to take on more passengers, Andrew moved Stead's luggage to cabin 87. As he hung the suits in the closet, the journalist launched an interrogation.

"You're the Scotsman?" Stead had a good memory.

"Aye," Andrew responded.

"The Steads settled in Yorkshire in the fifteenth century. Nothing wrong with the Scots, though. A solid race."

Behind Stead's hoary beard Andrew detected immense physical and intellectual energy. He was a Viking of a man, a man to be cautious around.

"Are you married, my boy?"

Andrew didn't fancy personal questions. Not that there was anything notable about him to reveal. He pulled back his shoulders. The newsman had a reputation for being exceedingly generous, and Andrew was prepared to give him his life's story if it meant a fat gratuity when they docked in New York.

"Yes, sir," he said. "Married ten years now."

"Thirty-eight years for me. I could not have wed anyone but my Lucy. Give your wife a valentine every year — that's the secret to marital longevity."

"Excellent advice, sir." Andrew hadn't given Emily a single valentine, but she was a forgiving woman.

"Your wife did not accompany you on the cruise?" Andrew figured since Stead had asked about his wife, he could ask about the journalist's.

"Not this voyage," Stead said. "Sea travel gives her anxiety."

"Understandable." Andrew couldn't blame her — *Olympic's* mishaps had raised his own misgivings.

"What is your religion, young man?" Stead leveled his eyes at Andrew. Talk of religion was out of bounds for a steward, but courtesy called for an answer.

"The Kirk, sir."

"I've been a member of the Congregational Church all my life." he said. "I enjoy the hymns, even though I'm told I sing out of tune. I'm sure the Lord doesn't mind."

"No doubt."

"Do you believe in the afterlife?"

"Sir?" Andrew sensed that Stead wanted to continue the conversation he had begun at dinner.

"Life after death. The spiritual realm."

"Never thought much about it, really." Andrew had enough to think about in this life, working twenty days straight, home for four days, and then off to sea again.

"We're all heading in that direction, young man—some of us sooner than later. You would do well to give it some consideration."

"Of course, sir." His jaw ached from gritting his teeth. He knew how to stow luggage efficiently without seeming hurried, but he wished for a blessed release from Stead's cross-examination. It was not wise to consider the afterlife on a ship's maiden voyage, and he flashed back to the Scottish blessing he had taught Sandy about the sheltering angel. He prayed she was protecting his family from harm, no matter whose spirit she represented.

Irish Home Rule and the Ulster Covenant
The Manchester Guardian, April 11

"Bradley," I said, "I think I'll skip lunch. I'm just not up to another big meal."

"You hardly ate this morning, Florrie." Bradley had a way of Boring into me when he was concerned. I wanted to put him at ease, hoping to put myself at ease as well. In truth, Mr. Stead's tale of a ship hitting an iceberg had taken my appetite.

"I'm fine, really. It's probably all the rich food we've eaten in the last weeks."

"Very well, but I'll have one of the stewards bring a little something for you to have in the cabin in case you're hungry later."

"I may go up and have a look at the Irish coast when we anchor at Queenstown," I said.

"A capital idea. Might as well get a last glimpse of land before we take off across the ocean."

When I reached the A deck promenade, a gentleman emerged from cabin number 37. He wore a clerical collar and was carrying a leather suitcase.

"Good morning, Father," I said.

A slight fellow about Bradley's age, he lifted his hat and a shock of canary-colored hair fluttered over his forehead. Setting down his suitcase, he pressed a hand over his head as if to calm the feathers.

"I don't believe we've met," he said. "Francis Browne." He offered an outstretched hand. "Episcopal church of Ireland. You may call me Reverend — or just Francis."

I heard a brogue. He must have been on his way home to Ireland. I had been around men of the cloth all my life. If anyone knew the inner workings of religious orders, it should have been I. At one point I thought I might marry a minister like my father — one with perhaps more sense of humor.

I shook his hand and gave my name. "My father is a Unitarian minister."

"I'm sorry, then, that we haven't had a chance to speak. There are similarities between Unitarians and Episcopalians."

"I would never have thought that."

"Sure there is. We accept worshipers for who they are, as do you Unitarians."

Except for those who intend harm on others, I thought. But the hallway of a ship was no place for a proper discussion of religious beliefs.

"I would enjoy a deeper conversation with you, Reverend, but it looks as though you're leaving us in Queenstown."

"Afraid so. My uncle bought me a ticket to sail from Southampton to Queenstown. Bragging rights, I suppose, for a sail on the newest ship afloat."

"A pity you've had such a short trip," I said.

"I've taken plenty of photos to remind me of the experience. I'm a photographer — amateur, mind you." He pivoted to show me the camera case hung over his shoulder.

"Ah — well and good," I said. "I'm sure people will be interested in seeing them."

"I wonder, though, if I'm making the right decision," he said.

"What do you mean?"

"Last night, one of my dinner table companions in the first-class saloon offered to pay my way to New York. When I telegraphed my uncle about the opportunity to continue across the Atlantic, he advised me to leave the ship in Queenstown."

Curious, I thought. "Why would he not want you to visit America?"

"Can't be certain. The telegram simply said, 'Get off that ship.' He ended with the word 'Providential.' The message sounded urgent."

"Have you any idea what he might have meant by providential?"

"He's the Bishop of Cloyne—in closer touch with the Almighty than most of us. I don't argue with him." The priest gave me an unconvincing grin.

I hoped he was joking. Probably the uncle had church business for his nephew to attend to. At the same time, the skin prickled at the back of my neck. What did the bishop know that the ship's officers didn't?

"Well, best of luck to you, Reverend," I said.

"And to you, Mrs. Cumings."

Irish Passengers Board Titanic's Last Port of Call
Queensland Record, Thursday, April 11

Just before noon, the *Titanic* reached the southern coast of Ireland and dropped anchor two miles outside Queenstown. The city nestled inside Cork Harbor and was protected by several islands impossible for a large cruise ship to navigate. Andrew knew the system from his service on *Oceanic*. White Star tenders and other small boats carrying mail bags and cargo would have to motor to the ship waiting at Roches Point.

Sid was on duty to serve lunch, so Andrew went down to E deck to help with boarding. Latimer had told him that only three would be traveling first class, none of them under his assignment. Seven held second-class tickets, and the rest would be assigned to steerage — one hundred twenty-three passengers in all.

He lined up half a dozen passengers to disembark. One of them appeared to be a priest. Just as the tenders reached the ship, a firemen bulled his way through the group.

"Coffey," Andrew called. John Coffey had been with Sally Caveney and the other firemen when they saved him from muggers in New York. "You're leaving the ship?"

"Aye," he said.

He seemed agitated, swiveling his head as if looking for someone who might stop him. Andrew wondered who had given him permission to go ashore.

"But why?" Andrew asked.

Coffey's eyes shot daggers at him. "Go below and bloody see for yourself."

The fireman's departure would leave one fewer stoker in the furnace room. With the two who had missed the launch at Southampton, some of the firemen would have to do double shifts, a nearly impossible strain under the furnace room's blistering conditions. Coffey's threat about whatever was happening in the furnace room, Stead's talk about the supernatural, and his own misgivings about *Titanic's* maiden voyage had him out of kilter.

After new passengers staggered up the swaying gangway to E deck, the seven disembarking passengers boarded the waiting tenders. One of the third-class men brought out an instrument, an Irish elbow pipe. The sound was similar enough to the bagpipes of his Scottish home that his fears began to dissolve.

"Who is that?" Andrew asked a woman.

"That's Eugene," she said. "Eugene Daly. We boarded in Queenstown just now, and I reckon he couldn't wait to play the pipes. That one's 'Erin's Lament'—do you know it?"

Andrew knew the song—a slow and soulful dirge. It seemed an odd sendoff for what he expected would be a happy voyage.

If he had calculated correctly, with the Queensland people there were now 1,316 passengers aboard *Titanic*, about half the ship's capacity. At exactly 1:30 p.m. by his watch, *Titanic's* whistle blew and the tenders answered, backing off to return to dock. For a few seconds he wished he had been aboard one of them.

The clanging of chains raising the monstrous anchor drowned out the mournful strains of the pipe music and Andrew waited one more moment before turning to his duties.

Berkeley Alum Warren Craig and Wife Travel First-Class Aboard *Titanic* Maiden Voyage from Europe
The San Francisco Call, April 12

I looked out the window of our cabin at the misty morning. It was as if a thin gauze of gossamer had been laid over the sea. So calm, it might have been a field of grain on a windless day. Except I knew we were over water—an endless and bottomless amount of water.

"Ready for breakfast, dearest?" Bradley was at the mirror, smoothing his straight hair with his palms. He turned his head to the right and left, checking his image. I would never understand what attracted such a handsome fellow to a plain girl like me.

I kept to the simple Parisian style of breakfast—a pastry and creamy coffee. Eggs so early made my stomach queasy. Besides, I was still full from last night's supper. Bradley had an appetite, and I was happy to linger at the table with him and nibble my shortcrust.

On the way back to our stateroom, we passed the open doorway of Edith Craig. She was still in her dressing robe.

"Oh," Edith said, "you're the Cumings couple, aren't you?"

"We are, yes," Bradley said. The dressing robe gaped open to show Edith's pale calf, and I watched my husband's face flush with embarrassment.

"I'm looking for the steward," Edith said.

"Andrew is serving breakfast," I said.

"Oh, pooh." Edith drew her mouth to the side.

"May I be of help?" I offered.

Edith flickered a tiny smile. "I wonder—might you come in? Just for a moment or two."

I looked at Bradley with raised brows. He understood.

"I'll be in our cabin. Please don't be long, Florrie."

When I entered the Craig's stateroom, there was no sign of Mr. Craig. The bed was mussed but otherwise looked as if it had hardly been slept in, and the heavy scent of perfume choked the air.

"Warren was out late at the card table. Fortunately, we can afford for him to lose—which he usually does." She pulled out a chair at the little table. "Please sit. Where are you from?"

What did the woman want? She didn't seem to be distressed.

"Boston," I said and then corrected myself. "But we've lived in New York for the past dozen years."

"Warren and I are from Montana but we live in California now." She flapped her hand at the stateroom. "Please excuse the mess. We're not persnickety." She sat across the table, a wine goblet with some dark liquid in front of her. I suspected Edith Craig had no need of anything—she was just lonely.

"Just to show how unfussy we are, Warren was at Berkeley six years ago when that horrible San Francisco earthquake destroyed the city. The college was spared, and he helped set up dormitories on campus for the survivors. All of the downtown was nothing but fire and rubble."

The wine, if that's what it was, had loosened her tongue.

"Three thousand people died. I imagine it was horrible. I was in Montana at the time."

I tried to think of a way to escape from the woman.

"After that ordeal, I honestly think Warren and I can endure anything."

"I trust your troubles are behind you." The perfume was an expensive brand I had sampled in Paris but decided we couldn't afford. Hairpins littered the bureau, and at first I thought the crumpled handkerchief was a wilted rose. I hoped Edith Craig would run out of chatter, but such was not the case.

"We're on our honeymoon. We went to Naples and Egypt, but I prefer Paris. There's never enough time in Paris." Her eyes glazed over.

"How nice for you." There was no point in telling her about our own visit to Paris. Edith Craig, had no interest in anyone but herself. And even though she glowed with youthful beauty, she was childlike, her needs simple — to be recognized and listened to. A mourning-dove sadness weighed on her, immense and heavy, as if she were too fragile to bear it. I felt sorry for her. Usually the groom was attentive to his bride. Where was her husband? And what was his wife doing drinking wine in the morning?

"Actually, we've been married for nearly three years." Edith sighed. "You know, you never foresee what you're going to get, do you?"

I pretended not to have an opinion about Edith Craig's question. When I married Bradley, I was absolutely sure what I was getting, and even now I was astonished at what a prize I had won.

"It's not really a honeymoon, you know," Edith said. "I mean for Warren and me. More like a vacation."

I had met enough upper-class men like her Warren to determine they wore masks, and the masks were all the same — dignified and expressionless — except for Bert Marckwald, that was. For women, though, words could be misleading. Edith Craig, by her wilted posture and her slow movements, was an unfulfilled woman. Her rich husband probably made love to her in the most proper manner, relieving himself quickly and efficiently. Her trunks may have overflowed with silk dresses and strings of pearls and her etiquette and good form were impeccable, but she was a woman locked in a silver urn, suffocating under so much money, dying a slow death.

"We have a son," Edith said. "He's nearly two. Do you have youngsters? By the way, what should I call you?"

"Florence will do." I judged Edith to be barely twenty-five with doe-like eyes, ivory skin, and impossibly high cheekbones. In spite of her sulking and self-absorption, she was quite attractive. "I was named for the Italian city. I don't know that my parents ever traveled to Italy, but my father studied Latin. Florence means flourishing, I believe."

"How nice." It was clear Edith Craig didn't care a fig about Latin. Her life of luxurious travel bored her—I was sure of it— as did a husband who preferred card games to his wife's company. With so many opportunities, she had only her wine and frivolous chitchat with a total stranger.

"Children?" Edith said.

"Oh, yes. Three." My chest ached to think of home. The thought occurred to send the boys a Marconigram over the wireless. Wouldn't that thrill them? It cost a dollar and a half for just ten words, but Bradley wouldn't mind. What ten words would I send?

"My Robert is an incredible child. Very intelligent and sweet. We're rushing back to California to celebrate his second birthday. My mother and a nurse are with him until then." She sighed and tilted her head toward me. "I hope you have someone remarkable taking care of your little ones while you're away."

"Yes, they're well cared for. One is away at school," I said. "Jackie is very independent." It tore at my heart to say the words.

Edith scanned me up and down. Why wasn't she with her husband, wherever he was? As if she had read my mind, Edith said, "Warren's going to lose everything to those card sharks in the smoking room, I'm afraid."

I was beginning to understand why her husband preferred the company of card players.

"I must go." I started to stand. "We're meeting the Astors at noon."

"Can you believe Colonel Astor has eighteen motorcars in his garage?" she said. "I like a man who knows how to get what he wants."

I sat back down. I was concerned about Edith. When she stopped talking for a second, I leaned toward her to see if she was all right. She was resting her head on her hand, elbow on the table, and I thought she may have fallen asleep. But then her head snapped up and she began again, as if she had just had a clever thought.

"That millionaire Ben Guggenheim has a flat in Paris where he entertains women. A marquise was one of the most recent, and now here he is on the *Titanic* with some French singer and her maid. Honestly, I don't know how his wife bears it."

By minding her own business, I wanted to say.

"Mrs. Craig, I'm sorry but—" I rose from the chair again.

"Please call me Edie. We're much more informal than you New Yorkers. I hope Warren doesn't want to dally in New York. It's such a long train ride to the West Coast. I'm eager to get home—for Robbie. I mean, I am and I'm not." She rolled her eyes up at me. "You don't know what I'm talking about, do you?"

I had no answer for her nor any interest in knowing what she was talking about. My hand was on the doorknob when Edith said, "One more thing—if you happen to see our steward, would you ask him to check for a wireless message for me? My friends in Los Angeles are probably wondering about me."

"Of course," I said. "I'm sure they wonder about you."

Andrew flagged Sid down in the middle of the hallway.

"Sid, my mate! Just the bloke I was looking for. Be a good man, won't you, and check on a wireless for Mrs. Craig. I've got my hands full with the Bronson ladies."

"Sod off, mate," Sid said. "Do your own running about."

"As your superior, I could make it an order."

Sid gave Andrew the evil eye. "I understand the fair lady asked specifically for you. Wouldn't want to disappoint her."

"I could mark you down for insubordination," he threatened.

Sid turned and tossed his final remarks over his shoulder as he scuttled down the hallway. "Then you'll have a mutiny on your hands. Wouldn't want that either, would you?"

Blast Sid. Between the Bronson ladies and Stead, Andrew was practically on a run.

In the Marconi room, Jack "Sparks" Phillips was tapping away on the machine. The wireless lines were strung like invisible clotheslines across the ocean as if hanging out greetings and orders to dry like ladies' laundry.

Harry Bride's fingers pounded the typewriter, writing up incoming wires.

"Slow down, will you, Sparks?" Bride said. "Everything's so urgent you'd think we were in the midst of some sort of disaster."

"I've got a pile of messages to send, and if I don't make thirty words a minute, I'll never reach the bottom," Phillips complained.

"Sorry, men," Andrew interrupted, "but anything for Edith Craig in cabin C-89?"

"Blimey," Bride said. "I think there is a message. I'll thank you to deliver it, Andy." He handed Andrew a half sheet of paper. He had typed so hard that the periods had made holes in the onionskin. "Envelopes are there." He snapped his hand at a box and got back to his typing.

"Oh," Bride added, "I think there's one for you, too." He flicked his fingers toward a pile of telegrams.

Halfway down the stack, Andrew found the Marconigram addressed to him.

"A wire—from my wife. That's odd."

Bride had his head down, focused on his work. Andrew considered why Emily would go to the expense of sending a wire. Was something wrong with one of the bairns? His hands shaking, he tore into the message.

HAD NIGHTMARE ABOUT TITANIC. BE CAREFUL. ALL WELL HERE. LOVE.

A nightmare? Andrew had never known her to have bad dreams. She must have been worried about the maiden voyage. He had dismissed his own qualms, and a dream was not a prophecy—just a worry. He hoped Captain Smith would set new records getting *Titanic* to New York and back so he could put Emily's mind at ease.

Then he remembered the message for the Craig woman. What could be so urgent that it couldn't wait five more days until they reached New York?

Andrew took the Marconigram and envelope into the hall. Before he folded the paper, he glanced at it. What was the harm?

ROBBIE WELL. CRIES FOR YOU. GRANDPA VISITS DAILY. MOTHER.

Just drivel. Nothing pressing, but he supposed he had to deliver it nonetheless. He slipped the paper into the envelope and sealed it shut.

When he knocked on C-89, Edith Craig opened. She had on a day dress, cinched at her tiny waist. He handed her the envelope and backed away.

"Just a minute, steward," she said. "I may need to send a response." She pulled out the message and when she read it, she burst into tears.

Andrew tried to look sympathetic, but he wanted to get on with his business.

Leaning against the doorframe, she said, "It's about my father-in-law. He's not fond of me."

"I'm very sorry, Miss," he said, hoping she was finished. No such luck.

"He controls thousands of acres of sugar beets and railroad and banking investments. And he thinks I'm incompetent—and my mother too. As if one of us might drop my boy on his head."

She took a handkerchief from her sleeve and wiped her nose. "Oh, we never should have left little Robbie."

The week aboard ship slowed passengers down and in the lull some of them—women especially—reflected on their most unhappy circumstances. Edith Craig was not the first woman whose tears had dampened his jacket.

"I'm sure everything is fine at home," Andrew offered. "Your son will be happy to see you."

She sniffed. "Yes." After thinking a second, she rolled her dewy eyes at him. "Do you have a wife?"

He was taken aback by her question. None of her business, he wanted to tell her. Then he thought of telling her about the Marconigram but that was none of her affair either.

"Yes," he said. "We have a son and a daughter."

"Oh," she said. "Does your wife ever get—blue?"

"I don't recall her getting blue, no." Emily was not one to pout.

"That's really why we went away, Warren and I. He thought a few weeks on the Mediterranean would cheer me up—the sun and all. We've been gone for two months and I don't feel the least bit cheered up. Oh, it's all very nice to be petted and feasted, but—"

Her lilac perfume was splashed on too generously and nearly made him sneeze. Andrew may never have missed Emily as much as he did at that moment.

"You might take a walk through the lounge," he said. "It's modeled after the palace at Versailles and quite grand. Always lifts my spirits."

Actually, that was a lie. He found the lounge tawdry.

"I've been to Versailles," Edith Craig said. "Imitations are cheap."

At least they agreed on that. He tried again to escape the maudlin woman's clasp.

"Have you had your lunch, then?" He checked his watch— early for the midday meal, but in first class, passengers could dine whenever they wished. We're serving meats, soups, pastries, sweets—whatever you desire. You might feel better after you've had a bite to eat."

She thought a minute. "All right—if you'll walk me to the saloon."

He was about to answer when Warren Craig rushed up, his face twisted with contempt.

"I'll escort my wife to lunch, steward," he said.

"Of course, sir," Andrew said, elated to be relieved of that duty.

As Craig took her elbow and led her down the hallway, Andrew heard him reprimand his wife. "Don't be so familiar, Edie. It's unattractive."

Andrew couldn't have agreed more.

The Effect of the Combustion of Coal on the Climate
What Scientists Predict for the Future
Popular Mechanics, April 12

Before the midday meal, Bradley and I went to the boat deck for a breath of air to settle my stomach.

On the port side, a crewman leaned over the railing and dropped a rope to which a bucket was attached. When he hauled up the bucket, he stuck a thermometer into the water.

"What's the reading?" Bradley asked.

"Thirty-six Fahrenheit," the crewman said. "Cold enough to shrivel your dick."

"Oh, dear," I said. Bradley forced a laugh and guided me down the promenade, away from the vulgar man.

"Is cold seawater anything to worry about?" I asked.

"Not at all," Bradley said. "Cold water is denser than warm water, dense enough to keep heavy objects afloat—objects like iron ships. That's one of the reasons big cruise ships take a northerly route." He winked at me. "Learned that tidbit of information from researching your subsurface torpedo boats."

The air was warmer than the water—forty-five degrees, I guessed. Warmer still in the sun. The sea was glassy calm, the only breeze coming from the ship cutting through the atmosphere.

"I suspect with these calm waters the captain will test the ship at her full twenty-three knots before we reach New York," Bradley said.

"Good. The sooner we get home, the better." I looked at the silky water. It was uncannily still. Not even a dolphin disturbed the surface. We were sure to make good time.

Fire Caused by Spontaneous Combustion in Wet Coal
The Charleston WVa Advocate, April 1912

Andrew still owed Jimmy and Sally for saving his hide from the New York thugs. He had a few minutes to give them a bit of relief.

When he reached the boiler room with the bucket of cool water, the stokers were shoveling at a pile of smoking coal. He nearly choked at the stench of sulfur.

"What's up, Sally?" he asked. The stoker was bent over, heaping smoldering chunks into a rolling bin. He stood up and when he used the tail of his shirt to wipe his face, his bare belly glistened with sweat.

"Some wankers loaded on wet coal in Souf'ampton. Now we're in fer it."

The stokers knew the properties of coal and having been raised in a coalmining town, so did Andrew. Freshly mined coal—especially when wet—takes on more oxygen than coal that has dried. Oxygen causes the coal to heat up and if it doesn't catch fire, it sends off toxic fumes.

"I'll call for the captain," Andrew said.

"Don't bovver. Few years back, a coal fire blew up a battleship in 'avana 'arbor down Cuber way," Sally said. "Nofin' cap'n kin do 'bout it." He hefted another shovelful of smoldering stuff.

Even in the dusky light of the boiler room, Andrew saw the metal inside the ship's wall had buckled, most likely due to the hot fuel. The metal was still seething. That's what Coffey was talking about.

"Don't fret, Andy boy," Sally said. "The stokers is usin' the 'ot coals fast as we kin get 'em into the ovens."

Using up the coal? Was there a chance the ship would run short of fuel? Sally must have read the look on his face.

"But dere's plenty enough to get us to New York long as we don't slow down," he said. "We slow down and it'll take 'at much more to get up to speed again." He wagged his head. "It's a thorny business, I'll tell ye."

Thorny indeed. Andrew's inklings had been right—officers shifting around, Stead's talk about icebergs, a compromised hull, and now a fire. Lady Liberty was going to be a welcome sight—if they could get to her.

Sally shook a finger at him. "Whatever you do, lad, don't be spreadin' word 'round. No need ta git ever'body nutter about it. The black gang kin take keer o' it." He turned back to his work. "G'won now so's we can git back to it."

Backing away, Andrew took one last look into the hell of the boiler room. The ship's wall didn't look good—not good at all.

Dollar Holds Strong Against Europe Financials
The Evening Standard, April 12

"I'm going up to the purser's office to give him some of these French francs," I said. "We'll exchange them once we get to New York."

Bradley was reclined on the bed, his feet up. He had drawn a blanket over his legs.

"How many francs do you have?" he asked.

"I don't know — five hundred or so."

"That's about a hundred American dollars, Florrie. With card sharks and other scoundrels on the ship, it might not be a bad idea to secure the francs with the purser. Do you want me to come along?"

My husband's eyes drooped. He looked like a reclining Ramses, and I suspected he had no desire to climb stairs.

"No, darling — you rest. I can't possibly get lost on a ship."

When I reached the grand staircase, a young woman stood with a perplexed expression on her face. It was the Bronson girl, if I wasn't mistaken. I wished her good morning — or was it afternoon by now? So hard to tell with the time changes as we sailed west.

"I'm looking for the purser," Emma Bronson said.

"I'm on my way there," I said. "Why don't you come along with me? I'd love the company."

"If you don't mind, I'd like to see if I have a message first. Do you have any idea where the telegraph office is?"

"I believe it's on the boat deck," I said. "We should be able to find it."

Emma stepped gingerly, clutching the banister and wobbling in her high-heeled shoes. She nearly lost her balance once, and I grabbed her elbow to steady her. Those dreadful shoes with pointy toes young women wore these days were a hazard. Paris fashion was sure to be their downfall. Emma started up the stairs again then hesitated, gazing up at the enormous dome overhead.

"Do you know the story of the Wizard of Oz?" she asked.

"Yes. I took my sons to the play in New York." I had heard the Bronsons were from outside Manhattan and I was pleased to discuss anything relating to home. "The story is about a girl named Dorothy who visited a magical land."

Emma heaved a sigh. "If I were Dorothy, I wouldn't click my heels to go home. I'd go immediately back to Paris."

"I enjoyed Paris, too," I said. It was true—not the shopping but the museums, the galleries, and the parks.

"The *Titanic* is a sort of Oz, don't you think?"

I laughed. "Let's hope we don't have any wicked witches aboard."

"Well—" Emma pursed her lips and gave me a sideways glance. "There *is* my guardian."

When we reached the Marconi office, I stepped into the doorway. The room had a masculine odor—hard and oily. One of the men was focused on tapping at a little machine, shrill long and short beeps that meant nothing to me.

"I wonder if you have anything for Miss Bronson?" I said.

Harry Bride had his back to us, frantically working the wireless.

Bride snarled. "Here's another bloody notice about bloody icebergs."

I glanced at Emma, a puzzled expression on her pretty face.

"Not to worry," I whispered to her. "I'm sure they're all out of harm's way."

Bride babbled on. "The *Californian* won't stop prattling on about bergs ahead of us. You'd think the end of the world was at hand. They reported about the French liner *Niagara* striking ice near Newfoundland. Sprang a leak, but another ship heard the S.O.S. and came to the rescue. Filling up the airways with rubbish," he spat.

"There are icebergs?" Emma asked. "We'll go around them, won't we?"

Bride had on his headphones and apparently didn't hear her, but the other fellow — Phillips was his name — tapped him on the shoulder.

"What?" Bride shouted. His mouth dropped open when he saw the two women.

"Oh, sorry." Sliding off the headphones, Bride fiddled them in his fingers. "Just wireless talk. Pay no mind."

"Is there really ice ahead?" Emma asked.

Phillips piped in. "You'll be lucky to see an iceberg off in the distance. They're quite beautiful. But we won't get close to one. The captain will be sure of that. And we've got first-rate lookouts just to be double safe. Nothing can hurt a ship like *Titanic*."

"Thank goodness," Emma said. "Mother and Daisy will be relieved."

Icebergs — I considered that ice was why the water was so cold and the temperature dropping.

Phillips jumped in again. "I wouldn't spread rumors. No sense in making a fuss."

"All right," Emma said. "If you say so."

I doubted that Emma Bronson could keep such a secret.

"That's an order, Miss," Bride put in, giving her a charming smile. "And if either of you wants to send a wireless, just let old Harry Bride know — that's me. I'll tap it out for you — no charge."

The young operator had charisma, that was obvious. Under other circumstances, he and Emma would have made a handsome couple.

"Anything for Emma Bronson?" I asked again. "Or for Bradley and Florence Cumings?"

Bride rifled through a stack of papers. "No, afraid not."

"We should get along to E deck," I said to Emma. "That's where the purser's office is."

When we reached the purser, Emma opened her bag on his desk and handed him a fistful of bills.

"I believe that's seven hundred dollars, but I'd appreciate it if you'd count it again just to make sure."

The purser took the money without so much as a blink. For first-class, I imagined that less than a thousand dollars was hardly worth the effort.

"Seven hundred exactly," he said and began to fill out a receipt.

"You're sure the money will be safe?" Emma asked. "It was a birthday gift and I'd be horrified to lose it."

The purser ignored her. I doubted anyone had ever given him a gift of that much money. He may not have made seven hundred dollars in an entire year.

He handed Emma the receipt. "I assure you your money will be perfectly secure for the remainder of the voyage—or for all eternity, if it comes to that."

"Eternity?" My voice was not more than a whisper. I wondered about the *Titanic's* metal hull, who had forged the metal and fashioned the rivets. If a wheel is not attached to the hub of a carriage tightly enough, the wheel will begin to wobble and eventually will fall off. With all its metal and tons of coal, what little must it take to plunge such a ship hundreds, maybe thousands of fathoms below? Would it take more than a floating piece of frozen water? I had to believe that when ice and metal meet, metal will triumph. But according to William Stead, history showed otherwise.

"Don't you have some money to deposit, Mrs. Cumings?" Emma asked.

"No—I've changed my mind. I won't be depositing anything."

Wife and Daughter of
American Can Company President
Will Arrive in New York
aboard the Magnificent *Titanic*
The Greenwich News, April 12

When Daisy Bush didn't answer Andrew's knock, he let himself in and cleaned her stateroom. Then he went to C-91, the Bronsons' suite. Daisy came to the door after his knock.

"Emma and I are having a lesson," she barked. "We could move to the lounge if we're a bother, steward." He suspected she was one of the underclass who considered herself above her station, as if she were a friend of her employers rather than their help. Of course, he had to be gracious to all his passengers.

"Very nice of you, Miss Bush. I've finished in your room if you'd prefer to go there. Or I'll come back later."

"Oh, Daisy," Emma said, "can't we be done for today? I'm sick to death of Latin. When will I ever use it except in heaven?"

Gladys Bronson was perched in a Bergère chair. A buxom woman, her hips overflowed the sides, hands folded over a book on her generous lap.

"If Latin is used in heaven," she said, "then it's worth knowing. We'll all go there sooner or later."

Emma rolled her eyes. "Hopefully later, Mother. Much later."

"Well then," Daisy said, "I'll be in my room when you're ready to continue." She elbowed past Andrew, nearly colliding with the cleaning cart.

"Is the ship on schedule?" Gladys Bronson asked. "We seem to be poking along."

"A big ship such as the *Titanic* does appear to move slowly," he said, "The White Star Line won speed records with its other ships, but the *Titanic* is more concerned with amenities." He glanced around the elegant stateroom. "I trust you and your daughter are comfortable?"

"Oh yes." Mrs. Bronson rolled her eyes around the room as if searching out details to criticize. "We could well be at a fine European hotel if I didn't know better."

"The *Titanic* is a lady of grace, not to be rushed in a propeller race across the Atlantic." He had to be careful. The Bronson ladies and their governess could be testy.

"Well," the older woman said, "as long as we're back in Greenwich by Wednesday."

"Greenwich?" He hadn't heard of the American city.

"It's on Long Island Sound but outside New York's dirt and din. A marvelous place."

"I've no doubt it is." All the Americans were from marvelous places. They spoke in superlatives — everything was splendid and grand. Of course, when one has money, how could circumstances be otherwise?

"And steward, take the flower vase and freshen the water. It's murky."

"Right away, Mrs. Bronson," he said. Cheerful — always be cheerful, he told himself.

"Could you bring some tea on your way back?" Emma asked. "It's quite chilly."

"Certainly." Vases, tea. Doubtless there would be more he'd be asked to do for these pampered hens.

"Did you know paper cups were invented in the second century for serving tea?" Emma asked.

"I did not," he answered. Her father, Latimer had told him, was a big investor in Dixie Cups.

"They're hygienic." Emma fixed a smug smile on her face.

Andrew had no interest in paper cups. Sanitary maybe, but he didn't like the idea of using a drinking cup that couldn't be washed with hot, soapy water.

"My father mostly invests in iron and steel. Much sturdier than paper."

"Then I'm glad *Titanic* is made of steel rather than of paper." Neither of the Bronson ladies laughed. Apparently they didn't get his joke. "I'll bring the tea straight away," he said and hurried out, taking the vase of flowers with him. He felt like the rabbit in Alice's Wonderland, always in a hurry, always running late.

On his way to fetch their tea he stopped at the first-class lounge to check that things were in order and was surprised to find Violet studying the mahogany bookcase. Most of the books were titles he had read on *Oceanic*—some he'd even read twice. Second-class had fewer books, and the passengers preferred playing games to reading.

"How are you faring, Violet?" he asked.

"I need a good story to warm me up," she said. "Cold as blazes in second class."

"Isn't the heat on?"

"The heating system is a blooming aggravation. Spoiled damsels in the first three cabins whined they were fairly frying, so the heat was shut off entirely. Now the rooms are like icehouses. Feel my hands." When she pressed cold fingers to his cheek, Andrew flinched.

She rubbed her palms together. "I started stewarding on ships in the tropics. Must've been barmy to sign on for a North Atlantic cruise."

"Aren't there electric heaters?"

"Not enough to go 'round. Besides, where would I put an electric heater? The berths in second are built into the walls with just enough room for a washbasin. Can't even open a steamer trunk without people crawling into their bunks first." She planted her fists on her hips. "If I get a call for room service, I have to leave the food cart in the alleyway and take the plates in one by one. Why they'd want to eat in the deep freeze is beyond me. The food's cold by the time they stick a fork in it." She shook her index finger at Andrew as if the next infraction were his fault. "Not only that, but the gates are locked at night so the second class isn't caught mingling with the toffs. What do they think we're going to do, steal a biscuit off their half-eaten plates?"

Violet was a mite melodramatic. Andrew was tempted to tell her about the scoundrel Kozlov who would indeed have stolen biscuits if he could've gotten away with it, but he let her have her moment to grouse.

"Sounds horrid," he said, feigning sympathy. "I can't imagine how you survive."

Stead walked in, eyed the pair, and took a seat at a table. The journalist must have wanted more elbow room. Either that or he enjoyed the opulence of the lounge with its carved mantelpiece and marble hearth and the ceiling edged in gold leaf. He opened a notebook and began writing.

Violet leaned toward Andrew, glancing at the old fellow. "Mrs. Shelley sent me to the chief to ask for a room transfer. Claims she was ill from the cold. It took four stewards to carry her and her haberdashery to the new room, which was just as cold. Mark me if she doesn't take to her bed the whole trip just to keep from getting stiff."

"Must be bloody awful down there." It was a weak gesture at consoling her. Andrew had his hands full with his own lot to deal with.

"If you're going to be sarcastic—"

He cocked his head playfully. "Help me out with the Bronson hens and their employee Miss Bush and I swear I'll be sympathetic to your plight."

"Never mind," she said and turned on her heel.

"Violet, wait." He opened the glass doors of the book cabinet and took out a volume. "Flaubert has some reading that'll put some color in your frozen cheeks." He handed her the novel *Madame Bovary*.

"Oh, you are a chump, Scottie," she said.

Swiss Geophysicist de Quervain
Launches Expedition Across Greenland
to Measure Shrinking Glaciers
New Yorker Volkszeitung, April 13

"Bradley, the telegraph operator says there have been warnings of icebergs in the area." I kneaded my hands, wanting him to tell me there was no danger, that the ship was safely on course.

He swung his legs over the side of the bed. "What were you doing in the telegraph room? I thought you were going to the purser."

"Never mind that." I dropped onto a chair. "What about the warnings?"

Bradley stood and looked out the porthole. "This is the ice season. The Canadian Coast Guard patrols these areas. We'd have received a warning from Newfoundland if there were danger."

"What about the captain?"

"What about him? Smith has been the commodore of the White Star Fleet for at least eight years. He's got more than forty years of sailing experience. I think he knows what he's doing."

"Then why is it so cold?" I slapped my gloved hands together.

"We'll be near Greenland in another day, darling. Greenland is all ice. Put on another layer of clothing if you're cold."

I sometimes found my husband's stoicism maddening. Although—the weather was calm and clear, and there were lookouts in the crow's nest. And I wouldn't want Captain Smith to slow the ship and delay our arrival in New York. So why couldn't I dispel a troublesome uneasiness?

Clara Barton,
Founder of Red Cross Society, Has Died
San Diego Evening Tribune, April 13

"Good game, my man." Astor and Bradley Cumings came out of the squash court into the gym where Andrew was pulling at the rowing machine.

"Of course you'd think that," he heard Cumings say. "You walloped me."

As lanky as he was, Astor apparently could slam the ball.

"Another go tomorrow?" Astor said.

"Absolutely. I'll be on my game next time," Cumings told him.

Astor headed for the Turkish bath and Cumings wandered toward the rowing machine where Andrew was working out.

"That fellow's quite a competitor, especially for such an old chap," he said. "Doesn't say much except for a few swear words when he loses a point. Almost had him once, but he edged me out."

Andrew paused his rowing. "You'll get him tomorrow, sir." Cumings was a fine-looking fellow. Liked to stay in shape. He admired that in a man.

"I'm still puzzling over your name—Cunningham. What part of Scotland are you from?"

"Shotts—east of Glasgow."

"That so? Do you know Cumings Castle—a few miles south of Glasgow?"

"Heard of it, yes," Andrew said. "Built by the Normans. Eleventh century, I believe. Not much left of it now but stones and a dry moat."

"That was my ancestor's home. John Comyn—the original name—was one of the guardians of Scotland. Known as The Red."

"I know of the Comyn clan," Andrew said. "The Cunningham clan were allies and fast friends."

Cumings slapped his knee. "Knew there was some link with you. The Red's uncle was king of Scotland—that is, until the English king sent him packing for demanding Scotland's independence."

"I read about that in school. I believe it was early 1300s when Robert the Bruce claimed the throne."

"Precisely. The Bruce wasn't even Scottish—he was a bloodthirsty Viking. You can imagine my ancestor opposed him. I'd hope your Cunningham clan stood with us."

Andrew started rowing again and raised his voice over the drone of the gears. "T'was not good business to oppose the Bruce."

"So The Red found out when he met the Bruce at a church in Dumfries to settle the dispute. They argued, tempers flared, and the Bruce drew his sword and ran The Red through." Cumings shook his head and tugged at the towel around his neck. "The bastard took possession of the Comyn land and castle and declared the Scottish throne his."

Andrew figured his exercise was finished and got up from the machine. The Cumings bloke was confiding in him, reaching back to his roots as if they were brothers, of a sort. It was an unnerving feeling, having a stranger ask to know about his background. At the same time, he wasn't at all unnerved. It may have sounded strange to Sid—or anyone else, for that matter—but Andrew felt as if he had known Bradley Cumings before—before this life. But that was as crazy as Stead's spiritualism and he shook it from his head.

"I hope you'll not hold the distant past against me, sir," he said.

"Not at all—let's leave such unpleasant topics behind us, shall we? Say, what's your first name again?

"Andrew, sir."

"Jolly good. Say, Andrew, what's the news? I'm starving for anything from the home front." He flopped onto the bench next to the rower.

"You mean the financial news?" he asked.

"No, no—I've been over all that. I mean the less dreary news. Something I might use to cheer up Florrie. She's suffering a bout of—malaise, shall we say."

"Sorry to hear it. Seasickness is not unusual at this point in the sail. Most recover in a day or two."

"I'll let her know. Any good news, then?"

Andrew thought a second. He wanted a shower and a shave and was surprised Cumings even recognized him out of uniform.

"I'm sorry to say your American nurse Clara Barton died last night," he said.

"Clara Barton, the Red Cross founder? A true humanitarian, that woman. But what have you heard about Boston? That's where we hail from originally, Florrie and I. We've been in New York less than a decade. Once a Bostonian, always a Bostonian, I say."

"I believe the wireless operator did give me a snippet of Boston news. The baseball park—"

"The new Fenway, yes. Have they opened the season?"

"The team—what's its name?"

"Red Stockings—best team in the league. I've lost count of how many games I've sat through in my life. I'll be getting season tickets when I get back to New York—box seats." He winked an eye. "My boys should have the same experience I had. Cracker Jacks, frankfurters, and all the rest of it."

"You'll be happy to know your Red Stockings triumphed over Harvard College," Andrew said. "An exhibition game, I would guess."

"Triumph, you say? As a Harvard man myself, I'm torn by this news. How bad was the beating?"

"Two-naught, I believe."

"Ah. Nothing to be ashamed of. I'd expect the Red Stockings to get the best of Harvard's youngsters. Their chief sport is intellect." Cumings smacked his chest with his palm. "When I was at Harvard, my game was tennis." Glancing toward the shower room, he lowered his voice. "I'd have trounced Astor in a match with a tennis racket."

Andrew moved to the punching bag hoping to give the bloke a message to end the banter. "I'll put in a word for a tennis court on the next White Star ship, then."

"That's the spirit." Cumings headed for the door and then stopped. "Say, Andrew, do you have an elixir you can bring Florrie? She's a bit—" He hesitated, searching for the right word. "—bound up."

Andrew jabbed the bag. "Right away, Mr. Cumings," he said.

"Finish your training first. No rush."

A knock came on the door of the cabin. Bradley would have burst in—who would be calling late morning, I wondered? I hoped it wasn't the cleaning crew. The way I was feeling, it would take all my determination to go out while they made up the room. My stomach was positively doing somersaults.

"Please come in," I called from the bed. I would have gotten up to open, the polite thing to do, but I couldn't muster the energy. At least I had gotten myself dressed.

The door opened and our steward Andrew pushed in a cart.

"Hello, Andrew." I noted his surprised expression. Most first-class passengers couldn't be bothered remembering a steward's name.

"Mr. Cumings says you're not feeling well. I've brought you some tea that might help." He moved a small table near me and set a dish of stewed prunes on it with a spoon and a linen napkin. Three prunes in purple juice. They looked like little turds. I turned my head away.

"Maybe some tea? I find ginger helps settle the stomach."

"Don't fret about me," I said. "I'm fine, actually. My husband worries for no reason." But I was glad for the tea—and the company.

"It's my job to fret." He put a cup and saucer on the table then dropped tea leaves into a pot of hot water. "I'll wait while it steeps."

I sat up and pointed to a chair. "Sit with me. It's dreary being alone."

Andrew pulled the chair close to the table. Using silver tongs, he pinched a cube of sugar and dropped it into the empty cup.

"There's as much company as you want down in the lounge," he said.

"Oh, I don't need that sort of company. I have friends enough in New York."

"I'm sure you do." He sounded sincere. Honestly, I hadn't any close friends in the city. There were those I knew from charity work and the women at the club, but I preferred the companionship of my sons to any of them. My boys gave me such joy.

I sighed. "I'm just missing my family. We've been away nearly six weeks, and I can barely wait to get home."

"I understand," he said. "I have tots, too. Miss them terribly when I'm away."

I didn't usually focus conversation on myself, but Andrew was so friendly and had family of his own.

"Jackie, my oldest, is fourteen. Wells is the middle son, and Thayer is just eight."

"Three—that's a lucky number." He poured the tea and stirred the sugar around. "Let this cool before you try it."

The ginger smelled delicious.

"Do you sing to your children?" I asked.

"My daughter sings to me. At night, mostly. Lullabies her mother taught her."

"My boys loved lullabies when they were younger." I closed my eyes and started to hum a tune, one of my favorites.

"English, isn't it?" Andrew asked.

I nodded and began to sing. "Lavender's blue, dilly dilly, lavender's green. When you are King, dilly dilly, I shall be Queen."

The cabin door opened quietly and Bradley's voice rang in ahead of him, harmonizing with me. "Who told you so, dilly dilly, who told you so? 'Twas my own heart, dilly dilly, that told me so."

Andrew stood when Bradley was in the cabin.

"Sit, sit," Bradley said, waving a hand downward.

I beamed at him. "Hello, darling." He still made my heart flutter whenever he entered a room. He came to the bed and kissed me on the cheek.

"She's got a good voice, don't you think so, Andrew? Plays piano, too. Damn well, I must add."

"Oh, stop, Bradley," I said. "How was your match?"

"Horrid. I do believe Astor cheats."

I laughed. For all the years Bradley and I had been married, I still felt like a newlywed.

"I should be going," Andrew said. Bradley's show of affection must have made him feel awkward.

"Nonsense," Bradley said. "Stay for tea." He glanced at the table and raised his eyebrows at the single cup. "Maybe I should ring for tea?"

"I'll bring a cup right away," Andrew said.

"No, no," he said. "Stay with us a little longer." He perched on the edge of the bed. "Besides, you need to be sure Florrie drinks this concoction you've brewed."

I sipped the tea and smacked my lips. "I'm feeling better already."

"Andrew and I go back centuries, Florrie," Bradley said. "May even be related."

"Do you know your tartan?" Andrew asked.

"The Cumings clan wears the red and green plaid, a thread of white for good measure." He looked again at me. "A pity we don't have a piano in our stateroom." He puffed out his chest. "I think we need a good old Scottish song to commemorate this reunion."

"I'll see about using the piano in the lounge," Andrew said.

I shook my head. "Oh, I never entertain. I play just for family and friends."

"Then we'll go a cappella," Bradley boomed. "Shall we sing 'Donald Where's Your Troosers'?"

"Heavens, no," I gasped. "What will Andrew think of us?" I did my best to keep my husband tethered to the earth. Otherwise he might have taken flight, but that was what I loved about him.

"What I will think of you," Andrew said backing out of the room, "is that you are the best people on the ship."

But I was too beguiled with my husband to register his compliment.

"Where the bloody hell have you been?" Sid pushed his knuckles into his narrow hips. "Bells are ringing, telegrams waiting to be delivered, and Stead wants to give me a lesson in clairvoyance. I could use a little help, mate."

"Sorry, Sid," Andrew said. "Mrs. Cumings was feeling a bit manky. Had to hold her hand."

"Sure you bloody did." Sid waved an angry hand down the alleyway. "We're almost at lunch service and we haven't picked up the breakfast trays. Why these toffs won't eat in the dining saloon, I'll never know."

"No need to get touchy. I'll get the trays. You deal with the telegrams — and with Stead." Andrew grinned at Sid.

"Smashing," Sid snarled. "Just smashing. "And when you get the trays delivered to the galley, you're scheduled for lunch duty in the café."

"My pleasure, mate."

Sid shook his head. "Cunningham, you are absolutely daft."

Can She Make Good as Our Queen of Society
New York Fashionables Ask of Astor's Young Wife
New York Times, April 13

By the luncheon service, I was feeling much better. Madeleine Astor sent her maid to invite Bradley and me to sit with the Astors at Café Parisian. Madeleine was nearly half my age, but we would be neighbors when the young woman moved into the Astor house on Fifth Avenue. The four of us might as well get acquainted.

Bradley helped me into an afternoon dress, simple with high neck and sleeves—no need to put on a show for the richest couple in America. When we reached the dining saloon, Andrew showed us to a table in the verandah dining room.

"Welcome," he said, pulling out a wicker chair for me. Sun poured through the glass of large picture windows and warmed the room, and I could gaze out at the tranquil ocean on this chilly spring day. Calm water meant the ship could set a good pace and the sooner we would get home. Home—oh, how I loved that word.

Andrew placed menus in front of us. "You look as though you feel better, Mrs. Cumings," he said.

"Your prunes and ginger tea worked magic," I said. "I'm as good as new."

"I'm glad to hear it."

"Andrew—my ally!" Bradley declared. "I'm famished. I do hope the food's good today."

"Always good, sir," Andrew said.

"Could you bring two more menus, Andrew?" I said. "The Astors will be joining us."

I heard a woman whisper that J. J. Astor and his wife had arrived. Andrew pulled out a chair for Madeleine, shook out her napkin and placed it on her lap. From her swollen belly, I guessed she was five months along.

"Be a good chap and bring us some wine, will you, steward?" Astor said, barely glancing at Andrew. "White."

I wished Astor would address the stewards by name. Papa had taught me that all are equal in the eyes of God. And it cost nothing to be cordial. I looked at Andrew sympathetically, but it would have been rude to say anything against Astor. To him, Andrew was just anonymous galley staff whose sole purpose for existence was to be at his service.

Andrew brought the menus and the wine and showed the label to Astor—a chardonnay. He dribbled a taste into Astor's glass, and when there was no objection, Andrew poured for me.

"That's fine, Andrew," I said when the glass was half full. "And I would appreciate some ice."

"Of course," he said. Even though the verandah room was cool, I enjoyed the crystal tinkle of the cubes against the glass.

When Astor said, "No wine for Mrs. Astor," I saw Madeleine pout.

Andrew stood ready to take orders.

"I think I'll try the chicken a la Maryland." I was starting to feel hungry. Or maybe it was the prospect of being back in New York within the next few days.

"Just consommé," Madeleine said.

"Maddy," Astor said, "you've got to eat something."

"I'm not up to it, really."

"Nonsense." He glanced at Andrew. "Bring her some dumplings and one of those egg dishes. She missed breakfast."

Madeleine's puffy lips gave the impression she had been crying. Her father had agreed to the marriage, and the obedient schoolgirl had been thrust into wedlock with a man who was a stranger to her. And what did Astor know of her other than her youth, as if by association he would be thought youthful and virile? I supposed a rich man is able to buy even admiration. Hold onto your self-respect, I wanted to tell Madeleine. Find joy in small moments. Better yet, find yourself.

Bradley and Astor both ordered the mutton chops—Astor with baked potato and Bradley potatoes mashed. I knew my husband so well I could have ordered for him. There was a certain delight in knowledge of the man one loves.

Astor and Bradley lighted on the subject of tennis. Maurice McLoughlin was favored to win the Newport Casino tournament. Astor liked McLoughlin's serve, but Bradley told him not to count out Wallace Johnson—he had won NCAA championships when he was at Penn. Bradley knew more about tennis. It was lucky Astor didn't initiate the subject of automobiles. Bradley would have been out in left field, as they say, although he had been yearning for one. Automobiles were a bother, if you asked me—gauges, levers, and the crank to get the things started. And there was the horrible smell of petrol. I'd just as soon walk.

Andrew set down my plate first and then the dumplings and eggs for Madeleine along with a cup of consommé. When he served the men, Madeleine brought her napkin to her nose.

"Are you all right?" I asked. Madeleine shook her head.

"Oh, for heaven's sake," Astor said. "Pull yourself together, Maddy."

"It's hormones," I said. "I've been through it three times." I curled my arm around Madeleine and helped her up. "Let's take a little walk," I said. "Bring some quinine water, will you, Andrew? We'll be on the promenade. Mrs. Astor needs some fresh air."

Because of the cold, most of the windows on the promenade deck were closed, but at the far end, the glass had been slid open on one of the windows. I stood with Madeline, and we took in the brisk air. Andrew brought the goblet of water, and Madeleine took a sip and leaned on the windowsill.

"I wish we could travel forever." She sighed. "People are so awful. They say I broke up Jay-Jay's marriage. It's as if I'm some sort of horrid villain."

I pulled a hanky from my bag and handed it to Madeleine. She dabbed at her eyes. "I don't want to go back to New York."

Andrew coughed into his fist. We had forgotten to dismiss him.

"May I bring you anything else?" he said.

I raised a finger toward him. "Wait a minute, if you will, Andrew."

Madeleine took another sip of the water and then as if a gust of wind took it, the goblet slipped from her fingers and fell out the window.

I gasped. "Oh dear."

Before the goblet reached the water, the *Titanic* had passed by.

"Oh, well." I put my hand on Madeleine's back. "Your lipstick will be imprinted on the glass at the bottom of the North Atlantic forever."

"Not to worry," Andrew said. "Plenty more in the galley."

Madeleine touched her forehead with the back of her hand. "I don't feel well at all."

"Andrew, would you be good enough to tell Mr. Astor I'm taking his wife back to her cabin?" I said.

"Yes, of course. Shall I go with you?"

"No need," I said. "This is a woman's affair." I offered him a pleasant smile. "I'm sure you understand."

Champion Quoits Tourney
to take place in Cynon Valley
The Wales Aberdare Leader, April 13

In a pause between service calls, Andrew stopped at the stewards' galley. It was always warm there, the air scented with spices and meats. Cooks left soups and stews heating on the stoves, to which stewards could help themselves. Next to the gratuities, the food was the best advantage of working aboard ship.

He was sitting at the table slurping a bowl of chicken soup when Sid came in.

"What's happening in the boiler room?" he asked. Andrew had told him about the seething coals.

"All under control, mate. When I took water to the stokers late last night, they were jolly well drunk, but Sally said the fire was confined to bunker six. Should be no problem from here on." Andrew was careful not to raise an alarm.

"Let's hope so," Sid said. He ladled soup into a bowl and sliced off a hunk of bread.

Violet came in, blowing into her cupped fists. "Can it get any colder?"

"It does seem the temperature's dropping," Andrew said. "Still no heat in second class?"

"Not a degree above fifty down there." She hugged herself. "Any of that gruel left?"

"Help yourself," Sid said.

"I'd like to curl up with one of your people in first-class." She held her hands over the pot to warm them. "The heaters work up here. Have you got anyone interesting?"

"I suggest you knock on C-87," Sid offered. "Mr. Stead will keep you entertained."

"I'm afraid not," Andrew countered. "He's writing and doesn't want to be disturbed."

"There must be some generous, friendly soul." Violet got herself a bowl of the soup, wove her hands around the steaming bowl, and brought it to the table.

"I rather like the Cumings couple," Andrew said.

"Mr. Cumings is a dapper fellow, isn't he?" Sid said. "His wife is rather reserved, though."

"Florence is a capital woman." Andrew got up to fetch hot water for tea.

"Florence, is it now? You think the passengers are your friends." Violet blew on a spoonful of broth. "But once they're off the ship, they won't remember your name." She sucked from the spoon. "I once had a passenger who poured out her woes and tribulations to me. In fact, she insisted I visit her in Manhattan the next time the ship docked. Two weeks later I looked her up." Another spoonful of her gruel. "When she came to the door, I said, 'Good afternoon, Mildred.' She looked puzzled, and I realized she'd forgotten who I was and with the audacity to use her first name as if we were long lost sisters. But she let me in anyway. She was having a luncheon with lady friends. When she tried to introduce me—." She waved her spoon over the bowl. "Well, it was humiliating."

Violet frowned at Andrew. "Ship relations are temporary, Scottie. Six days. After that, it's as if you never existed."

Andrew wished she'd talk about pleasing things—like Lady Duff Gordon's line of lingerie. But Sid couldn't resist giving her a rejoinder.

"Violet, when the rest of us are gone, I've no doubt you'll live to tell the tale. So could you manage to raise your spirits just a tad?" The lad got up to refill his bowl.

Just then Jenny, the ship's cat, wandered under the table and rubbed against Andrew's leg.

"Has Jenny caught any rats today?" he asked, changing the subject.

"The rats are probably staying warm in the boiler room." Violet smirked. "But there are little two-legged rats playing quoits up on the boat deck. That's one place where classes mingle."

"Democracy at its best," Sid said from the stove.

"It's fine for the third class to mix with the second class. That line sometimes blurs," Violet said. "But woe to any second classer bold enough to cross the line into first."

"I'm no snob," Sid put in. "I don't hold anything against the underclasses."

Violet pulled her mouth into a sneer. "You're second class at best, Sid. Weren't you a shop clerk before Scottie got you the steward's job?"

Sid sat down again, careful with the contents of his bowl. "Well, yes. In fact, I was. But there were circumstances—"

She ignored him. "The middle classes are always on alert never to say or do anything that might be thought in poor taste. They'd like to pass as the smart set, but the toffs do whatever they like. In fact, they invent the social rules."

"Rather a simplification, but can't say I don't agree with you, Violet." Andrew said.

"One needs to know what one's dealing with." She dared a look at Sid.

"It's crude even to speak of class distinctions." Sid would never miss an opportunity to put Violet in her place. "One is what one is."

His tone set her off.

"You might not be so sure of yourself, Mr. Siebert, if you were part of the working class." Violet lifted her chin toward him. "They labor on the farms and in the factories and wait to be told what to do and when to do it. Just ask anyone in steerage."

"I believe anyone with sufficient ambition and imagination should be able to improve his lot in life." Sid wasn't one to end an argument without having the last word, but in this contest he had met his match.

"Exactly," Violet said. "Which is why there are seven hundred third-classers who've packed all their belongings, kissed their relations goodbye, and are on their way to America."

Andrew sighed. "I'm glad you both agree on one issue, at least." He was always the peacemaker, however aggravating the argument.

"My brother-in-law's a third-class steward," Sid said. "Charlie says steerage doesn't have it so bad. They get three meals a day, and it's decent food. Their cabins are clean and they have a smoking room and a library. No one complains there's a single bathtub for the lot of them."

Andrew leaned back in his chair. "From what I've heard the last couple nights, steerage is having a rousing good time. The Bronson girl even asked if she might join in."

"Did she?" Violet asked. "That would be highly unseemly."

"Her governess quashed it," he said.

"That was wise. I'd hate to have her spoil the party."

"Speaking of party," Andrew said, pushing to his feet, "I'd like to have a look at that game of quoits on the boat deck. Shall we go up?"

"Go ahead," Violet said. "I've got cabins to tend. A woman's work, as they say—"

"Maybe that will keep you out of trouble," Sid jabbed, getting in the last word after all.

While steward Siebert cleaned the cabin, I thought I would take Mr. Bride up on the telegram he offered to send. What could I say, keeping it simple—ten words?

HOME IN FEW DAYS. FLYING ON WATERY WINGS.
LOVE MUZ

I wanted to sign Daddy's name, too, but I had used up the word limit. Anyway, the boys would know Bradley sent his love with mine.

In the telegraph room, Harry Bride and Jack Phillips both had heads tucked over the machinery. Harry fiddled with wires and tapped on the telegraph lever.

"I have a message to go out—" I started.

"Can't you bloody well see nothing's going out?" Bride interrupted. When he recognized me, he stopped. "Very sorry, madam, but the apparatus has been down all afternoon. There's this pile of telegrams—" He bounced his fist on the stack of paper. "Orders for stocks and bonds, notes to friends and family. Nothing pressing except for Major Butt. He's expecting to hear from the U.S. President. The major's been in here three times."

"Germany's poking its nose into North Africa," Phillips added. "If things get out of hand, Butt's got to stay in touch with Taft." He wagged his head. "Taft's better off using carrier pigeons until we get this confounded thing operating again."

"Oh," I said. "I suppose mine will wait."

The ship must have been nearly in wireless range of New York, and I suspected the messages back and forth would only get busier. But Bride and Phillips were clever young men. They were sure to figure out the dilemma. They had to. If *Titanic* encountered problems, the Marconi could be the only lifeline.

I put my message on top of the others and backed out of the room without either operator aware I had gone. There was no point in telling Bradley about the wireless being down and cause him concern. Something wasn't just off kilter — it was far worse.

Andrew's scraggy mate Sid said he didn't want to catch a chill and would rather stay behind and answer bells. When he went by the wireless room, Bride yelled to him.

"Andy! Got a minute?"

"Is the thing up and running, Harry?"

"Afraid so." He handed me an envelope. "You'd better get this message to the captain. If he's not on the bridge, give it to one of the officers. Sounds urgent. I'd take it, but I'm so backed up here we'll be docked in New York before I've sent out all this drivel."

Andrew took the envelope and rang for the lift thinking he might as well say hello to Freddy, the lift steward. He was a teenager with a shock of blond hair, a good looking fellow and exuberant about his first voyage at sea.

"You going up to watch the game?" the boy asked. Seventeen, Andrew guessed.

"I am, Freddy. Have you played quoits?"

"Sure. Quite good at it, too. I wish I could go out there and show them a thing or two."

Andrew slipped the telegram into the pocket of his trousers. "I could mind the lift for a bit if you like."

The lad tilted his head, considering. "Better not. But thanks."

When the gate opened at the boat deck, Freddy said, "Odd, isn't it, that on this gigantic ship I'm confined to this one small room. Feels almost like a coffin."

Patting him on the back, Andrew said, "Keep up the good work. We'll be in New York in two shakes of a cat's tail."

Outside it was a glorious day. Not a cloud anywhere and the skyline crisp and straight as a line drawn with a ruler. Laughing youngsters pushed each other aside for a turn at tossing a rope ring over a wooden pin, cheering whenever someone got a ringer. Girls dressed in English linens tossed rings next to boys in homespun knickers. English, Irish, Armenian, American, Russian — they saw no difference. Eventually they would be taught to envy the rich and shun the less worthy.

Andrew's own father couldn't afford even a second-class ticket on the *Titanic*. Not that his Da had any desire to sail to New York. He was content to toil in wood, a proud Scotsman who had taken an honest road to make a good life. Too much money robbed the soul of any aim other than to stuff the pockets with more money, he once said. As far as Andrew was concerned, idle riches were nothing to be self-righteous about.

Money matters aside, Andrew couldn't deny the pleasure of the sun's warmth soaking into him. Strolling past lifeboats at the port railing, he stopped ahead of the wooden cutter. The cutters were the forward boats at starboard and port, suspended over the water in case of emergency. If someone were to fall overboard, a cutter could be lowered immediately. They were smaller than the other lifeboats with a capacity of forty, although Andrew thought the little boats would be overloaded with that many. Lifeboats on the starboard side were oddly numbered, even numbered at port. Number four was fixed directly behind cutter number two. He would rather have bet his life on the bigger boat that held sixty bodies, but he told himself it wouldn't come to that — not with a ship as seaworthy as *Titanic*.

He leaned on the railing and watched the glint of sun on the water. On eastbound crossings, he lost half a day. Time was arbitrary on an ocean liner. It took two days for his body to adjust to the change. When dawn was breaking in New York, it was already noon in England. At midnight in Southampton, New Yorkers were having pre-dinner cocktails. Andrew took to ignoring time altogether, eating when he felt hungry, sleeping when his duty ended, and soaking up a wee bit of sun when he had a minute.

"Extraordinary, isn't it?" Charlie Lightoller came up beside him.

"It is extraordinary, yes," he answered.

They stood, Lightoller squinting into the sun.

"How long have you been in this business, Andy?" he asked.

Andrew thought a minute. "I hardly believe it—a decade and a half."

"I shipped out at thirteen," Lights said, "after my father left."

"You were just a lad. What did your mother think?"

"Died when I was born. I never knew her. My father must've thought I could handle things on my own." He heaved a deep breath and propped his forearms on the railing. "In twenty-five years aboard these vessels, I've encountered cyclones, shipwrecks, and ship's fires. Still can't resist the Siren's song."

"I've had a few run-ins myself," Andrew said, but he didn't want to think about disaster. Not on this sail.

Lightoller went on as if he hadn't heard Andrew.

"I believe water is a woman," he said, looking down at the ocean. "Mysterious, alluring and teeming with life. She can be furious enough to throw lances of lightning, and at other times she hides pouting in a fog."

"I rather like her as she is today—sparkling and bright."

The officer emptied his thoughts aloud. "I've been in four shipwrecks. The sea isn't wet enough to drown me." He raised his index finger. "But a word to the wise— she'll swallow any other man in an instant and think nothing of it."

"I'll consider that, Lights."

Andrew suddenly thought of the telegram and pulled it from his pocket.

"Harry Bride asked me to deliver this. It came about twenty minutes ago."

Lights took the envelope and ripped it open, glowering at the paper.

"Another ice alert. Second one we've received." He surveyed the sky. "It's going to be a moonless night. The only way to spot a berg when there's no moon is by the foam at its base. But by then you're too close." He snapped a finger at the paper. "I'd better get this to the captain. Remember what I said about the wicked sea woman. Best keep on your toes, Andy."

"Aye, sir." Andrew watched him walk away. Yes, he would keep an eye out for icebergs, moon or no moon. But he wouldn't be afraid of the sea. Fear was a man's downfall. Fear paralyzed a man and turned him into prey. It wasn't the sea that was the enemy, nor the icebergs either. It was fear, and he wouldn't allow it to creep under his collar.

Even on a ship the size of *Titanic*, claustrophobia set in after a few days. I could eat only so much, and our cabin seemed to grow smaller by the hour. I prodded Bradley for a stroll on the boat deck.

Open to the sky, the still air carried a chill. I ran my eye across the straight line of the horizon and the crystalline water, relieved not to see any sign of ice. Would it pop up like a Jack-in-the-Box and stand in our way? The French called the toy *diable en boîte* because of an English prelate during medieval times who captured the devil in a boot in order to save his village. Where is the prelate who was going to save *Titanic* from a devil of an iceberg?

On the deck, a children's game was in progress—quoits, I believed it was called, a sort of horseshoes contest with rings of rope tossed toward a peg. A boy tore past on a run, a girl in a striped dress chasing him. From his newsboy cap, I deduced he was probably from steerage. Bradley was about to grab the youth and no doubt shake a finger at him for running on deck when the Bronson's governess ambled into his path, apparently unaware of the boy. At that moment the lad crashed smack into her, nearly knocking her over.

"Uf!" the governess gasped. She shoved the youth away from her as if he were a wild animal. "Watch where you're going, young man."

The boy tottered backward, panting. His hat had fallen off, and he snatched it up from the deck.

"Sorry, miss. Meant no harm."

"Your type never means harm, do they?" She drew back her gloved hand and swung forward, catching him across the cheek. The glove muffled the slap, but the boy's head snapped to the side. "Someone ought to rope and tie such a slapdash hooligan." She jeered at a huddle of steerage mothers watching the game.

I rushed to the boy and laid my hands on his shoulders. Looking into his teary eyes, I asked if he was all right. He was a handsome youth, brown hair curling over his ears and falling onto his forehead. He rubbed his cheek and flicked a look at the governess.

"There was no call for that." It was unlike Bradley to speak in such a manner to a woman, especially a woman he didn't know.

Her brows rose with indignation. "*I'm* the one who took the brunt of it." She brushed off her skirt as if the boy had soiled it. It was clear she was none the worse for wear.

I pressed my hand on the boy's back. "What is your name, young man?"

"Seamus Cleary, m'am."

"Well, Seamus Cleary, you might do well not to run on deck again." I knew how to reprimand children without hurting their feelings. With firm but gentle guidance, I hoped my own sons would turn out to be good men.

"Gee. Sure, missus." He blinked at me and walked back to his friends.

Bradley addressed the governess, waving his hand toward a deckchair. "May I help you to a seat, Madam?"

The governess raised her chin. "It's Miss. But no, thank you."

Seamus rejoined the quoits game, and we watched for a few minutes. When I hugged myself for warmth, Bradley suggested we make our way back inside. As we passed the governess, I saw the woman's spiteful glare narrow at Seamus.

"Cheeky delinquent," she muttered.

I wanted to tell her Seamus Cleary was just doing what boys do. My own boys liked to run through Central Park with reckless delight. But I dared not criticize another passenger. If I had, no doubt the governess would have accused me of being cheeky as well.

Now I realized what Emma Bronson meant when she said Oz's Wicked Witch of the West was aboard *Titanic*.

Those In Peril on the Sea
Human Ingenuity May Be Destroying Sea Gates
The Economist, Sunday, April 14

Early Sunday morning when Andrew followed his usual pattern of heading to the pool for a few laps, he was surprised to find Archibald Gracie splashing back and forth in the heated water. The gym and pool were open to guests beginning at 9:00 a.m. but Gracie was a cousin of former U.S. President Teddy Roosevelt, so policy was ignored. Andrew stood against the wall and waited while the walrus grunted through laps. Looking at the clock, he realized if he swam at all today, it would have to be late at night when passengers' bellies were too full to keep them afloat.

Gracie stopped at the pool's edge. If seas were rough, deep water could shift to the shallow end, so designer Andrew Thomas thought it best not to install a diving board.

"Say there," Gracie called to him. "Be a good chap and toss me a towel."

Gracie was a history buff who knew details—too many— about Civil War battles. The writer had sailed on the *Oceanic* on his way to Europe and had bent every ear he could catch to tell the tale of his father's demise while fighting with the Confederate army. Just the other night he had cornered Edith Craig in the dining saloon. She spent half an hour looking for an escape from his unending monolog about the battle of Chickamauga. Andrew could have rescued her, but he rather enjoyed watching her exasperation.

Passengers would be settling at tables for breakfast soon, and it was his morning to serve. He figured he'd better get into his uniform, laps or no laps.

"Should we skip the service this morning, darling?" I asked. "It's dreadfully cold."

"You've been sailing in Maine, Florrie," Bradley said. "Nothing colder than being in a boat on a reach."

"All right, but when we get back to New York, we'll attend the Unitarian service and thank the Almighty for our safe journey." I didn't mean to whine. Really, I told myself, what was there to worry about?

"Anyway, what would Reverend Thayer say if he knew you wanted to dawdle instead of singing the Lord's praises?" Bradley said. "And did I not promise your father that I would keep you on the straight and narrow?" He held up my coat and I climbed into it, glad for the fur at the neck.

"I suppose a little peace that passeth all understanding is a good idea."

He kissed my cheek. "Of course it is, my dearest."

At breakfast Andrew had distributed notices listing services. In steerage, a Catholic mass was conducted every day in German and Hungarian. In second class, mass was held in English and French and the purser led a Church of England service. Baptist minister John Harper, a second-class passenger, offered the protestant service. Harper and his young daughter were on their way to Chicago where he was to be a guest preacher at a church there, I had heard. He must have been hoping to convert the nonbelievers.

At eleven o'clock Captain Smith offered a Christian service in first class. The service was scheduled for half an hour, and worshipers stood while he read meditations from White Star's prayer book.

Andrew came in a few minutes late and I motioned for him to stand next to me.

Captain Smith asked the group to turn our prayer books to the hymn "For Those in Peril on the Sea." I liked Andrew's deep voice as he sang the verses: "Eternal Father strong to save / Whose arm has bound the restless wave / Who bids the mighty ocean deep / Its own appointed limits keep / O hear us when we cry to Thee / For those in peril on the sea."

"That was a rather gloomy hymn," Bradley whispered.

"Most hymns are," I answered.

"Really? I thought they were supposed to be uplifting."

I blinked at him. "You are what uplifts me, darling."

When the service ended, I took my husband's arm and turned him toward the grand staircase. Officer Lightoller had been standing behind us during the service.

"I'll be sure you get an extra blanket tonight," he said. "The temperature's plummeting. Could be a bitter evening."

"Any idea why it's getting so cold?" Bradley asked.

The officer rubbed his forehead. "A warm winter caused Arctic ice to break away from glaciers, and the current is carrying chunks of it into our navigational route. I suspect that has to do with the nip in the air. The water temperature this morning was twenty-eight Fahrenheit. The air will be near the freezing mark tonight."

"Could there be ice in the area?" No matter how I tried to dispel the thoughts, the floating hazards racked my brain.

"I'm sure the lookouts would have spotted it," Bradley answered quickly. He was putting up a good front. Officer Lightoller had just confirmed ice—chunks of it. He didn't say how large those chunks might be.

"The lookouts know their business," Lightoller said, "and we'll be out of harm's way by daybreak." He gave a nod and ducked his cap on his head. "Have a good afternoon, Mr. and Mrs. Cumings."

When he was gone, Bradley said, "There ought to be a lifeboat drill."

"The captain canceled the drill because of the cold. And all that work getting into life jackets, queuing up, herding us to the boat deck," I said. "I'd rather not." But even as the words were out of my mouth, I couldn't dispel the niggling sense that a lifeboat drill would be a good idea.

British Women's Tennis Champions
Charlotte Sherry and Ethel Lacomb
To Face Off at Wimbledon
London Times, April 14

When Emma Bronson rang for a hot bath to be drawn, Andrew came into her stateroom with fresh towels and looked around for her mother or her governess.

"Mother has gone to the library," Emma said. "She's found a beam of sunshine coming in on the ship's southern side. What do you call it?"

"Port side," he said.

Emma looked perplexed.

"The word 'left' has four letters," Andrew explained. "And so does the word 'port.' That's a trick to help you remember." He grinned. There was a childlike quality about her, a beguiling purity.

"Aren't you clever," she said, but he didn't believe she had listened.

"Would you like your bath drawn now?" For some women a bath was an all-afternoon undertaking. He was surprised she hadn't asked him to warm the towels for her. As for drying and dressing her, the governess would have to tend to that.

She nodded. "This cold makes me dreary. Hot water will do wonders."

Andrew went into the bathing chamber and focused on opening the taps. Passengers, especially young women, tended to get fidgety the fourth day aboard ship. With any luck, a bath would make her drowsy enough to nap under warm blankets.

Each bathing room on the *Titanic* had hot running water, an improvement over lugging tubs of hot water from the *Oceanic's* galley. He filled the tub and checked the water—not too steamy.

"All ready for you, Miss Bronson," he said. "Will there be anything else?"

She tapped a finger to her cheek. "I wonder—Madeleine Astor is so young to be carrying a baby. Goodness—I haven't even thought of such a thing."

Emma Bronson was surrounded by female guards. A fellow would have to be damned cunning to find his way under her petticoats.

"When two people marry," he offered, "such things happen."

"Have you any idea how she caught such a prize?"

"Prize?" What Andrew had seen of Astor was unmistakable snobbery. He supposed she meant wealth. Wasn't the Bronson family wealthy enough? When, he wondered, did the rich reach contentment with what they had?

"I mean such a—prosperous gentleman. Colonel Astor, I mean."

Andrew knew enough to keep his mouth shut. But when asked a question, regulations required him to give a polite answer.

"I heard the colonel first fancied his wife when he saw her playing tennis at her boarding school." Gossipmongers had a field day with tidbits of news about them. Even on the *Titanic*, when the couple took a walk on the promenade, tongues wagged.

"Oh," Emma said, her face drooping with disappointment. "I don't play tennis."

She must have wished for a fairytale of her own—Cinderella or Rapunzel. For nineteen years she had been locked away in her family vault. Within the next year or two, her parents would choose a respectable husband for her, someone who would continue her captivity.

"I'm sure you could take lessons," Andrew offered. "I hear tennis is a cheerful sport." He gave a wee bow of his head and with a formality he had practiced, he said, "Now, if you'll excuse me. Enjoy your bath, Miss Bronson."

1912 Renault Coupe De Ville
Steals Hearts of the Wealthy
Life, April 1912

With but a few days left until *Titanic* docked, I told Bradley we should take advantage of the offerings aboard the ship. I was well over my seasickness and feeling elated about sailing into New York. At dinner we ate, drank, and conversed with our fellow diners as we nibbled our way through the eleven-course meal. I ate only one of my oysters, and Bradley finished them. For the second course, I paced myself with the consommé and Bradley had cream of barley soup. I ate half the poached salmon, but Bradley pushed the salmon away and munched a cucumber in mousseline sauce. For the fourth course, we both chose the filet mignon rather than the sauté of chicken—and why not? In a few days we'd be back to Ciara's lean meals.

Bradley finished the fifth course of lamb with mint sauce—I had roast duckling—with new potatoes and creamed carrots, and Andrew was setting the sixth course in front of us, punch romaine palate cleanser. There was no hurry—we had all evening to sample the galley's sumptuous repast.

William Stead, seated at our table with four others, lectured Margaret Brown about the British Museum's controversial cursed mummy of a high priestess of the Temple of Amen-Ra.

"Every person who has come in contact with the coffin has encountered ill luck," he said. "Maiming, illness, madness, and even death. I have looked upon the face depicted on the cover and determined that it represents a living soul in torment."

For the life of her, Mrs. Brown couldn't get a word in. Once or twice she raised a finger to make a point, but Stead rambled on.

When he took a breath, Marian Thayer broke in. "Have you encountered bad luck, Mr. Stead?"

He lowered his head to glare at her. "The only unpleasantness was being declined my request to hold a séance in the room where the mummy is housed."

While Stead blathered on about the mummy, John Thayer, a quiet sort, listened. Astor went on about squash, probably without a clue that Thayer, across the round table from him, had in his day been a university baseball player and first-class cricketer on the Philadelphia team, so Bradley had said.

While Madeleine Astor folded and unfolded her napkin, Marian brought up private school for her son.

"Jack just graduated from St. Joseph's in Philadelphia," Marian said. "He'll matriculate at University of Pennsylvania in the fall. We're awfully proud, aren't we, John?"

A man of few words, her husband nodded.

"And where is your Jack?" I asked.

"He's off with a new friend this evening," Marian said. "Probably dining on the verandah."

"Our two younger sons will follow their brother to St. George's School in Rhode Island," Bradley said. "Family tradition."

"But of course the boys might develop special interests," I said. "Wells might want a school with a stronger music program, but the focus on the arts at St. George's would suit our youngest son Thayer."

"Where were you educated, Mrs. Astor?" Bradley asked.

"Spence School in Manhattan," Madeleine said.

"Not far from home, then." I hoped Bradley was paying attention. Certainly there were fine schools closer than Newport.

Madeleine dipped her head. She had waved away most of the courses and still her plate was full. "That's where I met J.J."

From what I knew, Madeleine was an excellent tennis player and an accomplished horsewoman. She was a good match for Astor's lifestyle.

She brightened. "You might consider Browning School for your boys, Mrs. Cumings. It's just a few blocks."

"A wise idea." I looked at Bradley. "They could live at home. Wouldn't that be wonderful?"

"Jackie's already at St. George's, and Wells and Thayer will go there, too," Bradley said. "St. George's will make fine men of them."

I could make fine men of them, but I wasn't going to draw Madeleine into a debate about the future of our sons.

Leaning in, I looked around Bradley. "There's quite a gathering of *Titanic* nobility in the Ritz tonight," I said, changing the subject.

"Isn't that the Wideners?" Madeleine said. "It looks to be a private party."

"Captain Smith and Bruce Ismay are at the table. Some Philadelphia millionaires, too," Bradley said. "Company business, I would guess. George Widener's father is on the board of the bank that controls funding for the White Star Line. I'm sure the captain and Mr. Ismay thought it useful to accept the Wideners' invitation."

"Don't bother about them, darling," I said. "Nothing to do with us."

Bradley glanced toward the private room where the company's dignitaries were gathered. "They invited that fellow Carter."

Andrew set down the palate cleanser in front of Bradley.

"Is it true Carter brought along his chauffeur to drive that good-looking Renault Coupé de Ville I saw being loaded into the baggage department?" Bradley asked.

"I believe so, yes. Quite a nice car," Andrew agreed.

"Twenty-five horsepower engine and crystal vases inside," Bradley said and took a sip of his wine.

"Why wouldn't the Carters enjoy freshly cut flowers when they ride?" Marian Thayer said. "Can't say I blame them." She was an attractive woman and a bubbly contrast to her husband's reserve.

Bradley pursed his lips. "I heard the Renault cost him five thousand dollars, an ungodly sum."

"Oh, but it's a pittance for the Carters," Marian said. "His father is a coal baron."

"Wouldn't mind an automobile like that myself." Bradley was not ready to let the subject go.

"What would you do with an automobile in Manhattan, Bradley?" I said. "We've no place to keep it. Besides—" I shook my head. "Don't you think it's—ostentatious?"

My husband drummed his fingers on the table. "Bert has an automobile," he said.

"Bert Marckwald lives in New Jersey. One can have that sort of thing in Short Hills."

His lips curled at a new thought. "We could drive to the summer house in Maine. Take in the countryside."

I glanced at Andrew and then blinked sweetly at my husband. I could not deny that man anything. But I could delay the inevitable, at least.

"A car would be convenient, that's true. But let's discuss your automobile when we get back to New York, shall we?"

I was relieved when Andrew redirected the conversation.

"The orchestra starts up in the Palm Room right after dinner. It should be a merry evening."

"Ask them to play 'Let Me Call You Sweetheart,'" Bradley said. "That's one of Florrie's favorites." He covered my hand with his.

"If they play it," I said, "we shall have to dance."

Bradley winked at Andrew. "In that case, we'd better order another bottle of wine."

Harry Bride darted into the saloon and shoved an envelope toward Andrew.

"Get this to Captain Smith right away," he barked. Then he turned and dashed out.

The message was sealed—in case the envelope should fall into the hands of a passenger, Andrew guessed. Never raise an alarm, no matter what mishap threatens.

Andrew took the message to the verandah dining room. Half empty wine bottles sat in silver bucket stands by the round table, a dozen guests elbow to elbow. Eleanor Widener was leading conversations, talking first to the person on one side of her and then the other. There was a hardness about her face as she challenged each guest to join the discussions. Her wideset eyes had a wildness about them, like a nocturnal animal that can see through the dark. Andrew stood at the edge of the table, stiff under her steely stare.

Captain Smith had a glass of water in front of him. With the ice warnings, it made sense he would want his wits about him tonight. Andrew slipped the envelope beside his plate. When the captain unfolded the paper, Andrew saw it was a notice from the *Californian* and read the words, "Ice ahead. Advise slowing speed." Smith passed the paper to Ismay, who looked at the message then slid it into his coat pocket.

Andrew waited for instructions. None came. Slowing down would use more of the ship's dwindling fuel supply, but to stay the course with ice warnings was not just careless—it was negligent. The words were in his mouth, but he held them there and let them melt on his tongue.

He cleared his throat. "I'll call for the first officer." Someone had to issue an order, and Murdoch took the helm when Captain Smith was busy elsewhere.

A robotic smile slit Ismay's face, a look meant for the dinner guests rather than for Andrew. "That will not be necessary," he said.

Captain Smith cocked his head. He looked terribly uncomfortable.

"Perhaps we should—" he began.

Eleanor Widener broke in. "Is anything the matter, Captain?"

Ismay answered for him. "Nothing to concern yourself with, Mrs. Widener." He lifted his palm toward Andrew. "That will be all, steward."

Halting the engines would mean a delay in getting to New York. With so many influential men and women aboard, a delay was out of the question. In the spring seasons when *Oceanic* had received ice alerts, the captain stopped the engines for the night and let the ship drift. But Ismay had a lot to prove with his investment in the *Titanic*. So, with or without the captain's agreement, the ship forged into the darkness at twenty-two knots.

After the roast squab, the cold asparagus vinaigrette, the foie gras, French ice cream, fruits and cheese, coffee and port, Bradley's lids drooped. He leaned back in his chair as if to release the stiff dickey pressing on his very full belly. But tea was being served in the Palm Room as the orchestra started, and I wanted to hear the music.

"If you insist. Music is night's reverie, my dear," Bradley said, taking my hand.

The Palm Room had a tropical look, even though the temperature outside was anything but. Dressed to the nines— men in tuxedos, women in silk and lace down to their ankles— it was a night tinkling with gaiety, a fitting evening to show off one's prosperity.

Men danced their charming partners to "Shine on Harvest Moon" and "Moonlight Bay." When the band played "Put Your

Arms Around Me, Honey," Bradley led me in a perfect two-step around the floor. I could hear Margaret Brown singing in her booming contralto, "Huddle up and cuddle up with all your might." Mr. Gracie even took a twirl with young Emma Bronson, and I was happy her petulant governess had taken the night off. We were more than halfway across the ocean, sailing on a monarch of a ship and mingling with the world's most prominent people. I refused to believe anything could darken this brisk and starry night.

It was nearly eleven when Mr. Stead retired to his cabin, but Major Butt, George Widener and several other men retreated to the smoking room. Warren Craig joined several men in a card game, and his wife went to their chamber alone. Gladys Bronson led her daughter off to bed, and still I wanted to linger in the gaiety.

"We have tomorrow, my darling," Bradley said.

"I suppose we do. I've been wishing to be home, but now with just two days left on the cruise, I want to savor each moment."

His lips by my ear, he whispered, "You'll savor it better with a good night's rest."

In actuality, I knew it was he who needed the rest. And after the socializing, the food and the wine, I had to concede.

"All right," I said, "but hasn't it been delightful?"

Andrew had never before wanted a cruise to be over as much as he did this one. A melancholy threatened to strangle him. He was restless and doubted he could sleep. Sid was on duty to answer bells, but there probably wouldn't be many requests. Most of the first-class passengers had worn themselves out dining and dancing. He thought a walk on the deck might relax him before he headed to his bunk.

Outside, the air bit his cheeks. Flickering light from thousands of stars speckled the heavens and reflected off the ocean. He wondered why there was no moon. The navigators talked about a phenomenon called refraction when light reflects off smooth water, making it seem like a mirror. Stars sparked on the water's surface almost as clearly as if he were looking at the sky. This sort of night could make a bloke think something was out there that wasn't — or the other way around.

He heard a splash a ways off — probably a dolphin or bluefish — but in the darkness he saw neither the animal nor the ripples left after its sounding. Even large objects were undetectable on such a night — whales, for example. Or icebergs.

The engines rumbled beneath his feet and he listened to the faint swoosh of the ship cutting its way through the Atlantic. The sound of happy squeezebox music sawed into the night. Hands clapped and voices hooted and hollered. The ruckus was coming from steerage. While first class was settling down, third class was revving up.

The toffs would probably sleep in tomorrow morning, so what was the harm in having a look?

After days in close quarters, a group of people tend to give up their individuality and become like-minded, taking on a single shared intelligence. Obvious with the first-class millionaires, most all of whom sought to be recognized and revered, the single-mindedness was also true of steerage passengers. What they lacked in refinement they made up for in jollity. Jackets cast off, men exposed their suspenders, sleeves rolled up to the elbows. Hatless women lifted skirts above ankles in high-stepping footwork. Locking elbows, they twirled each other, some falling dizzy to the floor. Strands of sweat-soaked hair tumbled about elated faces. Kozlov's squat-kick dance drew a circle of hand-clappers egging him on. Those who weren't playing music or dancing swigged from glasses of ale. The air reeked of beer and sweat.

Among the dancers, an auburn-haired woman shuffled in quick circles with a slender man, their faces contorted with laughter. Violet Jessup was a blur of movement, her arm linked with Charlie Savage's. Stewards dancing? In all his ocean crossings, Andrew had never seen the like. And yet, the music seeped into him, too, and he found his foot tapping to the rhythm. The tune went on and on, as if the musicians were boosted by the energy in the room. He wondered if the party would last through the night, the merrymakers exhausting themselves before the sun rose over the watery horizon.

He was about to head to the glory hole when Violet looped him around.

"Scottie!" she panted. "What brings you down to the slums?" She wiped the back of her wrist across her damp forehead.

"I might ask the same of you, Violet," he said. Charlie nodded a sweaty greeting.

"Just letting off some steam," she said. "Come join us. Or are you afraid you'll catch some horrible disease from the deprived and depraved?"

"And Violet'll carry it up to second," Charlie said. "Then it'll creep up to your first-class toffs. We'll have to sink the ship to stem the contagion."

"Don't be ridiculous," Andrew said. "Bruce Ismay swears the *Titanic* is incapable of sinking." He was trying to make a joke, but Violet missed the point.

"Then we'll set fire to it." She did a little jig as if her feet were afire.

"Violet, have you been drinking?" he asked.

"Me? No—just having some good fun. Life's short, Scottie. Loosen your collar and for an hour forget about those stuffed shirts upstairs."

"Those stuffed shirts will be up and ringing their bells in the morning, and I'd better be ready for their beck and call."

"We'll be in New York in a couple o' days," Charlie put in. "You can catch up on your rest then."

Violet didn't wait for an answer. She wrenched Andrew onto the dance floor, tugging him into a two-step. The deck vibrated as feet stomped in rhythm with fiddle bows scraping over the strings. A current surged through him and fatigue fell like a heavy cape from his shoulders. He looked at Violet's pretty, jubilant face. If she wanted to dance, he would catch this fever and dance with her. Pulling her toward him, he pressed his hand to her waist. Her dress was dank from the heat of her skin. He wove her through the others, spiraling her around. Once she nearly stumbled, but he caught her and lifted her off her feet.

"Goodness, Scottie," she panted. "Full of surprises, aren't you?"

He laughed. How long had it been since he'd let his hair down and had some fun? When the fiddlers took a break, he caught his breath.

"That's it for me," he told Violet, pushing her toward Charlie.

"Spoilsport," Charlie chided.

"Enjoy the party," Andrew told them. "I'm bushed."

When he walked out onto the deck, a scent in the air stopped him. It was like earth after a downpour of rain. His mind must have been playing tricks on him. The ship was in the middle of an ocean and solid ground was miles away in every direction, even miles below. Fatigue must have been getting the better of him.

Lying on his bunk that night, Andrew thought of Emily. If she had been in steerage, he'd have stayed up all night with her. His chest ached to hold her again. He could almost feel her silken hair against his cheek. He remembered brushing a strand of that hair from her forehead, and then he kissed her there, above the eyebrow. As they lay together, her hand on his chest, the curve of her body matched his as if they had been molded for each other. He drifted to sleep that way, imagining her wrapped in his arms.

The Greatest Ship Hits Iceberg
The Patriot, Monday, April 15

"Are you coming to bed, Florrie?" Bradley was in his pajamas and robe.

"In a few minutes." I sat on the bed and started to remove my shoes. Bradley would have to help me out of the dress.

Then I felt a jolt. I stopped, bent toward my feet. Was it my imagination?

The unearthly screeching that followed sounded like the cry of a forest animal caught in the death clutch of a predator. Or it could have been a thousand creaking hinges. In the quiet of the still night, I thought I detected a popping as well—as if metal were being torn apart. A natural inclination when hearing threatening noises is to run from the danger. But where does one run when in the middle of a ship's cruise miles from safe ground?

"What the devil?" Bradley said. He had heard it, too. I wasn't imagining.

I stood up, grabbing the table edge. Out the porthole I saw a tall sail passing, gleaming in the reflection of the ship's lights.

A ghostly white. An unnatural white.

What was a sailboat doing so close to the *Titanic*—and in the north Atlantic?

With no wind.

When the sail passed, blackness closed in.

Thoughts ran through my mind. A propeller had gotten fouled somehow. Or a bolt on a smokestack had loosened a metal plate that had fallen to the deck. What else would cause a jarring like that?

A *diable en boîte*. Bradley was right—the devil had escaped the box.

Hard as I tried to erase the idea of icebergs from my mind, the reality was inescapable. There had been warnings. Ismay and Captain Smith knew the ship was headed for trouble. Maybe they expected to push a few lumps of ice out of the way. But what I had seen was more like a frozen mountain. Not even *Titanic* could shove a mountain aside.

There was a sudden whoosh of escaping steam and then no noise at all. Not a sound.

"The engines have stopped," Bradley said.

Slow and low I said, "You'd better get back into your clothes, Bradley."

Andrew wasn't sure if he had slept for minutes or hours when he was shocked awake by what sounded like a band of wailing banshees. Surely the party in steerage hadn't turned into a riot. No—he recognized the scraping of metal. He had heard it the night of the Kincora accident. But there was no fog tonight and no other ships in the navigational route.

Wide awake now, he fumbled into his tweeds because he was not on duty. When he went to the hallway, Stead was standing outside his cabin.

"What's happened?" he asked.

"I'm not sure," Andrew said honestly.

"I saw it," Edith Craig panted, still dressed in her evening clothes. "It must have been fifty feet high. Blue—no, silver. I went to the smoking room to tell Warren. Was it an iceberg?"

If she saw an iceberg from C deck fifty feet above water level, the thing must have been the height of a ten-story building. And who knew how much of it was hidden underwater?

"An officer told Warren that we struck some ice but we're on our way again," Edith said. "Funny that I don't hear the engines. The officer said the watertight compartments are closed and there's no danger of any kind." She caught her breath and blinked. "Warren went back to his card game."

George Widener appeared with a life vest buckled around him.

"Aren't you a nervous fellow," Edith said, laughing at him.

Widener interrupted her. "There's been an order for all passengers to put on life jackets." His face was stony.

Edith swiveled to Andrew. "Is that true?"

"I'll find out what the situation is. Stay where you are, all of you." Now he was giving the orders. Suddenly everything had turned on its head.

He started toward the grand staircase when Charlie Lightoller stopped him. Charlie's words tumbled over each other.

"Wake your passengers, get their life jackets on them, and take them up to the boat deck."

"How bad is it?" Andrew asked.

"Bad enough."

He read alarm in Lightoller's eyes. The damage was serious. But he had to stay composed. He had to see to his passengers.

"Tell them there's no danger," Lights said. "Tell them we're simply taking precautions."

Andrew frowned at the second officer. "Level with me, Charlie."

Lights blew out a breath. "Six of the watertight compartments have been torn open. Water's pouring in, spilling into the transverse bulkheads. That's all you need to know."

"I need to know the truth," Andrew said.

Lights hesitated, his eyes searching Andrew's. "We could've stayed afloat with five compartments flooded, but not six." He shook his head. "We're going down."

Andrew swallowed. There were sixteen lifeboats and twenty-two hundred souls aboard. He couldn't do the exact math that quickly, but he knew a lifeboat's capacity was sixty-four. They couldn't save everyone.

"How long?" he asked.

"I don't know." Lightoller's face was blanched. "Less than two hours."

"Two—" Andrew started.

Lightoller looked past Andrew at the passengers waiting for news, for instruction. "Now get moving," he said.

As Andrew was about to turn, Sid ran through the alleyway carrying a hunk of ice the size of a cricket ball.

"Ice crashed all over the top deck," he blurted. "Some fools are putting it in their drinks. He belted out a crazy, nervous laugh. "A few of the second-class drunks are playing football with chunks of it. Did you see it? The thing was taller than the ship's funnels, and shiny."

The lookouts must have alerted the bridge of the berg because Andrew felt the ship turn hard to port. If *Titanic* had hit straight on, they might have had a chance. But it was too late for second guesses.

"Never mind that," Andrew said. "Help me with the life vests. You tend to the Bronson ladies and Daisy Bush. Then get them up to the boat deck. I'll take care of the others."

Sid froze and stared at him. "It's just practice—right, Cunningham? I mean, it's just a drill."

In a split second enough was communicated between them. This was no drill.

"I hear voices in the hallway," I said, thinking everyone was as curious as I.

When Bradley opened the cabin door, I saw stewards rousing passengers — Archibald Gracie, Mr. and Mrs. Strauss, Madeleine Astor's nurse, some in nightclothes and others still in gowns and tuxedos. The Astors' staterooms were on the port side near the Wideners and Thayers.

"Get them to the boat deck — port side," Andrew called to the other stewards. "Keep everyone together."

Mr. Stead had on his overcoat. "I'll go and see if I might be of help," he said.

"Help with what?" Bradley asked. No one paid him any attention.

"Your life vest, Mr. Stead," Andrew said.

"I'll come back for it," he called over his shoulder.

Behind Bradley, I glanced into Stead's cabin and saw the floor, the table, and the bed littered with papers. He must have been working on his speech.

"What's happened?" Bradley asked Andrew.

"Get dressed. Warm clothes." He edged past Bradley and pulled two life jackets from above the closet. "Put these on, both of you. And be quick. We're wanted on the boat deck immediately."

While Bradley climbed back into his evening clothes, he grumbled about why in damnation the captain had changed his mind about the lifeboat drill. I fastened my shoes back on and struggled into my coat. I wished I had time to change into my wool suit, but we were ordered to hurry. Andrew helped me get the vest over the coat. The life jackets were made of bulky cork, and I felt as if I were climbing into a straitjacket.

Tying on the life vest, I grumbled, "I can't move in this thing."

"All you need to move for the moment is your feet, Florence." Andrew addressed me by my first name. He was no longer my steward — he may have been my protector.

"Do as Andrew says, and let's hope this is much ado about nothing." Bradley was buttoning himself back into his tuxedo as if whatever was about to befall would call for formalities.

When I stepped into the hallway, Edith Craig was clutching her coat closed, looking as if a brute had clamped its paws around her. She had put on her hat, and the feathers wiggled over her head. Her husband was probably still in the lounge.

"Won't it be awfully cold on the boat deck?" she asked.

"Yes," Andrew told her. In no mood for a chat about the weather, he shoved her life vest at her. "Now put this on."

Bradley looked at me. "We'd better go with the others."

"Of course." I didn't want to leave. The cabin was warm. There were my things, clothing and toiletries I had carefully packed. Souvenirs I had bought in France to bring back to the boys — Voltaire's *Candide* in French for Jackie. He was on his way to mastering the language through his school classes. French candies for Wells, which I would insist he share with his younger brother. Several postcards for Thayer, and an églomisé box for myself. I started searching for the bag with the gifts. Had I put it in the wardrobe?

"Florrie, this is not the time," Bradley said. "Leave everything."

Yes — but leave for what? For where? I had removed my brooch — my grandmother's diamond one, and before I went out I plucked it up and dropped it into my coat pocket.

Andrew and Siebert led the way up the grand staircase. The polished mahogany shone under the electric lights. I noticed fingerprint smudges on the banister and thought the cleaners ought to have polished the wood. What absurdity that seemed now.

When we reached the landing, the clock began striking midnight — the witching hour. I had read my sons a folktale about the witching hour. The story went that in the middle of the night the veil between life and death thins and spirits cross into the realm of the living. When was the last time I was up at this time of night? And what realm was Andrew taking us to?

I caught a glimpse of Edith Craig dashing toward the lounge, no doubt looking for her husband. Andrew yelled after her, "Meet us at the port bow." I doubted the woman knew port from starboard or even bow from stern, but hopefully she and her husband would find us.

I almost laughed at how seriously the crew was taking this exercise—if that's what it was. Nice of them, though, to schedule the drill for just after passengers were in their cabins rather than waiting until we were sound asleep. In dire circumstances, I knew the directive was always women and children first. Men followed if there was space. There had to be space—I couldn't possibly leave Bradley.

Titanic, Greatest Steamer,
is Afloat, Badly Battered
The Tampa Daily Times, April 15

The parade of stewards and passengers passed the Marconi office, and Andrew saw Harry Bride bent over his machine, tapping away.

"Give it up, Harry. Let's go," Andrew said.

"Cape Race needs to move their arses," Bride said. "We're not in range of New York—we've got to forward messages through them."

"Cape Race in Nova Scotia?"

Sparks spoke trancelike, quick, every cell of his being focused on the machine. "The *Californian* kept interrupting—some rubbish about an icefield, but our lookouts never saw a bloody thing except for that one berg we grazed."

"We didn't just graze the berg, Harry. It tore us open."

If he heard Andrew, Bride ignored him.

"I'm trying to rouse the *Californian*. She's five miles out and could be here within the hour." Bride tossed a hurried look toward the door. "They've been sending warnings for two days and now they're not answering our signals. Probably all asleep." His hand shook as he waved Andrew away. "You go on. I've got to get through to them."

"Don't be a hero, Harry," Andrew said.

"I'm no hero," Bride answered. "I'm trying to save my own arse."

Before he bolted off, Andrew heard Bride tapping frantically, talking into the mic. "Hello, hello! Wake up, you sots!"

From the boat deck the heavens twinkled like diamonds thrown against a black curtain. Below, the sea heaved slow breaths. Andrew made out what looked like a ship's lights in the distance. Must have been the *Californian*. It was past midnight now, and most of her crew had probably turned in.

The berg must have popped up out of the water like a monstrous buoy. Or else Satan himself tossed it out of hell.

Beyond the bow, Andrew saw a strange glittering stretching from port to starboard. What the *auld mahoun* was it—what they called a mirage in the desert? Maybe just starlight reflecting on the water—or maybe the ice field the crew of the *Californian* had warned about.

With no moonlight, the stars were like silver fireworks. How could nature be so glorious with so many lives at risk? One of the songs the orchestra had played that very night came back to him. "We were sailing along," it went, "on Moonlight Bay." Was Andrew crazy to think such a happy thought when around him was chaos? He needed to keep his mind in the moment.

"Port side?" Sid asked.

"Is that what I said?" There were boats on either side, yes, but a steward shouldn't forget details, even under pressure.

At that moment Violet broke between them, her life vest around her.

"Cut the chitchat, you blokes," she said. "We've got a situation on our hands."

Leave it to Violet to slice through crisis with her saber wit.

"I'm getting my folks into starboard boats," she spat out.

As she was turning to leave, Sid swung his arms around her.

"That's for good luck," he said.

Violet pulled away and took a second to catch her breath. "Well," she said, "take care of yourselves, blokes." She waved and was sucked into the throng.

"Port side," Andrew said, remembering.

Lifeboat number four was thirty feet long, I guessed. Nine feet wide and quite deep, made of wood painted stark white. About the size of our sailboat in Maine. If a mast and sail were stowed aboard, at least I knew how to rig out a sailboat. Secure the halyards before raising the sail. The last two feet of the mast are the most difficult to hoist and I may need to ask for help, especially with cold fingers. I had to remember to keep my head out of the way of the boom. I doubted there would be a jib but I wouldn't have bothered with it. Anyway, what was the use of a sail without wind? I had never experienced conditions like tonight—the air so still I wiggled my toes to keep them from going numb.

Andrew pointed to number four. "You'll find flares, blankets, and some provisions in the bow," he said.

"You sound as if we might be in the lifeboat for a long spell," I said. "Anyway, I don't intend to get into one of those deathtraps."

"They're called lifeboats for a reason, Florrie," Bradley said. "*Titanic* is the deathtrap. Do as Andrew says."

I thought of the purser's comment about eternity. I wasn't ready to face eternity—not tonight.

Four pine benches were bolted across the gunwales—for rowers, I guessed—not enough seating for the number of people who would have to crowd on. Some could sit on the bow and stern platforms but others would have to stand or settle on the bottom, which would be wet from rowing. Ten boats on the port side and I guessed as many at starboard. Twenty boats for so many people.

"Heaven help us," I murmured. I tried to swallow my outrage even though at that moment I wanted nothing more than to slap Bruce Ismay across his smug face. Hate is heavy, my father had said. Love is light. But this was not the time to forgive. To live was all that mattered. To live for my family.

Andrew, Lightoller, Gracie, and Stead helped women board. Edith Craig and Emma Bronson teetered and swayed trying to get into the boat in their long dresses and high heels. Even holding the men's hands, boarding the lifeboat was a lost cause.

"Siebert, Cunningham—get them all down to A deck," Lightoller ordered. "We'll hold the boat even with the windows to make climbing aboard less of a gymnastic feat."

"Is that wise?" I said. Women were loading into other boats, some of them looking awkward as they struggled, lifting skirts to heave one leg over the side. Lowering number four would take time—maybe time we didn't have.

"Follow Andrew," Bradley said, and he took my arm.

The stewards were like pied pipers leading children away from Hamelin—except the piper's brood were never heard from again.

Around us, men and women raced by, searching for a source of salvation—one that didn't exist on a sinking ship. A man with a washed-out face turned his head as if searching for deliverance. He cried out for a life vest, his protruding eyes making him look like someone possessed by a demon. Two women started in one direction, halted abruptly, and turned the opposite way, fighting past a tide of other passengers, a turbulent river of humanity.

"Keep calm," someone yelled above panicked voices. But calm with doom pressing down on our heads was too much to ask for.

The windows on A deck were closed against the cold. When Andrew tried to slide one back, it wouldn't budge.

"It's painted shut," I said.

Astor shoved Andrew out of the way and pushed his weight against the slider. It wouldn't give. Bradley stepped forward and pounded on the frame. Still nothing.

"We'll all have to go back up to the boat deck," I said. Now even in the midnight cold, I felt hot, trapped, and I struggled to breathe as minutes ticked by.

Young Harry Widener spoke up. "I'll have a try." He had a large book in his hand. I suspected it was one of the precious first editions he had purchased in Europe. The name Charles Dickens was stamped in gold letters on the leather binding.

Harry swung the Dickens volume back and struck the window casing with it. Once. Twice. On the third hit, the frame came loose, but the book fell apart and pages of *Hard Times* scattered over the deck. His face held a stuporous expression, as if he had committed accidental murder.

Andrew struggled to hold his balance as the deck tilted. He grabbed a deck chair, folded it, and placed it under the window to use as a step. Left foot on the chair, he put his right leg out the window and into the boat to hold it steady. Then he reached for Eleanor Widener's hand.

"What about Harry?" she said.

"He'll stay with me, Ellie," George Widener said.

"You'll both take another boat, won't you?"

"They say there's another ship a few miles off," he said. Then he added, "We'll be fine."

"Don't worry, Mother," Harry said. "Just do as you're told."

Harry Widener had the same demeanor as his father — straight posture, the air of decorum even in the face of calamity. Not a sign of trepidation on their chiseled faces.

The Widener maid boarded next, followed by Gladys Bronson and Daisy Bush.

"Hasn't this drill gone too far?" Gladys Bronson was indignant.

"It's not a drill, Mrs. Bronson," Andrew told her.

"There's no real danger, is there?" she said. "We'd be safer aboard ship than dangling over the sea in a lifeboat."

"In you go," Lightoller said, nearly shoving her into the boat.

Daisy Bush followed her. "I smelled it," she said. "I've been in an ice cave. I know what ice smells like."

For once, Daisy Bush may have been right. The scent last night, like the air after a hard rain—it must have been ice. The ship had been surrounded by bergs.

Gracie was at Emma Bronson's side helping her climb over the gunwale.

"Wait!" Emma cried out. "I have to go to the purser."

She must have put money in the safe. A few hundred dollars was a mere trifle to the Bronsons. So many were about to lose so much more.

"It's too late for that," Gracie said. "Water has flooded the boiler rooms and the mailroom as well."

Andrew guessed the baggage compartments were underwater, too—along with William Carter's precious Renault and millions worth of valuables—valuables the sea would claim within the next minutes.

People rushed by, pushing, heads twisting, calling directions, no one sure where to go, what to do, a wild chorus of voices. A woman yanked a crying child by the collar, hurrying him along to who knew where. The only safe place on a sinking boat was another boat, and even that was questionable reasoning.

Above them, Andrew could hear the band. They had come out onto the deck and the melody of "By the Light of the Silvery Moon" reached him. But there was no moon, not even a slim crescent of silver. When they started in on "Good Night Ladies," Andrew thought of the irony. This was not at all a good night. But they were cheerful melodies meant to quiet the rising dread. The band members were all men and would not be allowed into lifeboats, so they played on.

Where had Sid gotten to? He was probably looking for Charlie Savage. Andrew hoped they had both found a way off the ship.

Astor had hold of his wife's arm with one hand, the Airedale's leash with the other.

"Jay-Jay," Madeleine pleaded, "come with me." The ermine coat fell to her ankles and hung open over her swollen belly.

Astor leaned toward Lightoller. "My wife is in a delicate condition," he said. "I should stay with her."

How was it that a ship's officer is given the sovereignty to bestow a pardon on one soul and sentence another to death? And how does the officer summon the nerve to pass a sentence on a man like John Jacob Astor?

"I'm very sorry, Colonel Astor," Lightoller said. "You know the directive."

Astor passed his wife's arm to Lightoller, and Andrew helped her board. The Airedale stayed with her husband.

"You're in good hands, Maddy," he said to his wife. "Be brave. I'll meet you in the morning."

From what Andrew had seen of her, Madeleine Astor was a woman used to getting her way, but on a sinking *Titanic* she was beaten.

"Take a seat—and stay there,"' Lightoller yelled to her. Andrew saw her lips quiver and then pout. He couldn't tell if she was afraid for her husband or angry about being told what to do.

John Thayer helped his wife up onto the makeshift step after two women from second class. A ship in trouble takes no measure of social status. When Marian Thayer was in the boat, she turned toward the tangle of passengers shoving each other along the promenade.

"What about Jack?" she asked.

Thayer lifted his head to look over the helpless multitude. Jack Thayer had probably gotten swallowed by the hordes trying to board the boats. He was only seventeen, but he might be resourceful enough to save himself.

"I'll see to Jack," Thayer said. "We'll be all right, Marian."

"Do be careful," she said.

"Of course I will. Now sit tight and don't fret."

Andrew was used to witnessing intimate moments between passengers. Rather than being embarrassed, he had practiced letting their emotions flow through him as if he were a screen in a breeze. If he had absorbed every sorrow, every regret, every passionate embrace, he would have been a wreck. But tonight, when two thousand lives faced disaster, he had his own existence to think about. For the Edwardian men, dying was nobler than the shame of cowardice. For Andrew, whatever means it took to stay alive was more than bravery — surviving depended on the force of his will.

"You may need this, Edie." Warren Craig broke through the crowd and shoved a wad of bills at his wife.

Edith broke into a sob. Her husband's gesture was as loving as an heir to a family fortune knew how to be. But money wasn't much use to a woman in a lifeboat. Craig must have thought his cash could change the course of the universe. He was a ridiculous man.

The fashion Edith was wearing had a skirt cinched close around the ankles, but with the tight skirt she couldn't step into the boat. Before Andrew could decide how to be of help, Colonel Gracie stepped forward and together they lifted her and heaved her in like a sack of grain.

"I'll meet you in New York," Craig said. There was no kiss, no goodbye.

"You'll hurry, won't you?" she called. Craig's response was lost in the shouting.

Arthur Ryerson assisted his wife, her maid, and their two daughters into the boat. Andrew had heard the Ryersons were hurrying back from a European vacation to the funeral of their son, a Yale student who had been killed in an automobile accident. Already they were in mourning, and a second tragedy was about to tear them apart.

When their younger son John tried to board, Lightoller held him back.

"Women and children only," he said.

Ryerson stepped forward, still in his tuxedo. "He's only thirteen," he said. "He's just a boy."

"Lights—" Andrew remembered turning thirteen, how excited he was to be a teenager. Barely five feet tall then, he wouldn't branch up another foot for several more years. He had dreams of being a competitive swimmer, a sailor in the Royal Navy, even a ship's captain. Always the sea played into his imaginings.

Lights looked into the man's pleading eyes. "All right," he said, "but no more boys."

Andrew watched Ryerson nod to his son, giving permission to go with his mother and sisters. May you live to make your dreams reality, young man, Andrew thought.

Florence Cumings stood with her husband against the metal wall of A deck.

"Florence," Andrew said, "let's get you into the boat."

She held Bradley's arm but didn't move.

"What about the third-class passengers?" she said. "Only first and second-class women are boarding the lifeboats."

Andrew held her eyes. He didn't need to speak what she knew. The third-class section was locked every night to keep the riff-raff from wandering to the upper decks and spreading their contagion of poverty among the elite. They had paid the fare expecting a safe passage, and their souls were as valuable as those of the men and women wearing tuxedoes and silks. It was not their fault the captain and Ismay had made fatal decisions that sentenced them to certain death unless they were released from their steerage prison.

"We're running out of time, Florrie," Bradley said.

Her eyes shot bullets at Lightoller. "I'm not getting into a lifeboat until the third-class compartment is opened."

"Mrs. Cumings," he started. "Please be reasonable."

"I have never been more reasonable. Release them immediately."

First Officer Murdoch materialized next to Lightoller. He was a Scotsman with years of maritime experience under him, a trustworthy fellow.

"Water's coming in—probably forty feet every second." Murdoch yelled at Lightoller over the screaming of voices. "The mailroom and squash court are flooded, and they can't hold off third class any longer." He pressed two fingers to his forehead, remembering his duty. When he spoke again, his voice broke. "She's—" He cleared his throat. "We're going down—within minutes."

Third class—Charlie Savage with them. Hundreds of them in steerage.

"Lights—" Andrew started. "Mrs. Cumings is right. We've got to unlock the gates."

Lightoller pressed his lips into a tight line. Then he pointed to Murdoch.

"Let them out," he said. "And be quick about it."

Bradley plumped the fur collar of my coat around my neck.

"Now go, darling, and keep warm," he said. "There's not much time."

"I'm not leaving you, Bradley."

He pressed his hands to my shoulders and searched my face.

"You have to think of the boys." His voice caught.

The boys—his boys. The thought he would never see them again, never tell them how much he loved them, tore at my heart. My legs threatened to collapse and I leaned against him. My breath came in sips and I held back tears. But of course he would get through this ordeal—he had to. At least at this hour the boys were tucked safely into their beds, and for that I felt overwhelming gratitude.

"You'll get in the next boat," I said.

His face did not reflect the inevitability of what lay ahead, the horrible inevitability I could not allow myself to believe.

"I'll be with you again soon, my darling Florrie."

My eyes bored into his. "Give me your word."

"I promise—I will join you soon."

As Andrew helped me into the boat, I turned back to my husband. His expression of confidence—even if it was a lie— masked any other emotion. I had never been more proud of him.

"No matter what happens," Bradley called to me, "you will always be the one true love of my life."

I refused to lose my composure—no crying, no clinging. I would show Bradley I, too, could be brave under grim circumstances. What a fortunate woman I was to have had him by my side all these years—how many years was it? I couldn't think. Time melted into one moment—this moment, these seconds, the ultimate instant of goodbye.

A shot whistled three times and flares rose into the dark sky. The captain must have ordered the distress signals. If Harry Bride had gotten through, the *Californian* should have been here by now. Why would the ship ignore distress signal flares? Captain Smith set off three more flares. Surely the ship could see them, but its lights came no closer. Most likely because of the ice her captain had ordered the ship to cut its engines and wait for daylight. A chunk of glacier could do little harm if it bumped a drifting ship. Why in the name of all that's holy had Captain Smith listened to Ismay?

Andrew pulled his attention back to the lifeboat. William Carter's wife was ushering her eleven-year-old son to boat number four.

"I said no more boys," Lightoller growled.

Lillian Carter jerked off her hat and shoved it onto her son's head.

"This is my daughter," she said. "She's coming with me."

With an exasperated wave of his hand, Lights signaled them to board. Officer Lightoller — executioner one minute, redeemer the next.

Stead reached for Ida Straus's arm, but she drew back.

"Go on, Ida my dear." In his late sixties, Isidor Straus's beard was frosting in the cold air. He was the owner of Macy's department store, a New York landmark that would prosper even without him.

Straus must have forgotten the wire spectacles he always wore, and he squinted toward his wife. In that moment Andrew saw himself as Straus's age, Emily holding his arm — if he lived that long. If he lived at all.

"Charlie," Andrew said, "protocol aside, might Mr. and Mrs. Straus both board the boat?"

"Under the circumstances — " Lights started.

"No — I won't go before other men," Straus insisted.

"And I will not leave my husband," Ida Straus said. "In all our years of marriage, we have not been separated. As we have lived, so we will die." She shrugged out of her fur coat and draped it over her maid's shoulders.

"Take this, Ellen," she said. "I won't be needing it. Now go get into a boat at once." She tucked her arm back into her husband's and they stood against the officers' deckhouse, watching together while other passengers were loaded.

There were now forty people in the boat. Lights put quartermaster Walter Perkis in charge and told him to take a couple other seamen with him to row.

Andrew could have rowed. By God, he could have rowed his heart out. He grabbed Lightoller's arm. "The boat's not full, Lights."

"Most of the others are gone," he said through gritted teeth. "We've got to get this one away.

Lifeboat number four started to lower and then lurched to a stop. I grabbed the gunwale to keep from falling backward and tumbling onto my rear end. The boat was still a long way from the inky water. Even with light reflecting off the surface, it looked like the gate to hell, open and ready to welcome the small boat and its passengers into its fiendish underworld.

Andrew struggled with the tackle holding the lifeboat aloft. Mr. Gracie tried his hand—no luck. The lines were twisted. When Officer Lightoller yanked on the ropes, the boat jerked but refused to give way.

"They're hung up on the sounding spar," Andrew yelled.

"Then free them, for pity's sake," Marian Thayer shouted. "And be quick about it."

I recalled the metal reel bolted to the deck for extending the spar away from the hull. Bradley had told me the spar was used for dropping a weight to measure the depth of the water. How did the engineers think the lifeboat was going to be of any use with such an obstacle in the way?

Other boats already were afloat. Number four would go down with the ship if we didn't get away in the next few minutes. I reached for Madeleine's hand. Mine were cold, and I was grateful for her warmth. Madeleine had two reasons to stay alive—her baby and herself. My three reasons were waiting for me in New York. The fourth was still on *Titanic's* tilted deck.

A wave of nausea washed over me. I swallowed to keep from heaving last night's rich dinner courses overboard, but I would be well rid of my stomach contents if I were forced to swim.

"No use getting the lines loose," Office Lightoller called. "We'll have to cut away the spar."

Over the screams from passengers left aboard *Titanic*, I heard Andrew shout, "I'll find an axe."

Where was he supposed to find an axe on a ship? Then I remembered—attached to the wall of every deck was at least one glass case with a fire axe inside. What good would an axe do in a fire? Break into a locked cabin or shatter a window, I supposed. I had to trust that Andrew knew where the closest case was located.

Already the ship was pitching forward and toward port, surrendering to the inevitable. Why couldn't I wake from this nightmare? We had been getting ready for bed, hadn't we, Bradley and I? He had gotten into his pajamas. Maybe I had fallen asleep in my dress. I had dreamed about an iceberg. Any minute I'd roll toward my slumbering husband, kiss his cheek, and fall asleep again by his side.

"Officers' quarters." Lamp trimmer Sam Hemming pointed toward a doorway. "Just inside."

The door was uphill, and Andrew climbed at a staggering run, pressing his palm against the metal wall. When storekeeper Jake Foley rushed by him, Andrew grabbed his sleeve.

"Jake! Get me an axe!"

Foley looked at him as if he had gone mad. Who would ask for an axe on a sinking ship? Then the storekeeper came to his senses.

"In here," he said and tore through the doorway.

A passenger frantically hobbled by, an older gentleman dressed in a tuxedo and carrying a silver-tipped walking stick. Andrew yanked the stick from the man's hand.

"Sorry, sir." Even in an emergency, Andrew remembered courtesy.

The fire case was directly opposite the entry to the officers' quarters.

"Jack, stand back." Andrew pushed Foley aside. Taking one swing with the cane and then another, he succeeded in breaking the glass and knocked shards clear. Then he snapped the axe loose.

"Could use some help at boat number four," he shouted to Foley.

When the two reached the davit, Sam had already climbed over the railing and was working his way to the spar by rappelling down the lines. Foley didn't ask questions. He took the axe from Andrew, cradled it under his arm, and followed Sam.

Captain Smith had chosen his officers well. He read a man's potential for bravery even before a crisis warranted it. Andrew had never felt more pride to be among a ship's crew.

I recognized the storekeeper who hacked at the spar, and then the trimmer they called Sam took the axe and worked on the other side. When at last the wood broke free, Sam dropped the axe into the sea and climbed back on deck with Foley. The axe had served its purpose and would be a burden to a man trying to swim for his life.

Gracie helped Lightoller get our lifeboat to the water. Two men smudged with soot who must have come from the furnace room shimmied down lines and stepped into the boat. Grabbing oars, they set about to row. Too near the ship and the lifeboat could be sucked under when *Titanic* sank. The *Titanic* was sinking—even as the ship listed to port, it was ridiculous to think that the stoutest ship ever built would go under. Nothing, I was horrified to realize, was infallible.

At the rudder, Perkis steered the boat alongside the wounded ship, searching for open doors where he might load on more passengers.

Bradley might have anticipated the opportunity—but the openings were empty and the lifeboat turned away. Marian Thayer and Madeleine Astor took up oars beside the stokers. In a disaster, the ship had no class barriers. Life was valuable no matter what one's situation.

I caught sight of Sam spidering down a line of the wrecked ship. He jumped into the water and swam toward our boat, which by now was out the length of a football field. As the rowers hauled Sam aboard, I looked toward the ship and thought I could make out Andrew—still standing on the leaning deck. Why hadn't he gone for it the way Sam had? But his job was to save passengers even to the bitter end. Oh, Andrew, find a way to save yourself—and my Bradley!

Andrew lurched up to the boat deck and stood with Cumings, Astor, and John Thayer. At the railing, Officer Lightoller clenched the metal rail, and Andrew imagined the gears turning in his mind. Was there nothing to do but watch and wait for the hand of fate to sweep them all into the ocean?

He checked his pocket watch. It was nearly two—one fifty-five, to be exact. Two hours and fifteen minutes since the ship had hit the iceberg. Lightoller glanced his way. There was no panic in his expression, for which Andrew was grateful.

"If we're lucky, we've got half an hour," Lightoller said, his voice full of supreme sadness.

Third-class passengers were spilling in. They clung to small children and huddled on the promenade, too horrified to move.

The band had retreated to a dry area on the boat deck, instruments clutched in their hands. Their sprightly songs had ended and Wallace Hartley and three other string musicians were now playing solemn hymns. Astor saluted the band members. The musicians were unshakable in these last moments before eternity swooped upon them—upon everyone left aboard.

"Gentlemen," Andrew said to his first-class passengers, "we'd best get the vests on you."

"Why haven't you left the ship?" Cumings asked.

Why indeed. He had run out of alternatives—except the least appealing one.

"Your vest, sir?"

"Gave my vest to a woman. Might do her some good."

Andrew took off his own vest and held it up for Cumings. "Put this on," he said.

"Good of you, Andrew, but save yourself. I'm in fine company here." He turned toward his fellows in their tuxedos.

"Sir," Andrew said, "I intend to swim. The vest will be an encumbrance. I must insist you put it on."

Cumings stared at him as if considering.

Andrew returned his glare. "I'm in charge here, sir." He took hold of the man's arm and stuffed first one and then the other into the vest.

"Confound it." Cumings's hands were shaking and when he fumbled with the straps, Andrew helped him get them tied.

"What will you do, sir?" Andrew asked.

Cumings sighed. "What is there to do? I'm going to go to find a bottle of the ship's best whisky."

"Won't you swim for it?"

Cumings shook his head. "Swim for what?"

There were a few seconds of tense silence between them. Then Cumings clapped Andrew on the shoulder.

"Florrie likes you. If you make it, look after her, will you?"

If he made it—if any of them made it. Survival was never a sure thing. A heart attack, tuberculosis, tripping down a flight of stairs—survival could not be counted on.

"I will be sure to look after her," he said.

It was a hard moment, a torrent of feeling beneath the courtesy of their words.

"Do you think God is laughing at us?" Cumings said.

Andrew thought a second. He hadn't considered God, hadn't even considered praying. He had a job to do and that job occupied every second of his consciousness. But Cumings had asked the question, and Andrew was obliged to answer.

"Not laughing, no—not if you believe God is merciful." He had to believe in a merciful God. In the next moments, he had nothing else to rely on.

"Yes." Cumings looked at the deck, already wet with seawater. "Yes—merciful, no doubt." He may have wanted Andrew to stay, two clansmen, allies to the end. But Andrew was not going to surrender, not as long as he had any flicker of hope. Finally, he broke the tortured silence.

"Well," he said, "good luck, sir."

Cumings took his hand and shook it. "Good luck to you, too, Andrew. You're a fine Scotsman."

Heavenly Father, I entreat you with every fiber of my soul to protect my husband, John Bradley Cumings. I beg you to find a way—a miracle, if that's what it takes—to bring him to safety. To bring him back to me.

There comes a moment when the situation in which one finds oneself is so enormous as not to be believed, as if the mind is incapable of making sense of it. This was one of those times. Andrew knew it was futile to think, to try to reason out what was happening. The only option in the face of such upheaval was to act, even if blindly and by pure instinct.

It must've been 2:00 a.m. Andrew reckoned the steerage decks were underwater by now. The stern was rising higher above the water. He took the ladders to C deck then scrabbled up to B deck and searched the hallway. Through an open door he saw a gentleman struggling into his tuxedo jacket. Saltwater splashed around his ankles. His valet tried to help him, both men fumbling with the formal attire. When one meets his maker, Andrew thought, he wants to make the best impression.

"Mr. Guggenheim," Andrew said, "you should have on your life vest." Most likely his mistress had gotten into a boat.

"That'll do no good." He wagged his head.

Slowly and carefully, Benjamin Guggenheim went to the bureau and reached toward a vase of red roses about to slide off the surface. He broke off a rosebud and stuck it into the buttonhole of his lapel. Then he leveled his eyes at Andrew.

"Now—if you would be good enough to show Mr. Giglio and me where we may find a bottle of brandy, we won't trouble you any further."

"Best of luck to you, sirs," Andrew said.

He raced up to A deck lounge and found Sid arguing with William Stead. A life vest lay on the table in front of them.

"He refuses to put it on," Sid said.

"Mr. Stead—" Andrew pressed.

A glass rolled down the floor, and Andrew heard things falling, clattering, breaking. In front of the hearth, Thomas Andrews stared blankly, hypnotically, at the cold firebox, his body leaning toward the mantel as he struggled to stay upright. The ship's architect must have been aware that he missed the fatal flaw in his design and now was about to pay with his own life. Above him, the mantel clock read two-oh-eight.

Stead pushed the life vest toward Sid.

"Here, young man. Take this and put it on. I know where I'm going, and I'm happy to go. May the Almighty be with you both."

"Take it, Sid." Andrew was commanding him again. This time Sid didn't argue. "Now follow me and stay close."

They worked their way back to the boat deck, shoving through a crush of hysterical people pressing forward, looking for a miracle. In shirtsleeves, thin jackets, nightclothes, leading young ones, carrying babies, they searched for family members lost in the pandemonium.

"Johnny! Johnny — where are you?"

"Jesus-Mary!"

"Johnny!"

"Have you seen a little —"

Screams came from women tumbling to the deck. Angry voices, pleading voices.

"Our father who art —"

"Please help!"

How may I be of help, madam? Let me assist, sir. You rang for a steward, señor? Right away, senator.

Andrew shook his head. There was no way to give help on this night.

When they reached the boat deck, the ship groaned and cracked so that Andrew could hardly hear Sid.

"Cunningham, you wouldn't believe it of me, but I do pray. Used to be, I'd pray for myself, but now I bow my head and ask for protection of my family."

"If you pray, Sid, this is the time for it." Andrew grasped the railing so tightly his knuckles were pasty, the gold of his wedding ring out of place against the white paint. The cold metal stung his fingers, fingers that still carried the scent of French perfume from the hands of the first-class women he had helped into lifeboats. At least the wives of the American millionaires were safely afloat.

Icy saltwater licked at the cuffs of his trousers. Within the quarter hour, the ocean would swallow the most brilliant ship ever built. He had to keep his head about him. Desperation bred futility.

Who was to blame for the ship foundering—the captain? The shipbuilders? Or the iceberg that popped up like a demon in the path? But laying blame did no good. All he had was this minute and the next, wherever the whims of fate took him.

The frosty air bit his cheeks. His ears rang with the shrieks and curses of people clinging to the hopeless ship. They clawed at the deck or lost their hold and skidded toward the ocean. A workman with his life's savings in his pocket watched his dreams of a new beginning vanish before his eyes. A woman wearing a knitted shawl embraced her small child as they held on to dear life. Andrew thought of his own children and bawled up gratitude to heaven that they were not aboard this wretched vessel. Captain Smith would not live to regret his incompetence. But he—Andrew Cunningham—had to find a way to defeat the inevitable.

The water was up to his shins now, water cold enough to freeze had it not held so much salt. He kicked off his shoes and watched them fall into the North Atlantic.

"Come on, mate," he called to Sid. It was good to have a mate, good not to be alone in this dismal moment.

They climbed toward the stern, away from the ocean nosing toward them like a dog teasing a bone. Below, the water was dotted with heads bobbing in life jackets. They might have been waterfowl resting on their northbound migration. From where he clutched the railing, the drop was maybe twenty feet. When the ship was fully afloat, the distance was four times that.

Above the officers' quarters, Andrew saw a frantic second officer trying to unlash the last collapsible. Lightoller had gotten boat D freed and there was a rush of men loading into it. The purser fired his pistol into the air and yanked men from the seats so women and children could take their places, but it appeared no more women were in the area. Most of them had moved to the ship's stern, which was now as steep as a ski slope.

"We could get into that boat," Sid said. The words were not out of his mouth before Andrew saw Bruce Ismay and William Carter step in. Lightoller watched them board then turned his attention to freeing collapsibles A and B, his face rigid with determination. Whacking at the lines, he stripped the cover off boat B and loosed the ropes, but he lost his grip. The collapsible rolled overboard, capsizing when it hit the water.

Thunder growled from the bowels of the ship. They had maybe seconds left. There was more Andrew wanted to do, more he should have done. Watch his children grow. Be of more assistance. But he was no savior, and he wasn't the one who sentenced them all to die. All of them on this flawed *Titanic* in the middle of a voracious ocean were taking their precious last breaths.

He thought of Emily, how she'd be furious with him for dying and leaving her with fatherless children.

"I've got to find Charlie," Sid yelled.

"It's too late," Andrew said. "You have to look out for yourself now."

He tried to rip Sid's life vest from him, but it was knotted around his waist.

"If you hit the water strapped in cork, the jolt could break your neck or your collarbone," Andrew shouted. He hoped Sid had heard him over the screams of the dying.

"Are you mad?" Sid said.

"Just get out of the blasted thing."

Sid tried to wiggle out of the vest, but he fumbled to get it unfastened. Andrew was afraid he'd sink without the vest, but wearing it might kill him.

"Never mind the vest." Andrew said. "Climb over the railing. When you reach the water, swim away for all you're worth."

Sid perched like a gangly bird about to take flight. He wriggled his arms out of the vest, and the cork flapped behind him like tail feathers.

"Probably not the time to tell you, Cunningham," Sid said, "but I don't fancy swimming."

"Bloody hell, Sid!" Andrew focused on the water rising toward them. "Follow me, then."

"Right."

False courage was better than no courage.

The bow was sinking faster now. They had two options — jump or go with the ship to a watery grave. Jumping into frigid water could mean drowning or hypothermia. But it was idiocy to stay on a sinking ship. The fancy men in their evening clothes were accepting their fate with ludicrous formality. Andrew may have been undignified, but he wasn't about to give in to ill fate.

He hooked a leg over the icy bar. The moment was now — or never.

With a glance at Sid before he jumped, he bellowed, "Death can bugger himself!"

Band Played Till End
Newburyport Morning Herald, April 15

Through the wailing voices of dying, I heard the band still playing. I recognized the melody of "Lead, Kindly Light," which I had played many times on the parsonage piano. The words—what were they? "Amid the encircling gloom lead thou me on." As if I had a choice other than to pitch into the water to freeze with the thousand other souls. But Bradley had admonished me to think of our sons, and I pulled my thoughts from the plight of my husband and placed it on the young men who would grow into proper gentlemen—like their father.

The mind, however, is disobedient. Hundreds of women still in evening gowns—others barely clothed, having been dragged from their beds—all had scrambled for the boats. If only there had been more boats, more time to board them, more heavenly hands to reach down and keep the damaged ship afloat.

More lines of the hymn came back to me. "The night is dark, and I am far from home." I could remember no more, my thoughts muddied by the cries of distress.

The sea opened its jaws and gulped Andrew down as easily as a seal tosses a fish down its gullet. His lungs contracted. Cold stabbed his chest and slashed at him like a wild animal. Thrashing with his legs, he felt for a bottom he knew was too many fathoms beneath him. It was pure futility to fight so immense a body of water, and he tried to relax. Better to surrender. Once the sea believed she had conquered him, she would lose interest. At that moment, he'd make his move.

When he became aware of a loud humming, he wondered if his eardrums were bursting. He opened his eyes—nothing but blackness. The sound, he realized, was his own blood rushing through his veins, desperate for oxygen.

Panic pressed against him, but panic was a killer. He looked skyward, toward the water's surface, and saw a blush of light—how far above he wasn't sure. When his descent slowed, he pressed his palms together the way he had taught Sandy to say his bedtime prayers and kicked himself upward.

Half a minute more passed before his lungs began aching with a ravenous hunger. He willed them to be patient, promising a feast in another few seconds. When the pain in his chest became unbearable, he suddenly popped like a buoy above the surface and guzzled delicious air, panting like a sprinter crossing the finish line. But this race was far from finished.

Shaking water from his eyes, he found himself in the middle of a host of drowning creatures. No, not drowning—there was no struggling. Their life vests kept their heads above the glacial water. He knew body temperature drops twenty-five percent faster in cold water than in cold air. In thirty-degree water, a person will lose consciousness in fifteen minutes. At last check, the water was colder than that. He hadn't much time.

A few yards away, Sid's head punched through the surface. He wheezed and spat.

"That's it—don't swallow water, mate." Andrew said. Swallowing saltwater would do him in. First cramps, then nausea, and finally delirium.

"Uhh—bollocks, it's cold," he grunted.

"Move your legs," Andrew told him. "No matter what, keep moving."

But Sid was right—it was inhumanly cold. Luckily there was no wind. In the still air, moans and cries echoed across the water. A mournful wailing, too, muffled by the sea. At first he imagined the sound was coming from the floating bodies, but slowly he realized that it was the ship itself—singing its doleful song of death.

The salt held him buoyant and he treaded water slowly, conserving energy.

The engineers must still have been aboard, keeping the ship's lights on, hoping the *Californian* would understand their urgency and come to their rescue. The light shone on the water where Andrew saw a man stroking hard toward the capsized collapsible. Just as he was about to reach the small boat, the *Titanic* shook under the weight of the water, breaking loose one of the forward funnels. The huge cylinder crashed to the deck, crushing screaming people beneath it, then rolled and fell straight toward the bloke in the water. He ducked under, the funnel barely missing him, and came up next to the collapsible. A dozen men stood single file on the upturned bottom. The boat had sunk low enough to wet their feet and Andrew wondered how long they could stand ankle deep in frigid water before rescue came.

When the men pulled the soaked chap from the water, Andrew saw that it was Charlie Lightoller. Once again, he had escaped the sea maiden, and Andrew was glad the second officer had made it. But the *Titanic* had been mortally wounded. The proud Achilles shuddered and a rasping crack pierced through the cries of the dying. Andrew thought at first the ship had been torn in half, but the hull was an inch thick. How could it be possible?

In seconds the bow dipped into the ocean. Then the stern rose straight into the air, its propeller reaching for the starry sky. The aft hung like an enormous waterfowl inverting itself to catch food under the water, only its tail visible. There followed a loud gurgling and the stern began to slip down. Human forms took to the air and fell like confetti.

As the ship dove, its lights blinked once and then went out. There was no suction, no gigantic spout of water. She had yielded to the ocean as peacefully as a sleepy child climbing into bed.

From beneath the water, Andrew heard the muffled creak and sigh of the ship drowning. How long would it take her to find her resting place on the black bottom? And how many would join her in the soggy grave?

Around him, people struggled for their lives. Their fearsome voices sounded like the high-pitched hum of locusts. But no— locusts lived in trees, and trees were thousands of miles away.

In the distance Pastor Harper splashed in the water, saving souls.

"Believe in the Lord Jesus Christ and thou shalt be saved," he shouted.

"Are we going to die, Cunningham?" Sid's voice was childlike.

Andrew thought of the book of Genesis and a verse, the one used at funerals—"dust thou art, and unto dust shalt thou return." But the body was made up mostly of water, so it was more logical that when a person died, he would return to water. When a body is submerged for a time, eventually the skin softens and peels off like a glove slipping from a hand. But Andrew was going to find a way out of the liquid grave. It wasn't his time— he knew it wasn't yet his time.

He had to keep Sid together. It was less the cold than the bleak darkness that threatened to break them.

"No, mate, we're not going to die tonight. But it's black as the Earl of Hell's waistcoat."

Our lifeboat was far enough away from the broken ship that I saw the explosion of fireworks cascading into the sky before I heard the crack of the gunshot. Had I not known better, I'd have thought the lights were a celebration. If only that were true. But

I understood the captain or the first officer was signaling for help.

Save Our Souls.

The *Titanic* itself was beyond saving. In its blinking lights, I watched the ship vanish porthole by porthole into the murky water. Taking with it the grand staircase. The carved mahogany and glass dome. The china and silver. The priceless treasures. My own woolens and silks. But not my husband. My husband had found a way off the ship. I would believe nothing else.

Perkis ordered the rowers to take the oars. The ship was so large that when she sank she would take lifeboats and swimmers down with her—even for miles around her. And if we weren't pulled under, the boilers could burst and tear us to bits.

Our lifeboat faced the ship's port side, and I watched as E and C decks submerged. The strains of music from the orchestra became faint, as if the instruments were filling with water. Over the music, cries of terror rose from the decks. Oars splashed in the water, adding discord to the shouts and moans. And then the music ceased and an inscrutable blackness enveloped us. Overhead, cheerless stars mocked the dreary congregation.

Next to me, Emily Ryerson buried her face in my shoulder.

A faint light flickered a short distance off. The light came close to a face. Someone was about to smoke a cigarette. Someone in a lifeboat.

From the boat, voices reached him. Scolding, calling orders. Andrew couldn't make out the words, but he heard a tone of urgency.

He shouted and waved. "Ho! Ho there!"

It was only a shadow, but yes—the shadow was close enough to reach if he made enough effort.

"Sid, do you see me?"

"You there, Cunningham?" he answered through clenched teeth.

"Aye, mate. Swim with me, Sid."

"Swim the bloody hell where?"

"Never mind that—stick by me."

"Righ—." Sid's voice was barely a huff of air.

Andrew pulled through the water, fighting to avoid muscle spasms, every sinew in his body alert. He had to stay loose. If he tensed up, he'd cramp—and cramping meant paralysis. He pressed his eyes closed and thought of *Titanic's* saltwater pool, the leisurely laps he swam there in the early mornings before the passengers awakened. But the pool was never this wretchedly heartless. He tried to imagine a warm hide of a powerful animal, but the water's sting brought him back to the dreaded present.

Lifting his head, he roared. Roared to drown out the hopeless cries. Roared for his children and his wife. Roared for his life. The roaring left him thirsty. So much water yet not a drop to quench his thirst.

With each stroke he thought of Scotland and his father. "Be careful on that ship, Andy," his Da had said. "Those rich sods'd just as soon see a boy like you in the drink." His Da was right, except they were all in the drink—rich, poor, and working stiffs alike. Andrew vowed to tell him as much if he ever got out of this blasted ocean.

When the water threatened to pull him down, he wished again for the life vest—or a coat. A dry wool coat. Wiping water from his face, he turned over and swam on his back. The sky's diamonds fell toward him—or was he rising toward eternity? He became confused about what was above him and what below. Confusion was a bad sign. He had to clear his head.

He forced his mind on something else—anything else. Sundays in Shotts. The way the Kirk's bell rang late in the morning. He could almost hear the dong-dong-dong calling worshippers to the service. Every Sunday he went with his family to the Kirk. He had always striven to be above reproach. Was this where a virtuous life had gotten him?

His watch was waterlogged, but he guessed it had to be near three o'clock. Back in Southampton it would be eight in the morning. Sandy and little Gloria would be waking, maybe jumping on the bed while Emily heated water for tea. Perhaps he was dreaming. The sunken ship, the biting cold, the dismal darkness—all a miserable hallucination. He could swear he heard fish parting the water, filling their gills, sucking oxygen from the sea. Shells and barnacles cracked against each other, and octopi crept across the ocean bottom fathoms below. The sounds of the sea drowned out the pitiful, haunting cries of people preparing to die.

Sid splashed toward to him. At first Andrew thought Sid was challenging him to a foolish water fight. But in the starlight he saw him drop beneath the surface. His life vest must have come loose or slipped over his head.

"Sid!" he shouted, reaching into the opaque water. Nothing. He splayed his feet out wildly, feeling through the liquid. Six seconds. Seven seconds. Eight. Then he sensed rather than felt him, dipped under and grabbed hold of hair or cloth and pulled upward. Sid's head bounced into the frosted air.

"Uh—uh," he grunted. "Can't feel my hands. Feet either."

"Don't give up, mate," Andrew shouted. "There's a boat just ahead."

"I'm done in," he gasped.

"No—we're almost there, Sid." Even as his own lungs constricted, Andrew called reassurance to Sid. He was breathing—he knew that much. He had to keep Sid breathing, too.

He swam sidestroke and dragged Sid toward the little vessel.

"Kick, Sid!" he shouted. The water felt like mud. Quicksand sucking them down. Fatigue pummeled him, but if he stopped fighting, they would both be ruined. What was inside him was all he had left—beating heart, blood flowing through arteries. Slowing, but not stopping.

He was alive. He had to stay alive. Exhaustion would not win. Cold would not win. He would not let even the night defeat him, and he pulled harder through the water.

Then he heard a child's voice. A child nearby. He looked around. Where was this bairn?

"A sunbeam to warm you. A sunbeam to warm you."

Maybe he was losing his senses, but slowly he felt the cold lift and a strange current of warmth surrounded him. He sensed a presence—was it Sid? No—he knew Sid's life was draining from him. It may have been the people in the lifeboat. They were closer now, but even a dozen yards felt like miles.

The voice again. "Nothing can harm you."

New life surged through him. He stroked faster, towing Sid beside him. The void vanished and he was holding onto the gunwale, rising from the bitter water into the bitter air. With a last burst of will, he kicked his way upward and felt himself being lifted.

I heard a sound different from the whimpering of the dying—a voice close to the lifeboat. At first I thought it might have been a creature from the sea lifting its head from the water. Maybe Madeleine's adored dog, panting from the exertion of reaching its master. A cough, a choking sound. A word forming.

"H—H—Here."

No dog.

Hands clutched the gunwale for dear life. I reached down and pulled not one but two people into the boat. I don't know where I found the strength.

If only—if only—

A blanket fell over Andrew. Not a blanket—a wool coat. With fur. So warm. Never in his life had he felt such gratitude. When he opened his eyes, in the faint light he saw a face. A woman's face. An angel's face. The face of Florence Cumings.

His mouth refused to move. He tried again, his tongue between his teeth, and found strength to utter two words. The two most important words of his life. "Thank you."

There was wood under him—unless he was dreaming. The slats were hard beneath him, so solid that he might have imagined them. No—he was in a lifeboat, of that he was convinced. A *Titanic* lifeboat. Lifeboat number four, the one he had helped Florence Cumings and the other women into. They were drifting atop water that was miles deep, water that could reach up and take them at any moment with no rescue in sight.

The coat covering him stopped his shaking but he had no feeling in his extremities. If frostbite didn't take them, his fingers and toes would ache and burn. The water probably kept his skin from freezing. But without sensation, he was clumsy. When he tried to pull the coat tighter around him, it slipped from his grasp.

He felt movement against his knees.

"Sid?"

No answer.

"Sid, wake up, mate!"

Andrew knew if Sid fell asleep, his organs would shut down. He had to move even in as little room as they had in the boat.

He touched Sid's arm, his head. Ice in his hair, his face stiff with ice.

"Come on, chum." Andrew crooned as if he were speaking to his own son. "There's a ship on the way. It won't be long." He pulled Sid toward him and rocked, giving him the warmth of his own body.

"Hold on, Sid. Hold on a little longer."

Andrew tucked the coat around him. When he put his hand on Sid's chest, he sensed a shallow rise and fall.

"That's the fellow. You're my best mate, the best mate a bloke could ever have."

Sidney Siebert had become his first companion back in Liverpool. Over the years they had taken wives and fathered bairns. They had lived through mishaps at sea, fought and forgiven each other. It was Sid who lightened his dismal moods, Sid whose antics got him across the Atlantic when they had the most aggravating passengers to deal with.

"Sid." Andrew squeezed his mate's wet body to his own warmth. "Sid," he said again.

Leave me be—a bit of a bloody nap is all.

Had Sid spoken? Still holding his mate, Andrew felt him sigh as if in surrender.

"No," Andrew whispered. "No, mate. Come on—come on." He couldn't die. Not Sid, so full of life.

Then Andrew felt a hand on his back. A tender hand.

"It's all right, Andrew." It was Florence. He was at her feet in the boat and realized it was she who had dragged them in.

"There is a poem by a writer named Rilke." Her voice was soft. "It begins, 'Before us great Death stands, our fate held close within its quiet hands.' No words were ever so true."

"He's resting," Andrew said. "He's tired. We'll let him sleep a while. Then he'll be right."

She patted his arm.

"Yes," she said, her voice barely a whisper. "Let him sleep a while."

No Hope Left: 1535 Dead
New York American, April 15

No one spoke, and I heard no voices from the other boats. The people in the water, too, had quieted except for susurrations of weak prayers.

I looked up into the pitch of night. A tapestry of sequins hung overhead. I thought of Bert Marckwald and wondered whether he had heard about the *Titanic*. His secretary must have come into his office, her mouth open as if she were trying to tell him something but couldn't speak it.

"What is it?" Bert would ask.

The secretary would try again. "That ship. The *Titanic*. It hit an iceberg."

"The *Titanic*—I think Bradley and his wife might be on that ship," he would say. The *Titanic* was a battleship of a vessel. Bert would believe it skimmed the berg and kept on its way, no harm done.

"It's sinking," the secretary would say. Bert would dismiss her as a foolish woman and wish he had hired someone older and with more sense. She would tell him to check the ticker tape, and he would burst past her to find paper rolling out, mostly stock prices, snaking into a wastebasket. He would thread the paper back a yard or two. And there it would be: "TITANIC HIT ICEBERG. NORTH ATLANTIC. SHIP FOUNDERING."

He would tell the secretary to send a wireless to Bradley right away, asking him to report that he was well. The iceberg was a stroke of bad luck, nothing more, Bert would think. Bradley was due back in the office at the end of the week. He would walk through the office door as he had always done. He would get to work refreshed from the trip.

If Bert sent a message, I doubted Bradley received it.

Andrew took the coat from around him and pushed it toward Florence.

"You must be cold," he said.

"I'm fine," she answered, and he believed her.

In the starlight he could made out Madeleine Astor pulling at an oar, her gown aglow like a swan's feathers. She was coatless. He glanced at Sid's body. It was Madeleine's fur covering him.

"Are there blankets?" he asked Florence.

"At the bow, I think," she said. "Go around the boat, Andrew, and find out who's on board."

His job was to take orders, but this was more than a frivolous request. Florence was giving him a task to take his mind off Sid. She wanted him to focus on the living.

He fumbled his way forward, asking each man for a name. Greaser Thomas Ranger was next to Madeleine Astor at the aft set of oars. Mrs. Thayer, too, clutched an oar. The first-class women—widows now—pulled as hard as men.

Storekeeper Frank Prentice and greaser Alfred White worked the forward oars. Walter Perkis stood at the rudder. Sam Hemming and fireman Tom Dillon had been plucked from the water drenched and huffing from the cold.

Andrew nearly fell over a man, his body limp as a rag.

"Who's this?" he asked Sam.

"Able Seaman Bill Lyons," Sam said. "He swam but didn't make it, poor fellow."

Able seamen were deck crew trained at operating lifeboats. Lyons must have seen to it that all boats were safely away — without him aboard. He was twenty-six years old.

Most of those in boat four were from first class. Four women and two little boys were second-class passengers. Andrew counted forty. After grabbing a blanket, he reported that number back to Florence.

"We have room for more," she said.

Andrew covered Sid with the blanket then put the coat around Madeleine and climbed in front of her.

"I'll take over here," he said.

When she let him have the oar, he saw that her palms were bleeding, but she said nothing. She pulled the coat around her, smearing red on the fur. Then she growled an order at Perkis.

"Turn the boat and search for survivors in the water." Climbing toward a seat next to Florence, Madeleine with her white coat and bulky belly resembled an adolescent polar bear.

Andrew spotted two more swimmers, and Florence helped Madeleine haul them aboard and wrap them in blankets.

After spending so many early mornings in a ship's gym, rowing felt natural for Andrew. Slowly he began to believe that everyone — the living, at least — in lifeboat four would make it through the night — if only they could endure until daybreak.

"What number are you?" Perkis called out. He had caught sight of another lifeboat.

"Fourteen," came the answer. "Can you take a few of us? We're overburdened."

"Yes," Madeleine called. "Perkis, tie us together."

Young people like Madeleine robbed stamina from old age. But she was pregnant — a condition her husband described as delicate. Astor had underestimated his wife.

Perkis lashed the bowline to fourteen, and White secured the sterns. Five more people groped their way into boat four and found spaces to pack into. If they took on any more, the newcomers would have to stand, making the little vessel unsteady. A sudden billow and they could capsize. Luckily the sea was glassy and the night peaceful.

Fifth Officer Harold Lowe, a Welshman, was in charge of lifeboat fourteen. It had been the thirty-year-old's first trip across the North Atlantic. Andrew hoped to catch sight of Violet, but she wasn't among those in Lowe's boat. Knowing her, she would have been with second and third class people in one of the very last lifeboats to launch.

Someone passed Andrew a bottle of water, and he drank as if he'd been stranded for days among desert dunes.

A lantern lifted in boat fourteen. I stood and searched the faces. Bradley might have gotten into that boat.

"I'm sorry, Florence," Madeleine said.

There was no sound now from the water. Under starlight, I was certain I saw spirits rising—drenched at first and then glowing and dry, walking on the surface and then rising above it. As a girl, I had seen my grandfather's spirit lift from his bed when his heart stopped, a transparent soul but still full of life. These spirits, too, lingered among the living.

A man tied into a life vest drifted close by but not raising his hands for help. My breath caught—Bradley? He had sunk into the vest, his forehead glistening. I thought how odd that the gentleman would perspire in such cold water. He should have been struggling, but he was motionless, his arms floating at his sides. He stared up at me, teeth bared in his gaping mouth. In the dim light, I understood the folly of my thinking. The glistening on his forehead was ice.

With a sense of guilt, relief swept over me—it was not Bradley. My husband was still out there.

We did not take the dead man aboard.

Out of the darkness, another lifeboat came toward our two.

"What boat are you?" Perkis called out.

"Twelve," came the answer.

When we were within reach, someone in the bow grabbed twelve's line. Tied, we had a better chance than drifting alone. I studied each face.

"Is Bradley Cumings with you?" I called. No one responded.

"How many aboard twelve?" Perkis asked.

"More than fifty," came the answer. "Picked up a few from the water. Will you take some of us?"

"Yes, we will." It was Madeleine Astor.

Carefully, people were redistributed so that boat twelve was relieved of its extra burden, but now boat four sank low in the water. How could we refuse to help?

Eventually collapsible D found us and joined the cold gathering. We must have been a miserable sight.

"What time is it?" Andrew asked. He was no longer needed at the oars. We had nowhere to go now.

"Must be close to four," I said.

Sidney Siebert's body was at his feet, and I watched Andrew reach down and cover his friend's pale face with the blanket. I prayed no one would have to do the same for my Bradley.

Oh, my dear – be warm and be well.

It was cold enough to snow, but there was not a cloud in the vast sky. From within my chest, I felt a hymn rumble and I let it take wing into the unfriendly air.

"Let the lower lights be burning! Send a gleam across the wave!" Others joined in, and their harmony was a comfort. "Eager eyes are watching, longing –"

I stopped singing when I heard a shrill whistle coming through the night. The other voices faded out, and I pointed toward the sound. "That direction. Someone's calling us from over there."

"Untie us, Perkis," Madeleine said.

"Pick up the oars, men!" Perkis ordered.

As wet as he was, I witnessed a strange buoyancy possess Andrew. He dipped his oar into the water and pulled in rhythm with the other rowers. He was rowing with all he had — with even more than he had. I had immense admiration for him.

While lifeboat four glided toward the whistle, I prayed, "Let him be there."

In the east, I made out a faint thread of pink. "The nearer the dawn, the darker the night," I murmured.

"Who said that?" Madeleine asked.

I wasn't aware I had spoken aloud. "Longfellow, I think."

"Pray for the dawn, then." Madeleine squeezed my hand.

I thought of rocks. I thought of boulders, solid and immovable. I thought of mountains reaching into clouds, of tree roots tunneling deep into soil, of sticky April leaves emerging from winter's bare boughs and unrolling their greenery. I thought of earthworms, how the deeper they dig underground, the more severe the coming winter. I thought of grass and gardens and honeybees, of bears emerging groggily from hibernation, of new fawns being born. I thought of anything earthly, anything except this damned darkness, this damned cold, this damned boat swaying over an ocean and holding sixty sad souls.

Several minutes passed before I began to make out silhouettes of people. Shadowy lumps clogged the water. At first I thought it was a herd of curious seals. But so many and so close to our boat. Then as the sky grew lighter, I saw they weren't seals at all but men and women in life vests. Number four plowed through them, pushing the lifeless figures aside as easily as if they were lily pads on a pond.

Ahead, Andrew thought he recognized one of *Titanic's* smokestacks floating in the water. Metal floating? But as they drew closer, he made out the overturned collapsible. There were twenty men standing on it now, young Jack Thayer among them.

Lightoller was blowing a boson's whistle, trilling into the early light. Colonel Gracie stood on the boat along with the two Marconi operators. Phillips slumped over, and Bride supported him. The rest were all crew, mainly firemen dressed in sleeveless undershirts, no chance to find warm clothes before leaping from the fiery furnace room into the hostile water. From the heat of Hades to the frozen arms of Boreas, the god of winter who sank hundreds of ships, there was no respite for the black gang.

The collapsible's canvas collar was saturated, and the boat was about to succumb to the sea. The lifeboats had arrived without a second to spare. Lightoller, Thayer, and a dozen or so others got into number twelve. Jack Thayer was quaking violently. In the gloom of night, neither he nor his mother must have recognized the other. Number four took on several more, including the wireless operators. Two men helped Phillips in and laid him on the bottom. Andrew knew he wasn't going to make it.

In the dawning, he saw both boats were now crammed with survivors hunkered into one another. Several women got up to give the new passengers a seat. Emma Bronson kneeled to wrap a blanket around Harry Bride's frostbitten feet. Andrew's own hands were numb and he tucked them into his waistcoat, hoping the damp wool would give a little warmth. He'd need to be able to grip the oar if — no, when — a rescue ship came.

Had to stay positive. Had to believe.

"Harry, did you get any last messages before—?" he couldn't finish.

Bride struggled to speak. "That light we saw five miles away. The *Californian*. No answer. But *Carpathia*'s on the way. They were fifty-eight miles out. Coming full speed. Should be here soon."

"Oh, thank the dear Lord!" Madeleine said.

Bride — their salvation. A sob of gratitude heaved from Andrew's chest.

"The sun's coming up," Florence said. "Everyone keep an eye out."

As the stars blinked out and the sky lightened around the grim boats, icebergs seemed to grow up out of the water, frozen monoliths luminous in the morning sun. Ahead, a field of ice stretched across the horizon — at least thirty miles of it.

"How could the lookouts not spot them?" Florence said.

"We had a dozen warnings," Bride said. "A dozen at least."

Andrew cursed Bruce Ismay and Thomas Andrews for urging Captain Smith to keep going. Had he not done as they asked, Smith might have been discharged from White Star service instead of enjoying a well-earned and honorable retirement. The two men were overconfident about *Titanic's* capability. Andrews said the ship was as perfect as designers and builders could make her. He hadn't considered the possibility of weakness — the possibility of utter failure.

Chunks of ice littered the sea, and ice walled in the weary party of lifeboats. Andrew wondered how a ship would ever reach them through such a maze. And yet if he drew his attention from the watery graveyard and faced the rising sun, there was a hopeful feeling about the morning. They had made it this far and he turned from the dismal past with a faint optimism toward the minutes that lay ahead.

"A ship!" Perkis yelled. Did Andrew dare believe? Then he saw it, like a vision — a vessel a few miles off. It had a single smokestack — a steamer. A big one, albeit not nearly so large as the *Titanic*.

"Oars in the water!" Perkis called. Andrew pulled at the oar again. It had been a long night and now began the slow journey toward deliverance.

Carpathia, Rescue Ship, Nears Goal In Silence
Chicago Daily Socialist, April 15

Icebergs stood in the way of the rescue ship reaching the lifeboats. We survivors would have to row our way to deliverance. Wind was picking up, raising a chop and threatening to capsize the boats. We had to hurry. I watched as Andrew and the other men worked at their oars—lean and pull, lean and pull.

"Time?" Andrew asked.

"It must be after five by now," I said.

"I feel as if we've been in this boat for days," Madeleine said.

No one responded. Days, weeks—eternity.

The Cunard flag quivered from *Carpathia's* mast. What a sight she was, this benevolent liberator. A David compared to the Goliath *Titanic*. And yet our survival depended on the small passenger ship. The icebergs around the ship were frozen mountains. Divine providence must have guided *Carpathia's* captain in maneuvering around them. I held out hope that the same hand was guiding my love.

Oh, Bradley, may grace lift you up.

The *Carpathia* crew dropped ladders and boson's chairs from the gangways for the exhausted survivors to climb aboard. Two of the ship's own lifeboats were brought out to help.

The lifeboat carrying Bruce Ismay and William Carter was the first to reach the ship. How had they been permitted to board a lifeboat, I wondered? Shameless wealth and privilege? But who was I to judge when my greatest hope was for another man's survival?

Behind them, boat number one waited. It could easily hold forty but I counted only twelve aboard — Cosmo Duff-Gordon, his wife, his secretary, and two other first-class passengers — both men. One of the lookouts stood at the rudder. The rest were rowers. Twenty-eight more lives could have been saved. Why the dear Lord hadn't the boat picked up more?

It took hours to unload stranded passengers onto *Carpathia*. I waited in the stinging air. The cold was bearable compared to what Bradley must have been suffering in the water. I scanned the surface for a splash, listening for his voice calling to me, but wind ruffled the water, muffling sound.

Eventually there were only three lifeboats left to unload, our number four and Officer Lightoller's number twelve, towing number ten. The crewmen in boat ten must have been too fatigued to row, so Lightoller had tied their bowline to his boat. Counting seven or eight women from first class, a dozen from second, another dozen from third class, and others I couldn't identify, there were nearly fifty people aboard number ten. Pulling two boats forward, Officer Lightoller's men worked the oars hard enough to break their hearts.

When lifeboat four reached the steamer, Andrew asked again for the time. Madeleine checked her brooch watch.

"Seven-thirty."

I sighed. "I wish we could turn back the clock to last night. We were having such a lovely time."

William Carter leaned over the railing of *Carpathia's* top deck and scanned the incoming lifeboats. Andrew saw Florence watching Carter, too. On her face he saw the despair of not finding her own husband — a despair that looked nearly to crush her.

Carpathia's crewmen helped women climb the rope ladder to the deck. Not one of them wept or even complained. They must have been grateful to be alive, hopeful their husbands were alive as well—suffering maybe, but alive. Andrew helped Bride into a sling because of his frostbitten feet. When Bride was on board, the sling was lowered again, and Andrew loaded Phillips and then the body of Bill Lyons. Finally he lifted Sid, the blanket still covering him.

"We'll be home soon, mate," he whispered.

When only three were left in lifeboat number four, they argued about who would climb the ladder first. Sam insisted Andrew had swum farther and should go before him. Walter Perkis was the last to leave the lifeboat.

Andrew boarded on one of the lower decks, which felt no warmer than the lifeboat. The captain had probably turned off the heat to direct more fuel to the engines, taxing his ship to get to the survivors. He thought of the *Californian* so close he could see her lights. If the ship had come at the first distress signal— but what was the use of laying blame at that point?

He joined the line to have a purser write down the names of those from the *Titanic*. When his turn came, he announced, "Andrew Orr Cunningham." His name felt strange on his lips, as if this Cunningham fellow were an ancestor who had crossed centuries to get to this place. Whoever his brawny forefathers were, Andrew thanked them for bequeathing him enough endurance to get through this endless nightmare.

He spelled out Cunningham, wanting to make sure that when the wire went out his name would be accurate. Families were waiting to hear if their loved ones had been rescued, and he ached to think of Emily worrying about him. If he hadn't made it to the lifeboat, she would be a widowed mother like Florence Cumings and Winnie Siebert. The thought was more than he could bear, and his head dropped, heavy with grief.

After he had signed in, Andrew caught sight of Duff-Gordon taking some bills from his wallet. He handed a bill to each of the stokers who had been in his boat. As Sally Caveney stuck the five-dollar note into his pants pocket, Andrew grabbed his arm.

"Duff-Gordon paid you to row the cutter?"

"Paid us, aw right," Sally said. "But not ta row." He jerked his arm away.

Andrew gritted his teeth. "What do you mean?"

"A man gots ta eat, boy. Gots ta feed his family."

"Is that why you didn't pick up more people? Because Duff-Gordon paid you not to?" Andrew said, spit flying at Sally.

Sally laid his calloused paw on Andrew's shoulder. "Whyn't you find someplace ta get in a few winks," he said. "It's done wif."

That was it—the wealthy could buy whatever they wanted, even human lives. And the poor did their bidding or else be part of the sacrifice. It was an unjust bargain, and it turned Andrew's stomach.

Carpathia's captain had supplied blankets, soup, sandwiches, and brandy for the *Titanic* passengers. While the crew manned the davits to lift *Titanic's* lifeboats to the deck, I asked Andrew to help me find the infirmary. If Bradley were on the ship, he'd most likely need a doctor, especially if he had been in the water.

I was feeling weak and leaned on Andrew—or rather, we leaned on each other. Neither of us had slept in a day and a half.

Captain Rostron was in the dining saloon greeting the shipwrecked and offering his condolences for our losses. I held out my hand to thank him and he took it gently.

"We came as promptly as we could," he said. "I apologize for not arriving sooner." A slender man with regal posture, there was a boyish, almost shy look about the captain.

"There may be others out there still," I said. "Now that it's light, you'll look for them, won't you?" I didn't try to hide my desperation. "We'll all look for them."

"I'm very sorry," the captain said.

Sorry wasn't good enough.

"There might be rafts. Or a small boat."

The captain cast his eyes at Andrew as if asking for his help.

"I am—" He corrected, "Was—steward for Mrs. Cumings."

"I'd like Mrs. Cumings, Astor, Widener and Thayer to use my cabin. Will you see that the women are settled in?"

Andrew said he would. Then the captain looked at Andrew's bare feet.

"Some of the passengers have given their extra warm clothes," he said. "Find a pair of shoes for yourself." When he saw my evening dress, he said, "There should be some warmer clothing for you, too, Mrs. Cumings."

"Thank you," I said. "But I'm fine." I had grown used to the cold. Maybe we all had. There were so many more important things.

"Where are we bound for?" I asked.

The captain raised his eyebrows. "We were on our way to Trieste, but after consulting with Mr. Ismay, we'll reverse route and make our way back to New York. Shouldn't take longer than three days. This ship holds three thousand passengers but we boarded half that number in New York. There will be plenty of provisions for everyone."

"I'd like to be of help," Andrew offered.

"I suggest you both see Doctor McGee first. He has medicines to treat any wounds or frostbite you may have. Hot drinks are ready for you. A cup of coffee cures a number of ills." He pointed to the table laid out with coffee urns and platters of food.

"Later today there will be a worship service and then a meal," Rostron said. "But first things first."

Captain Rostron had thought of everything—an exemplary captain.

"I'm too tired to eat," I said. "But I'd like to speak with the doctor."

Andrew led me to the infirmary where a line of women waited to be examined. No men. If he were on the ship, Bradley would have searched me out. He would look until he found me.

"Let's find the captain's quarters," Andrew said. He led me to the door and said, "Send for me if you need anything at all." I told him I would.

Inside, the other women were settling themselves.

"Do you think they made it?" Madeleine asked.

"By the grace of the Almighty, my son Jack is on board." Marian Thayer said. "He wasn't with his father, so heaven knows where John is."

Eleanor Widener wagged her head. She wasn't ready to consider what had become of her own husband and son.

"Yes, they made it." I said. No matter how long it took, I would never give up.

Someone had hung sheets to screen the infirmary area and Andrew took a seat and waited his turn with the doctor. While he stared into his coffee mug, he heard someone calling him. Not his name—but "Scottie!"

Violet was flesh and blood, her cheeks pinked from cold. Seeing her brought reason to the insanity around him. He gave her a good long hug.

"I worried about you, Violet."

"Murdoch ordered me into lifeboat sixteen," she said. "Barely made it before we launched." She was carrying a bundle, and inside the cloth some live thing squirmed and protested—a baby.

"Whose?" Andrew asked.

"I don't know. Someone shoved her into my chest then turned on her heel and ran off." The child fussed, and Violet swayed back and forth, cooing to her. "Poor little thing."

He hadn't thought Violet had a maternal bone in her body. But who would give up a child? A woman panicked in the chaos. A woman who had to search for another child lost among the mobs.

"Are you all right?" he asked. "Not hurt are you?"

"Shaken, like everyone else." She glanced around. "Did Sid make it?"

Andrew couldn't answer. He wasn't ready to accept the truth.

"I'm sorry, Scottie. Really I am."

A woman surged into the saloon with a shawl around her, anxious eyes searching. She came toward Violet, looked at the baby and gasped. When she reached for the child, Violet pulled it against her chest.

"Oh, my Ruthie," the woman cried. "Give me my child." Without a word of thanks, she plucked the child from Violet and dashed out the way she had come.

Andrew shook his head. "I don't think anything will shock me ever again."

"I guess I can get some shut-eye now." Violet laid an arm around his neck and touched her cheek to his. "I'm very glad to see you, Scottie," she breathed.

"And you as well, Violet," he said.

At the infirmary, Doctor McGee pressed two fingers to Andrew's wrist and watched a clock on the wall.

"You've been in the water, I take it?" he asked.

Andrew must have been a sight—clothes still damp and crumpled, hair plastered to his head.

"Yes, sir," Andrew said. The cruel water. The murdering water.

McGee brought the stethoscope to his ears, opened Andrew's shirt, and pressed the chest piece against his skin. He listened, his brows drawn into a frown, and then put the chest piece against his back.

"Take a few deep breaths," he said. Andrew did as he asked. Then the doctor straightened and looked Andrew over.

"How long did you say you were in the water?"

He had been in the water for decades. On the water, over the water. But he knew what the doctor meant.

"Most half an hour," he said.

McGee pulled at a corner of his mustache. "Floating in a life vest?"

"No, sir. Swimming for a lifeboat. I was taken aboard."

"Swimming? How far, approximately?"

"It was dark. Half a mile, I'd say."

The doctor shook his head. Had McGee thought Andrew was lying?

"At that temperature, you should have had hypothermia within fifteen minutes. But your pulse is strong and your lungs are clear."

"I'm glad to hear it." Except for fatigue and nerves, Andrew was holding his own.

The doctor clicked his tongue. "What you have survived, young man, is nothing short of a miracle."

Andrew wasn't sure he believed in miracles. He believed in a strong body and a strong will. He believed in luck. And after last night, he wouldn't count out help from another realm.

When the doctor released him, Andrew found the smoking room where men were trying to get comfortable in chairs and on the floor. Stewards brought in dry trousers, shirts and sweaters, and he chose items that looked to be a close fit. The only shoes were a pair of leather slippers. They were small for him, but he wedged his feet into them. He had shed his jacket before he leaped into the water, but his waistcoat was nearly dry by now. There would be an investigation in New York—questions, meetings. He would have to find a suit.

He unbuckled his own trousers, good wool of a London tailor. Emily had bought them for him on one of her trips to

London. She often squeezed a few shillings from the household allowance to buy him a special treat, a gift to show how much she loved him. Maybe the trousers could be salvaged. He checked the pockets and found his wallet missing. Down in the deep, no doubt. The White Star Line was sure to take care of him until he could return to Southampton. He didn't remember putting anything in the back pockets, but he slipped his hand into each of them. In the second pocket, he felt a piece of paper and pulled it out—a creased photograph, the outlines of his wife, his daughter, and his son, all barely visible. His family had been with him on the ship and in the sea—with him even now. He pressed the picture flat, put it in his waistcoat pocket, and patted it.

The passenger's trousers were short for him, but they would have to do. In dry clothes he wandered to the open air of the deck. Some had taken empty cabins, but dozens came to the boat deck, wanting, as he did, to be near others who shared a common grief. They all gazed at the sea that had pardoned them, expecting the *Titanic* to pop up out of the water alive and pulsing with music and laughter.

Toward the stern, a group gathered around the bodies of four men laid out on bulwarks. They had been stripped of their clothes, and Doctor McGee was examining each man with his stethoscope, a grim look on his face. A man with a clipboard followed the doctor.

Andrew half expected Sid to have recovered and was now stuffing his jowls at the food table, not lying naked under the scrutiny of these strangers. He had seen Sid fresh out of the bath dozens of times and had struggled to keep from laughing at his bony shoulders, the way his cock swung as he climbed into his union suit. He still had the lanky body of an adolescent. And yet, there was an elegance about him—and grace, too, in his loyalty to their friendship. Andrew couldn't let Sid suffer such indignity.

"For fuck's sake," he yelled, "cover him!"

"It's no use," one man said. "Doctor's signing the death certificates."

Andrew stared at him. The words "death certificate" had no meaning. Sid, the wisecracker, the madcap, couldn't be gone.

"No—" His throat closed.

"Let's get you to a chair," the man said.

Andrew jerked his arm from the man's hand. "I have to stay with him."

"No point, lad," he said. "We'll take care of him now."

"He's my mate—" Andrew couldn't finish.

"Go on up to the bow," the officer said. "That's an order."

Andrew stumbled along the deck and found Violet on a lounge chair, curled under a coverlet. He sat on the planks next to her, and she fanned the coverlet over him. Neither of them spoke. Even though the ship was solid under him, Andrew had a lingering fright. When he closed his eyes, they stung behind his lids. Violet reached down and patted his chest.

"Hey there, Scottie," she murmured, and he drifted off.

In the captain's quarters, my shoes sank into soft carpeting. Not that I could feel my feet. My senses had pushed beyond what my mind could tolerate. The carpet was deep blue. I wished it to be any other color but that of the sea. I had seen enough of the sea.

Tall windows flanking a wide roll-top desk let in weak morning light, and I loosened the curtain fabric to darken the room and block the view of the frothing waves. I should have felt fortunate that the wind had waited to churn the swells. And yet, if Bradley had been pulled under, I'd have wanted to drown with him.

"We should try to get some sleep," Madeleine said. She lowered herself onto the settee and worked her feet out of her shoes. Blankets were folded on one end of the settee, and when Madeleine brought her feet up, I billowed a blanket over her.

Eleanor Widener took another blanket and fell onto the fainting couch.

"Mrs. Cumings, you and Mrs. Thayer ought to take the captain's bed," she said. "It's wide enough for you both."

Marian Thayer was standing in front of the chifforobe's tall mirror.

"I look a fright," she said. The salt air had frizzled her curly hair, and spirals of it hung around her face and clung to her neck. When she failed at patting the tendrils into place, she declared, "Oh, what's the use."

What was the use — of anything? At least we were on our way back to New York. At least there was that.

I huddled next to the heater and tried to warm my hands. When I licked my lips, I tasted salt. Even my hair was sticky with damp, salt air. The cabin had a private washroom, but I was too tired to draw the water that would wash away the brine of last night's horror. A weight pressed on my spine. I drew back my shoulders to be rid of the heaviness, but the burden slid down my back, growing heavier until my knees buckled. Marian caught me as I crumpled.

"Come lie down." She whispered so as not to wake the others. Marian was a few years older than I, but she was incredibly strong. I took her hand and turned it to look at the palm, swollen and blistered.

"It's you who should lie down," I said. "You pulled at an oar for most of five hours."

"Did I?" Marian regarded her own hands as if she had just noticed them. "I hardly remember." She led me to a chair. "But sit. We're all in shock."

I should have gotten up to search for Bradley. He might have made it to *Carpathia* by now.

As if she knew my mind, Eleanor Widener murmured, "If they find our husbands, the captain will send them to us, won't he?"

There was no answer to the pointless question. Eleanor should have said "when"—*when* Bradley is found. *When* he boards the ship. *When* he takes me in his arms again.

"Mrs. Cumings," Marian said, "let's get you out of those shoes. You've brought a pint of the ocean with you."

I saw that she had taken off her own shoes and placed them by the heater—expensive shoes, probably purchased in Europe and now ruined by salt water. I remembered now that our lifeboat had taken on water. I remembered the wet rising around my ankles, remembered ignoring the cold sensation and the numbness in my toes. Now my feet were aching, and Marian bent to help me release my senseless feet from the useless shoes.

When I stood, pain shot through my feet and up my calves. I tried to walk but fell forward and again Marian caught me and helped me to the bed.

"You must lie down, Mrs. Cumings," she said. "I'll lie with you. We can warm each other."

I thought I might never sleep again. Or if I did sleep, I wished never to wake to this living dread.

"Just close your eyes," Marian said.

Slowly, I sensed the spirit returning to my body. My thoughts drifted to the cemetery in Paris, how at Chopin's tomb I had asked Bradley about the soul. What was it he had said? *When I am in the tomb, my soul will rise and seek you out.* Maybe that was the weight I felt, my husband's soul seeking and finding me.

With that thought, as if from a towering height, I fell into a silent and bottomless depth.

A tremor. An earthquake? No—he was on water, not land. The ship shuddered, struggled. Going down.

Andrew bolted awake.

"Easy, Scottie," Violet said.

"How long have I slept?"

"An hour, I'd guess," she said. "There's a service in the main lounge for survivors. We should go."

Andrew shook his head. His forehead throbbed and his whole body hurt.

"You must be brave," Violet said.

He wished he could be as brave as this young woman — and as strong. Leaning on her, he got his feet on the deck — the dry and solid deck.

I leaned over the side of the lifeboat and reached for my husband.

Take my hand, Bradley. Don't let go. Whatever you do, don't let go. Your skin is slick with salt water, but your body is buoyant. If you relax, you'll rise. Then I'll lift you into the boat where you'll be safe. Don't fight the water, darling. Please don't fight or I'll lose my hold. But why are you so heavy? With all my strength, I can't manage to heave you up. Even now you're slipping from my grasp. I can barely see you through the murky water. Don't let your wide eyes lose sight of me. I'll find a way, darling — I swear it. How long has it been? Seconds? A full minute? Why is someone not oaring the lifeboat toward you? Row! Row, damn it! But the others don't hear me. My voice is gone. Can't they see you drifting away? Bubbles are rising through the water around you. Wait for me, Bradley. I'll swim to you, swim through this torturously cold water. I would give you breath, but my own lungs are burning. I want to scream, but my tongue is frozen. Am I dying with you, Bradley? The water is smooth as black silk. I can't lose you. I can't!

"No!" I screamed.

"Mrs. Cumings? Mrs. Cumings, wake up." Marian Thayer held my hand. I gasped for air and pressed a palm to my throat. Had I swallowed seawater?

"You were dreaming," Marian said.

"Did he get on the ship? Is Bradley here?" I asked.

Silence answered my question.

"Captain Rostron is having a service in a few minutes," Marian said. "We have to get ready."

"A service?" Was I still in the nightmare—this nightmare that seemed to have no end?

Andrew wound his way between lifeboats that cluttered the deck like hard whales. At the railing, he saw small pieces of wreckage in the water. Patches of yellow cork, fragments of steamer chairs, pieces of pilasters, cushions, and dark objects rolling beneath the surface. Captain Rostron was guiding his ship over the graveyard of fifteen hundred souls.

A hundred yards out he thought he saw a wooden deck chair but when the ship got closer, he realized it was a person in a life vest. The man had turned on his side, his face in the water. The *Carpathia* cruised by without stopping. It dawned on Andrew the captain had arranged the worship service inside to keep the survivors from seeing what he was witnessing, from reminding them of the ultimate horror of their lives.

Someone was standing close to him, their sleeves touching. At first he didn't recognize Charlie Savage. His hair was tousled, and the once crisp serving jacket drooped around him. He was twenty-three, but the previous night had put years on him. He had become a middle-aged man.

Charlie was the only fellow Andrew knew who had known Sid longer than he had. Andrew was glad to see him.

The younger man raked his eyes over Andrew's face.

"Andy," he said, "was you with Sid—" He couldn't finish.

Andrew nodded. A thing trapped inside him banged against his ribs, struggling to get free. He swallowed to keep it from erupting.

"How'd you make it out, Charlie?" He had to change the subject even though he knew there was no other subject.

"I was starboard on A deck helping second class into boats. First Officer Murdoch ordered a few of us stewards into boat eleven to help row." He bowed his head. "Must've been seventy of us in the boat. We could barely pull an oar without it catching on a coat and nearly tossing 'em out."

Resting his forearms on *Carpathia's* railing, Charlie said, "Not many in steerage got out."

Andrew leaned next to him. "You couldn't have taken on any more."

"The little ones was scared of the dark," he said. "We had ten, I figure. Mrs. Rosenbaum brought a toy with 'er. Darndest thing. A little pig with grey fur. When she cranked its tail, it played music — a happy tune. Lifted our mood — even mine. She called it 'er lucky pig. It was lucky, too — kept the kiddies quiet." Charlie dropped his head. "Only half of them got out, I hear."

The kiddies — Sid had an unborn child who would never know his father — never know what a fine man his father was.

"You'll see about Winnie, won't you?" Andrew asked.

"Sure I will." Charlie waited a minute before he spoke again. "Winnie was going to name me to be godfather. But I expect now she'll want you to do the honors."

It was good to think of agreeable things.

"Of course," Andrew said. "I should be proud."

He sighed. "I'm hopin' fer a little footballer."

Andrew patted his back, but neither of them could muster more words.

The service must have ended and the minister came to the deck, followed by the crew and a few dozen survivors. Eight crewmen brought the four who had died, each of them covered in a sheet and laid on a skid. Andrew remembered once finding Sid resting on a deck chair after New York passengers had disembarked from the *Oceanic*. He had thought it a ridiculous sight, Sid lounging like a member of the upper class. He had asked, "May I get you anything, Mr. Siebert?" Sid had enjoyed the joke. But now it was time to put aside the joking. It was time to say goodbye.

Someone had hung a weight from the feet of each corpse. The sheets made it impossible to identify them, but Andrew knew one of them was wireless operator Jack Phillips who had died after being hauled aboard the *Carpathia*. Another was a stoker picked up by a lifeboat. One was Bill Lyons, and the last was his mate Sid.

The *Carpathia* crewmen stood at parade rest, hats secured under an arm. Andrew had lost his own hat to the sea and stood with hands at his sides. *Titanic* survivors clustered themselves, arms around one another, sisters in adversity. Madeleine Astor stood close to Florence Cumings. Marian Thayer was with them.

As the minister spoke, Charlie hung his head.

"Unto Almighty God," the minister intoned, "we commend the souls of our brothers departed, and we commit their bodies to the deep in sure and certain belief in their resurrection into eternal life."

From the back of his mind Andrew pulled lines from a poem by John Greenleaf Whittier that fit the moment. "The dark night is ending and dawn has begun," the poem went. "Rise, hope of the ages, arise like the sun."

"Sid," he whispered, "wherever you are, shine like the sun."

Then the crewmen lifted the skids and held them side-by-side atop the railing. At the captain's salute, the figures slipped from beneath their drapery with only a whisper into the North Atlantic. They were all four good men. They would be mourned and commemorated in their hometowns. As for Andrew, he would be listed as one of seven hundred survivors of the ill-fated ship. He wished no more acknowledgment than that.

Captain Rostron stood next to the minister, holding his hat over his chest. When the dead were overboard, he moved his lips as if pronouncing his own private prayer. The gloomy gathering waited.

When the captain raised his head, he said, "May the deceased rest in peace." To the women who had lost their husbands he added, "And may the living have peace in their hearts."

Charlie stared with Andrew at the water where the four men they knew were on their way to the bottom of the ocean two thousand fathoms down to join the ship they had served. It was Monday. The *Carpathia* would arrive in New York by Wednesday evening. Andrew wasn't sure how long he would be in the city or how he would get back to Southampton. All he knew was that he was going to see Emily and his children again.

As the decks throbbed with the labor of the engines, he composed a wireless in his head: "Darling Emily. Am safe. Love, Andy."

Margaret Brown sent around word to gather *Titanic's* first-class passengers in the lounge. I regarded the bedraggled lot, most of them widowed just hours earlier. Like the rest, I scoured the room, searching for the face most familiar to me. Other wives would accept that they'd never see their beloveds again and already were considering what comes next — loss claims, wills, estates, disbursements of money and possessions. But those were legalities I wasn't ready to face — not yet. First I had to find my way home, bathe, sleep, recover. I wasn't about to grieve. Bradley was not dead. He would not desert me. When I found him, my worry would dissolve in a puff of smoke and gratitude would fill my very soul.

I saw Andrew wander in and stand in the back. My heart pained for him. Captain Rostron said only sixty stewards had been rescued. Sixty out of hundreds. There was no assigned section for stewards aboard *Carpathia*, but as far as I was concerned, Andrew deserved to be with first-class passengers. I was glad to see him there.

Mrs. Brown raised her arm to get the attention of the group.

"I am hereby forming a survivors' committee," she announced, "and I nominate myself as chairman. Any objections?"

There was weak applause.

"Some of the second and third-class survivors have only the clothes on their backs," Mrs. Brown continued. "They have no money, no one to meet them at the dock, and nowhere to go. I, for one, appreciate how that feels."

It was well known Mrs. Brown came from bleak poverty. After she married a prospector who struck gold, she found her way into companionship with the moneyed. I suspected it was her bank account, not her breeding, that invited her into their circles. From what I observed, the wealthy regarded Mrs. Brown as a sort of amusement. But she was a woman who got things done, and I liked that about her.

The gold heiress swept her arm over the disheveled survivors. "Who'll be the first to cough up some dough to help 'em out?"

We were all victims of tragedy now—the rich as much as those with nothing.

Colonel Gracie had been meandering around the decks, making sure people were warm and comfortable enough under the circumstances. His was the first donation. The others followed with pledges in the hundreds of dollars. Madeleine Astor offered two thousand dollars. Mrs. Brown wrote down names and amounts and put the money into an envelope.

"We've got nearly ten grand," she said. "That'll help."

I found a bill in my purse and as I handed it to Mrs. Brown, I whispered to her.

"Sure," Mrs. Brown said.

Andrew turned to leave the lounge when Mrs. Brown tapped him on the arm.

"You'll need this, son." She pressed the bill into his hand. "Get some clothes in New York—you look like hell."

I suspected he wanted to tell her to give the money to someone who needed it more, but Mrs. Brown interrupted.

"Good luck to you, son," she said and spun around, trotting to hand out money to needy passengers.

I watched him look at the bill with the number one hundred printed in the upper right corner and a picture of John Knox on the left. Then he scanned the room. When our eyes met, I gave him the subtlest nod. Nothing else was necessary.

During the sail to New York, the sea was choppy and the wind blew cold. On larger ships Andrew had hardly noticed the dips and swells of rough water, but he felt every drop rolling beneath the *Carpathia*. For as long as he could stand it, he crowded into the smoking room with other men, despite all of them being in desperate need of bathing. When the stench of tobacco smoke and body odor overwhelmed him, he went back to the deck for fresh air and salt spray.

Since he was not employed by the Cunard Line, there was no call for him to steward and he had time to think. Too much time. His father had called him a dreamer. If he was a dreamer, then it was dreaming that kept him out of the coalmines of central Scotland. Dreaming saved him from working in wood—sawdust under his nails, in his hair, his lashes—making railings and stairs he would never climb to better himself. Dreams had taken him from coal dust to the coal furnaces of the most expensive and luxurious cruise ships afloat. Dreaming opened doors to wealth and class and a style of living he had never imagined. And it was dreams that kept him alive when he had faced certain death in the worst maritime disaster in history.

Whenever a man gets on a ship, he gives his fate over to the indifferent and unpredictable sea. She is jealous and avaricious, yet for Andrew her lure was irresistible. Each time the sea threatened to overtake him, only his dreams saved him.

Carpathia is Plunging Toward Port
With Remnant of *Titanic's* Thousands
Cleveland Plain Dealer, April 17

After interminable hours, land appeared off starboard. The sighting of New York's coast had always gotten Andrew's blood racing. Passengers were ushered off so the workers could begin the odious task of cleaning up their messes. But not this night.

Clouds hid the mocking moon and no stars glittered, but through the damp mist Andrew saw lights blinking from Long Island. An army of ferries, yachts and steam launches swarmed the *Carpathia*. Half a dozen tugboats led the ship through Ambrose Channel. When it neared the harbor, New York's Mayor Gaynor stood aboard a tug, waving with a welcoming party of dignitaries. The tug blasted its whistle, which started a barrage of bells, sirens and noise from every boat in the bay. In Battery Park, thousands cheered. It was enough to choke a man up, this salutation for no more accomplishment than surviving.

Lightning flashed followed by rolls of thunder. When rain showered down, Andrew stood with Charlie under one of *Carpathia's* lifeboats.

"Beats anythin' I've ever seen," Charlie said. "Does the whole world know what we've been through?"

"Seems they do," Andrew said.

Charlie gaped at the throng. "You'd think we was heroes."

"A hero sacrifices himself for others. We saved ourselves." A fierce pain ripped through Andrew's chest. How ironic, he thought, to die after surviving the *Titanic* disaster. He pressed his palm to his ribs.

"You all right, Andy?" Charlie asked.

Within seconds, the pain eased. "Sure mate — right enough." Andrew couldn't achieve even a bogus smile. He wasn't all right. He'd never be all right again.

Rain trickled down his face like tears. He hadn't wept, even though he had every good reason. When the sprinkle turned into a furious downpour, he let the rain wash the salt out of him, a baptism into life.

The Statue of Liberty drifted past. Andrew had seen the tall lady hundreds of times, but it had never occurred to him before what a symbol of freedom she was. He understood now how the immigrants must have felt when they first saw her lighted torch, a beacon welcoming stragglers and strugglers to safe port. Now he was one of them.

From a tugboat, he heard a voice blast through a megaphone. "Will you anchor for the night?"

Captain Roston raised his own megaphone. "No," he called. "I am going into dock. There are sick people on board."

The tugs guided the ship into Pier 59, the White Star dock. The *Titanic* should have been tied up at this berth by now, but she would not be there on this night. Her home now and for all eternity was the bottom of the sea.

People packed the wharf. So many — thirty thousand or more, all standing in the downpour. Some held up brollies. Others let the rain soak them, their faces filled with anticipation as they lifted homemade signs with names of passengers — their loved ones. Most of them would turn home dejected.

"What time is it, Charlie?" Andrew asked.

"Close to nine, I'd guess."

Exactly four days ago Andrew's passengers were drinking expensive French wine with the most sumptuous meal of their lives. Five hours later, they struggled to save themselves — and the lives of their fellows. Six hours after that, those still above water waited, prayed, and watched for rescue, some realizing they would never again touch the cheeks of those they most loved. Hours and days had no meaning except some part of him wanted to keep track of each precious moment, moments when Emily had no knowledge of whether he was dead or alive. He drew a breath and thanked whatever force allowed the blood to keep pumping through his veins.

He and Charlie watched as crewmen hooked *Titanic's* lifeboats to the davits and lowered them, other men rowing them off to tie up out of the way. One of the lifeboats was marked with the number four.

"They'll be picked clean by mornin'," Charlie said. "Anythin' with the name *Titanic* on it."

"That's wretched," Andrew said. "I don't want even a splinter of those boats."

"Those boats—" Charlie choked out. "Those noble boats saved us, Andy."

The noble boats, he wanted to tell Charlie, saved only a paltry number of them. Not that he wasn't grateful. Grateful, stunned, and outraged all at once.

When the lifeboats had been unloaded, tugboats nudged *Carpathia* two blocks south to the Cunard slip at Pier 54. As the crew pushed gangways to the dock, a battalion of police held back the onlookers while two others ushered six men aboard. Andrew suspected they were White Star officers, men with stern faces. They must have known there was going to be hell to pay.

Captain Rostron directed survivors back to the dining saloons where they were given the names of hotels holding rooms for them. Vouchers were passed around for cafes that would serve them food. There was to be a hearing, Rostron said, and he read a list of those who would be called to testify. Bruce Ismay, Charles Lightoller, Colonel Archibald Gracie, Harold Bride, Samuel Hemming, and Andrew Cunningham were among the dozens of names. It looked like Andrew would be in New York for a good while.

I opened the door of the captain's quarters to find Andrew waiting.

"It's quite a circus out there," he said. "I'll see you to the dock."

"That's kind of you, Andrew." I took his arm and realized I was one of the lucky ones. Rescued, dry, free from the clutch of the frigid deep. I was wearing dry clothes and had bathed in a sea captain's bathtub. Who would know I had nearly died? Who would know what I had lost? Now I was almost home. Almost with my precious sons. And if there was a benevolent God, almost home with my Bradley.

When we came out onto the deck, I drew back and raked my eyes over the hordes of people, looking for one face—a face I cherished. An impossible hope, but what did I have besides miracles?

A barrage of newsmen pressed toward the gangway and shouted questions with hungry wolf eyes. It was late, and they were on deadline.

"What was it like?"

"Can you describe the ship when it sank?"

"How'd you survive?"

I pressed Andrew's arm tighter. Crewmen formed a line to hold back the newspapermen, but one slipped by and dashed aboard. Captain Rostron locked onto him, his usually gentle face knotted with rage.

"Under no conditions are you to speak to these passengers." Rostron turned to his first officer. "Mr. Dean, take this chap to the bridge and hold him there while the passengers disembark." I was grateful. I would answer no questions. I would never speak of the tragedy. Let the others tell the story if they felt so moved.

It was nearly ten o'clock when we crossed to the dock and walked the aisle formed by greeters. Behind the police line, the curious strained forward to take pictures. At the end of the dock, I didn't recognize Bert Marckwald at first. He was not the man I was searching for.

"Florence Cumings!" He rushed toward me, catching me as I fell against him. The *Titanic* sinking and the voyage on *Carpathia* had been dreamlike, as if I had been in a novel almost as fantastical as *Don Quixote*. Bert had found me and brought me back to the world. He would have questions in the way a person would ask about the book I had read. But retelling it would require reliving it, and that I couldn't bear.

Bert helped me to his waiting car and held the door open. Before I got in, I remembered Andrew.

"You must come to see me," I said.

"Yes," he said. "Of course I will."

"Bert, give Andrew my address." Then I crumbled into the car.

Through the windshield I saw Bert speak to Andrew.

"Albert Marckwald," I heard him say, and he shook Andrew's hand. "I'm Bradley's partner at the brokerage firm." He glanced at the car, checking on me. "Is she all right?"

"As can be expected," Andrew said.

"I sent a telegram when I heard the ship was damaged. I don't suppose Bradley received it?"

"I don't think so, no," Andrew said. "It was too late."

Bert asked a few more questions. Had he seen Mr. Cumings? Did he know what became of him? How had he seemed?

"Bert!" I called out the window. "It's raining. Ask Andrew if we can drop him at a hotel."

"I'm fine," Andrew said. "Take Florence home."

"I'm sorry for your trouble," Bert said. "The Cumings address is fifty East Sixty-Fourth. A brownstone."

Then Bert got into the car and we left Andrew standing in the wet cold wearing a stranger's slippers.

Tragic Details of Sinking of *Titanic*
Given By Witnesses
Staunton Virginia Daily Leader, April 19

White Star Line put up a hundred *Titanic* crewmen at the Seaman's Relief Center, a chunky brick hotel overlooking the river in the Meatpacking District. Andrew's room measured not more than five by seven feet. He wasn't squeamish about small spaces—life aboard ship had cured him of that. Still, it felt like a casket, and he planned to retreat to his bed only to sleep.

With the money Florence had given him, he bought a suit of clothes and a hat, a razor and shaving cream, a toothbrush and toothpaste, a comb. He kept a few dollars in his pocket, stashed what was left in a Gideon's Bible, and hid the Bible in a drawer under his bunk. He was taking no chances with hoodlums.

The U.S. Senate had scheduled an investigation into the *Titanic* sinking even before *Carpathia* docked. While he waited to be summoned to the hearing, he found a shoe store and spent two dollars on a pair of oxfords. He put them on, paid for them, and left the lifeless slippers on the counter.

In his new shoes, Andrew walked around Greenwich Village, glad to have solid ground under his feet. The last decent meal he had eaten was on the rescue ship, but he didn't feel hungry. Salt water had dried his throat, and all he wanted was to quench the thirst that water couldn't satisfy. When he passed a pub with a sign over the door that said Landmark Tavern, he wandered in. Men in tweed newsboy caps, thread-worn jackets over sweaters—working men—sat at the bar, glasses of beer between their propped elbows. There was a vacant seat, and he took it.

"What'll it be?" the bartender asked. Andrew must have looked puzzled. What would Sid have ordered?

"Mister?" the bartender said. The buttons of a tweed vest strained over his barrel chest, a black tie knotted neatly at the collar of his shirt.

"I—" Andrew started.

A mug of sudsy ale materialized in front of him. "This ought to do you." The bartender's bushy hair refused to cooperate with the pomade the fellow had used to slick it down, and gray sparked through his red mustache.

Andrew tilted up the glass and guzzled half the ale. Suds drizzled down his chin, and he wiped it with a handkerchief—a new one he'd bought that day. Then he lifted the glass again and emptied it.

"Thirsty, are you?" the bartender asked. The fellow couldn't know how parched Andrew had been just a few nights earlier. How exhausted and traumatized.

"Have another?"

"I wouldn't mind." The bartender didn't force him into conversation even though he wanted to pour himself out, to air the wound. That would have been improper, of course. How well he understood that the bartender was paid to be considerate.

He stared into the fresh ale. For once he didn't have to ask how much a thing cost. He deserved a quaff—even two. He deserved at least that.

The Seaman's Relief Center had a fancy bar dripping with red velvet decor in a space big as a ballroom. Every night stewards and survivors from second and third class sidled into the bar, but Andrew wanted to evade the woes of *Titanic* stories. Instead, he took a stool at the Landmark, hoping no one would occupy the seat next to his and spark a conversation. A bloke could be anonymous at a bar. A man at a bar lived in the moment. No past, only the drink in front of him and the bartender who kept them coming.

Once or twice he was the first patron of the afternoon and found the bartender wiping glasses for the night's business.

"Evening," he'd say. "Welcome back."

One night he offered his name. "Joe." That was it—just "Joe."

"I'm Andy." It seemed like the name of some working stiff who would frequent such an establishment. He was a working stiff—or had been until a week ago. Who knew what the future held for him now?

The first glass was always on the house. He paid for three or four more after that. Later in the evening, a sociable fellow might buy him a pint or two because he looked like "a decent guy." Once in a while he heard talk about the investigation into the ship that had sunk, but he stared straight ahead rather than get involved—except when he heard words like "pity" and "travesty."

"The hell you know!" he yelled down the bar.

The blokes stopped their gossiping and gawked at him as if he'd lost his mind.

"Easy man," one of them said. "You know somebody who was on the ship?"

"Right," Andrew said. "A bloody lot of somebodies."

"Then have a drink on us, buddy," another said.

A drink became two and then three, and it was late when Andrew staggered back to his bunk.

On Friday the hotel clerk slid a message across the desk. Andrew Cunningham was to report to the Waldorf Astoria the next day. He thought about staying dry, but if ever a bloke needed help with nerve, it was that evening. Joe put a drink in front of him before he asked for it. Andrew told him he had a challenging day ahead.

"Anything to do with that ship sinking?" the bartender asked.

Andrew circled his mug with his hands but couldn't speak.

"Listen, Andy," Joe said, "your money's no good tonight. Whatever you want, it's on me."

Andrew didn't recall how many he had, but it was well after midnight when he found his way back to the hotel.

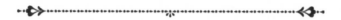

I didn't remember sleeping, but I must have because in my dreams I was dancing with Bradley, safe in his arms. When I awoke, I tried to hold onto him.

"Don't go, my love!"

Once, I must have called out and awakened Wells, and he came into my bedroom.

"Muz, are you all right?"

"Where's your father?" I asked, not sure whether I was awake or still asleep.

"Go back to sleep, Muz," he said.

Yes, sleep. Dreams were sweeter than reality.

In the morning, Andrew dressed carefully. He tried to tell himself that he worked on the railroad or was a bartender like Joe and hadn't been on the *Titanic* at all. Maybe he was a millionaire who didn't have to work—anything to get distance from the horror he was about to plunge back into.

Under an overcast sky, he ambled up Forty-Fifth Street through Hell's Kitchen. He was early and not in a hurry. When he turned up Fifth Avenue, the Waldorf Astoria came into view. Built by the Astors, the Waldorf was the grandest hotel in the world. With its stonework, balconies, and turrets, it might have been a European castle. The Astor name meant money, but money was of no use to the Astor floating in the Atlantic belted in a life jacket.

Inside, the hotel's gilding was more ornate than even that of the *Titanic*. The ceilings were higher and the columns thicker, anchoring the building to the earth. Andrew found comfort in that. A swarm of people shuffled toward the East Ballroom where the day's hearing was getting underway, and he crammed in with newsmen and spectators.

It was the eighth day of interrogations. James Moore, captain of a Canadian passenger ship, was the first to speak. He was testifying that his ship, *Mount Temple*, had been less than fifty miles away when he received *Titanic's* distress call. Bride hadn't mentioned contacting the ship nor that the *Mount Temple* was on its way. But what Captain Moore reported stunned Andrew. When his ship was within twelve miles of *Titanic*, he had seen a floating island of ice with a breadth of five or six miles and extending farther than the eye could see — twenty miles or more. He had counted forty or fifty icebergs as well, some as high as two-hundred feet above the water.

Andrew felt sick to his stomach and swallowed the phlegm building in his throat. He heaved a deep breath, trying to stay calm. Icebergs, he knew, could carry rocks. Icebergs the size Captain Moore was describing could carry boulders as big as small mountains. A sharp spur of ice under the water's surface had the chance of ripping open metal, but a rock of that size surely could.

Captain Moore's ship, had he been able to navigate through the ice field, would have arrived too late. In fact, the *Mount Temple* never arrived at all.

When Captain Moore was dismissed, Andrew heard his name called. He squeezed his way to the front where a gentleman asked him to raise his right hand and pledge to tell the truth. He said he would — the truth as he knew it. The hearing seemed like a farce to him. No testimony was going to bring the dead back to life.

Senator Smith, a white-haired lawyer, asked Andrew to state where he was from, his age, and what his job was aboard *Titanic*. He answered the questions like a machine, without emotion.

"After the ship struck the obstacle, what did you do?" Smith asked.

"We didn't receive any orders, but I helped six or seven of the ladies put on their life jackets. Afterward, I went down to E deck to see how things were there. The water was flooding the post office." His voice was flat. He could have told the senator so much more. He could have described the terror, the chaos.

"As far as the passengers, was there any signal given within their staterooms?"

"Yes. About half-past twelve, the stateroom stewards came to our stations. All my passengers had been roused." Andrew wondered if Smith was trying to find him guilty in some way, although he knew he had followed his duties to the letter.

"Do you know whether there was an emergency alarm on the *Titanic*?" Smith asked.

"To call the passengers?" Andrew wanted to be sure he understood the question. It was important to be precise.

"Yes," he said.

Andrew's head hurt. The room was too warm and he wanted to shrug off his coat. His throat was gritty. But he had to answer.

"I don't think so."

"You do not think they had an alarm?"

"No, sir."

Smith scratched his forehead, thinking. "In the absence of such an alarm, how would the passengers be awakened in case of distress?"

Andrew was sure of the answer to this question. "Each stateroom steward would go around and call them himself." He could have said to hell with the passengers and stowed away in the bottom of a lifeboat or stolen one of the collapsibles. Most aboard the damaged ship were doomed anyway — the men, at least. But he couldn't have lived with himself if he hadn't done what he was trained to do.

"Then, if passengers were apprised of serious danger," Smith said, "they would be obliged to depend entirely upon the vigilance of the stateroom steward?"

Funny, now that he put it that way. "That is so, sir."

Senator Smith fired the next questions at him. Whom had he seen in the staterooms after ordering everyone to the boat deck? How long did he linger on C deck before going to the boat deck? What was every action he had taken before jumping into the water?

And then questions about the water.

"When you struck the water, what did you do?"

Andrew pinched the bridge of his nose to will away the thudding ache in his head.

"I swam clear of the ship, about three-quarters of a mile. I was afraid there would be suction when the boat went under." He hadn't mentioned Sid — he couldn't.

"How long had you been in the water before the boat sank?"

Forever, he wanted to say. It seemed like forever, but he told Smith half an hour, as he had told Doctor McGee.

"And then what did you do?"

Andrew described swimming to lifeboat number four, about being hauled aboard. He was struggling to control himself, but the senator was patient. When Andrew hesitated, he heard the breathing of the thousands of witnesses packed into the room — breathing like some giant beast waiting to gobble up his next words. How did one speak of cradling one's best mate as he lay dying? Instead, he spoke of Florence Cumings asking him to identify the poor souls in the boat. That much he could handle.

"Did you hear Hemming's testimony when he said a quarter hour after the ship struck the iceberg his shipmate came to his room and roused him and told him he had only fifteen minutes to live?" Smith was working into a fury. "He testified the shipmate said this information came from Mr. Andrews, the builder of the ship and Andrews told him not to say anything to anyone. Had you heard that information?"

"No," Andrew answered. "I never heard that until I saw it in the paper. Last night, I think it was."

"Did Hemming say anything to you about what his shipmate told him?"

"No, sir." He wasn't about to incriminate Hemming or his mate. The iceberg was at fault and as far as he was concerned, so was Bruce Ismay for not heeding the warnings. It was the fault of the wankers who had loaded on wet coal and a fleet of others who had rushed to get the ship finished, who had skipped details, who had overlooked weaknesses. It was the whole clutch of White Star Line execs whose lust for money had driven them to launch a ship before she was ready and who had sailed her at full speed toward her ruin.

The questioning went on for another twenty minutes. At times Andrew wasn't sure what had been said or even what he had experienced the early morning of April 15. He just wanted the grilling to be over.

The Ship That Passed in the Night:
Norwegian schooner *Samson*
Reported in the Area of Titanic Sinking
Washington Post, April 19

Jackie took leave from boarding school to be home with me. We had a service to plan for his father, but not yet. I held to the belief that Bradley might still find his way back to us.

Jackie kept abreast of the news and reported snippets to me. The hearings were going to go on for another two weeks. More than eighty passengers and crew of both *Titanic* and *Carpathia* were scheduled for questioning. Women had been excused from testifying, but I imagined Andrew would be interrogated. Nothing about the disaster was his fault, but he could shed light on how events occurred. He promised to come for a visit while he was in New York, but, honestly, I wasn't up to seeing anyone other than my boys.

When a knock came at the door, I heard Jackie answer and Andrew introduce himself.

"Are you the steward?" Jackie asked. I had told him how highly his father regarded our steward, about how centuries ago their families were allies in Scotland.

"Yes," Andrew said. "One of the stewards, anyway."

Even though it was good to hear Andrew's voice, I was in no condition to make my way downstairs.

"I mean the steward who was in the lifeboat?"

The very word "lifeboat" froze me.

Andrew must have acknowledged that he was the steward I had spoken of.

"I'm Jackie—John Bradley, Junior. Muz told us about you."

He invited Andrew into the foyer, and I wondered what he thought of our place, the marble fireplace with pictures of the family on the mantel—Bradley and I at our wedding, photographs of the Maine house and the three boys.

I had closed the lid on the black piano. Since the disaster I hadn't played it at all. Neither had I sent notes of gratitude for the flowers erupting from a dozen vases, unopened notes among the blossoms. Sympathy, condolences, prayers.

"I'm sorry about your father," Andrew said. "Before the ship—I mean, I promised him I'd see about your mother."

I heard Jackie say, "She's not well, I'm afraid. The doctor has been to see her and advises rest."

"Of course. She should rest," Andrew said.

Like a good host, Jackie offered coffee or tea. When Andrew declined, he said, "May I ask you a question, Mr. Cunningham?"

Andrew must have agreed. I understood Jackie would want to know about that night, the night his father—I refused to use the word "died." But I didn't want to hear their conversation, didn't want to hear another word about *Titanic*. I'd rather have pulled the pillow over my head or plugged my ears with paraffin. Should I call out to Jackie and tell him that if they must talk, to go out onto the porch and close the door behind them? No, that would seem ungracious. I wouldn't embarrass him.

"Did you happen to see a sailboat that night? Maybe one of those sailing barques? Muz says she believes my father would have gotten in one. She says she was sure she saw a sail. Is it possible?"

With all my will, I wanted Andrew to confirm the sighting of the sailboat. There had to be a sailboat. I had seen it, hadn't I?

It seemed eons before Andrew answered.

"There was no wind," he said. "No wind at all and no way a sailboat could have gotten to the *Titanic* before she sank. I believe what your mother saw was an iceberg. The one the ship collided with was shaped like a giant sail."

Andrew was mistaken. Hadn't there been wind earlier? And wasn't *Titanic* in the North Atlantic shipping route? Wouldn't ships—even sailing ships—have been in the area? Andrew had been in the water, but I had the better vantage point from the lifeboat. It was a sail I had seen, not an iceberg.

"I see," Jackie said. "But she keeps saying my father was saved and will be coming home. She'll need to face reality eventually."

Reality was my adversary. The reality I wanted was my arm through my husband's, strolling along Avenue de Champs-Élysées, or sitting in the brownstone reading to one another, laughing at one of his funny anecdotes.

"I mustn't stay," Andrew said. "But please tell Mrs. Cumings I came by."

"She'll be happy you did," Jackie said. "Stop in again, won't you? In a couple weeks when she's back on her feet, Muz would enjoy seeing you, I'm sure."

"Then I'll return in a couple of weeks," Andrew said. "That's a promise."

I heard the door click closed and felt regret press down on me. Only Andrew knew the loss I felt. I shouldn't have rebuffed him. The next time he called, I would pry myself from bed and greet him.

Andrew had been honest when he told Florence's son he hadn't seen a sailboat. He hadn't seen it, but Captain Moore had testified about the *Mount Temple* passing a schooner a dozen miles from where *Titanic* sank. Maritime law required steam-powered ships to move out of the path of a sailing ship, and the maneuver had trapped the *Mount Temple* deeper in the ice. It's possible that Captain Moore and Florence saw a fishing ship illegally in the maritime navigational route, which might explain why it wouldn't have helped with the rescue. It was dark, of course, and Moore had detected only the schooner's lights. There was no point in raising hopes. No point at all.

Convinced they had said all they had to say, Senator Smith released the *Titanic* crew from the investigation. White Star Line gave Andrew and the other stewards hardship settlements of a month's pay and passage home aboard the ship *Lapland*. Andrew wasn't keen to get on a liner again, but if he wanted to get back to his family, he had no choice.

During the crossing, he barely slept. It would have been better if he had been put to work rather than sitting idly. He read a little and played a few hands of whist with the other stewards, but he couldn't keep his mind on either. He wondered if his Da and Mum were worried about him. Surely they had been in touch with Emily. He ached to have her at his side again.

From the *Lapland's* deck he watched the water, expecting a crag of ice to rise up in front of the ship, but the captain steered clear of floating icebergs.

When finally they reached the Southampton dock, thousands of waiting eyes searched faces as the passengers disembarked. Andrew looked for only one face. And then there she was, hair tied back, collar of her coat up against the chill English spring. He embraced her, kissed her, warmed her cheek with his own.

"I don't know how you survived," Emily said, "but I thank heaven you did."

Andrew couldn't answer. How could he tell her what it was like one hour to be on the greatest ship ever afloat and in the next hour have it become a tomb? How could he explain what it was like to witness the suffering of fifteen hundred people, people who minutes before had been dancing, drinking, laughing? How did one describe simultaneous terror, denial, and hope? And how could he make her believe in angels?

They walked to Colton Street, a good way but it was a comfort to have the soil of home under him.

"Have you visited with Winnie?" he asked.

"She's ill with grief and worried about her baby," Emily said. "Charlie thinks it best to move her back to Brightlingsea where her family will help her, especially when the time comes. They'll leave within the week."

"Yes," Andrew said. "For the best."

At home, his bairns were cautious around him, as if they sensed a change in him. And they were right—a close encounter with death changes a man. Emily cooked, but Andrew barely ate her meals. While she got Gloria and Sandy ready for bed, he had a habit of slipping out to the Pig & Whistle where he kept the innkeeper company. A man is welcome at a tavern. No questions asked except for a single word—"Another?" There was always another.

"You've become a stranger," Emily said when he stumbled home.

"I'm sorry, Em," was the only response he could summon. His body was home, but his mind was still slipping on the tilted deck—slipping toward the cold, black water.

At night he sat in the darkened parlor staring at ghouls dancing in front of him. He was always cold. If he slept, his teeth chattered and he thrashed the icy water. The sea pulled him under and he held his breath until his lungs ached. He kicked and tried to swing his arms, but they were fastened to his sides. He was freezing but he had to breathe. Somehow he had to breathe.

He woke writhing and gasping, blankets tossed about him like frothy waves. In the moonlight he made out the bedside clock—two in the morning. That was typically when the terrors choked him awake. He stared panting at the ceiling, alternately shaking with chills and sweating with fever. Above him, fifteen hundred spirits rose and hovered, beckoning him to join them. The name Andrew Cunningham should have been among theirs, the fifteen hundred lost in the *Titanic* sinking. He belonged among them more than he belonged in this Southampton house with his two children and steadfast wife who welcomed him home from a living hell.

Each wakeful second was a sledgehammer to his skull. Between strikes of the clock, he questioned why he was spared when so many were taken — passengers, crew, even the captain. But why was the enemy. It stalked him like a leopard in the night. He saw its hungry eyes glisten as it slinked closer, its teeth sharp and iceberg white.

The nightmares bled into day so he could barely tell whether he was awake or asleep. It didn't matter, really. He had shut a door and was alone in the terror. Em saw it. He knew she was trying, but she couldn't reach him, couldn't pull him from the dark room where panic, guilt, and helplessness wrapped itself around his bones and crushed his lungs. He wished for death to escape the memories that plagued him. But there was no escape. Emily was right — he was a stranger, even to himself.

Capt. Rostron Guest of Mrs. J. J. Astor
New York Times, June 1

Andrew had been in Southampton for two weeks when he received a letter from the White Star Line offering him a job on the *Olympic*. He wasn't ready to go to sea again. He would never be ready, especially on a ship so much like *Titanic*. Emily said going back to sea would be good for him—like getting back on the horse after being bucked off. If only it were that simple.

An animal suffering from trauma hides itself in order to heal, but Andrew's family needed income. Stewarding was all he knew, and so he took White Star's offer. Violet had sent him a message saying she would be working in *Olympic*'s second class. If she could stand getting back on a ship, so could he.

He boarded *Olympic* and went through his stewarding duties like a mechanical creature, feeling nothing and answering bells without joy. He missed Sid and believed Violet did, too, although she wouldn't say so. When they crossed the North Atlantic without encountering ice, the walls of his prison began to crumble. He noticed beauty in the blue of the sky and its cotton clouds, sun glimmering on the water, the clean line of the horizon.

On May 26, halfway to New York the Marconi operator shoved a telegram at him. "LUNCHEON AT ASTOR FRIDAY NOON," it read. "MRS. CUMINGS WISHES YOU ESCORT HER. BERT MARCKWALD." Florence must have had Marckwald track him down. The fellow would have checked *Olympic*'s schedule and found that Andrew would be in New York on Friday. Marckwald could have offered to take her to the luncheon, but she must have known her husband's business partner could never grasp the pain of her loss — the loss of all the survivors.

When he rang the doorbell at the Cumings house, a boy close to Sandy's age opened the oak door. He ducked his head when he saw Andrew and stepped aside for him to enter.

"Wells? Did you answer the doorbell?"

Andrew knew that melodic voice. Florence Cumings was standing in the parlor. She was a column of black from neck to shoes. Andrew didn't remember the silver streaking her dark hair, done up in a loose knot atop her head. Her face was drawn and pale, her eyes crinkled with lines.

When he reached out his hand to her, she pushed it aside and embraced him. He hadn't realized how small she was, how fragile, until she was against him. In those silent seconds he knew she was gathering nerve not to break down. Even though he was wearing a suit and not a steward's uniform, his presence must have brought back the horrible ordeal.

"I don't want to go," she said, drawing back. "but Madeleine insisted. She has more pluck than I do."

"I doubt that," he offered. Madeleine, Florence, and the other women had stood up against the North Atlantic cold, a few of them rowing lifeboats with lifeless men at their feet. It didn't get any braver.

Florence introduced him to twelve-year-old Wells and the younger boy Thayer, who peeped his head in from the other room, a woman behind him. His governess, most likely. There was no formality, no protocol. They were just a family — a family minus one.

"The Astor house is on Fifth Avenue across from Central Park," Florence said. "It's only three blocks, but we shouldn't be late."

"Shall we walk, then?" Andrew was thinking the sunshine would do her good. She probably hadn't been out of the house in weeks.

"No, Wells will call for a taxi." She stood in front of the foyer mirror and fixed her hat on her head. "You'll understand when we get there."

From Sixty-Fourth Street, the taxi turned right onto Fifth Avenue. There was no mistaking the Astor mansion. Not only was it an immense stone monstrosity that took up half the block, but it swarmed with newsmen and photographers, some taking moving pictures for the newsreels.

I sighed. "Whenever the Astors have an event, word leaks out."

"Bootlickers," Andrew growled.

"Perhaps. But I don't envy Madeleine. The limelight has had her in its eye as the new wife of the wealthiest man in the country. Now she's a widow gravid with his child." Gravid with decisions about the future, I might have added, and gravid with her inheritance.

"She'll have to find the mettle to deal with what's ahead," Andrew said.

"Have no doubt about her mettle." I sighed again.

I was less than a decade older than Madeleine, but I felt ancient and brittle, webbed with cracks that at any moment might shatter me.

"Are you up to this?" Andrew asked.

I nodded. But no—I was not up to it. I could not have faced the pack of newshounds without Andrew at my side.

The spectators parted as the taxi pulled around the horseshoe driveway. Footmen dressed in brass-button livery opened the taxi door. Andrew exited first and held his hand out to me. Then two footmen swept us between the tall bronze gates and through the wide portal into the reception area with a glass dome ceiling three times the size of the *Titanic*'s. There it was again—I feared the ghost of *Titanic* was going to follow me for the rest of my life.

Both dressed in black, Madeleine and Marian Thayer stood waiting for us. Madeleine wore a beaded choker and a double string of long pearls, her hair done in a chignon. Her face was pallid, her belly rounding under her loose dress.

The women each kissed my cheek. If Madeleine was surprised to see Andrew accompanying me, she hid it well.

"I'm sorry Mrs. Widener is unable to join us," Marian said. "The trip from Philadelphia would have been too much for her."

I knew how Eleanor Widener felt. Here in this grandiose mansion no one but we surviving wives knew what it was like to be thrown into a lifeboat and to watch those very men most dear to us perish. Yet we held up our heads under the weight of anguish, even if we wanted nothing more than to wither away. Tributes had to be paid and expectations met.

"Shall we wait in the library?" Madeleine asked. "Captain Rostron and Doctor McGee will be here soon."

The library was immense, the walls gilded. I had never been in the Astor's house before, but I imagine Madeleine must have felt small and insignificant here. None of it—not the giant paintings, the velvet furniture or the oriental rugs—belonged to her. She looked as uncomfortable as Andrew must have felt perching on the red sofa.

"They should be here any minute," Madeleine said again, flashing her eyes toward the doorway. She was still standing, her hands fidgeting over the bulge of her belly. I was sure she wanted to dash out of the place as badly as I did.

"Your house is remarkable," Andrew blurted. It was kind of him to say so, even though I suspected he didn't care a dead rat about the house. But Madeleine lighted on the topic.

"Jay-Jay's mother lived in half the house until she died. Then Jay-Jay opened it up." She called him by his pet name, as if Andrew and John Jacob Astor had been old friends. Tragedy was the fundamental equalizer.

"There's a ballroom for parties, but of course I haven't used it." She swiped her gaze around the room as if seeing it for the first time. "I doubt there will be parties after—"

"Perfectly understandable," Andrew put in. There was no need to finish the thought.

"Anyway, Vincent will end up with the house. I don't want it."

I leaned toward Andrew. "Vincent is her stepson," I said.

"It feels odd to call him my stepson. He's only a year younger than I am." Madeleine frowned, fighting back tears. "Vincent loved his father. He was up all night when he heard about the — ship." She couldn't get the word *Titanic* through her lips. "The next morning he went to the Associated Press office and then to the Marconi Company to try to find word about him." She dropped into a French style chair. "Poor Vincent. He offered to give his entire inheritance for news that his father was safe."

In the pause that followed, a footman escorted the *Carpathia* officers into the library, both of them looking distraught.

"Very sorry to be late," Doctor McGee said. "The taxicab lost a tire and skidded onto the sidewalk. Nearly threw us on end. Thankfully, the driver got the automobile under control and no one was hurt."

Frank McGee had treated the frostbite of survivors. He had examined unresponsive corpses and declared there was no more to be done for them. I breathed up gratitude that one of those corpses was not my husband. Better to linger in hope than in certainty.

"We didn't intend to make such a dramatic entrance," Captain Rostron said, an apologetic grin on his face.

Please don't laugh, I wanted to say. Today is not a day for laughing.

Madeleine invited the guests into the dining room, another grand space that made the dining table seem absurdly tiny. The table was set with gold-rimmed luncheon plates. Two vases spouted pink roses and gladiolas. A footman pulled out a chair for me, and a servant stood against the wall watching Madeleine for her nod to begin serving.

The server set a salad of simple greens in front of each diner. Before I lifted my fork, Doctor McGee thanked Madeleine for having him to lunch.

"I'll never forget this experience," the doctor said. "Everywhere we've been people have cheered and honored us."

"I'm gratified by the enthusiasm of you Americans," Captain Rostron added, "but it's rather embarrassing to be thrust into the limelight simply for doing my duty."

"You saved the lives of hundreds of people," I said. "You deserve to be honored."

"I wish the number had been greater," the captain said.

I, too, wished the number had been greater — greater at least by one.

A few seconds of silence followed, and I wondered if I had spoken the thought out loud. When a pot clanked in the kitchen, Madeleine raised her eyes and frowned at a servant. She nibbled at her salad and said, "My husband stood at attention and saluted as our lifeboat rowed away." She blinked, and I knew she was no longer with her guests. "He was a colonel, you know." She might as well have been alone, speaking of their private wedding seven short months earlier at the Astor home in Newport, the secrecy because of Astor's divorce scandal. Most women talked out their feelings of sadness with a confidante. For me, Bradley had been my compassionate ear. Who would care to listen to me now?

"Jay-Jay believes marriage is the happiest condition for a person," Madeleine said. Speaking of him as if he had not died was excusable even though the recovery of Astor's body had been all over the newspapers. Astor had been found floating in a life vest, wearing a tuxedo with thousands of dollars in paper bills and gold notes in his pockets.

The server took away the salad dishes and brought out plates of steak frites. I picked at the food, moving the meat and potatoes around. How could I eat? Tears threatened my eyes, but I held them back. There was no use for tears.

Madeleine waved a hand at the servant, who removed the plates to the kitchen and came back to the mantel where there were two small boxes. One he placed in front of Madeleine and the other before Marian Thayer.

Madeleine rolled a pearl of her necklace between thumb and forefinger. She started to speak and then stopped.

"Are you all right, my dear?" Mrs. Thayer asked.

I stood and went to her. When I laid a hand on Madeleine's shoulder, the younger woman tilted her head up and took a deep breath. She would go on. We all would go on.

"Captain Rostron," she said, "in appreciation for what you did for my comfort and for all the survivors of the *Titanic*, I would like to present you with this gold watch."

As he opened the pocket watch, Marian Thayer presented the other box to Dr. McGee—a gold cigarette case.

Captain Rostron uttered his appreciation and said he was delighted to have had the pleasure of meeting with us before his ship sailed again.

"I'm sorry to have to take leave so soon, but we're due in Philadelphia to visit Mrs. Widener," he said. "Doctor McGee and I have events to attend and the schedule is, well, tight."

"Mrs. Thayer has arranged a private rail car for you," Madeleine said. She turned to Andrew. "Will you accompany Mrs. Cumings home?"

Andrew, always the gentleman, said of course he would.

When they reached the brownstone, Andrew followed Florence into the foyer.

"I'm sorry to put you through that, Andrew." She removed her hat and placed it on the foyer table.

"I'm glad to have gone," he said.

Pinching the tip of each gloved finger, she worked the gloves off and rested them atop the hat. Then she released a breath, as if unburdening herself of the adornment had been an effort.

"Andrew," she said, "I want you to know Bradley thought highly of you."

Was it the first time she had used past tense when speaking about her husband? So — he would not be back. Not on a sailboat, not swimming through the cold North Atlantic, not ever.

"I thought the same of him."

"Wait," she said as if remembering. On the table was a small box, and she lifted it and handed it to him. "This is for you."

When he started to protest, she held up her hand to stop him.

"That night — you kept asking me the time — do you remember?"

"Yes. The time seemed important then. I'm not sure why."

"This one is not as costly as Captain Rostron's, but it was one of Bradley's and I'd like you to have it."

Andrew hinged the box open. The watch was silver with a leather band. Watches for the wrist were a new idea, and it looked as if Bradley had never worn it.

"Shouldn't one of your sons have the watch?"

"They have enough" was all she said.

When he laid the watch over his wrist, she turned up his hand and fastened the buckle. For a moment longer, she held his hand between her own.

"Bradley used to say that service is the highest calling. Wealth and status — none of that matters. But to be of service to others is the best we can do in our sojourn on earth. You won't forget that, will you?"

"I won't forget."

A strange sense came over him, as if he had returned from a long journey. The thing welled up in his chest. When he forced out the words, "I ought to go," they came out as a whisper. He had no desire to leave.

"One more thing," she said. "When you sail back to New York, I want you to come and visit me. Whenever you're in New York. Promise me that."

"You have my promise." He tried to resist the overwhelming urge to hold her, to soothe her. Instead, he leaned toward her and kissed her cheek. It felt natural, as if he had done it a thousand times, his lips on her skin, soft as a ripe pear. Before he pulled away, he inhaled her scent, yeasty and flowery.

She uttered "oh," not more than a breath. "Must you go?"

"I'm afraid so." He wanted to add "dear," but it was not his voice and they were not his words.

She studied his face as if looking for someone. Andrew knew he was not the one she sought, but for a fleeting few seconds he wished he were. No—he had a duty and a family of his own. Even so, again words formed that he didn't intend to speak, and yet they spilled from him.

"But I'll be with you again soon, my darling Florrie." He had never called her by that name before. It sounded foreign yet intimately familiar. And in that moment he meant them with all his heart.

When Florence closed the door softly behind him, he stepped into the afternoon sun. Lines from the old Scottish tune came to him, the song he was singing at Hogmanay when he first met Emily. He hummed as he walked downtown.

And there's a hand my trusty friend,
And give me a hand o' thine,
And we'll take a right good-will draught,
For auld lang syne!

Titanic Engineers Memorial Unveiled
BBC News
Southampton, Friday, April 15, 1932,

"You're limping, Andy." Emily wrinkles her brows at him. "Should we turn back?" For a woman in her fifties, she has only a few lines in her face. If he were to meet her today, he'd still fall in love with her.

"The common's just ahead," he tells her. "We'll stop there." He pulls her arm under his. "After thirty years, don't mind if I lean on you, do you?"

She tilts her head playfully. "It's thirty-one years. You've lost count."

Andrew is closing in on sixty, but he feels much older. He must have traveled millions of miles in his four decades on ocean liners, indentured to the rich, answering to their whims, treated as if they see through him unless a demand needed to be met. The sore hip and aching back are his penance, but he has made a good living for his family. He has been luckier than he deserves.

"I would live each minute with you over again if I could."

Emily laughs. "You've always been a romantic."

"I guess it's the Scot in me." He pats her hand. "I miss those moors sometimes, Em. The dawning light shining through the mist, the bells ringing from the Kirk on Sunday morn. It's an earthly heaven. Don't you think so?"

"I'm a London girl. But yes, I do love Scotland." She presses her breast against his elbow. "That's where I met you."

"'Tis true, although it was so long ago that my memory lags."

She stops and fixes her fists on her hips, a gesture that brings a smile to his lips.

"Andy Cunningham!" she scolds. "Shall I slap some memory into you?"

"Nae." He draws her to his chest and kisses her hair. "How could I forget such a thing?"

They saunter down Hill Lane and through Southampton Common.

"You used to bring Sandy here when he was just a boy," Emily says.

"I did," he says. "Whenever I was home. The lad loved the ponds."

"I was cross with you for naming him after your friend Sid, you know."

She never ceases to surprise him, even all this time. "You never said so."

"Never mind," she says. "It suited him."

Across the common children are playing on the lawn. The years have flown behind them like autumn leaves in a wind. Even in this beckoning spring, he feels winter's chill.

"I could do with a cup of tea," he says.

"There's a teahouse on the corner," she says.

They go in and take a table by the window. Andrew orders tea and two biscuits, the shortbread Emily likes. The table is set with porcelain cups and saucers. He prefers the heaviness of these cups to the thin china they serve tea with on the ocean liners. Things with substance last longer. Emily has never been a frail girl. He admires even how her figure has become more solid since having the two bairns. He needs her firm footing now that he's feeling rusted.

The waiter brings a tray with two pots, one with steeping tea and another with hot water for diluting it. Emily likes her tea strong, but he prefers his weak with plenty of cream. The waiter sets the teapots on the table along with a bowl of sugar cubes and pitcher of cream.

"There's no strainer," Andrew grumbles.

"Everyone's using teabags now," Emily says. "It's more convenient, more modern."

"I'm not keen on modern ways. Tea should be a ceremony."

"You're not in first class now, Andy. I wish you'd relax a little."

For the past twenty years, he has found it impossible to relax. The shriek of a train whistle, the sudden croak of a crow, the blaring horn of a bus all make him bristle. At night he wakes flailing and crying out. It happens so often that in the early days Emily took to crawling into bed with Gloria to get some rest. When Sandy grew up and moved out, she started sleeping in his room and Andrew had to sneak in like an Arab visiting one of his concubines.

The waiter places a plate of biscuits on the edge of the table. Andrew moves it to the center. He's used to doing things a certain way.

Emily nibbles a biscuit. "I think I'll pay Winnie a visit while you're away on the next cruise."

He begins pouring the tea, which he thinks the waiter should have done.

"All the way to Brightlingsea?"

"Winnie hardly ever leaves Brightlingsea. She likes to be near the memorial to Sidney. Her brother Charlie saw it was placed in the town green."

"You'll go, won't you?" he asks. "To the memorial, I mean."

"Of course." She puts two sugar cubes into her tea and stirs. "Winnie will want company."

"Give her a kiss for me. And tell little Constance to come and see her old godfather."

"Little Constance will be twenty in December. But I'll tell her," Emily says. "And I'll give Winnie a kiss."

Outside in the sunshine, Andrew steadies himself against his wife's arm as he limps along.

"Let's walk through East Park, shall we, Em?"

"Yes. We haven't been there in ages."

He keeps his eyes straight ahead, no longer strolling with his wife on a spring afternoon. He is in the glacial North Atlantic under a canopy of stars. His head is ringing with the screams and moans of the dying. He's freezing, and he's swimming for his life.

In 1914 he was at the unveiling of the memorial to *Titanic*'s engineers. Ten thousand people had jammed into East Park to see the bronze statue of Nike, the goddess of victory, standing with her wings spread before the curved granite wall. When they reach the spot now, he stops and faces the goddess. Beneath Nike a carved relief of two engineers holds the names of the thirty-five who kept the lights burning until the second they went down with the ship.

"Are you all right, Andy?" Emily asks.

He's not all right. He'll never be completely right. He stares down at the grass, a spring grass, not the deep green of the ocean. It seems he marks everything by the *Titanic*. Before the *Titanic* he had a best mate, a friendship that gave him stability even in the middle of the Atlantic. After the *Titanic* there is only guilt and regret.

Emily slips her arm through his. "Shall we go?"

He looks at her, silver strands mixing with the gold of her hair. It is because of this woman that he swam to lifeboat number four. Because of Emily he clutched life, held on, and fought his way back.

Across from East Park, a granite plaque to the *Titanic* musicians is affixed to the library wall. "They died at their posts like men," the inscription reads. He can hear again the final song they played. "Nearer My God to Thee," a hymn of farewell. The name of bandleader Wallace Hartley pierces through him along with the names of the other musicians.

"All of them—lost," he chokes out. "I should have stayed with them—Bradley Cumings, William Stead, Captain Smith, the officers, engineers, musicians. Even Colonel Astor."

"What about Officer Lightoller?" Emily says. "And Bruce Ismay. Charlie Savage, too. Lots of men survived."

"We all died that night—even if some of us made it back."

Emily tugs his arm. "I'd like to wander through the gardens." She has a way of clearing the air, and he is grateful to her for that. Although he breathes in the fragrance of gardens blooming with yellow and red blossoms, he's feeling out of sorts. He doesn't want to worry his wife, but not much escapes Emily's scrutiny.

"We'll take a taxi."

"No. I'm fine—just tired." He sits down on a bench, and Emily perches beside him. Pulling back the cuff of his jacket, he checks his watch and rubs his finger around the crystal. Quarter past twelve.

"That old watch is worn out," Emily says. "Whatever happened to the new one I gave you ten years ago? I don't believe you ever took it out of the box."

"This one suits me," he says. "Still runs all these years later."

"If you retire from stewarding, you won't have to concern yourself about the time."

"What would I do in Southampton? I'd be underfoot." He has to admit the crossings are more challenging now than they were when he was younger, but as long as he's able, he intends to keep his pledge to Bradley Cumings—and to Florence.

"I could go with you on the next voyage," Emily says. "We can only afford second class, but at least I'd be near you."

He wags his head. Fewer than half in second class were saved the night of the tragedy. He doesn't want his wife to get on a ship—ever.

"No one goes through life unscathed, Andy. You above all should know by now that life is not a fairytale."

"You're wrong about one thing, Em." He nuzzles her cheek. "Life with you has indeed been a fairytale—a very charming one." He puts his arm around her and she leans into him. They are still a perfect fit.

AFTERWORD

When the *Carpathia* docked in New York on April 18, Margaret Brown stayed behind to assist survivors of the *Titanic* sinking. When she finally disembarked at three o'clock in the morning, newsmen asked her how she had gotten through the disaster. "Typical Brown luck," she said. "I'm unsinkable." Later she gave Captain Rostron a silver cup and gold medal for his rescue mission.

At the White House, President Taft presented Captain Rostron with the Congressional Gold Medal. In England, King George V knighted him. He was promoted to Commodore of the Cunard fleet and retired from service in 1931.

After the tragedy, Bruce Ismay suffered from psychological maladies. As he aged, he developed diabetes resulting in the amputation of a leg, leaving him wheelchair-bound. He died of a stroke in 1937 at age 74.

The character of stoker Sally Caveney is based on Billy Nutbean. Stoker Jimmy Birdsall is based on Johnny Podesta. Both Nutbean and Podesta survived the sinking.

Gladys and Emma Bronson are based on Edith Graham and her daughter Margaret of Dixie Cup wealth. Margaret's governess was Elizabeth Shutes, who claimed to have smelled the iceberg before it was struck.

Warren and Edith Craig are modeled after first-class passengers Walter and Virginia Clark. After Walter died on the *Titanic*, Virginia returned to Los Angeles to be with her son. Five months after being rescued, she remarried. Her father-in-law sued for custody of his grandson and was awarded the child six months of the year. Virginia died in 1958.

The only black passenger on *Titanic* was Haitian engineer Joseph Laroche, who perished in the sinking. His French wife Juliette, pregnant with their third child, was rescued with her two daughters and in May returned to France where she gave birth to a son whom she named Joseph.

Marian Thayer returned to Philadelphia after the disaster. She never remarried and died at her house in 1944 at age 71 on the thirty-second anniversary of the sinking of *Titanic*.

During WWI, Violet Jessop was working on His Majesty's Hospital Ship *Britannic* when the ship was sunk in the Aegean Sea. She went into the water and suffered serious injury when the propeller struck her head. When she recovered, she continued to work as a ship's stewardess until she retired in 1950, and she died of heart failure in 1971 at age 84.

In August 1912, Madeleine Force Astor gave birth to John Jacob Astor VI. Her husband's will awarded three million dollars to the child and to Madeleine one hundred thousand dollars and income from a five million dollar trust, so long as she did not remarry. In 1916 she relinquished the inheritance when she wedded her childhood friend, banker William Karl Dick. Four months after her second marriage ended in divorce, Madeleine married Italian boxer Enzo Fiermonte, but they divorced after five volatile years. Madeleine died in Palm Beach, Florida, in 1940 at age 46. In 1926 the Astor mansion was torn down and in its place now stands Temple Emanu-El, the largest synagogue in the world.

The body of John Bradley Cumings was never found. In May 1912, a funeral service was held for him in Boston. Florence Briggs Thayer Cumings had a memorial inscribed on the family monument at Mount Auburn Cemetery with the words, "*Sacred to the memory of John Bradley Cumings - Born September 26, 1872, Lost at Sea on S.S. Titanic, April 15, 1912 – 'Greater love hath no man than this – that a man lay down his life for his friends.*" The couple's middle son Wells entered the Marines in World War I and on June 30, 1918, he was killed in action at Belleau Wood, France. He was 18 years old. Their youngest son Thayer became a New York advertising executive. Eldest son John Bradley Cumings II served in France during World War I and afterward became a banker and stockbroker, following in his father's footsteps. In 1921 Florence married Chester O. Swain, vice president of Standard Oil Company of New Jersey. He predeceased her in 1937. Florence donated money to charities, especially the

Children's Aid Society to help orphans. Florence Cumings Swain lived out the rest of her life in an apartment on Park Avenue in New York City, a country home in Bedford Hills, and a summer place in York, Maine. She died peacefully in 1949 at age 76. [Photo from family collection]

Andrew Cunningham continued to work as a first-class steward on cruise ships, including Cunard Line's flagship *Beregaria* on which the Prince of Wales was a passenger in August 1924. He lived in Southampton with his wife Emily, and for the rest of his life after the *Titanic* tragedy he kept his promise to visit Florence Cumings whenever he was in New York. In September 1932, he died at Royal South Hants Hospital in Southampton surrounded by his wife and children, Sidney Andrew and Grace, and was buried in Hollybrook Cemetery near his home. He was 58 years old. [Photo from *Titanic Encyclopedia* website]

In Southampton more than 500 households lost loved ones. Out of the 421 stewards on the ship, only sixty survived. Of the 330 bodies that were recovered from the water, only fifty-nine were claimed by relatives and were buried in locations around the world. The rest of the dead were interred in Halifax, Nova Scotia, or were buried at sea.

As for the *Titanic* itself, according to the *New York Times* (August 21, 2019): "Resting on the icy North Atlantic seabed more than two miles down, upright but split in two, the fragile mass is slowly succumbing to rust, corrosive salts, microbes and colonies of deep-sea creatures."

More than a thousand songs have been written about the *Titanic* sinking. More importantly, the disaster resulted in modifications to maritime policy. Ships are required to carry enough lifeboats to accommodate everyone aboard, and lifeboat drills are now mandatory. Wireless offices are operated twenty-four hours a day, every day. The International Ice Patrol cruises the North Atlantic searching for icebergs that might endanger ships. Hulls are built with double thickness to ensure bulkheads are watertight. Thanks to these changes and increased vigilance, to this day there has never been another accident at sea as catastrophic as that of the *Titanic*.

ACKNOWLEDGMENTS

For years I heard my mother-in-law, Lea Cumings Reynolds Parson, talk about her grandmother Florence Cumings who survived the *Titanic* sinking. Even in the confusion on the early morning of April 15, Florence, grounded by her fierce Bostonian blood, kept her wits about her.

Lea inherited her grandmother's stalwart nature. For many years, she visited elementary schools near her home in Hamilton, Massachusetts, to tell students of her grandmother's courage. What I know of Florence comes from Lea's memory of her and the weeks she stayed with Florence at her home in New York City. Although Florence spoke very little about that fateful night, Lea sensed the effect the traumatic events had on her grandmother. Since I first heard the story, I've felt it is one that needs telling.

Coming from a middle-class family myself, I'm interested in societal rules and traditions that isolate the classes from each other. During the Edwardian era, one had to be born into high society in order to be acceptable among the well-to-do. Anyone middle class who aspired to the upper class would be carefully scrutinized if not soundly rejected. A relationship between a ship's steward and an Upper East Side New Yorker would have been looked upon warily. Florence, however, had no concern about what her society friends thought. Her connection with Andrew Cunningham was grounded in their surviving the most horrific tragedy of their lives, a tragedy that made them aware of their common humanity.

When I perused transcripts of the 1912 Senate Investigation of the *Titanic* tragedy, I stumbled onto the identity of the steward Florence Cumings saved. At the Waldorf Astoria, Andrew Cunningham spoke of his passenger Florence Cumings and her request that he identify the other people in lifeboat number four. Lea Cumings Reynolds Parson, her son Harrison Reynolds, and her nieces Sandy Cumings Sullivan, Susan Cumings and Sarah Cumings Morse, a member of New York's *Titanic* Society, gave me permission to use the actual names of Florence and Bradley Cumings.

Charles Brown, grandson of Sidney Siebert and great-nephew of Charles and Winnie Savage, and Pat Gilbey, Siebert's great-niece, gave permission to use the names of their ancestors in the book. A. Hunter Marckwald, great-great-grandson of Albert Marckwald, gave permission to use his ancestor's name. Vickie Green, local studies assistant at Southampton Public Library in England, graciously tracked down Andrew Cunningham's records in the Merchant Seaman's Register, which included his height, weight, eye color, and tattoos, and his service after April 15, 1912. She also provided information about Cunningham stewarding for the Prince of Wales who later became King Edward VIII.

The Encyclopedia Titanica and Titanic International Society were two valuable websites for information. John Maxtone-Graham's annotations of Violet Jessop's memoir, *Titanic Survivor*, supplied me with a wealth of information about the life of a steward. *The Ships Steward's Handbook* by J. J. Trayner, published in 1955, was a great help. Andrew Wilson's book, *Shadow of the Titanic: The Extraordinary Stories of Those Who Survived*, helped flesh out the personalities of the survivors. Owen Mulpetre's website, "W. T. Stead Resource Site" offered in-depth information about Stead's life, his work, and quotations from his writings. Articles from the archives of the *New York Times* reported about the Astor luncheon in June 1912. Dozens of other websites and videos were invaluable in supplying details about *Titanic's* layout and design, the lifeboats, and the possible reasons for its sinking and information about some of the notable passengers and the treasures they brought aboard.

Heaps of thanks go to my writing group members Sally Baldwin, Dora Coates, Linda Cruise, Michelle Houghton, Ann Kensek, Stephanie Miraglia, Tina Scharf, Harriet Szanto, and Jacqueline Tuxill for their careful editing, their honest and insightful critique, and for not letting me get away with lazy writing. Humble thanks to Black Rose publisher Reagan Roth, who believed in this book enough to shepherd it into print. Gratitude and love always to my spouse Harrison Reynolds, a member of the Cumings clan, without whom this book would not exist.

ABOUT THE AUTHOR

Louella Bryant holds the MFA in Writing from Vermont College and Master's degree from George Washington University. After publishing two young adult historical novels, Bryant taught for a dozen years in the graduate writing program at Spalding University in Louisville, Kentucky. Her other books are *While In Darkness there Is Light*, a Vietnam-era biography, *Cowboy Code*, a WWII novel set in Southwest Virginia, *Hot Springs and Moonshine Liquor*, a memoir, and the historical novel *Beside the Long River*. She also has published a collection of short stories and numerous essays, poems and articles appearing in anthologies and literary magazines. Visit her website at http://louellabryant.com.

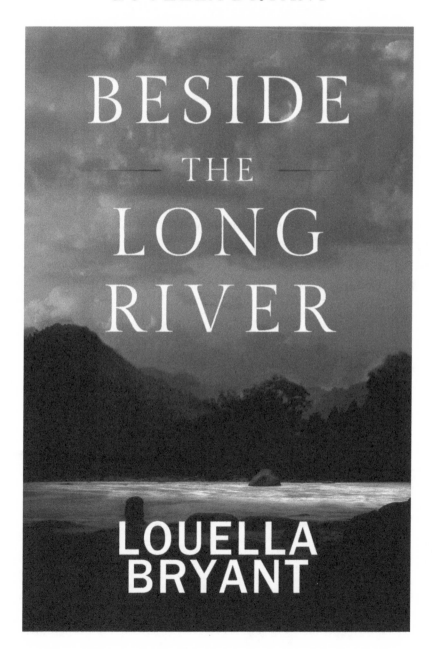

BESIDE

— THE —

LONG

RIVER

LOUELLA
BRYANT

NOTE FROM LOUELLA BRYANT

Word-of-mouth is crucial for any author to succeed. If you enjoyed *Sheltering Angel*, please leave a review online — anywhere you are able. Even if it's just a sentence or two. It would make all the difference and would be very much appreciated.

Thanks!
Louella Bryant

We hope you enjoyed reading this title from:

www.blackrosewriting.com

Subscribe to our mailing list – *The Rosevine* – and receive **FREE** books, daily deals, and stay current with news about upcoming releases and our hottest authors.
Scan the QR code below to sign up.

Already a subscriber? Please accept a sincere thank you for being a fan of Black Rose Writing authors.

View other Black Rose Writing titles at
www.blackrosewriting.com/books and use promo code
PRINT to receive a **20% discount** when purchasing.